THE OTHER SIDE OF THE COIN

This is a story for all those who have traced their family histories and wish to know more of the times in which their ancestors lived and the lives they led.

It was a time, in 1815, when fear over the end of prosperity in agriculture prompted Sarah Dodds to say, "We saw the good side of enclosure in the war. Now the wars are over, we'll see the other side of the coin. You mark my words!" Readers must guess whether, with growing hardship, their ancestors would have followed the mysterious Captain, who urged them to fight for equality and a say in government, or believed, with the Colonel and the gentry, that they should stand against change. Perhaps they simply accepted their lot or, like Sam Stevenson, had few concerns beyond outwitting gamekeepers and watching bare fist fights with other followers of the of the fancy.

But it was not only national events which affected lives; attitudes and beliefs played their part. Readers may wonder whether their ancestors would have comforted Beth Stevenson, or accepted that any handicap was a sign of God's displeasure. They may wonder, too, whether their forebears would have seen John Stevenson as an upstart with ideas above his station or as a man who, having been to the wars, had a right to improve his lot in life and to marry a woman others considered to be too good for him.

Whatever readers decide, it is certain their ancestors shared hopes and joys, disappointments and tragedies very similar to those known to the Stevensons and the Dodds.

Other books by the same author

THE ADVENTURES OF
NATHANIEL SWUBBLE

The story of a parish boy's childhood

www.swubble.co.uk

ISBN 978-0-9555497-1-7

Printed and bound in Great Britain by Heronsgate Print Ltd, Basildon, Essex.

HOUSE
PUBLICATIONS

Published by InHouse Publications
Rose Farm, Top Road, Wingfield, Diss, Norfolk. IP21 5QT

www.swubble.co.uk

THE OTHER SIDE OF THE COIN

LILIAN SPENCER

IN
HOUSE
PUBLICATIONS

CHAPTER ONE

The sudden cry made Frances stir in her drowsiness and jerked her half awake. For a few minutes she could not recall where she was. She looked and listened and tried to urge her mind to gather sights and sounds together and make sense of them. Where was the familiar room she usually saw when she woke and where was her mother's voice calling to her to get up? She would have sunk back into her uneasy sleep, but the crying grew stronger and more urgent. Several people were talking at once. Something different was happening and she must not miss it. With a great effort Frances struggled to drag herself from sleep, spurred by the biting, burning pain of her cramped limbs.

At last, Frances made sense of her surroundings. She was sitting on the bottom step of the stairs. Around her was darkness, but as the erratic flame of a candle flickered against the white washed walls, she made out figures moving in the room above.

"It's a lovely little boy," a woman's voice announced with satisfaction. "Beth Stevenson, you've got a lovely little boy. Fought his way out like a real, strong man."

With a great swell of pride, Frances felt herself part of the drama again. She had been strictly forbidden by Mrs Fletcher, the midwife, to go into the room and, as Mrs Fletcher's word was law, Frances hesitated to go against her.

"Billy," she whispered, turning to where her young brother lay, still asleep, on the steps beside her. It was always wisest and safest to have a partner in crime to share the punishment. The little boy did not stir.

In the upper room, the excitement continued. Her limbs now less stiff and painful, Frances could not resist creeping up the stairs on her hands and knees and peeping into the bedroom. Grown-ups looking after grown-up business would not notice. There stood Mrs Fletcher wiping her hand across her sweating brow and then adding its grime to the already grubby and bespattered apron. Her work almost over and completed in absolute sobriety, she now took a long drink from the gin bottle provided to help the mother through the birth. No mother ever protested. Gin left over meant that Mrs Fletcher had seen to it that they had had an easier time than they had feared.

Elizabeth Stevenson lay back. Her fair skin looked sallow in the candle light and the brown curls, which escaped from her cap, clung damply to her cheeks. In the stifling heat of the room, she watched her mother and Mrs Fletcher wrap the child and prepare a bowl of pap for him.

"Three hundred and twenty he makes," the elderly midwife declared, aglow, by now, with pride and gin. "Tenth set of twins last week."

"Seeing double?" Elizabeth suggested, managing a smile.

"Just resting before we start on the second one." Mrs Fletcher liked to get her own back straight away so there were no hard feelings.

"That's no joke to any woman, Martha Fletcher," Sarah Dodds, the new-born baby's grandmother, told her.

"You're a sensible woman, Sarah," Mrs Fletcher appealed to the older woman. "Wouldn't you like him swaddled?"

"He's Beth's child, not mine." Her sharp tone suggested there had been many family arguments on this point already.

"No, I'm set against it," Elizabeth answered with as much determination as she could muster. "So's my husband."

"What do men know about babies?" the midwife demanded, expecting no answer for it was so obvious. "That's what I ask myself when I hear about them men midwives what's all the fashion these days."

"Men midwives!" Eliza Braithwaite, Beth's friend, for once a spectator at an event where she was usually the centre of the scene, giggled unbelievingly.

"All the fashion with wealthy ladies," Mrs Fletcher assured them.

"What respectable woman would have that?" Mrs Dodds wanted to know.

"What husband would?" Elizabeth guessed what Charles would have to say on the subject.

"Wish I had a guinea or two to spare," Eliza sighed. "Might be worth going through it all with a man midwife. Now what about that young Dr Gray?"

Elizabeth said no more on the subject. She could see her mother's face set in disapproval at the turn the conversation had taken.

"He's the vicar's son and a respectable young man." Having corrected Eliza, Sarah Dodds added, liking to remind everyone that her youngest daughter, as the child of a respectable small farmer, had found employment at the vicarage, "Becky says he's turned out very serious and ambitious."

"Don't see children with lovely straight bones anymore." Mrs Fletcher returned to her original subject. "All the twisted little bodies you see now-a-days. Just because some physician in London sets against swaddling, I dare say." Picking up the bowl of milk and flour pap she went on, "Everyone knows best these days. Everyone wants to be in the fashion and the good's thrown out with the bad. Even the pauper hussies what ain't married give their orders. Young bits of things with no shame. 'No swaddling for my baby,' they say. 'My baby!' Wouldn't you think they'd be ashamed to own it?"

Eliza Braithwaite was quiet. The old hag was getting at her.

"Do you know what one said?" Mrs Fletcher went on. "'Don't give my baby that mess.' I was giving her little bas..." She suddenly noticed Frances taking everything in and changed the word for young ears. "Baby," she continued, "what I'm giving yours now." To illustrate her point, she brought another spoonful of pap to the child's mouth, deftly sweeping her grubby thumb around the chin and pushing back between the gums any mixture which threatened to dribble out.

The talk turned to Dr Gray's taking work from the apothecary, Mr Wright, and the chance that Mrs Fletcher would, in turn, lose work to the apothecary.

"If he skims off the apothecary's cream, there'll be less work for you, Mrs Fletcher."

"How many of our neighbours can afford an apothecary's fees?" Mrs Fletcher replied with a question. It was a question she had asked herself in the many hours she had spent considering the turn of events in which there was less money about and these new gentlemen physicians took work from the less revered apothecaries and the apothecaries took work from women like her. "They'll come to me like their mothers and grandmothers came to my mother and grandmother and pay a penny for medicines he charges a shilling for."

"And Dr Gray charges a guinea," Beth was quick to point out in gratitude for the midwife's services.

"That's human nature," Martha Fletcher explained. "Must be better if it costs more. No, my neighbours are my neighbours," she went on, passing on the conclusions she had reached in her own thinking on the subject. "People don't like strangers in their houses at times like these."

Such thoughts had not occurred to Eliza Braithwaite before, but now they struck home. "Fancy having to clean and tidy up, just when you was feeling at death's door."

"I'm sure," Sarah looked around her, "Beth's home is as clean and tidy as a palace."

"It's not that." The full horror of the situation was dawning on Eliza. "It's having to be on your best behaviour in front of a gentleman. 'Yes, sir.' 'No, sir.' 'May I die now, sir?' Just fancy!"

"There's many a little job I've done for the dying," Martha declared with satisfaction, taking, as usual, little notice of Eliza. "And message I've given. What physician or apothecary would do that? They pocket their fees and they're off. The dead won't pay later for favours. Anyway," Martha showed her trump card, "a woman needs help from another woman in sickness and trouble, that's what I say."

The midwife looked at her companions and was glad to see the readiness with which they agreed with her. Although of average height, average weight, average looks and just about average everything, Martha Fletcher provoked extreme reactions in others. The gentry and the prosperous tradespeople, while not above calling her in to their servants, were repulsed by the smell of stale blood and gin which impregnated her dark clothes and were never completely masked by the scent of herbs. They condemned her for her ignorance and superstitions and tut-tutted over the hold she had on the minds of the common people.

To the villagers, the small tradesmen, the cottagers and labourers, who turned to her at birth, illness and death, Martha Fletcher was as ordinary as they were. Her clothes were soiled by honest work as a shepherd's was after lambing and the smell of her craft hung about her just as the blacksmith's and the baker's did. Her gin, refreshment at the end of her task, was no more nor less than the harvester's ale or the physician's glass of wine in the rich people's houses. While the apothecary and physician might bow and scrape to the gentry, she came into their houses as a neighbour, with no need for ceremony or keeping up appearances on either side. As she worked, they deferred to her, lending a hand as they watched, as they would with the carpenter or the wheelwright. That was the way it had been for generations and there was no cause to start changing things now.

"There are too many new-fangled ideas about these days," Sarah Dodds agreed with feeling.

"What's new-fangled about illness?" the midwife demanded. "It's as old as sin and so are the remedies. Old pills in new boxes, that's all the apothecary or physician can offer."

CHAPTER TWO

Frances had been looking and listening silently to everything. She had, of course, been taught not to butt in when adults were talking, but she loved to listen quietly, storing facts and information to think over later and fit, piece by piece, into the picture of the world she was building up in her mind. Her grandmother came towards her.

"Come and see your second little brother, Frances."

Aware, like everyone else, of young William's reputation for disobedience, Eliza muttered, "'Ope he's a bit better be'aved than the first one." The distress on Beth's face made her regret her words immediately and she covered them with action. Lifting Frances onto her mother's bed, she cooed at the baby.

Elizabeth, realising how left out her little girl must feel, urged, "Come on, love. See your little brother." With one hand she straightened the coverlet and, with the other, patted the bed beside her. Frances nestled closer, flinging her arms, around her mother's neck.

The jolt on the bed made Beth wince, but she kissed her daughter on the cheek and together they looked down at the baby, which Mrs Fletcher had placed in his mother's arms. Her mother's movements, as she eased the white cloth away from the baby's face with her finger tips, were so gentle that Frances suddenly felt jealous. The tiny face was revealed. It was red and wrinkled, not as pretty by half as her and Billy. It was an ugly, miserable looking little thing and no one could possibly prefer it to her, yet they were all fussing over it. The midwife, her mother and her grandmother and Eliza acted as though it were beautiful and adorable. They smiled down at it cooing and gurgling and, worse still, they kept on about its being a boy.

At that moment, Frances heard a click of the front door latch and she felt a rush of cool air into the oppressively hot room. They all heard the slow, slightly limping footsteps crossing the parlour and coming up the stairs.

"It's Charles," laughed Beth, anticipating her husband's delight. Frances jumped up and ran to the top of the stairs to throw herself in her father's arms, as she so often did when he returned from work. He had picked up Billy and she waited for him to scoop her up in his other arm as he always did. With hardly a glance towards her, he walked past to the bed and

5

hugged his wife. Then, standing back and balancing Billy on his arm, he had Mrs Dodds carefully place his new child on the other. Delightedly, he stared at him for a moment until, overcome with joy, he danced around the room, while the women called to him to take care and mind the baby's head.

"Three men in the house now," Charles crowed, ending up sitting beside his wife as they both laughed and gazed lovingly at each other and the new born child.

Frances watched, her joy in the baby fading and her expression growing sad and dejected. Even William, her playmate, was patting the baby gently and laughing with his parents in a happy family group which did not include her. She did not care. Unnoticed, she walked to the door and, closing it behind her, began to go down stairs. Too late she realised the door at the bottom of the stairs was also closed.

The journey on the stairs was one Frances never made without begging for the door at the bottom and the door at the top to be left open to light her way and let her know her mother or father was close at hand, for she knew for certain that this was the territory of ghosts and bogey men. When people tried to reason away her fears by asking what she was afraid of, she could not say. She dared not give her fears shapes and bodies, but they were terrifying nonetheless.

Dejectedly, knowing she would never ask her parents for anything again, Frances continued on her way, her arms outstretched to steady herself against the side walls, pausing at every step to feel the next with her heel. As she neared the bottom of the stairs, Frances began to pray and pray that someone would think of her and open the door, but no one did. Well, they could have their precious little boy and she would look after herself. Still she dreaded the last step, for she knew of old that this was the most dangerous spot of all. Here, her courage exhausted by holding down the terrors which had assailed her on every step, she had to stop and stretch up to feel for the latch on the door which led to safety and the sanctuary of the parlour. There could be no running or rushing to evade the eyes which would be watching her. Trying not to listen, in case she heard a step creaking behind her, and trying not to feel, in case a hand brushed her shoulder, she desperately felt over a wider area. Where was the latch? In the darkness, Frances began to lose her sense of direction. Had she wandered into some strange and terrible land away from everyone she knew? At last, she had it.

The latch lifted in her hand. She fell into the parlour and, by the fire light, stumbled across the room to the table, put her head on her arms and sobbed.

In her loneliness, even the warm, fire-lit parlour offered no sanctuary. A flame spurted in the fire, making the shadows dance briefly on the wall. Through her tears, one shadow on the wall caught Frances's attention. It was moving, not just with the flickering coals, but by itself. Larger and larger it grew, looming over her. Sobbing, Frances turned towards the fire to face the terrible object that could make such a shadow. It was her cat, Nelson. Unaware of the fear he had aroused, he rubbed against her, purring with love and devotion. As she stroked him, the cat threw himself at Frances, rolling over and stretching his neck to be tickled. Nelson was hers. She had found him, a wet, bedraggled, skinny kitten, his eyes streaming and half-closed. With her care, he now looked a sleek picture of health.

"Suppose you want some food, so you can go out after some Lady Hamilton," Frances said, repeating, without understanding, her father's joke. Giving him a scrap or two put aside for him, she picked Nelson up and put him outside. "If that wasn't enough, you'll have to find yourself a great fat rat," she advised him, as his black body merged with the darkness and disappeared.

About to turn back into the house, Frances heard footsteps and her grandfather's voice called to her to leave the door. The smell of soot and smoke caught at her throat. Frances loved her grandfather Stevenson, but, leaving the door, turned and went back into the house without waiting for him. She had given up being a little girl and did not want anyone making a fuss of her.

"Don't tell me you can't stand the smell of smoke, now," he complained. "It's bad enough your Ma always moaning at me without you starting as well." He stepped into the room. "I'm as clean as a new pin, today." By the light of the fire, the old man displayed, like a child, his strangely clean face, small and lean with alert, green-brown eyes. His hands, too, were stark white, but, where the water had trickled along his wrists, pale grooves shone through the black grime.

"So no one's taking any notice of you, eh? What is it?"

Knowing only too well to what he was referring, Frances snapped, "A baby." She could be as awkward as her grandfather when she tried. Her mother was always telling her that.

"So that's it?" Edward Stevenson laughed at the little girl. He slipped a coin into her hand. "Never mind. That means you are still my only little lady." He waited to see a trace of a smile and then set off upstairs. "Young 'Enry's coming any minute," he told her. "Just taken the soot 'ome."

CHAPTER THREE

Those few days in early September, 1815, were to see other arrivals to add to the paupers, labourers, craftsmen, tradesmen, farmers and gentlefolk of Abingfield. Through the long, hot days of August, John Stevenson had been walking up from the South Coast after his discharge from the army. On the ship, returning to England, he had planned to take his time, see the countryside and towns, even go to London, but, once on English soil, he had made straight for home. Reaching the neighbouring parish of Stebbingbourne as dusk fell when, unbeknown to him, his nephew was being born, John had slept beneath a hedge in an orchard.

The early morning squabbling of sparrows and the harsh squawk of pheasants now made sleep impossible. John lay, wide awake, planning the last few miles of his journey in his mind's eye. This particular route was a round about one, but it entered the village over the ridge of Hangar Hill, from where the whole of Abingfield could be seen. Ten years earlier, about to set off for war and suddenly overcome with a sadness and regret he had not expected to feel, he had climbed to the top of these hills and, gazing down, had promised himself he would return to see this view again.

The ridge of the hill was about a mile ahead of him now. Taking up his few belongings, John climbed to the top. There, over to his right, was the river, widened and deepened for barges when he was a child, running its course from North to South. The ridge of the hill, where he was standing, skirted the village on its western side. The church stood out as it had always done and there was the chapel a little way along the main street, in among the straggling row of workshops, cottages and farm houses. But, stretching out from the street, where there had once been three huge fields, there were now small fields, separated and hugged possessively by neat thorn hedges and fences. Here and there, straight lanes cut their way between the fields on their way to the toll gate and the highway. Thinking back, his memory jogged by familiar land marks, John realised that the small, enclosed fields had encroached beyond the lines of the old open fields onto the common and waste land on the hills. The lands where, as a boy, he had stood to watch the kite hover above its prey and hidden to spy on the vixen teaching her cubs, had disappeared beneath the plough.

It was no surprise to find changes. John had seen many enclosed villages on his way home. It was just as someone had said. They taught you that God created the land and gave it an unchanging face. Then came enclosure and you realised that landowners in Parliament had the power to remodel it to their own design. Looking at the scene, John was reminded of his reaction at seeing a comrade's scarred face when the bandages were removed. It was disturbing to catch a remembered look, a fleeting expression from features which were at once familiar, yet strangely distorted.

As he had so often done as a child, John looked from chimney to chimney to see where his father was working. There, over on the roof of a large, new house by the church, was a brush being waved to someone below by a lad. Instinctively and in sympathy with the boy, John took a deep breath of fresh air. How often had he clung to a chimney stack, a child's fear of falling completely lost in the need to gulp in the air after the suffocating climb up the seemingly endless tunnel of the chimney?

This, John admitted to himself at last, was why, after making such speed in his journey, he was hanging back from the last mile. He was afraid that, stepping back into the village, he would step back into his childhood of being simply 'John, the sweep's lad.' Like the landscape, he had changed. In war, in foreign places he had been tested and had found himself, compared with other men, to be more able and quicker to learn than most. It had given him ambition and independence. But, John told himself, he was no longer that little boy at other people's mercy. He was a grown man not only well able to look after himself, but to improve himself, too, and get on in the world

Absorbed in his own thoughts, John, even with his experience of sentry duty, had not heard anyone approach. In a second, his memories were shattered as a tall, energetic man dashed from the bush behind him, snatched his belongings from the ground and, without a word, searched them. John jumped to his feet to defend himself and his possessions. Raising his fists and balancing his body for a fight, he glanced around to see if there was a stick or stone he might use as a weapon. As his eyes searched the ground, he saw the hooves and legs of a horse and, looking up, saw the muzzle of a Brown Bess pointed at him.

"Search him, Walker," the rider ordered. "I'll shoot, if I must."

For a moment, John had the wild idea of pushing the man back against his companion's musket and making a run for it, but he realised he was not being robbed. The men, master and servant, were out protecting game against early morning poachers and, although he was resentful of their assumption that they had an unquestionable right to search him, it was not a matter for which he would risk killing a man. He let himself be searched for snares and nets and waited while the dogs were called up to sniff around for a hare or bird he might have hidden in the bushes. All the time he regarded the man on foot with a deliberately contemptuous stare. He had even less respect for the man than for the master.

"I'm no poacher," John said, feeling a certain pleasure in their obvious disappointment at not having caught a culprit red-handed.

"He might be a lookout, Colonel." The servant ignored John's remark and addressed the man on horseback.

"I'm making a pretty poor job of it, then," John laughed.

"If you're not poaching now, you doubtless had that intention." The master had absolute faith in his own judgement. "Be on your way. We've enough rogues and paupers of our own home-grown variety, without foreigners. I'll tolerate no rubbish from other parishes adding to the burden of the poor rate. Get back to your own parish and let them support you."

"This is my own parish, sir." John spoke respectfully, partly from an instinctive feeling that the man was an officer and partly from the knowledge that it was masters like this who would provide him with work for the rest of his life.

"Another old soldier!" the man interrupted before John could identify himself. "Yet another hero! If all the men who claim to have been at Waterloo had, in fact, been there, the French would have been outnumbered twenty to one and Napoleon's army trampled into the mud without the use of canon or musket."

Carried away by his own mockery, the man went on, "Where's the wound which is going to prevent your working for the rest of your life? Left leg? Left arm? It couldn't be the right arm — unless you raise your tankard with the left." John laughed without thought, as he did when an officer made a joke. The man seemed flattered by this and, for the first time, looked at John as though he might be an individual with his own name and character.

"You have the look of the old man Stevenson about you. That is, a Stevenson on a Sunday beneath the grime."

This time John ignored the joke, reflecting as it did on his father's trade. When he had first joined the army, he had referred to it with pride, as his

11

father always did, thinking himself a cut above the labourers' sons. He had soon found that most men saw sweeps as a subject for scorn and mistrust, having experienced them as thieves and hard masters.

"My father is Edward Stevenson. My name is John Stevenson."

"Then this is your parish and we have no choice but to put up with another penny on the poor rate to support you." This time, money being involved, the gentleman did not laugh at his own words. Turning his horse's head, he trotted away, whistling his dogs to follow.

"Come on. Look sharp, Walker!" John ordered the servant in a brisk tone. "Your master's calling you."

"Before the smile was off John's face, the gentleman reined in his horse and looked back. "That means you're Samuel Stevenson's brother." Looking sternly at John, he continued, "He's an idle thief. Follow in his footsteps and you'll hang as surely as he will."

Having stood and watched the men go, John made his way to where he had seen harvesters at work. He was not worried by what he had heard about Sam. It only meant he did a bit of poaching on the side and they would have to catch him at it.

Near the bottom of the hill he lost sight of the workers, but he soon heard their voices and found the field where men bent low, methodically and rhythmically cutting the corn, separating and supporting a bundle of stalks against each clean sweep of the sickle. Following behind, women stooped to gather the bundles to be stacked in row after row of neatly balanced shocks.

As John went through the gate, men and women looked up and stared at him. He had found country people everywhere stared at strangers in this way, their faces expressionless and their reactions hidden. In foreign places he had interpreted these looks as unwelcoming, even threatening, but he had come to learn that, in villages everywhere, such stares were uncommitted, neutral, just taking in the appearance and expression of the stranger. The first word might be welcoming or rejecting, but it would not be uttered until the inspection was completed.

"Is Charles or Sam Stevenson here?" he inquired.

The expressionless faces continued to stare, until one woman at last turned from him. "Sam, there's a stranger asking for you."

A tall, broad young man stood up and looked at him with the same blank stare, but it soon changed to a look of recognition. His sun tanned face was lit by the broad, easy smile of a man who accepted everyone as a friend and was well liked by everyone in return.

"John? Is it John?" the young man demanded. Facing his brother, absent for ten years, he was for once awkward and ill at ease. Turning around he shouted, "Charles, here's John, back from the war."

Charles did not hesitate. He was only two years older than John and the two had been firm friends as boys and youths. He hurried over, his right leg dragging slightly across the cut corn. With laughter and tears, the brothers hugged each other while others gathered around, until the leader recalled everyone to work.

"Do you remember how to use one of these?" Charles held out his sickle.

Without a word, John reached out, grasped it confidently and walked forward among the harvesters.

"It's not for killing Frenchmen," someone called.

"You'd think it was, the way he's using it," another answered.

Within a minute, John was cursing the tool which at first felt so uneasy in his hand. Gradually, he fell in with the rhythm of the harvesters, moving forward, cutting the corn and the last, flimsy, faded poppies, sending to the ground the nests of scampering mice and scattering to the four corners of the field the rabbits and hares who had waited, hearts beating ready to burst, in dread of his coming.

Snippets of conversation came to John as he bent over the corn. It was bare news and brief comment gasped by men who needed their breath for their work, except for the longer snatches of talk when men sharpened their tools and rested for a moment, rubbing back strength into their aching arms and flexing their fingers, stiff from clutching sickle and stick. It concerned matters he had noted for himself as he surveyed the village from Hangar Hill. How the landowners and even the small farmers had prospered from enclosure and the war. How the Big House had been built by the Hammonds from those profits in the grand style by foreign workmen who could not even speak a word of English. How, with the end of the war, prices were collapsing and it was the small farmer and the labourers who felt the pinch. There was complaint in their statements and discontent in their voices.

"There goes Lady Muck," a young labourer called, jerking his head in the direction of a lady riding by. "Lucy Simpkins. Been away to school."

13

Pulling the brim of his hat down over his ears to make do for a bonnet, he raised his nose and pursed his lips to imitate the lady's genteel and superior manner. "Remember the Simpkins?"

"Simpkins?" John remembered the name well. "Had a small farm. That was my first job. I lived in and ate with the family. Kept a good table."

"They've done well out of enclosure," the young man assured John. "A large farm now. And a grand house. No labourer would be allowed into their kitchen nowadays."

"There aren't many labourers live-in these days," an older man commented, with a tone of regret. "When the price of food went up, it was cheaper to pay a wage."

"Pay half a wage," a labourer sneered," and leave it to the parish to make up half the rest."

Then it was back to reaping and gathering with less and less talk as the clouds threatened to rain off harvesting for the day. Harvesting was paid at a rate fixed between master and men and the sooner it was finished the sooner everyone got back to his usual work and wage with the harvest money safely in his pocket. It was noon before the clouds had swept by and before some young men and women, and some old enough to know better, disappeared out of sight by the canal bank and the more serious and sober gathered in groups in the shade of a hedge.

Sarah Dodds, following behind the reapers, placed the last stook and straightened herself slowly, grateful to lean on Frances's shoulder. She had brought Frances and Billy out of Beth's way, but, while Billy played eagerly with the other children, Frances had begged to work and Sarah had given in at last, welcoming the help of young limbs.

Taking breath, Sarah watched her little granddaughter plodding across the field to fetch Billy, who had fallen asleep. The child walked straight and proud and had denied any tiredness, but Sarah guessed the little girl had been too stiff to bend down and re-tie the rags which had protected her ankles from the cruel cuts and stabs of the stubble, but which now trailed along the ground behind her, revealing red wheals on her skin. It was a pity children were always in such a hurry to grow up.

Stopping and putting her hands on her hips, as she had seen the women do, Frances called, "Do come on Billy. Don't make me have to come and fetch you or there'll be trouble." Her sigh of resignation and exasperation as Billy slept on could be heard by all the grown-ups watching her progress.

Billy was grabbed and shaken vigorously.

"Ouch!" John exclaimed, laughing at his niece.

"He'll take care of himself, you'll see," Charles assured him.

Startled, Billy shook his sister off roughly, but soon they were walking back hand in hand.

"Mind you," Charles told his brother, "she's the only one who can make him do anything. Tells him off, she does."

"It's you and Elizabeth should be bringing him up, not his sister," was Will Dodds' opinion on his grandson. He went on, "Even if he was talking, he'd not get a word in edgeways. She answers up for him, before he can open his mouth."

"He'll talk in his own good time," his wife said. It was second nature to her, now, to temper everything her husband said. "Our Jack, the one who went to America, didn't talk until he was three. Then it was great, long sentences like a scholar."

The children settled close to Sarah, gazing at John as they ate. He winked at them. Billy laughed, but Frances remained serious and a little shy of her new uncle. Watching John, Sarah thought, as many other mothers would soon think, that he would make a good husband for her unmarried daughter. There had been many suitors eager to inherit a share of her father's farm, but none had taken Becky's fancy.

"It's a struggle for the small man," Will Dodds stated suddenly, revealing the problems which troubled his mind every moment of the day.

"Do you want this last piece of cheese, Billy?" Sarah asked her grandson. Children and animals were always good for turning a conversation. Billy smiled and took the cheese from her outstretched hand.

"He understands every word. As bright as a button," Charles continued the conversation, realising Sarah was trying to keep her husband off his problems. They could tell John all about them later, without everyone listening in.

CHAPTER FOUR

It was time to go and find his father, John decided, and he asked about the new house by the church.

"That'll be the new vicarage," Charles told him.

"He'll have left there by now," Sam guessed. "He was going on to the Big House. The Hammond's place, over by the canal." As John walked away, he added, "Knock at the back door and ask for Alice."

As the men laughed, John called back, "In my day it was Margaret."

"Margaret!" Sam roared with laughter. "She's fat, thirty and has a dozen children."

"Once she was seventeen, fair with only two children," John assured his brother. Most of the houses in the village were deserted as John walked along, their inhabitants busy with the harvest, but there were sounds of hammering and sawing as craftsmen worked to mend the tools and carts for the fields. From time to time the noises gave way to the creaking of doors and the clicking of catches. People were watching him, John knew, and he became conscious of the slap of his boots on the dried earth of the path and the patter of stones scattering at his footfall. Soon everyone who was left in the village came out to greet him. He was invited to hold a piece of wood or hold the bellows for craftsmen who were eager to talk, but had urgent jobs to finish.

In Abingfield, as in any village, gossip was all things to all people, the sole occupation of the idle, the chief recreation of the industrious, the knowledge of the ignorant and the social chatter of the learned. It was the stuff of conversation of the spiteful and benevolent and the basis of predictions for the optimist and pessimist alike. Gossip, the great leveller, was the currency that the poor could possess in abundance and the inarticulate might recite with fluency, binding master to servant, man to woman and joining as neighbours those from the east and from the west of the parish. Gossip was harvested by the old woman at her door, the old man leaning over the canal bridge and the child scaring crows for a penny. It was gleaned by the eavesdropping servant and the solicitous mistress and gathered by the drinkers in the alehouse. Then, like any crop, it was flayed by skilled threshers to separate the corn from the chaff, fact from rumour. Finally, the kernels were stored or ground on the stones of prejudice and interest to be passed on at a suitable time.

Very soon, John found that he was being told far more than he was allowed to tell. His stories might be told on a long winter's evening, but they were stories, not gossip which touched the life of the villagers. He spoke of strange lands and events they needed time to accept, while their talk was immediate and relevant.

John pressed on. No one had news he had not already heard in the fields. Tired and hot, he reached the canal, with the park beginning on the other side. Going down the steps to the canal basin, he walked to the water's edge and knelt to bathe his face in the cool water. Without knowing why, John suddenly had the feeling he was being watched. Looking up, he saw a man standing by one of the barges, gazing at him. Thinking it was the usual interest in strangers making the man stare, John was about to turn away, when he realised the man was grinning at him. His hat was pulled down to keep the sun from his eyes, but, as John looked at him, he lifted it with an exaggerated bow.

"Tom Hutchinson," he announced, "Late of the Rifle Regiment."

John ran over to him. "Tom Hutchinson! How long have you been back?"

"Long enough to wish I was still in the army."

After the shortest of times, they were interrupted by a call from the warehouse.

"Get on with it, Tom Hutchinson." As the man who spoke continued, Tom mouthed silently to the oft repeated words. "Just because you're married to my daughter, doesn't mean you can take it easy. I've worked hard all my life and don't have to stand for your lazy ways." Tom was well prepared for the next bit. "What's that book you're always reading on my time? The Rights of Man? Bet they don't include the right to work." The man laughed, as usual, impressed with his own joke.

All Tom replied was, in a low voice to John, "Welcome home, brave and deserving soldiers, who saved England from the French Tyrant." He went on, "Have you noticed how no one is interested where we've been? They're all full of their own stories."

John laughed. He did not feel the resentment Tom felt. He had seen sights and done deeds the ordinary villager did not dream of, and it made him feel superior to them. Tom went slowly back to his work and John called after him that he would see him again, soon.

17

Having crossed the canal bridge, John walked along the front of the park, past the wide, high gates with the proud Hammond crest and on and on, to a smaller, more discreet side gate. He knocked at the gate house, but, when he could put forward no better reason than that he wanted to see his father after ten years, the keeper refused him permission to enter.

Only when they had chatted for a while and the keeper realised that his mother and John's had been second cousins, was he rather reluctantly let through. After walking along the path, over the ridges and valleys, past the carefully laid out copses and newly built ruins, through groves and shrubberies, he at last glimpsed the house itself, so remote and secluded from the village and yet so dominant in its affairs. The walls of the house were castellated, with turrets sprouting here and there, imitating in style the castles of old, but it showed a fragile, civilized face, without the harsh, robust look of earlier times. No rough men, pledged to fight to the death, walked its battlements or guarded its towers. This place had not risen to defend the land, but had been built by men, secure in their tenure, to enjoy the fruits of their kingdom. Going along the paths and through the more prosaic walled vegetable and flower gardens, John spoke briefly to a gardener and was directed to a small door.

It was certainly Alice who let him in and talked to him as an old friend the moment they met. She hurried along in front of him, through seemingly endless kitchens and sculleries and storerooms.

"I should be scrubbing pots," she mentioned, with obvious indifference, as they dodged maids and kitchen boys rushing this way and that. At last they were at the edge of the territory of the lower servants and beyond lay the territory of men in livery.

"I'm not allowed any further." Alice's voice fell instinctively to a whisper. "He'll be up there somewhere," she added vaguely. The upper rooms and their world were as remote to her as China.

John protested, "What do I do if I meet someone?"

Alice was already on her way back to her dirty pots. "Don't ask me. You'll think of something."

This was not John's world, either. He flattened himself against the sides of the passages and listened before daring to enter each of the rooms, strung out one after the other like gems on a necklace. In his confusion, the fine pillars, painted ceilings and staring portraits became a blur of golds and reds and blues against the shining hues of wooden panelling. It was to his immense relief that, through an open door, he saw furniture and carpets covered with sheets and saw his father standing by the fire place. The old man turned in his direction. A huge smile spread across his blackened face.

John was touched by his father's obvious pleasure at seeing him. Over the last few years, looking back at his childhood, he had wondered how any father could treat his children as his father had treated them, forcing them to work until Charles had injured his leg and he, himself, had grown to an age when he was too big to fit into chimneys and could earn more in the fields. Seeing the old man standing there, greeting him with such genuine pleasure, John warmed to him as he had as a young child. In those early days he had worshipped his father as a god who could do anything and knew everything.

The glow from the warmth of family affection was interrupted by a swooshing, scraping rush of noise from the chimney and a cloud of dust filled the room. Luckily for the lad at its centre, a thick layer of fallen soot covered the fire, deadening the glowing logs onto which he fell. The old sweep rushed to the boy, but John moved more quickly. Grabbing at the black, squirming pile, he pulled out a small boy. The child was covered with thick, black grime. It clung to his hair, to his clothes and every inch of his skinny body. At his knuckles and finger tips and at his elbows and knees, it mingled with blood from his raw flesh.

Holding the lad with one hand, John hit him on the back to make him cough up the soot he had swallowed.

"That's right," his father said, approvingly, glad to see his son had remembered so much from his own lessons. "Give him a slap and send him back up. You'll make a good master soon, son, when I can't go on no longer."

"Slap him?" John echoed, unbelievingly, turning in anger on his father. The resentment he had nurtured all these years against the man surged up again and overwhelmed him. "Beat him?" he screamed. "Yes, I could beat him. I could kill him with one hand. He's a half grown child and I'm a man four times his size. But I'd rather beat you — or her." John stopped at last, lost for the name of the housekeeper, who had rushed into the room to see what had gone wrong. Embarrassed by the argument and afraid her employers might be disturbed, she touched John's arm.

"It's wrong. I should have put out the fire. I didn't think. Master Frederick seemed to have a little chill this morning, and I wanted to warm the room thoroughly for him. I'll take your boy to the kitchen and Alice

19

shall wash him and give him a bite to eat. That soon cheers a boy up, in my experience."

Not to be so easily placated, John protested, "Look at his arms and legs. They're raw."

Outraged that his skill as a master chimney sweep was being questioned by his own son in front of strangers, Edward defended himself with vigour. "I've only had him a week or two. You must remember enough to know that it takes time to harden skin. I rub brine in night and morning. What more do you expect me to do?"

The boy was watching the argument, terrified. Shouting, in Henry's experience, could mean only one thing. He was in trouble. Strangely, he edged round not to John, but to the old man.

His anger suddenly leaving him, John commented, "Rather the devil you know, than the devil you don't."

In silence, they followed the maid who had been directed to take them to the sculleries. The sweep was in two minds what to do next. He did not want to encourage the boy to make mistakes by letting him gain by them, but food for the boy meant food for him and two less meals to provide from his own pocket. He decided that they would eat and that it would give him a chance to talk to his son. Not for a moment did it occur to him how deep was his son's resentment. He had never asked anyone to do what he had not done himself as an apprentice and it was up to him, as a good master, to teach his apprentice, in turn, a trade by which he could always earn his own living and grow into a man independent of the gentry's charity or the parish's handouts.

"You'll be coming to live with me, again, then son?" he asked, forgetting their disagreements already.

"I'll maybe see you later this evening." John stopped, thinking he would say what had to be said. "I'll never follow your trade, Pa. I've seen a bigger world and I'm going to make something of myself in it."

His father looked suddenly old and alone. "Don't worry about me, then, John," he said, convincing himself he meant it. "Have a good time on your first night back. We'll have a good talk later. We'll have a lot to tell each other after all these years."

It was always that way, John recalled, feeling ashamed of his anger. How ever much their father annoyed them, it was always he and his brothers who ended up feeling sorry for the old man.

CHAPTER FIVE

Just before Charles had left for the harvest field, he had placed the baby in Elizabeth's arms and she had fed her son and tucked him up beside her on the bed. Close to him, she was there to smile down on him whenever he opened his eyes, to rearrange the sheet and prop him comfortably when, fast asleep, he rolled into an awkward position. When he cried, she comforted him, putting him to her breast, rocking him gently in her arms and murmuring soft words just for his ears alone. At night, he slept in the small wooden cot by the bed for fear she might lie on him, but in the day time she liked him beside her, still part of her. In a day or two she would be back at her work again, caring for Charles and Frances and Billy and looking after the house, but these few days after the birth were hers and Timothy's — a time they would never have again and could never replace, once the chance was lost.

Elizabeth wondered what sort of day the men would have. With luck, Charles had said, they would finish harvesting and return to their regular jobs. Their usual money would be paid again and the harvest money would be there as a bonus. Charles would offer it all to her, but she would insist on him having a little back just for himself. He had earned it. She would enjoy spending that money. Once the rent was paid, if she was careful and looked around for bargains, she could manage boots for Charles and the material for winter clothes. With John chipping in now and again when he ate with them and with Sam's occasional offerings, they would see the winter out comfortably.

Turning back the bed clothes, Elizabeth eased her feet gently to the floor and slowly straightened herself. Two steps were enough to take her to the small, high window of the little room and she peered out to check on the weather. It seemed at first that the ground had come up to meet her. A foot or two below the window was the surface of a seemingly solid, pinkish mass. Only when her eyes had adjusted to the bright light reflected from it, could she make out, here and there where the sun's rays pierced the dense covering, wisps of mist gliding, swirling, struggling to stay together. Gradually defeated by the sun's brightness and warmth, threads of mist broke away, losing all shape and substance as they floated into the distance.

This contest between the mist, which had crept over the ground under cover of darkness, and the rising sun was one Elizabeth had often witnessed in the early hours of a summer's morning. Soon the trees, whose tops now looked like bushes growing on the white surface, would be entirely revealed. The shape of their branches and leaves would become sharper, their colour deeper, as the layers of obscuring mist peeled away. It would be a hot day. There was no doubt about that.

Feeling a moment's regret at missing the harvest, Elizabeth returned to her bed. Apart from the wages, she missed the friendship. Birds of a feather flocked together and, while there were always some women who took the chance of male company to make coarse jokes and disappear in the woods, there were others like her who kept themselves to themselves and just wanted to share a harmless joke and recall when they were children and girls together. Perhaps she would be up and out for gleaning.

At Elizabeth's side Timmy stirred. Easing him onto his side with one hand, she busied herself with the other tucking the sheets to make a cushion for his back. Looking at her baby, Elizabeth recalled when Frances was born and Billy, but she closed her mind to the tiny mites who had died. She had had such high hopes for her daughter, wanting to give her everything. A week or two after her birth, Beth had asked the school master how much it would be for Frances to have a year or two at school. He had pointed out that, although it was tuppence a week, she had a few years to save and, if she put by a penny a week, she would have enough for several years' schooling when the time came. She must put the money by, he had told her, for trying to pay week by week never worked. Children missed in a bad week and then in two or three weeks together and that was the end of getting an education.

It had seemed possible at the time and, when things were good and her father and mother had helped her out, she had managed it for a while. Then she had dipped into the old wooden box when Charles had no work in bad weather and again when her second child was ill — not that the medicines had done any good. At last, one evening last winter when Charles was troubled with his leg and unable to work, she had given him the remaining coins and sent him to the ale house, preferring her own company to his brooding presence. She had told herself that it was not much for a man to ask for a pint of ale when he provided as well for his family as Charles did. Elizabeth made up her mind to try again. Frances wanted to go to school more than anything else in the world. Before she was old enough to even look in the schoolroom door and see what went on, Frances had determined she wanted to be a pupil. Heaven only knew where the idea came from, how it had taken hold of her mind. Her grandfather Dodds had had a little schooling, but no one else in her family and no one at all on Charles's side had stepped through a school house door. It showed what could be done, though, with John learning how to read off some of the other men while he was in the army. The thought reminded Beth of Frances sitting, serious and quiet, listening to her Uncle John's stories, taking in every word and storing up questions for later.

For a while, Elizabeth indulged in the luxury of daydreaming, until, seeing how quickly the morning was passing, she set about tidying the bed. This was the time when Miss Gray, the vicar's daughter usually called with a little calf's foot jelly or broth and everything had to be looking just so. Beth put the edge of her gown to her mouth, wetting it slightly, and carefully wiped around the baby's mouth until all traces of dried food had disappeared. Then she gave her own face the same quick cat-lick, thankful that her mother was not there to see.

Her toilet completed, Beth pulled up the covers and arranged them neatly around her and Tim. She had timed it just right. There were voices in the street below and people had stopped by the door. As Becky let herself in and showed Miss Gray up to the bedroom, Beth cast her eyes quickly around the room. There was that cobweb she had noticed yesterday and forgotten to do anything about. Her mother's eyes were not what they used to be. It was too late to do anything about it now, except hope that Miss Gray did not look into that corner.

Becky came in and kissed her sister. Beth, her attention on Miss Gray, pecked her in return. She always felt awkward being in bed when someone like Miss Gray called. It seemed so insolent just to lie there and not curtsy or pull up a chair for her visitor. Not that Miss Gray was not kindness itself and she did at least look at you and ask after your health before looking around and taking everything in.

"He's lovely Beth," Becky exclaimed, holding the baby close to move aside the thick wrappings and peep at his face. "Look, Miss Gray. Isn't he just like Elizabeth?"

"Some people think he favours Charles." Beth was determined to give her husband his share of the credit.

Miss Gray joined in the admiration of the baby, but, having left her gift

23

and seen that all was well, she hurried off to visit other, less fortunate, of her father's parishioners, leaving Becky to catch her up.

Becky hugged the baby, enthralled by his perfection and helplessness.

"Better hand him here, Becky. You're getting broody just holding him. You get married first."

"It's not for the want of trying, Beth." Knowing the truth of Becky's claim, Beth laughed.

"I dread one day I'll wake up and find I'm thirty and have no chance of a husband," Becky went on, reliving her nightmare.

"You stay at the vicarage in comfort for the rest of your life. You're not badly off, Becky."

"That's what you all say, married and sitting there with your babies. Anyway," Becky added, "I don't want to spend the rest of my life waiting on people and eating leftovers."

Beth lay back and laughed. "What do you think a wife does, but wait on her husband and children and eat what's left when she's filled their plates?"

Becky was no more ready to heed such warnings than any other young spinster in the village might have been. She rocked her nephew in her arms. "Blessed with children, that's what I want to be."

"Well, you live in the vicarage, Becky. It's the vicar who gives out blessings."

"Beth!" The sisters spoke in chorus, imitating the tone their mother used whenever she considered they had gone too far.

"Children are a mixed blessing, I can tell you," Beth told her sister.

Too deep in her dreaming to hear, Becky was walking around the bed as though setting a table. "When I have those lovely plates in my hand and set out the shining glass and silver, I long for a home of my own."

"Listen to your Aunt Becky," Beth addressed her baby son. "They tell you when you go into service that it'll teach you how to look after your own home. All it really does is give you grand ideas." She looked from Tim to Becky. "You'll have no silver my girl, and you'll be thankful. You'll find no time to clean it."

"You sound just like Ma," Becky protested.

"I begin to know how often Ma is right. So will you, one day!"

"There's Miss Gray back, and me still sitting here." Reluctantly, Becky returned to her work.

CHAPTER SIX

The rush of Becky's hurried footsteps down the stairs masked the sound of John's entering the house and he was half way up the stairs before Beth had a chance to prepare herself for another visitor. John looked round the door. "I did knock, but, when no one answered, I thought I would check and see if you were asleep."

"Come in, John. No, I'm not asleep, just daydreaming." She welcomed him readily, having accepted her brother-in-law at once as a member of the family. She had always liked him when they were children, but now she welcomed him, too, as a breath of fresh air, blowing the cobwebs from the routine of their daily lives.

"The Devil finds work for idle hands," he admonished her.

Although the imitation was a poor one, she recognised it at once as her mother's words and laughed with him. "There can't be any harm in day-dreaming."

"I certainly hope not, "John smiled. "I've done my share in the last ten years."

"Charles calls it scheming, not dreaming," she told him. "No," she added after due thought. No temptations to evil have entered my mind today. It's like when I'm ill or have an hour to myself on a Sunday " She began again, eager to explain herself to John. "Well, when I'm working in the fields, sewing, cleaning, cooking, a part of my mind — a part of my spirit — goes numb. With a minute to myself it comes to life again. I begin to plan this and that. A little schooling for the children. Enough to apprentice the boys to a trade. Enough to let Frances marry a shop keeper and be useful with the accounts."

"No harm in that," John agreed, as Beth knew he would. "Time to your-self lets the mind roam and the spirit breath. The gentry have the right word for it. They call it leisure, not idleness. It's precious. You can't toil just to keep the body alive all the time."

Beth felt at home with him. "Here's another dreamer," she laughed, as Frances came shyly past her uncle to kiss her mother. Snuggling up to her, the child waited to see if the grown-ups had finished talking before she spoke.

"What's the sea like, Ma?"

"Like a big river, I suppose," Beth ventured, appealing with her smile to John, to whom the question had really been addressed. "Your Uncle John's the only one in this family who's ever set eyes on it."

Searching for words they could understand, John explained, "It is like a big river — a great river so wide you can't see the other side. You can cross it for days and days and see nothing but water until you at last reach the other side."

The child's eyes fixed upon him and her eager silence made him go on. "There are waves." Again he searched for words to create a picture in their minds. "You know how the corn blows in the wind? You can see one row dip and then the next and the next until the wave ripples right across the field. Or it's like the tiny waves on the canal as the barges pass, only much wider and deeper — sometimes as deep, as high, as a house." He ended laughing, "That's when the ships bob about and everyone is sick."

"Do Spanish people look like us?" It was not that Frances's mind dived from one subject to another, but that she felt she had to ask all the questions which had arisen from her uncle's tales, while she had the opportunity.

"God made all men in his image," Beth ventured.

"Have you ever seen a Spanish person, Ma?" Since her uncle's return, Frances had decided her own parents and grandparents knew little of the world, but she checked to be sure before dismissing what her mother had said and preparing to accept her uncle's words as the real Gospel truth.

"No. Nor a Frenchman for that matter," Beth answered honestly. Eager, as usual, to pass on to her daughter any scraps of information she did possess, she recalled, "We had some Irishmen building the canal. That was when your Uncle John and I were children. Do you remember, John? They were a wild bunch. Always drunk and fighting and well, a wild bunch. But that's Catholics for you. Do what they like and get forgiven for it afterwards."

"Is Fred Roberts a Catholic?" Frances named the worst of the village's many drunks.

"He doesn't bother whether he's forgiven or not," her mother told her.

"He'll burn in Hell fire, then, for sure," Frances proclaimed. After a moment's silence, the little girl whispered something in her mother's ear.

"You ask him. You've got a tongue in your head."

"Come here," John beckoned, having heard, as was intended, most of the loudly whispered request for him to teach her to read. Taking her onto his lap, he promised, "Learning's precious, Frances, but not like money and jewels you keep to yourself and hide from thieves. It can be passed on again and again. I'll gladly share it with you, Frances, and anyone else who will treasure it as you will." Taking pleasure in her obvious joy, he added, "I'll borrow books, somehow, and we'll read of the seas and the oceans. And of lands and animals. Spaniards and Frenchmen."

"Oh, thank you so much, Uncle John." Frances, remembering that she had been told always to thank people properly, spoke very formally, but she responded with a great hug to the bear hug he gave her.

"Perhaps," Beth suggested, eager to promote John's dreams as well as her own, "Miss Gray — that's the vicar's daughter — will want help with her new Sunday School. You know what the gentry are — always starting schemes and never finishing."

Looking at John and her small daughter together, she added, "You'll want to settle down with a wife and children of your own."

"It will take time to find myself a wealthy wife." It was John's standard reply and generally led successfully to a change of subject, but Beth was sure he was not that kind of man.

Sensing the evasion in the answer, she talked around the subject. Laughing apologetically, she went on, "There I go. You'll have had enough of that sort of advice from mothers with unmarried daughters."

"It's not that." There, with Beth and her small daughter, pictures and impressions he thought long buried came as strong and fresh as the day they happened. For the first time he had confided to anyone, he said softly, "I was married, once."

Beth stared at him. When he had come home alone, no one had dreamed he had a wife. Frances was silent. She knew this was not a conversation for children to join in.

"My wife had a little girl who was near Frances's age."

Somehow, Beth knew they were dead and waited for John to speak about them in his own time.

"I told you, didn't I, that I helped the surgeon in our regiment after the fighting died down? Me and another few fellows. At first, we carried the wounded about, sorted out the half alive from the dead, piled up the bodies and made room for the next lot in the surgeon's tent." John paused, seeing the scene as it had really been, with sawn off limbs, the blood and dying men covered with flies. "We tidied up the tent, you could say, and held down men while the surgeon did his work. Few were so brave they didn't use their last breaths struggling and fighting to run from his knife, wanting just to die in peace. And a good many of them might as well have been left — they died anyway.

"This young man was brought in. You could hardly recognise what colour his uniform had been and what regiment he was in. How he hung on we never knew —for her, I suppose. He kept asking for, 'Sarah. Sarah.' and she must have been told, for she came to the tent to find him. She struck me as a little mouse of a thing and shy. I could see why he was so worried what would become of her." John stopped. The war was so far from Abingfield. How could Beth ever understand what it had been like?

He tried to explain. "Most soldiers are rough and ignorant. Being all together seems to make them worse, coarser, more like animals. Think of the worse drunkards and blasphemers and lechers you've seen in the harvest gangs and navvies who roam the country and you're part way to recognising the average soldier. Officers have them flogged to keep discipline, but if they think they'll not be caught, most have no morals or restraint. And the women — they get the women they deserve. The women swear, drink and sell — give themselves to anyone."

"Silent again, John sought the words to go on with the next part of his story. "Sarah was — there is only one word for it — respectable. The two of them had married young against their parents' wishes and he had joined the army to make a new life. A new life! They were babes stumbling about in a world they didn't understand.

"There were plenty of men dying and women weeping, but those two — I just kept thinking about them and watching them. He kept lingering on and she kept begging me to do something. 'Please God,' she prayed, 'let him have peace.' I don't think she thought for a second what would become of her and all the time he worried about her. It seemed her father had forbidden her ever to come back once she'd married. Anyway, they were miles from England in the middle of war and she'd be a young woman with a child who could do nothing once he'd gone but follow the army from battle to battle.

"I was going round with water that night and I lifted him up to drink. He pushed it away and grabbed my arm. His face was drained of blood and he looked like a man already in his grave. 'You're a decent man,' he begged,

'Take care of her.' I mumbled something. I can't think what, now, but he was desperate. 'Promise me. For Christ's sake, promise me.' What do you do? If it made his last seconds happy, there seemed no harm in agreeing. 'I promise,' I said. 'I'll take care of her.' He smiled and was dead in that second."

There was complete silence in the room. John was aware of neither the room nor the silence. He could see those scenes from the past as though living them again. "I told the woman she was always to come and see me if she needed anything, but she never did. Some of the fellows said I was slow and should take advantage of the situation. They were round her like bees round a honey pot. There were never enough women to go round. A widow could have her choice of husbands before the last one was in the ground.

"I kept thinking about her — about the pair of them. Usually I managed to make myself believe it was none of my business. Now and again, I'd see her and offer her money. She would refuse, but she'd take something for the child and I'd feel better for a while. Then I'd start worrying about her again. I couldn't just take her over — it was like taking a dead comrade's belongings, only worse. She had a mind of her own and she never asked me to help her.

"One day, I heard some of the men laughing about an officer pestering this young widow. I just went and got her. I mean, there was no chance of him marrying her. Marriage seemed the easiest way to get over a lot of problems which arose. She still loved the young fellow, I knew that, but I needed her more and more. She grew to love me. She told me so. Once she explained it. 'You don't have just so much love in you and no more. There's no limit to it. There's enough love for anyone you really want to give it to.'"

In the flames of the fire, John seemed to be gazing at her face. "She had a strength like no other woman in the world."

Elizabeth waited, minute after minute. There was no sound except the crackling of the wood and the gentle breeze blowing through the tiny window.

"And your family died?" Beth's voice was gentle.

John looked up, puzzled. He stared at her, hardly seeming to see her. "Yes. They died." He had been talking about those terrible times and their dying was an inseparable part of them. Didn't Beth know that they had died? Weren't their deaths a part of reality? But, then, no two people shared the same reality.

Elizabeth watched John, wondering why he had stopped. Was their end too terrible, too awful to relate? "How did they die John?" She felt she must know and share the burden with him.

"They just died," he said, briefly. Elizabeth thought he was going to say no more, but he added. "That's not quite true. They simply stopped living." Elizabeth did not know what he meant. She did not even know what question to ask. Frances was sobbing quietly, her head on her mother's arm.

John was speaking again. Elizabeth realised he was trying to find words to make her understand "Death is so dramatic," he began. "In battle, a man is strong and alive one moment and the next he is dead — his head blown clean off by a cannon ball or his body torn to pieces by musket shot. But he's a soldier and soldiers die. If a man dies in his bed, he seems to know he must put his house in order. Call his relations around him. Everyone is there to mourn his passing." John paused, trying to grasp again the thread he was trying to follow. "There, Corunna, during that terrible retreat, there was no sudden passing, no clear distinction between being dead and alive, and no mourners — just survivors."

Stirring, John placed his hand on Beth's arm, which rested on the bed cover, as though willing her to understand, to see the scene which would never pass from him.

"At first," he continued, "we were desperately hungry and cold. We scraped up raw turnips and potatoes or tried to beg a little bread and water. The Spaniards hid their food when they knew we were about to pass through. They seemed to like us no better than they liked the French. In the mountains the nights were bitter and the snow soaked our clothes. But after a while without food and warmth, you stop feeling hungry or cold. A numbness, a void, a lack of feeling is all that is left. There is no more moaning, no more complaining or cursing — only silence. Hundreds of silent people, soldiers and women and children, moving slowly forward."

"I was carrying young Mary," John said, talking of his wife's and child's death to Beth, as he had been unable to talk to anyone else. "I had buttoned her inside my great coat and tucked her bare feet under my arm and her little hands in close to my chest. She was desperately weak and she breathed as though every breath was painful. We had walked for some hours and people were stopping in groups to sleep for the night. A friend, who had chosen a shelter by a wall, saw us and beckoned us over. He got up to give Sarah his place and turned to take Mary from me. My hands were stiff with cold and, when he saw that, he unbuttoned my coat to take the child from my arms.

"'We'll try to find a spot where the soil's not too frozen to bury her,' he said, thinking I knew she was dead. There had been no sign, no word. There, hugged close to me, the little thing's life had just come to an end." Frances sobbed as though her heart would break. Her mother pulled her closer, thanking God in her heart that she had her own daughter alive and well. "Sarah, my wife," John went on, "poor, sweet Sarah. She took the dead child from my arms and nursed her all the night and carried her all the next day."

"Couldn't she believe the little girl was dead?" Beth asked, imagining how she would feel at something so cruel.

"We thought that at first," John answered, "but she just couldn't bear to think of the child lying there, abandoned in a bleak, cold country among strangers. Perhaps," he added, "she knew she would soon die and be buried next to her. She died — Sarah died — the next night. As the afternoon went on, she begged me to stop and tried to restrain me by dragging on my arm. I had only one thought, to keep going on, not to give in, not let ourselves die. Sarah summoned up what strength she had and stood in my path. I looked at her to plead, to coax, to urge her to go on, but I never uttered the words. There was a look about her, a look, not of despair or defeat, but of acceptance.

"Have you noticed," John suddenly demanded of Beth, "that when we are healthy we all dread death, but when illness has destroyed the body and death comes, a calmness and acceptance come with it?"

"God is merciful," Beth murmured.

"I didn't argue with her again. We sat in a field, in a kind of shed, like a couple parting before one went on a journey. As the day ended, as the sun set, Mary's life came to an end. The peasants had left the fields and led their oxen and mules to shelter for the night. I buried my loved ones together, young Mary in Sarah's arms.

"I remember a farmer coming to stare, thinking I was stealing his crops and, not speaking a word, he helped me with my task. Then I took my rifle and knapsack and joined that straggling, endless procession which had been passing all day long. A few people asked what had happened to Sarah and the child. When I told them they had died, they nodded and went on. Death was commonplace. The rest of us were not mourners, but people waiting our turn to die."

Beth put her hand gently on John's arm. "John, what you must have felt!

What you must have thought as you walked along!"

Turning to look at her, John said earnestly, "That was the strange thing. I knew I should have wept. I should have cursed God or called upon him for strength. I did nothing. I felt and thought nothing. Others were walking to the coast with no more thought than sheep and I was just walking with them. Some said afterwards that they walked because officers ordered them to, threatening them with a beating, or because they wanted to see England again or were afraid of being caught by the French.

"I walked because it was the easiest thing to do. If I'd had to refuse to march, refuse to obey an order, that would have taken an effort. Even lying down would have needed a decision to stop. It was easiest to sleep at night, get up each morning, walk each day. I'd been doing that day after day and it was easier to keep on doing the same thing than make an effort to do anything else.

"Only on the beach, I nearly gave up. I couldn't just keep on walking any more. I had to jump into the sea and swim to the ships. Feelings didn't really come into it. Only afterwards I began to realise what I had lost. Like when your leg goes to sleep. It's when the life begins to come back that the pain comes.

"We sailed for England and were landed at Portsmouth. Mothers and wives and sweethearts came down to the harbour and asked for news of their dear ones. They hadn't seen death as we had seen it. Death so casual and indiscriminate that it seemed commonplace. Death to these people was one death of a husband or son and they wept. And I mourned with them. Sarah, my wife, and Mary, our little girl, were lost to me for ever. I would never see them or hear their voices again."

Elizabeth put John's fingers to her lips and gently kissed them, just as she comforted her baby son.

"When the pain came, at last, I was afraid I could not bear it, afraid it would swallow me up, afraid it would destroy me. It was like being lost in a great open space, with no landmarks, no signs. 'How will it all end?' I used to ask myself. Their death was so final. How could my pain ever end?"

It was at this moment, as Beth held John's hand in hers and John was looking at her, trying to make her understand, that Charles walked in. He did not pause to take in the details of the scene or ask questions. He had noticed how warmly Beth had taken to John and he needed to know no more.

Feeling a hand on his shoulder, John, still lost in his thoughts, turned his head. By instinct, he moved to avoid the blow aimed at him and then stood, looking at Charles, seeing his anger and realising what he was thinking.

"Get out," Charles ordered. "Get out of my house. Is this what the army has done for you? Taught you to take your brother's wife?"

Elizabeth, having had cause in the past to know how possessive her husband was, was the first to realise what was happening. She was angry — angry that he should suspect her without cause, but far, far angrier that John's first attempt to find comfort from his family should end like this.

"How could you?" she demanded. She hugged the baby to her as though to leave the house and be alone, as she always did when there was no reasoning with her husband.

"Let it rest, Beth," John told her, too close to real sorrow to be affected by his brother's petty feelings. "I'll go, as he says. You see if you can bring him to his senses."

Charles, the first doubts about his conclusions creeping into his mind, stood aside and let him pass.

CHAPTER SEVEN

Charles, usually a quiet, diffident man, talked and talked on the way to the Navigators, the village ale house, anxious to make amends to John and to stifle his embarrassment and guilt at his own behaviour. Most of all, he wanted to make John feel that, although he had lost his wife and children, he had a loving family around him. To this end he described all that had happened to the family in the last ten years.

Only half listening and wanting to think his own thoughts, John asked just enough questions to prompt him to continue. "What's all this about your father-in-law, Will Dodds? he asked.

"Will Dodds," Charles launched himself into the subject, "did well for himself after enclosure, what with the war coming and prices rising. That was the time! Enclosure! All those gentlemen from London. Surveyors and lawyers trampling every where. Lots of legal talk and no one understood a word, I swear, unless it was 'profit'. Off they went back to London, to talk it over in Parliament, they said. Suddenly every farmer was given a few fields in a neat parcel instead of his strips, scattered here there and every where in the open fields."

"The trouble was," Charles went on, "He had to pay his share of the costs. There were fees to every Tom, Dick and Harry you care to name. And he had to pay to fence and hedge it in. It was no burden when prices were high, but where's he going to find the money now?"

His steps slowing as they approached the ale house, Charles concluded, "A few good harvests and he could pull through. A bad one or two and he's finished." With the last words Charles came to an abrupt halt and turned earnestly to his brother. "I do love her, John. More than life itself. I work every minute God sends for her and the children."

Before John could comment, Charles continued, "It's these black moods, John. They come over me — like stifling in those dark, close chimneys when we were boys. I take it out on Beth then, I know. I pick on any little thing. Billy's not corrected enough. The food's cold. It's not ready on the table when I come home tired after hours in the wet and cold. Then I gnaw away at it, John. Like there's a little devil on my shoulder goading me on and on." All the time he spoke, Charles looked at his brother, appealing for an explanation he could not provide himself.

At a loss, John murmured, "You take things too much to heart, Charles. How Ma and Pa can have produced both you and Sam, I don't know!"

"Sam!" Charles followed John's lead in changing the subject. "He hasn't a care in the world."

"Perhaps it's because he believes 'God helps those who help themselves,'" John laughed.

"He certainly believes that. And to prove it he's helped himself to many a rabbit and pheasant for miles around!"

In front of the ale house was the usual parade of pleasure seeking and pain avoiding humanity to be found at harvest time. After a head start of free ale and companionship in the fields, joy and oblivion came more rapidly than at more sober times of the year. Already, the preliminary taunting and daring long over, young men and women whispered and teased in a closeness which just passed for dancing. Older folk slept, heads on arms resting on the tables, some to refresh themselves for more drinking before the walk home and others, perhaps, to dream of the steps they had once trod to the music of a warm summer's night.

Dodging the stamping feet and jutting tables, John and Charles lowered their heads to enter. The smell of tobacco and candles, of beer and sweat hung trapped in the heat and made their throats long for the cool ale.

"Sit here, John," Carrie White called, patting the seat beside her. "Remember my daughter, Margaret? She's been saving herself for you."

Leaning over the high back of the chair, John winked. "Sorry, Mrs White. Can't oblige. I'm saving myself for a rich widow."

"There's more mantraps set by mothers than by gamekeepers," Sam laughed when John reached him. He began, with the help of his friends, to give John the form of all likely girls, sporting dogs and pugilists for miles around.

"You'll be working with Sam, will you John?" Sam's friend took it for granted that his trade of poacher was known to his brother.

"That's sport. It only takes the place of work for the rich," John answered. "I'm thinking of starting a school."

"He's turning into an old dame," Sam joked, expressing the embarrassment he felt at his brother's statement, before anyone else did.

His friends had too much respect for Sam to comment in his presence. The boldest was satisfied with, "There's not much calling for book learning in Abingfield."

35

Before long, the talk turned to boxing and when bets were being laid, John, with some years of hard learning in that school, moved on to other friends and neighbours and conversations. Heading for a table where Charles had sat down, John found himself with Will Dodds and his old friends Paul Low, the shepherd, and Stephen Ballom, the shoe maker. With them was Tom Hutchinson. As Tom waved a greeting, John raised his glass, as everyone had done in Tom's presence in the army, and toasted, "The Revolution!"

Will looked uneasily around. "That's enough of that. You're in Abingfield now, John."

"Do you remember, a good twenty years ago, Will." Stephen Ballom asked, "after those Frenchies started all that trouble? The landlord here used to read newspapers to anyone who'd listen. Pretty fiery stuff, it was. Revolution and rebellion ...."

"And what happened to him?" Will demanded, hoping to end that topic of conversation. "Lost his licence and turned out of the village."

"It was Tom and me fought against the French for you," John reminded them. "And for men like this," he added loudly, staring insolently at Ben Walker, the Colonel's servant, who had searched him at Hangar Hill the day he returned. Raising his voice still louder, he demanded of no one in particular, "Here's the monkey. Where's the organ grinder?"

Although Ben Walker's expression told clearly that his dislike for John had been as immediate and strong as John's for him, he came forward politely enough. "Any of you gentlemen dropped this? Just kicked it with my foot on the floor down there as I was passing your table."

"Let's see," Tom said, taking the paper and spreading it out on the table. "This is what I like to see," he announced, smiling at the contents as he prepared to read the pamphlet.

The chance to show off his new skill of reading was too much for John. "Here. I'll read it." Loudly, for everyone to hear, he read

"To all stout hearted Englishmen. Soldiers of the Peninsula, of Waterloo and America, the war is not over, the Tyrant Napoleon has been defeated, but greater tyrants rule England. Join the army of Englishmen who rise up and cry for Liberty and the blood of our oppressors."

"Throw it away, John," Will Dodds interrupted, but John had everyone's attention for his reading and he was not going to stop.

"They tax us, but give us no voice to protest. The Placemen and

Sycophants in London do nothing but get rich and fat on our Labour and Taxes. These Leeches live on our Blood and Sweat and keep us as Slaves. They shall pay in their turn with Blood. These Tyrants have no power, but a corrupt Parliament. We must rise up like a Great Army and destroy them.

"There is no wealth without Labour, no justice without Democracy and no Victory without the Common Soldier. Leave your ploughs and Tools. Take up your Swords and Muskets. Cut down the English Tyrants. Signed the Captain."

As John came to the end, only Tom cheered.

"Here, Ben Walker, take it away. That belongs to no one here," Will assured him, anxious to be rid of the thing. "There's no man here hides behind a make believe title. There's a colonel in this village, but no captain."

"No." John took the paper from Tom's hand. "I'll have that."

"Is it yours? Do you agree with it?" Walker wanted to know.

John did not bother to answer, but his manner made it clear that the man was not welcome to join their conversation. Reluctantly, the Colonel's servant moved away.

"What do you want with that?" Will demanded.

"The back's quite blank. Just what I need to teach young Frances her letters." Folding it carefully, John placed the handbill in his pocket.

"What do you make of all those words?" Paul Low asked.

"And these times?" Stephen Ballom added.

"Time for men to take off their blinkers," Tom was quick to answer, although the question had not been addressed to him. "Stop thinking it's the weather, or God who's to blame for all evils instead of those tyrants in Parliament. Until every man…."

John seemed to be contemplating the marks of years worn into the heavy oak table top, but he spoke up at last, ignoring Tom's predictable opinion. "Join together? For my part, I want to get on by my own efforts. No one to blame but myself and no one to credit. After the war is the time for a new start."

"You're more like your father than you'll ever admit," Tom commented with obvious scorn.

"So? Pa's got his faults, but he owes no man. He raised himself from the workhouse to being a master. And he'll see that young Henry does the same."

Tom was not impressed, but Will had no hesitation in agreeing. "Glad to hear you talking like that, John. I'd begun to think you were one of those wild young men — all for changing everything and having a say in Parliament."

"Precious little chance of that," Tom muttered into his ale.

CHAPTER EIGHT

"Better make our way to our homes," Charles suggested. It was usually only on such small, everyday matters that he expressed an opinion.

About to follow the others, John's attention was caught by a man beckoning to him from a table in the corner of the room.

"Hear you're a bit of a surgeon," a small, neatly dressed man called to him.

Flattered, John went closer and answered, "I had a bit of experience helping the surgeons in the Peninsula."

The man drank from his tankard, slowly nodding his head. "Quite a lot of them died, eh?" he suggested tentatively.

"They did, but most of them would have died anyway. The surgeons saved some who were at death's door. You see….."

This time the man did interrupt him, but politely, so that John could take no offence. "My name is Wells, John Wells. Same handle as yourself, I believe. I'm in the medical business myself." He hurried on, "I'm looking for an assistant — a strong, intelligent chap like yourself with ambition."

The heavy flattery did the trick. John was listening eagerly. "I'm certainly interested. I need work and if it's a job with prospects, that's better still."

"You'll do alright. I'm in the profitable side of the business. None of your medicines what everyone wants on charity." Mr Wells decided to venture into the open. "Had a bit of experience of dead bodies, have you?"

"Too much," John agreed. "Buried many a good man." A thought struck him. "What are you then, an undertaker?" he inquired.

"A bit the reverse, really," the man chuckled, as his companion, a large, dark man sniggered.

"The reverse?" John's face was a blank for a moment and then his eyes showed his horror. "Resurrection men. You dig up bodies for surgeons to cut up. Resurrection men!" he repeated, too astonished to think of anything else.

Mr Wells silenced John. "It's not something we shout around. Have a drink on me while you get used to the idea."

"I shouldn't think you would shout it around!" John refused the drink. He decided he needed a clear head. "Is this some sort of joke?" John felt the suspicion of town dwellers so often felt by countrymen.

"I know how you feel." Mr Wells was all calmness and patience. "You're revolted. Sick to your stomach. I felt just the same and you should have heard my dear wife when she found out what I did. But we got used to it and so would you. It's a business like any other. A case of supply and demand. Not but what there ain't ghouls in the business, but I wouldn't invite anyone like that to join me."

"Did Sam put you up to this?"

"Sam? Your brother, the young sporting gent?" Mr Wells laughed indulgently at the joys of youth and then leaned closer, his expression serious and sincere. "Have a drink and let's discuss this business like men of the world."

As he had begun to feel he needed a drink, John changed his mind and accepted. They settled down to serious discussion. Mr Wells leaned forward, his head a little on one side, his expression one of transparent sincerity and his voice nicely balanced between that used to reason with a child and that used for talking man to man.

"Now, John, my boy, did these surgeons of yours in the Peninsula ever save a friend's life? Are there men walking around today, even on crutches, who should, by rights, be as dead as this table?"

"Certainly," John agreed. "There were a good few friends of mine in the Rifle Regiment who should be dead, but lived to see their families again."

"Just so. Just so," Mr Wells murmured, giving John enough time to recall his injured comrades. "Now, how do you think those surgeons knew what to do?"

"They got a deal good of experience on the battle field." John made an obvious point and spoiled the one his companion was making.

Mr Wells adjusted his argument a little. "You wouldn't want them practising on you if you was injured, would you? It's like everything — you need to practise. Would you expect a blacksmith to strike a good shoe first time? Would you expect a clockmaker to take a clock to pieces and put it back together again first time he saw one? Course you wouldn't."

The man paused for a second before making his next point. "A surgeon's like any other skilled man, any artisan. He serves his apprenticeship and part of that is practice. Would you like to be dealt with by a surgeon who did not know where your bones were? Who didn't know how to shorten your pain by snipping off your leg in a few minutes?"

John could find no answer to this and, as he thought it over, the man rammed home his argument.

"We serve a great need in the advancement of medicine and healing. Without us no surgeon could learn his trade. How can you expect them to manage on a few criminals took from the scaffold?"

"Maybe," John conceded at last. "I can't argue against you, but my feelings are still revolted. What about the feelings of the relations, too?"

"Relations?" Mr Well's tone and face suggested he was greatly insulted. "What do they know about it? We're not plunderers. We're craftsmen — master craftsmen — and we leave as we find. Who, just tell me, is going to check on a body if there is no sign of disturbance? What old woman is suddenly going to toddle down to the graveyard to check if her Fred's body is still planted in its hole?" His large, dark companion sniggered, as usual. "And your feelings," Mr Wells continued, with contempt. "Didn't realise you was rich enough to have feelings. My apologies. Didn't know you was a gent of independent means — a gent with feelings." He doffed his hat, mockingly. "Thought you would be glad of a bit of money. Suppose you're one of those able bodied fellows who'd rather be on poor relief."

Stung by his words, John replied, "I'm no pauper, but I don't want to be hung, either. It's stealing — stealing pure and simple."

"Stealing!" Mr Wells spoke with open contempt. "Who am I stealing from? Whose body is it? The fellow himself has finished with it. He's gone off to heaven or hell, as the case may be, and he has no more use for it. Thrown off his — what do you call it? — vile body and he's up in heaven in saintly white. I'm stealing from no one but the worms."

John's mind was now in utter confusion. This man had made the most startling proposition, but managed to make it sound reasonable and matter of fact. There'd be good money to be made. He laughed, half aloud, half to himself. "Whew!" was all he managed to say.

"Think it over, lad," Mr Wells urged. "It does no one any real harm and plenty — including yourself — a bit of good."

As John stood up, the man gripped his arm. "Just between ourselves." There was a threat in his tone.

"I don't think it's for me, but I'll tell no one."

John left the ale house, the conversation going round and round in his head. Suddenly, he stopped and laughed. A resurrection man! A body snatcher! He walked on. It was best not to get involved. Once he helped, they would have a hold over him. There were stories, too, that they sometimes made their own corpses.

Along the lane, half way from home, John heard a noise behind him. Instead of stopping and facing it, he continued, all too aware of the darkness. All the talk of bodies and death had made his imagination take flight.

"Go home, John Stevenson," he said to himself. "You're as bad as Frances with her bogey men."

CHAPTER NINE

Each day, even each hour, in Colonel Benson's life had its preordained task. He knew that there was a time for every purpose and that tonight, Saturday night, was the time for men, their tongues loosened by ale, to let slip a word or name, which would identify the rogues who had burned down five stacks in the village within the last month. In this knowledge, a few hours earlier, the Colonel had sent his servant, Ben Walker, to spy on his fellow men in the Navigators.

Briefing him, the Colonel had handed him a pamphlet, which had circulated in the neighbourhood, instructing him, "Note if anyone betrays an interest in such foul, seditious nonsense."

Quick as ever to understand his master, the servant still spoke modestly and differentially. "You mean, sir, I pretend to pick it up and ask, 'Any of you gentlemen dropped this? Just kicked it with my toe, over there on the floor?'"

"Just so. Just so. Encourage them to read it and carefully note their response. Watch their expressions. They will betray themselves."

As Walker saluted smartly, the Colonel added, "Beware of the sly ones. A man may feign indifference, yet pocket the paper to circulate once again." Now, the Colonel stood waiting for his servant's return. Walker had never disappointed him.

As a young child, the Colonel, inspired by his idol, Marlborough, had dreamed of the day when, tall and handsome, mounted on a beautiful charger, facing an enemy superior in numbers and equipment, he would order the guns forward, direct the cavalry to attack and the infantry to stand firm and, bringing up reserves, would cut off the enemy's retreat to win an astonishing victory.

Reality had been so very different. The boy who played so eagerly with his toy soldiers, who listened so intently to his mother's stories of her great grandfather who fought for King Charles against Cromwell, had grown not tall, but of middling height, not handsome, but passable. He had, indeed, rejected his curate father's advice to join the Ministry and won the help and approval of a maternal relation and the gift of a minor commission in a minor regiment, but lack of money and family connections had inevitably curtailed his advancement.

In action, in the American Colonies — he still thought of them by that title — he had shown himself a steady, reliable officer, perhaps better suited to organization and to the care of supplies than to the leadership of men. Returning, not to applause, but to a life of managing the estates of wealthier and more fortunate men, he had retired to a small house in Abingfield with his sister as housekeeper.

After such a life, it might have been understandable if the Colonel had turned bitterly against the society which, while giving riches and position to less worthy, but better connected men, had not recognised his worth or rewarded his service. Instead, Colonel Benson's precarious financial and social position, only just above the tradesmen and artisans, had led him to cling more fervently and fiercely to the beliefs, manners and interests of the gentry and aristocracy than any favoured gentleman might. While others could proclaim their position by connection, fortune or estate, Colonel Benson could prove his only by his bearing, his behaviour and his values. Over the years, he had come to embody the established ideals and institutions of England, so that any mention of threat to them was a threat to his very being.

Fear of change had kept alive the Colonel's boyhood dream of saving his country in its hour of need. At the time of the French Revolution, he had felt that hour had come at last, but it was not to be. Now, the war against Napoleon finally over, he was certain that the forces of atheism, of radicalism and revolution stood poised to attack in England. He praised God that he had been spared to do his duty.

At the Colonel's feet, his dog raised his head, listened and let it fall again, reassured by familiar footsteps.

"A good evening's work, sir," Ben Walker reported eagerly. "It's just like you said when you first set eyes on him that morning at Hangar Hill. Stevenson's a troublemaker."

"The facts, Walker. Relate the facts. I'll judge their importance."

Briskly, Walker reported the facts as he saw them. John Stevenson had been talking with Tom Hutchinson, a well known radical. He had pretended indifference, but had pocketed the pamphlet. He had engaged in subdued, secret conversation with men who travelled the canal.

The Colonel almost smiled. Now, in his conceit at spotting Stevenson's real character beneath the soldierly bearing, he could almost admit his envy of the man's youth and strength, the battles he had fought and the enemies

44

he had defeated.

"I heard more than they knew," Walker claimed with satisfaction. "He's ambitious. Wants to marry a rich widow. And he plans to start a school."

"To spread his poison?" the Colonel snapped, answering the last point first. "We'll put a stop to that nonsense." After a pause, planning how he would accomplish that, the Colonel returned to John's other plans. "Ambition, Walker. That has been the downfall of many a man. Such men envy their betters and use weak, ignorant men for their own purposes."

Content with his servant's work, and, for all his pride in his objectivity, not questioning one word of it, the Colonel bent to pat the dog, which had risen and stretched ready for his walk around the woods and fields where poachers roamed.

"Wait, Smoaker." The Colonel walked to his desk. In each pigeon hole and on each shelf were tidy piles of paper, neatly tied with ribbons placed precisely around their centres. Each pile was labelled, for the Colonel labelled things and people alike. From one word, the Colonel could describe a man's whole character to his entire satisfaction. About to label John Stevenson 'radical', a short description for 'rogue, traitor and destroyer of property', he suddenly stopped. As he reached for another pile of papers to place with John's in a new pigeon hole, he addressed the dog.

"We'll hunt a brace of Stevensons, Smoaker, my lad. John and Samuel. One radical and one poacher. A fine pair of villains."

CHAPTER TEN

Golden days of harvest blurred into misty October. November, a moody month of bright, sharp days and sudden storms, gave way to December with its more constant chill. Animals and people, each species and rank driven by its own unthinking interest, fell in with the rhythm of the seasons, living their lives to the beat of short winter days and long winter nights. Visiting birds flew to display their finery in warmer lands, the gentry to show off theirs at hunt and ball. Farseeing squirrels stored their food for rainy days, the farmer his wheat for better prices. Animal hunted animal with all the cunning of the gamekeeper pursuing the poacher.

The Stevensons and Dodds, no less than the birds and the animals, turned their faces against the cold and sought food and warmth for the winter. In the fields, the men buttoned their jackets and, dodging from shelter to shelter, looked forward to the cottage fire and to the bowl of onions to warm the hands and scorch the breath. There, in the cottages with the women and children, they sheltered themselves from the harshness of winter yet to come with the joyful anticipation of Christmas. Of an evening, with the doors tight shut, they made their gifts and went over, time and time again, their plans for that special day.

As usual, they agreed, they would all gather at the Dodds' house. That had an oven by the side of the fire and a larger room than the other cottages. They would bring all the chairs and stools from Edward's and Beth's and, even if it was a bit of a squeeze, they would all be warm and comfortable with plenty to eat for everybody. There would be a piece of pork from one of Will's pigs, one of Sarah hens, which was past laying, and a ham from Edward. Charles and John could bring the ale and that and the homemade wine would wash everything down a treat.

It would be a day for the children, but the men would enjoy lying in and then there would be church. It would suit everyone best, they all agreed, if they had a little something in their own homes at midday, went for a good walk to build up appetites and keep out of the way and then came together to eat by candle-light with the blazing fire in the hearth. Presents? Beth decided it would be a good idea for the children to have just one first and save the rest for later.

Somehow, cooking pies and puddings and cleaning the house from top to bottom, Sarah had not caught up with herself on Christmas morning. When Frances burst in, she was still trying to ease the stiff arms of the small, wooden doll, which Will had made, through the arm holes in the tiny dress.

"Your limbs are as bad as mine, Amelia," she said to doll. "Whatever will they be like when you're my age?" Sarah put the doll into Frances's eager hands. "There, my love, you finish it. Your fingers are younger than mine."

Frances hugged and kissed her grandmother, but, as she worked quickly with small, supple fingers, the child paid no heed to her grandmother's remarks about her stiff fingers. That was how it was with the young, Sarah thought. It was only when you were old yourself that you knew what old age meant. Without experience to give them meaning, words were just empty sounds. Until the last year or two, old age had not been a thing which she had wanted to face herself. You really gained nothing by facing it. You could not out-stare it, out-scheme it or find a way round it. Once the pains pinched your joints, made your feet drag and made your hands feel bloated and awkward, it was best just to carry on. For a while, a little extra care, a little extra concentration would make up for the clumsiness, but for how long there was no telling. It was right that children knew nothing of that long distant future.

"Well, Ma," Beth asked, pushing open the door with the chair she was carrying, "have you said it yet?"

"I'm sure we all say many things," Sarah answered, pretending not to understand what her daughter meant.

"'It doesn't seem a bit like Christmas.' You say that every year, Ma. Has she said it yet, Pa?"

"Not today," was Will's carefully considered reply. "A hundred times yesterday. A hundred times the day before, but she seems a bit quiet today."

"Who's this 'she' you're all talking about?" Sarah inquired, trying not to let them annoy her with their teasing.

"What's the other one, Ma? 'I wonder what we will all be doing this time next year?'" Beth laughed. "As though anything will change from one year to the next."

"This time last year," Sarah reminded them, "Tim wasn't born and John was miles away. And you tell me it's a foolish thing to say."

Seeing the tears in her mother's eyes, Beth laughed, gently this time, and kissed her. "We're all together, Ma. Let's enjoy ourselves." She could not resist adding, "For the children's sake." This was another of her mother's sayings, which was often heard at Christmas time.

"Be off or I'll spank you as big as you are"' Sarah laughed at herself. She knew, as well as anyone, how to put her own feelings aside and put her family first.

By the time church was over and the meat set in the oven, Sarah was so into the happy mood of the day and so raised in her own spirits, that she surprised everyone by agreeing to walk to the woods with Beth and the children, while John kept an eye on the cooking.

"I'll be back long before it's done," she told John, but somehow, with Beth seeming to want to waste time stopping and talking to everyone they met, everything was just about ready when they returned. Without pausing even to take off her outdoor clothes, she rushed in and pushed Sam aside. He was standing, smartly dressed in his best clothes, casually lounging with his back to the fire. Sarah opened the oven and, ignoring the blast of heat except to half close her eyes, reached in for the nearest dish. In her surprise at what came forth, she very nearly dropped it in the grate.

"That's no way to treat a brace of the best pheasants," Sam chided her. "Whoops," he exclaimed as Sarah stumbled again, his expression as innocent as a little boy's.

Sarah looked down to the dish and then up to Sam. "Sam, I won't rest while they're in the house."

"They won't be in the house long, in a manner of speaking," John pointed out. "And we'll bury the carcasses as soon as we've picked them clean."

Putting his arm around Sarah's shoulders, Sam assured her, "Jacob Rush will have his feet under his own table by now." As she seemed ready to be persuaded, he went on, "You know how careful I am. There's not a feather within a mile of here. Everything's gone on a bonfire."

With the selling of game forbidden by law, even Sam would have been at a loss to explain how the birds had got into the oven if anyone came searching, but Sarah loved a slice of pheasant and she knew it was Will's favourite dish. No one could deny him a little treat after all he had been through that year.

"If you're sure, Sam," Sarah smiled, setting the dish on the trivet while she checked the chicken and the pork. "There's enough mouths to feed."

"Presents first," John announced. "Everything on the floor here. Come forward when I call your name." He made a great to-do of collecting the presents until the children could hardly bear it any longer. "Tim. Here,

Frances, you had better take this for the baby."

Frances took in her hands the beautiful, smooth, round, glowing orange, its smell the unmistakable smell of Christmas.

"Billy." Frances pushed her brother forward. The quicker he was finished with the sooner she would have her own orange.

"Help Billy peel his," her father told her. Sighing at the helplessness of boys of nearly three year old, Frances hastily peeled the fruit. By the time she had finished they had passed on to other gifts and everyone was smiling and swearing that they had expected nothing so lovely or costly as the useful handmade gifts they received. Only she and Henry had been forgotten. There was no sign of another orange anywhere. Step by step Frances sidled up to her mother, who was nursing Tim, and leaned against her. It was greedy to ask for a present for herself, but her Ma could ask for her. She waited.

Her Ma was giving her full attention to giving Tim a taste of the juicy orange.

"Yes, my love." Beth at last reached to pat the child head.

Not sure how to draw attention to her plight without asking outright, Frances skirted the subject. "Billy's nearly finished his orange, Ma."

"Did you want a piece of it, Frances?" Beth's expression suggested that she had suddenly realised what her daughter wanted.

"Don't tease the child," Sarah said at last. "She's been as good as gold waiting so long."

"Tell her what you've got for her," Will prompted.

John, who had been standing with his hands behind him, seemingly lost in thought, said simply, "Don't ask, don't want. Ask don't get."

Frances ran to him, stretching her arms around him to reach his hands.

With an air of surprise and innocence, he held out one upturned palm to her. "Nothing there. Look." Putting that hand behind him and holding out the other, he added, "Nothing there, either."

"Enough's enough," Beth said and watched, as they all did, to see the anxiety on her daughter's face turn to radiant pleasure. In his hand, held out to his niece, John displayed a small, tin box and in it rattled three farthings.

"There. Every week I'll add another — when I have work and a wage, that is — and when you're ten you can choose what you want to do with all the money in it."

"It'll be a fortune," her father told her. More than your mother and me will have put together."

"More than a child of ten will know what to do with." Sarah did not approve of allowing a child to decide such a matter. "It will do towards your bottom drawer," she told the girl.

"You can buy books, a dress, anything you like," John repeated.

With Frances sitting happily hugging her tin, there was silence for a moment.

"I suppose my old present isn't good enough for you now," Will observed.

"Amelia's lovely, Grandpa," Frances answered.

"Not Amelia. The other wooden present."

Her eyes taking in the whole room, Frances asked, "Where is it, Grandpa?"

"You're using it already."

There was nothing made of wood that Frances was using that she could see. She stood up, turning around to look behind her. John swung her up onto her chair.

"First you were sitting on it," he told her. "Now you're standing on it."

"The chair?" The present was so wonderful, Frances could not believe it. It was more than a chair, more than a chair which had belonged to her mother and her grandmother. It was more than a chair made out of oak by her great grandfather. The present was an acknowledgement that she was the oldest, that she was almost grown up and that she was too old to perch on a stool like an infant. Frances's happiness was complete.

At first pushing close to the others around the fire and gradually, as they busied themselves giving and receiving presents, retreating to stand and watch a little apart, Henry struggled to understand all that was happening. No one had thought to tell him what families did on Christmas Day and he had certainly never seen for himself. All he had been told in the past few days, when he had bubbled over with excitement, was that he would have to behave himself in someone else's house and he was desperately anxious not to offend. Seeing the last of the oranges gone and the other presents distributed, the boy had concluded, denying his disappointment, that presents were given only to relations and not to apprentices. It was Frances's being given a chair which made him realise, in one joyous moment, that his present was in the sweep's house. Without a word from anyone, he rushed out through the door and along the street.

The sweep's cottage had one room up and one down and, in the parlour just beneath the ceiling, there was the wooden bed where Henry slept. The board across the opening had been broken long ago by John or Charles or Sam larking about up there. John had promised to repair it and Henry was certain, as he ran along the lane, that he would find it mended now, as good as new. Once in the house, he ran to where the shaky ladder stood and stopped. The old ladder with the missing rungs was gone and, in its place, a new one rose, rung by perfect rung, to the bed enclosed now by a new plank. In the poor light there seemed to be a blemish on the plank, but, as Henry climbed level with it, he saw it was the letter 'H' carved in the very centre with a wiggly pattern around the edges. John had made it all secretly and fixed it in place while they were out walking.

More was to come. Neatly folded on the bed was a pair of breeches, a shirt and a jacket. It did not matter to Henry, it did not occur to him, that they were second, even third, hand. They had been bought, cleaned and lovingly sewn for him and for no one else. They were the first present he had ever been given in his life at Christmas time.

Impulsive as ever, Henry took off his jacket to put on his new clothes. Then he reflected that he would need a better scrubbing than he had given himself that morning before he could wear them. Carefully folding one on the other, he rolled them up and placed them under his arm. The others had their presents with them and he would have his. It would be no problem to him to eat his dinner with the bundle under his arm.

At last remembering that the meal would be ready on the table, Henry swung open the door and, head down, lunged into the lane.

"Steady, son." Jacob Rush, held his hand out to protect himself from being butted by the child. Backing away, Henry's first thought was to run off towards the fields hoping Rush would follow him, but there was no reason why the gamekeeper should be after him. He must warn the others. Dashing around the man, Henry headed straight for the Dodds' house instead.

The food was set on the table in the candle-light and everyone sat wondering whether to wait for Henry or go and fetch him. When he burst in, they were pleased to be saved the trouble and laughed, expecting to be thanked for the gifts.

"Mr Rush. It's Mr Rush," he yelled. There was time to say no more.

Heavy footsteps sounded close behind the boy and Will had hardly reached the door when, without even a token knock, Jacob Rush let himself into the room.

"You'll not enter my house without my permission," Will told him.

"I've the Master's permission."

"Sir Philip's not my master."

"He's my master and that's good enough for me."

The gamekeeper stepped further into the room and stared at the food on the table. There was no game on the table, but there was a space where another dish might have stood and Beth was wiping a dish on her clean, white apron.

"I told you, Ma, that this dish would be too small for the chicken. I've put it on a bigger one. I'll just put this away."

Jacob Rush knew, for certain, every bone in his body confirmed it, that, at last, he had Sam Stevenson within his grasp. Beth's trying to explain away the spare dish, the fear on the old woman's face, the sweep's boy with eyes raised to the ceiling, Charles holding Billy tightly in his arms with his face tucked down so that he could not look at the spot and, most of all Sam lounging in his chair, all told him he was right. Struggling, in spite of his father's efforts, Billy twisted his head over his shoulder to gaze from the empty space on the table to Frances.

"Stand up," Jacob Rush ordered the little girl.

Frances looked at her mother and tears swelled in her eyes.

"She's upset," Beth explained hastily. "She spoilt her best dress helping me take the chicken from the oven."

For a second, as the child stood up, sobbing, to reveal a greasy stain on her dress, the gamekeeper hesitated. Then, in a second, he realised what had happened. He grabbed Frances and stood her on her chair, expecting the evidence, a pheasant or rabbit, to fall from her petticoats. Charles moved towards him and Sam and John rose from their seats. A deep, threatening growl sounded from beneath the table, close by his leg. Rush groaned and swore under his breath. Too respectful of Sam's ratting dog to put his own hand towards it, he ordered Sam to call the dog out.

"Mind, Frances," Sam said, wasting precious seconds in lifting her aside and moving the chair.

"Get that brute out — and fast." There must still be some evidence, Rush prayed. Just a bone would be enough for a magistrate, who had himself experienced the harm poachers did to a gentleman's estate.

"Here, Cribb." As the command was spoken, Cribb, a close cousin to a mastiff, lumbered out, its long tail slowly beating the air and its mouth seemingly drawn back in a satisfied smile. Taking a candle from the table, Rush bent down, and, moving the light slowly from side to side, searched the floor. Not a scrap of flesh, not a bone was to be seen. There was not even a speck of grease, such must have been the speed and efficiency with which Cribb had dispatched the bird.

"Have we Sir Philip's permission to eat our own food, now, under our own roof?" Will asked. "It'll be cold before you've finished playing games."

Jacob Rush left without a word, but he heard the laughter which followed him along the lane. What he did not hear was the triumphant sound, loud and clear like a post horn, which Henry made as he unrolled the bundle under his arm and let one pheasant drop onto the table. It was the cock bird, not as tender as the hen which Cribb had enjoyed, but it tasted even better than Will had anticipated.

CHAPTER ELEVEN

For months all the ladies of Abingfield had interfered in Anne Gray's plans for a Sunday school in the village. Suddenly all had more urgent calls on their time. It was a sure sign that the school was, at last, about to begin. Miss Gray found herself alone in preparing the barn where the school was to be held and alone in preparing to face the children who were expected. The advice she had received at every turn, as she had walked the parish collecting contributions from the gentry, farmers and tradesmen, on how to deal with the sprigs of the lower orders was all she had to help her now the day was here.

"Be firm," Mr Simpkins had advised. "Start as you mean to go on. There's only one language these people understand. They respect you for it, you know."

"Tire them out," Sergeant Grant had told her. As a former drill sergeant he claimed, with some justification, to have had much experience of commanding the lower ranks. "When we weren't fighting, there was always trouble. Hanging around, doing nothing, that was always the time for drinking and a knifing or two, maybe. Drill — that was my answer. Keep them in the habit of obeying orders. Keep them working together, listening to you and following you. If I still had my leg," he had concluded, "I'd be there keeping order for you."

Anne had found that everybody had an excuse, most far less honest than Sergeant Grant's, for not actually being in the classroom with her. Everyone talked of our school, our subscriptions and our efforts, but, now Sunday was here, the scheme would stand or fall by her efforts alone.

Early in the morning, Miss Gray took Rebecca Dodds from her work in the vicarage and went to prepare the barn.

"Pooh!" Becky stopped at the door and held her nose against the smell of pigs and chickens and hay. "Some of the children will feel at home."

"A good country smell," her mistress told her, holding her handkerchief to her nose.

"The Donkins will fit in. All ten of them are coming." Becky was rewarded by a shudder from her mistress at this news. "Still, our Frances will help to make up for them. She's been sick with excitement as the day's got nearer."

Anne was experiencing the same feeling, but she was not convinced it was prompted by excitement. She wondered whether the whole thing was not, as her brother, Nicholas, said, simply the idea of a young lady with nothing better to do.

"It'll be alright, Miss Gray, you'll see. It's going to be a great success." In her heart, Becky knew she would not face the mob of children for all the tea in China.

"It's so different from my own school days," Miss Gray told her, looking around at the untidy, bare building.

"And mine!" Becky laughed. "Spent my school days in the kitchen and washhouse helping Ma."

"That was an excellent education for your duties in life, Becky."

The servant agreed, "Ma and Pa brought us up right." Then she went back to listing the children who would be attending.

"The Braithwaites are coming. Mr Hammond told them they had to come or there'd be trouble."

"I don't expect those were Mr Hammond's exact words," Anne laughed, imagining telling Richard what she had been told.

"You know what I mean, Miss Gray," Becky explained. "If you're in work, you do what your master says so that you stay in work. It stands to reason."

Anne Gray hastened to state the argument more clearly. "It is any employer's duty to set a good example and give good advice."

Becky continued her counting. "They'll be Eliza's four — just out of curiosity. That Jemima's too knowing by half. I should think all the labourers' children in the village will turn up the first time. She looked around. "Don't you need desks, Miss Gray, like the grammar school in Gressingford?"

"Dear me, no! The children do not need to write, Becky. They'll need no desks or even slates."

At the end of the barn, Miss Gray stood rehearsing the lesson without an audience. "I think I'll put a few letters on the blackboard and then I can start straight away without turning my back on the children."

"You've got the right idea, Miss Gray."

Anne wrote the first few letters of the alphabet. "Questioning is a good method to keep children's interest," she explained to Becky. "I shall begin by asking them which letter this is."

"It's A, isn't it?" Becky asked, quite pleased to be showing off her knowledge. When her mistress agreed, she added, "They'll tell you that's what the horses eat. Anyway, how can they answer questions before you've taught them anything?"

"Becky, I came here early to bolster my confidence and you are doing your best to destroy it. I can only repeat the method by which my brother and I were taught, by my father and my governess. It worked very well with us."

After early morning church, Anne hurried back to the barn, eager to begin. A little girl walked close by her and Anne recognised the child as Becky's niece. Seeing her eager, alert expression, Anne's spirits rose. Within a second, a young boy charged up, his feet stamping the ground and his tongue clacking in imitation of galloping feet. Frances was flung forward as Henry, ceasing to be a fiery steed, slapped her on the back, but, as soon as Anne looked at him, he hung his head. Billy, only three, rushed up like a young colt, only to become as silent and shy as his friend. Anne decided to leave it to a later lesson to teach them it was not seemly to rush about on a Sunday. They had so much to learn.

She greeted the other children who had been at church and who now caught her up, some showing off and others, shy and quiet, keeping their distance. From the barn as Anne and the young children approached, came loud laughter and shouting. A boy at the door dashed in as he caught sight of them and the noise stopped at once. Anne's heart sank, but she walked in. On bales of hay, the Donkins and Braithwaite families were seated, hats on the back of their heads and feet stretched out before them. Brothers, sisters, cousins, aunts and uncles, nieces and nephews, aged from two to twenty, stared insolently at Anne as she entered.

She was hardly in the door when there was a crash behind her and she turned to see Henry, the sweep's boy, flat on his face. Nearby, Joshua Donkins gazed at the ceiling and whistled a casual tune. His followers and admirers giggled excessively. Straightening himself and brushing down his best jacket, which he had been strictly instructed to keep clean, Henry made a move as though to attack. Joshua's clenched fists showed all too clearly what would happen if the youngster made a move. Wisely, Henry moved away. Anne was never quite sure what happened next, but there was a piercing scream from Joshua's youngest and smallest supporter by whom Henry happened to have stopped.

Hastily beginning her lesson in an attempt to gain the children's attention, Anne indicated the verse she had written on the board, carefully pronouncing each word as she pointed to it. "Frances Stevenson," she instructed, picking on one of the few children she knew by name, "read it after me."

Frances, who had a quick memory, repeated the verse with only a few promptings.

"Henry, now it's your turn," Anne ordered.

Embarrassed by hearing his name spoken before such a large gathering by a lady he hardly knew, Henry could get no further than the first word. The strange words and phrases of biblical language had meant nothing to him and he could not even guess at them. With whistles and jeers, Joshua and his friends mocked the boy's feeble efforts.

"Got soot in 'is 'ead, Miss," one volunteered.

"It's 'is 'ead, Miss. 'E 'it it falling down a chimbley," another called. "Knocked 'is wits out, it did."

Sidling up to him, deftly dodging the feet set to trip her and the hands reaching to pull her hair, Frances prompted him and Henry made a brave attempt to carry on. Anne tried to ignore the commotion, hoping it would die down once the lesson was under way, but she found that every time she looked at the board there were cries and shuffling, suggesting that Henry was being poked and pinched. Trying to look at the class, Anne found it impossible to follow the words on the board with her pointer. Angry at such treatment, which she had never known in her life before, Anne was determined the school would not fail. She pointed straight at Joshua.

"You will read next," she ordered.

The youth leaped to his feet, tilted his hat forward and leered at her. "Oo, Miss 'as chosen me." He flexed his muscles as he paraded up and down, pausing now and again to wink, muttering suggestions and invitations which made the other children snigger or gasp. His performance was greeted by the usual cheers from his followers and some began to stamp and whistle. Other children looked on in horror and waited to see what Miss Gray would do. The old sergeant's advice rang in Anne's ears. She must make them work together. She must gain their undivided attention. Perhaps, if she began some drill — she could not believe it would offend God on the Sabbath — the louts would leave and she could resume her lesson.

"Frances. Henry. Billy." She summoned those she knew. "Come to the front. The other girls line up behind Frances and the boys behind Henry."

Relieved to see most children obeying her, Anne Gray instructed them with a little more confidence. "Girls walk that way round the barn and the boys in the opposite direction." It seemed to be working. "Now run. Don't push!" The children obediently ran. "Now skip."

The sergeant had been right. Even the younger Braithwaites and Donkins were joining in. The older boys, bored, were considering leaving, the fun over. "Now walk on your toes."

The little girl near the front stopped suddenly, the rest of the line bumping into her and coming to an abrupt halt. It was Emma Braithwaite trying, with great effort and determination, to walk with one foot placed firmly on the toes of the other. Sensing everyone else was watching her, she looked puzzled and defeated.

"I can't do it, Miss," she declared. "I can't walk on me toes, Miss." Everyone laughed, not only Joshua and his gang, but even Frances and Billy. Henry, with Billy copying him, collapsed on the floor and rolled about in merriment.

Never one to miss an opportunity, Joshua picked Henry up by the scruff of his neck and began to spank him. "You naughty boy," he said in a high voice, apparently imitating their teacher, "you must not laugh on the Sabbath."

Like an eel, Henry wriggled out of his jacket and shinned up a supporting beam and across to a mullion window. Henry was an old hand at escaping from bullies.

Defeated at last, seeing her boasts, her hopes and her Sunday school disappearing beneath the laughter and jeering of the children she had so sincerely wanted to help, Anne cried. She hated herself for it, but they were tears of anger as well as sorrow and she could not stop them. A hush fell on the children. For a moment, Anne Gray thought they had seen her tears and soon the whole village would know. Then she noticed that the children were gazing up at Henry, murmuring in admiration at his skill and asking each other what he was doing.

"Henry's running away, Miss," a child informed her gleefully.

Henry, indeed, had his head and shoulders through the bars and was pulling his legs and body through. Was he leaving or was he shouting to someone who was passing? With horror, Anne imagined all the children screaming and calling and hanging out the windows. Joshua clearly had the same vision. Organising his followers, he ordered some to go after Henry and others to scramble like monkeys to the rafters.

Henry had disappeared. Anne stood helplessly watching. Suddenly, before her in the doorway, a look of complete triumph on his face, was Henry and behind him a man Anne knew by sight.

"With your permission, Miss Gray," the man said, politely taking off his hat as he entered the barn. Quickly deciding that Joshua was the ringleader, he clipped the youth's ears, wheeled him around and marched him to the back of the class. The small riot in Abbingfield melted away. The other youths fell over themselves in their haste to stand quietly in line looking towards Miss Gray. The younger children stood wide-eyed in front. Sunday school was the most exciting thing to happen in the village in their short lives.

All eyes on him and feeling at a loss for words now the action was over, the man took his hat from Henry. "I'll be just outside for a while, Miss Gray. Henry can fetch me if necessary."

For once, Anne was equally at a loss for words. There was no accepted way to thank someone who had just subdued your Sunday school class with blows and threatening glances.

"I'm quite sure I can manage, Mr..." The man's name would not spring to her mind.

"Mr Stevenson," Henry announced with pride.

"Mr Stevenson," Anne repeated.

John bowed like a man not much used to bowing and glanced quickly around the class in case anyone laughed at him. No one did.

"That's my uncle," Frances whispered to those around her. Uncle John knew everything — from what the sea looked like to how to box Joshua Braithwaite's ears.

"We shall make a fresh start," Miss Gray told the children. She had recovered her composure. Frances repeated the verse. Henry repeated the verse with much prompting. Joshua repeated the verse, even though the words seemed to stick in his throat.

"If ye be willing and obedient, ye shall eat the good of the land." Briefly explaining the verse, Anne told them to obey their parents' and masters' smallest wish with eagerness and speed, for God had set them in authority over children. Now the time passed quickly and Anne had scarcely time to touch on the A, B, C before it was time for the children to go home. Some children, well primed by their parents, thanked her kindly and Henry bowed, as he had seen John do.

As Anne Gray had feared, John Stevenson was waiting for her outside, seemingly proud of what he had done. "You got the measure of those lads in the end, then, Miss?"

"Most people have a better side to appeal to, I find," Anne answered primly.

"They knew you were outside, John," Henry boasted.

John did not deny his part in the happy outcome. "May I suggest, Miss Gray, you'd do better to start with just the younger ones — under thirteen, say? Strapping lads of sixteen and seventeen don't take kindly to being given orders by a lady. Many Sunday schools admit men and women, as well as children and they'd keep order for you."

Anne Gray did not intend to discuss the matter and she assumed that was the last word, but it was not.

"Then the men can keep an eye on the boys. Adults and children or just children, I would say."

Having been brought up never to argue with servants — and this was only Becky's brother-in-law— she answered shortly, "My father has the final say in such matters."

"I wish I'd had the opportunity to learn when I was young," John told her, falling in uninvited beside her. "My life would have been very different."

"It is certainly not my aim to make people dissatisfied with their lot," Miss Gray disclaimed, in haste, anything so irresponsible. "My aim is to bring contentment by bringing them closer to God."

"I don't know the rights and wrongs of it, Miss Gray," John said simply, "but I know reading is the key to the wide world. Do you know, Miss, there are countries I didn't even know existed? Animals and plants, the stars, history and geography. I've so much to learn"

Not seeming to notice Miss Gray was walking the more quickly to reach home and was giving him no encouragement to talk, John continued earnestly, "'God save the King' we all say. Do you know, Miss, there are many in this very village who do not know the King's name?"

"There are many more, I fear, who do not know the nature of God and have not shared the joy of following His commands. Bringing the common people to a knowledge of their Maker is my humble purpose, no more, no less."

Realising Miss Gray was about to disappear through the vicarage gate, John hurried to broach the subject of a school. "I wondered, Miss Gray ..." sensing her coolness, he began again, "Perhaps I should speak with Mr Gray. You see, Miss, I wanted to start a school. Just reading and writing and a little arithmetic and I..."

"Goodness me," Miss Gray laughed aloud in genuine astonishment. "What would happen to the work in the fields? And the children's wages? Would you turn their parents into paupers and throw them on the parish while their children sat in a school room?"

"But just the little ones — for a year or two. Little children like Frances."

"But what better schooling for life, Mr Stevenson, than learning their work in the fields? They must learn that he who does not work, does not eat." With great finality, she concluded, "My father would never agree and no school can be started without his permission. Only this morning I heard him assure Colonel Benson that there would be no day school in Abingfield while he was alive to stop it."

CHAPTER TWELVE

Sam's friends had been right, John found. There was little call for book learning in Abingfield. Those who wanted it for their children had no money to spare and Mr Gray and most of the farmers actively discouraged talk of any such idea. Just to earn money, he worked in the fields as a daily labourer, but, when the weather was bad and there was no work, he trudged the villages looking for an opening for a man with ambition who wished to improve himself. As one wild goose chase followed another, so another hope was destroyed. Soon, he would have to do what everyone was telling him he would have to do in the end, either be satisfied as a labourer, like every other man, or join his father as a sweep.

Walking along the lane, feeling so frustrated that he was even toying with the idea of joining John Wells, the old man who had approached him in the ale house, John thought back to how, as a boy, he had walked these fields, scaring birds. When he had grown tired of turning his rattle and chasing over the fields, he had stood, arms outstretched like a scarecrow. In his scruffy clothes, he had thought he might well be mistaken for the real thing. Was that all his future held?

As he walked on over the meadow in the lengthening evening shadows, John saw the big buck hare he had watched on so many evenings. Silent, still, it had lain in its form, its ears flat against its back, until he was almost upon it. Then it leaped within an inch of his boot. Over the brow of the hill it went, its running smoother and its stride longer as it fell into the rhythm of movement. Bending down, John examined the hollow in the clump of grass. The flattened, browning grass was warm to his touch. Startled by the animal's sudden leap, John's own heart was beating fast. How much faster the hare's heart must have beaten, John thought, as it had lain there watching his coming, feeling the ground vibrating and hearing the thump of his boots on the earth. No wonder the women folk thought witches entered the bodies of hares to disguise themselves from humans. Perhaps it was because the hare was so like a rabbit and yet so different that women had become suspicious of it. The animal had ears like a rabbit and yet the ears were longer, long enough, you could imagine, to hear men's thoughts. It could outrun most animals to disappear into thin air. Strangest of all, it lay above the ground as though it would stifle in a dark burrow beneath the surface.

Lying in bed that night, John was tempted to go after the hare. Restless and bored, like any soldier used to activity, he lay waiting for Sam to come home. For once Sam did not feel his way up the stairs in the dark, but lit a candle and sat on the edge of John's bed.

"Are you awake, John?" he whispered.

"Haven't been to sleep yet."

Keeping his voice low, as though a gamekeeper might be listening at the window, Sam asked, "Would you like to join us John? There's this fellow who can sell any fur or feather we can acquire."

"Don't think I haven't thought about it already, Sam. The trouble is, there doesn't seem to be anything I want to do if I can't be a school master. It's all I've thought about for the last year or two."

Sam did not press his offer. He dropped his boots to the floor one by one and blew out the candle.

"I saw the big buck hare again today."

"Don't touch it," Sam warned.

"You sound like the old women."

"It's Jacob Rush, the gamekeeper. Since we made a fool of him at Christmas, he's got together with the Colonel and that servant of his to set mantraps and spring guns just about everywhere. I hear the snap of those things in my nightmares. Serve them right if some gentleman walks right into one." It was more likely, as sometimes happened, that a dog would walk into one, but Sam could not bear the thought of that.

"Protecting game," John laughed. "It's all a game in itself."

"Maybe, but there's playing fair and playing dirty. I'd never use a gun against a gamekeeper. Just my fists. That's a rule I go by. Jacob Rush and that Colonel have no rules." A thought occurred to Sam, or perhaps it had occurred to him before and he was just trying it out on his brother. "We could lay in wait on a dark night and teach Jacob Rush a lesson he won't forget in a hurry."

"That's against my rules, Sam."

"So they're to get away with maiming anyone and anything that walks in the woods?"

"What ...?" John began, his mind racing with the joy of activity. "There might be a way of making them look fools without anyone getting hurt or us getting caught."

It was easy, once John had worked out the plan, to collect a few volunteers, as restless as he was and as set against Jacob Rush and the Colonel as Sam was, and gather outside the gates of the Big House. It was easy, too, to persuade the gatekeeper to let Sam and him in by saying that they had come to earn a few shillings boxing with Mr Hammond. It was less easy to persuade the man to let the other men through.

"Wait there," John told them. "We'll think of something." For once he had something to do and a chance to exercise his mind.

The gatekeeper had pointed out a thatched cottage not far along the path and the two brothers made their way there. The building had been a stable, part of a farm demolished as an eyesore when the park was being landscaped. Leaving it had greatly upset the planners, but Richard Hammond, commenting that, "Man cannot live by fox hunting alone," had asked for it to be left as a place where he and his friends could practise the manly science of boxing. His father, thinking it would keep him from London and other places where he might waste his life and money, had agreed. At last, the architect had thought of disguising the old stables as a cottage, in the modern, picturesque style, and everyone was happy.

Inside, the building was a copy of Tom Cribb's place in London. An ardent follower of fighting himself, Sam gazed around enraptured. The lower part of the building had been converted into one large training room and, at the far end, a sparring bout was being watched by a group of gentlemen. Lost in admiration and envy for what he saw, Sam walked around the room, looking at the prints and paintings of prize fighters which adorned the walls. "Come here, John. Read this for me."

Checking that the gentlemen's attention was still engaged, John joined his brother and read the magic names to him.

"Richard Humphreys. There's Gentleman Jack Jackson. That's Jack Carter against Tom Oliver at Gretna Green."

Most of the figures and poses showed a remarkable resemblance to each other, but Sam spotted the longish hair of one fighter.

"That'll be Mendoza."

Unable to list the kings of England, or its generals and admirals before Nelson and Wellington, and never having heard of Castlereagh or Canning, Sam could, like every true Englishman, rich or poor, list Cribb, Spring, Oliver, Carter, Jackson, Humphreys and the Game Chicken. He admired them, even worshipped them, as shining examples of the pluck, skill, strength, doggedness, heart, openness and all the other manly virtues, which made his country men stand without equal in the world.

"This isn't what we came for, Sam," John whispered, tugging at his sleeve and accidentally jogging the table on which stood replica silver trophies. Bored by the unequal struggle they had been watching, the gentlemen looked round to the noise. John did not attempt to hide his nervousness, but exaggerated it, twisting his hat and bowing awkwardly, with Sam doing the same beside him.

"What have we here?" Richard Hammond asked his companions. "A Johnny Raw and Dusty Bob, if ever I saw them."

"We've no work, sir," John said meekly, "and we thought we might earn a shilling or two sparring with the gentlemen."

"A shilling or two. We'll see." Richard Hammond was not going to throw money away. Contrasting his meanness towards them with his extravagance in dress and the expense of the building, John's conscience was eased.

"Let's see what you can show us," one of the gentlemen urged.

"Before we consider money," Mr Hammond said, "we'll see you spar. Come on. Strip down and let's have an exhibition of fisticuffs."

Doing as they were told and glad that they had swilled down under the pump before coming, Sam and John shed their clothes to the waist.

"Shall we put on mufflers, sir?"

"We want to see your spirit, my man, as well as your skill. Let it be bare fists and hard blows."

From sparring together and from John's having seen Sam fight whenever injury or insult required, they knew each other's style well enough to let the match go as they wished, with John showing some skill and winning at first, but with Sam appearing the pluckier and more promising of the two. The gentlemen were absorbed by the entertainment, following each blow with cheers and advice.

Sam hit John hard on the body. "What a stomacher!"

John hit back to the head. "That's it. Plant one on his knob!"

Sam landed a blow on John's mouth. "Right on the mug! Now pepper his sneezer."

Delighted, Richard Hammond told his friend Arthur Browne, "Didn't I tell you we had some fine native talent locally? Try a round or two with the younger one." Seeing John seemingly unable to beat Sam, Arthur Browne was dying to try his skill.

"Enough," Richard Hammond called and, putting his arm around Sam's shoulder, invited him to stand up against his friend. Sportingly, he suggested that Sam should rest awhile and agreed with John's suggestion that some of Sam's friends, who had waited at the gate, should be allowed in to cheer him on and place a bet or two.

Once the fight started, Sam showed his true skill and ability. Whatever their purpose had been in coming to the training room, all he wanted now was to win and knock the smile off the gentleman's face. He had won every fight he had been caught up in over the last year or two and it did not occur to him that he could lose this one, or, rather, it did not occur to him in the first half. Underestimating his opponent, he was deaf to John's warning to take it steady and hold something back until his opponent had weakened. The only thought in Sam's mind was to thrash the gent, quickly and thoroughly.

It was half an hour before, too late, Sam realised this fighting was quite a different matter from scraps in the ale house. Arthur Browne not only matched him in weight and reach and in strength, but outdid him in skill and training and, above all, in experience and stamina. As Sam, with only victories in short fights with village lads to his name, was panting and feeling his legs growing heavier and heavier, Mr Browne, who trained every day in London with prize fighters, was breathing and moving almost as easily as when he started.

By this time, Sam's aim had changed from wanting to win to wanting to show he had as much pluck as any man. He kept coming forward, he kept rising from the ground and he kept trying to hit the elusive figure who danced around him. Time and again, barely able to see through his swollen eyes, with blood running from his nose and cut cheeks, he protested whenever John tried to stop the fight. It seemed that, for the sake of Sam's pride and the betting, the contest would have to go on until Sam was unconscious, but, at last, Richard Hammond stepped forward.

"The gentlemen who placed bets on Sam concede victory to his opponent." Leaving John and a servant to tend Sam's cuts and bruises, Richard Hammond took a collection among his friends.

"Give generously. You'll seldom see such an exhibition of native skill and thorough bottom."

Five pounds were collected and, as Sam's hands were too battered to take the money, it was handed to John for safe keeping. Arthur Browne, content with the day's exercise and victory, stood and gave advice to John on how to treat Sam's injuries and to Sam on how to defend himself. Then he prepared to bathe and dress.

"My clothes," he called to a servant. "Fetch my clothes."

"They were here, sir."

"They're plainly not here now. Find them."

A prolonged search, increasingly thorough, failed to reveal the clothes. "They've been stolen," a gentleman announced, stating what was, by now, obvious to everyone.

"Run after those men," Richard Hammond ordered the servants and they hurried off. A few gentlemen went with them just for the fun, but they returned without the clothes. John and Sam stood ready to leave. As they had been in full view of everyone all the time, no one could suspect them.

"What are the names of the fellows who were here?" Richard Hammond demanded. Thinking hard, John named a few names. "They wouldn't have taken them, sir. I can't recall all of them."

"The coat cost a fortune," Arthur Browne complained.

"Look at it this way," Richard Hammond suggested. "Your tailor has lost a coat. I'm sure you hadn't paid for it, had you?"

"It was out of fashion, in my opinion," another gentleman stated. "You had worn it twice to my knowledge."

"Can't you recall the men who were here, Richard?" Arthur made a last appeal.

Richard Hammond reluctantly made an effort to conjure up the sea of grubby faces he had seen earlier.

"They all look alike to me."

CHAPTER THIRTEEN

Once the brothers reached home again, John took over the execution of the plan, with help from Beth and Becky. They swore the children to secrecy on pain of torture.

Early the next day, Jacob Rush, the Hammond's gamekeeper, sat giving careful thought to the night's events. While patrolling one side of the estate, he had heard a shot not far away and hurried over. Finding nothing, he had concluded it was a diversion and had made his way at speed to the other side of the estate. Heading there, he had heard a shot from another direction and changed his path. That was how it had been all night. They had led him right, left, forward and back, from one end of the estate to the other and back again. He was inclined to think it was someone with a grudge trying to give him a sleepless night, but he went over the plan of the grounds in his mind to see which area he had not been drawn into by the joker. He had not been sent on a wild goose chase to Hangar Wood.

Without more ado, the gamekeeper made his way there. Just as he was about to leave the lane and enter the wood Jemima, Eliza's eldest, ran up to him, her mouth wide open with fright. Grabbing his arm and tugging him after her, she gabbled words he could not catch.

"Calm down, girl. What is it?"

"Oh, mister, there's a man dead in the wood." Looking at him, an expression of horror on her face, she breathed, "A gentleman."

The gamekeeper's thoughts flew to the mantrap. He would be in trouble if a gentleman had been hurt. He would be blamed for setting the trap too near the road.

As though reading his thoughts, Jemima suggested, "Perhaps he walked in after 'is dog, or something."

"Where is he? How do you know he's a gentleman?"

"There's no mistaking a gentleman. Ma 'as gentlemen call sometimes. Some with titles, she sez."

The original purpose of his visit to the wood forgotten, Jacob Rush followed the child into the wood. She ran ahead, pointing with one hand and half covering her eyes against the sight which lay in front of them with the other. At a small hill, she stopped and pointed into the dip, thick with bushes, at the foot of the next hill. The gamekeeper's heart was beating as never before. That was just where he had set a trap. His skin was cold and he felt as though a giant hand clutched at his innards.

"There's the gent, mister. 'Is 'ead and shoulders is sticking out of them bushes."

Jacob Rush, no coward, had to force himself to look. The top half of the body rose from the bushes above the spot where he had set the trap. It was all too obvious what must have happened. The gentleman had been walking down the hill, had slipped and slid into the trap which had snapped to on him.

There the gentleman lay, twisted so that his face was buried in the hill side, with one arm above his head and the other limp at his side. The attitude was that of a lifeless body. Worse still, it was a gentleman's body. The girl was right. Those clothes were expensive, anyone could see that. This, Rush concluded, was the end of him as a gamekeeper. Charges would be brought and it would be the end of him. Trapping poachers was one thing to a judge, but trapping stray gentlemen was quite another.

Crossing the narrow valley, Jacob Rush prayed as he had never prayed before. He prayed that the gentleman had just fainted, not died, or that, in slipping, he had missed the trap and died of natural causes.

Jemima took up her position behind the gamekeeper, peering at the body through her hands. "I don't want to see all the blood, mister." As an after thought, she asked, "Will the gentleman's leg be snapped right off?"

"Be quiet." Rush knew better than to send her away. He might need someone to back him up in a story to get him out of this.

Pushing through the bushes, concentrating so hard on reaching the man that he did not feel the brambles and thorns, he turned the gentleman's head. The scream the gamekeeper gave rang out for miles. The gentleman had no face.

It was a pity, Jemima related later, that the trap had already been sprung, for Jacob Rush jumped so high he would have fallen into it himself.

When the gamekeeper recovered his nerve, he looked more closely. It was no gentleman, but a kind of scarecrow in a gentleman's shirt and coat and a gentleman's hat on its head. The lower half, hidden by the bushes, was just straw and was held tight in the man trap.

"You little bitch!" The gamekeeper turned to Jemima. She was the picture of innocence.

"I just spied 'im, mister, from the road."

69

It could not be true. The bush was not visible from the lane, but Rush smiled at the child.

"I'll give you a penny to keep this a secret between ourselves." When she did not answer, the bid was raised a penny at a time until Jemima had a shilling in her hand. Jacob Rush knew that her promise to die rather than tell was as false as the straw man he carried under his arm, but there was nothing else he could do. Nor, when the story of Gentleman Jack was spread through the parish, was there anything he could do, except swear revenge on the Stevensons.

CHAPTER FOURTEEN

Even the creation of Gentleman Jack had not relieved the boredom of his first months in Abingfield and John determined to renew his efforts to find congenial work. As the early morning light broke the sky, he woke Henry.

"Where you going?" the boy asked, staring at John.

"Where are we going?" John corrected him, having expected the boy to dance a jig. Instead, Henry sat and thought. There was no understanding the boy. Most of the time, now, he was like any lad, but usually more respectful and obedient. When he was excited, he had his mad moments, but seldom did any harm. You could give him his head and then calm him down. Just now and again, he reacted in an unexpected way, as though from a foreign land where things were done differently and nothing meant what it did to other people.

"What's the matter now?" John demanded. "Stir yourself. I want to be off to Gressingford to look for work."

"I'm coming." The boy's tone was grudging, but he swung himself out of bed and, ignoring the ladder, jumped to the ground. No one ever showed children that way of getting down, John thought. It was simply the way they preferred. He had discovered it himself when he was a boy.

"Do you know what I thought for a minute when you woke me up all quiet and sudden?" Henry asked, as he fell into the routine of getting breakfast for everyone.

"There's no knowing what goes on in your mind." John shook his head to show that he was completely mystified.

"I thought you was running away."

"Running away?"

"Yea. Up the Great House," Henry explained, referring to the newly and grandly built poorhouse, "When a boy ran away, 'e'd shake you to see if you wanted to go along."

"You're not up at the Great House, now," John reminded him. "Just hurry up or I'll pretend I'm the pauper master and give you a walloping."

Henry laughed and moved faster. They all pretended to bully him and scold him, but he knew from the tone of their voices and from their faces that they did not mean it. It was just teasing and you only teased people you liked a bit. Although he would have gone to the ends of the earth for any of them, that was all he asked in return.

"Put your Sunday clothes on," John told the child, "and I'll inspect you before we set off."

It was the only way, John had found, playing at military inspections, which could make the boy scrub himself and make himself smart. Sam had bought him clothes and Elizabeth had made them fit, but, left to himself, the child could manage to look like a sweep in anything.

Henry posed for inspection. "Do I look like a soldier now?"

"Like one who's been in battle," John sighed. "I meant you to look like a soldier on parade, not a casualty." He looked the boy up and down. "Go and give those boots a rub — with a rag, not your sleeve."

"Henry's movements seemed to become slower and slower. Soon John became short tempered with him. It seemed the cleaner the boy became and the smarter his appearance, the more hunched and dejected he looked.

"What's wrong with you?" John snapped.

"I like looking like a sweep," Henry protested. "What's wrong with looking like a working boy? People know I'm not on charity then."

John stopped and looked at Henry. Was the boy making sly hints about him having no permanent work? He decided at once he was becoming too touchy on the subject.

"Quite right, too," Edward commented on Henry's remark, pausing a second from noisily blowing and then swilling his tea.

Henry, looking thoroughly miserable, was weighing up whether to speak. At last, he ventured, "I'm grateful to you, John, for thinking of me, but don't you think I ought to stay with your Pa? 'E's all by 'isself. 'E may need me to fetch and carry."

"Do what you . .," John began and then changed his mind. "No, I've wasted enough time on you. Without you holding me up, I'd have been half way to Gressingford by now. Just move yourself, young man. You're coming with me and that's all there is to it." As Henry seemed about to speak, John added, "Not one more word! Not one, do you hear?"

In silence, they walked to the canal basin. There loading and unloading was progressing as busily as usual. Sacks of flour were being swung onto their shoulders by men who then, bending only slightly under the weight, carried them to barges moored on the bank. Barrels were rolled down boards to rattle crazily on the stones of the quay, coal was shovelled into slithering, clattering heaps and wood, half carried, half tossed, fell into ram-

72

shackle piles. Over the cobbles, carts and waggons arrived with wheat, oats, barley, hay and meat to send along the canal and, in return, carts and waggons clattered away with coal and iron for the blacksmith, wood for the carpenter and wheelwright and seed for the farmers. Men carried, heaved, lifted, dropped and barrowed goods this way and that, from barge to warehouse or straight into waiting waggons.

On upturned barrels and on sacks, old men watched and gossiped, while children played among the bundles, disappearing when sworn at, only to re-emerge later and continue their game. Only when chance offered, they stopped their play to watch goods or horses for a coin or two.

The sights made no impression on Henry. His poor spirits began to dampen John's enthusiasm for the outing. Thoughts of earlier disappointments suddenly made the journey seem a waste of time. As they boarded a barge, Henry seemed close to tears, but no words of John's could make him smile or show interest in the sights and sounds around them.

By the time they were approaching Gressingford, John was past caring how the boy felt. He should have come on his own. Now, instead of feeling confident and hopeful, he was becoming more and more convinced he was on yet another fruitless mission.

As the barge pulled into the bank, the children near Henry jumped ashore and John expected Henry to rush after them. Instead, he hung back, looking carefully around the quay to see who was about. For a moment, it entered John's head that the boy had been upset by something and planned to run away. If that was what he planned, John decided, it was better to let him try now, while he was watching him. He did not want to spend all day keeping an eye on him. Without a word, John walked off the barge, keeping the boy within his vision. It was not likely that Henry would want to start his journey in soaking clothes by jumping off the other side and swimming for it, and, if the boy made a dash along the bank, he would be ready for him.

Wanting to see what Henry had in mind, John waited on the bank, looking around as though casually watching all that was going on around about. The last person, a man a little older than John, left the barge. As he walked away, Henry jumped lightly over the side. John was poised, ready to give chase. To his surprise, the child came straight to his side, behaving like a well trained dog.

Impatiently, John grabbed the boy by the shoulders and looked at him.

There was no chance of Henry's avoiding his grasp or his eyes. "Right. What's it all about, son?" John demanded. "Let's waste no more of my time."

Henry stood, his eyes trying to avoid John's gaze, every inch of his body looking the picture of misery.

"Are you trying to run away," John prompted him.

The expression of complete amazement on Henry's face as he lifted his head told John he had made the wrong guess. The child's reply was blurted out with complete conviction and sincerity.

"What me? Run away? I ain't going to run away now I've got a proper 'ome."

Releasing his hold, John laid his arm around Henry's shoulders. "Let's sit down right here," he said gently, "and find out what the trouble is."

Henry began to cry. Never having seen the child sob like this before, John looked at him with fresh eyes, as he had never bothered to do before. Once it had become clear that the boy much preferred being a sweep to being in the workhouse, the family had considered themselves lucky in Edward's choice of an apprentice and teased him, spoiled him now and again when they were in a good mood, and rewarded him with a treat, when they had the time and inclination. By now, Henry had given up trying to stem the flow of tears and, made even more miserable by seeing them soaking his best clothes, he clasped his arms around his knees, let his head fall onto his arms and abandoned himself to sobbing, at first noisily and then in silence, as though he had not the heart to cry any more.

John was aware of the stares of the passers-by, but he patted the boy's head and tried to revive his spirits. "I'm not angry with you. You're a good boy."

His shoulders heaving, Henry turned his face to John. Tears streaked his cheeks and his toughness and perkiness had quite deserted him. John had never seen him as a child before. He had treated him as a child in some ways, sending him on errands and expecting obedience and respect, but he had never treated him exactly as he treated Frances and Billy. He had treated him as though he were simply a younger, smaller version of a man. Certainly, Henry was less knowing than a man, a little more innocent, but his life was already set on the course it would follow into manhood. He worked and slept and ate, day in, day out. When he was a man, he would marry and have children. That was about the only difference there would be. John had never seen him as he saw him now, a child belonging to the play world of childhood, a child needing time to be a child.

John hugged Henry to him, a gesture which, a short while before, would have been unthinkable and embarrassing to them both. "We're in no hurry, Henry. There's nothing more important in the world, at the moment, than making you happy again. Out with it. What's troubling you, son."

"What if 'e finds me?" Henry sobbed, his tears welling up again.

John was too taken aback to answer.

"It's alright when I'm covered in soot. Nobody knows me from Adam," the boy went on. "When I'm all cleaned up I look like meself. 'E might know me."

"Who might know you?" John had no idea what Henry was trying to say.

"Me Pa."

"But you haven't got a Pa."

"I must 'ave 'ad one." Henry pointed out the obvious.

"Yes, but . ..," John hesitated. He was not sure how to explain that even the boy's mother may not have known who his father was. Before this morning, John might have told him, as coarsely as he would have spoken to any young man, but now he found it difficult to explain to the child.

"Look," he pointed out, taking a different line. "No one inquired for you for seven years. Why should they start now?"

"I'm worth a bit now, that's why," Henry answered, his old pride coming back into his voice. "It does 'appen. People comes to claim you when you starts to work and bring in a wage."

John could not help smiling. "Is that what's been going round and round in your head all morning? And I thought I had troubles."

Taking Henry's hand, he said firmly, "I know about these things. No man could prove he was your own Pa after all this time. Do you think the parish would have fed and lodged you for six or seven years if they could have found anyone to pay for you? You are — you were — all alone in the world, believe me. Now you've got me and Sam and, as though that wasn't enough, you've got Pa thrown in as well. Can you imagine Pa letting anyone take the best apprentice he ever had? If there's a man wanting to claim you who isn't afraid of Sam's fists, he'd be afraid of Pa's tongue."

They both laughed, the tension and worry lifted from them. Crossing his heart, as the children did, John promised, "Nobody will take you away from us Stevensons." He stood up, pulling Henry to his feet. "The best thing we can do," he suggested, "is to take you to Tom Hutchinson's place. I can ask if they've heard of any work and you can stay and play with young Emma. His wife, Emma, is a good cook and she won't mind keeping an eye on you, if you're a good boy. You'll have a better day there than tramping around with me. You'll feel safe and cosy there."

Henry nodded, desperately trying to wipe away the evidence of his weeping by applying his sleeve and scarf to his cheeks.

"Let's wash your face in the canal," John suggested. "You take your time and tell me when you're ready.

CHAPTER FIFTEEN

At the Hutchinson's, Emma saw at once that Henry had been crying but, at a sign from John, she said nothing to upset him, telling her little daughter to fetch him a cake and take him outside to play while the men talked.

That done, Emma waited patiently for a pause in the men's conversation. "Tell John the news, Tom," she urged, having been longing to tell him since he came in.

"What news?" John asked. "Have you been invited up to London to give advice to the King's ministers?"

"They could do with it," Tom told him. "No. This news will seem far more important to you than anything to do with the country. It concerns you."

"Have you heard of work for me?" That was certainly more important to John than anything else.

"Mr Wright, the apothecary, had a long story about not taking any more apprentices, but wanting an assistant. I told him you had experience in the war and that you can read."

It was too much to hope for. An apothecary's assistant! That was a bit beyond his wildest dreams.

"I know no Latin, Tom, you know that."

"Have confidence in yourself. He was interested in you when I spoke to him and told me to send you round to see him. I think he'll be inclined to take you, unless you go and tell him you're no good."

"What do you think, Emma?"

Tom seemed surprised that his wife had been consulted. "Emma doesn't know much about an apothecary's work."

"I see more of it than you do." With John there, Emma found the courage to protest. "I'm as likely to be sick as you."

"More likely," her husband interrupted. Since expecting the baby, Emma had been complaining about feeling dizzy.

"I was saying," Emma continued, "I'm as likely as you to be sick and more likely than you to be here when he calls to see the children." She turned her attention to John's question. "You'll do well in any job, John, if you set your mind to it. You'll be able to pick up Latin. Tom can help you." Without openly refusing, Tom wondered how he would find the time.

There were political meetings almost every evening in some town or village.

"Will you walk over with me, Tom?" John asked, feeling it would be easier if there was someone with him to introduce him and start the conversation.

"Can't spare the time today, but I've told him all about you — all the good things, that is. He'll see the bad bits soon enough for himself."

"And what might they be?"

"They're quite visible and obvious. You're a bit stiff and wooden when you don't know what to say. You seem to think people who rank above you in society spend all their time thinking great thoughts and uttering noble sentences, instead of talking about the same things as you and your family talk about. When you meet them, you're so busy wondering whether to bow and what to say that you end up doing and saying nothing."

"Is that all?" In retaliation John let his mind dwell for a moment on all his friend's faults, but he kept quiet.

"Well, as you ask, John, like all Stevensons, you've no patience with fools and you're too critical. You seem to expect people to be perfect all the time. You expect people to understand and make allowances for your tender feelings even though you don't often confide what they are."

"Sorry I asked."

"Off you go," Emma urged him encouragingly. "We both wish you luck. There's no one more critical than my husband — especially where I'm concerned."

John still hesitated. He liked to know what to expect and have his mind prepared to cope with it. "What kind of man is Mr Wright?"

Tom had him well summed up, too. "Still belongs to the last century. Hasn't moved into the nineteenth century yet."

"Sounds like Pa."

"God-fearing. Much given to Bible reading, praying and church going."

"Not like Pa."

"Go on," Tom told his friend. "I don't know what you're worried about. He's not going to make you climb the chimney, you know."

At last, John began to walk to the door. "Is Mr Wright for reform, like you?"

Laughing, Tom tried to be fair. "Up to a point. He accepts all new ideas up to a point."

The buildings of the quarter of a mile and more of the High Street in Gressingford could be likened to several generations of a family standing in line, stretching from the few remaining timber structures at one end to the smart, classical edifices at the newer, more fashionable end. Common features of local brick and workmanship revealed a family resemblance, while a bow window or oblong window, three stories interspersed with four stories, flat roofs abutting gables, a small balcony here and a run of steps there gave each building its own, individual features.

The Street, as the High Street was called by the shopkeepers and customers too occupied with selling and buying to waste two words where one would do, was a matter of pride for the five thousand inhabitants of Gressingford and a joy for the many people who came by lane, turnpike and canal to sample its wares and pleasures. It was truthfully said that, between them, the buildings provided for all the wants and needs of mankind, all the body demanded and the soul desired. Butcher's stood next to watchmaker's, pastry cook's leaned against pie shop, draper's supported saddler's, bootmaker's faced cordwainer's, inn nodded to theatre and Church stared at Chapel.

To and fro, assistants dashed between strolling shoppers and clattering carts, along alleys and into courtyards, fetching and carrying and replenishing windows, so that purchasers would not be sullied by the dank cellars and stuffy workshops where apprentices and journeymen toiled from dawn to dusk. It was generally agreed by those who knew about these things that there was nothing which could be bought in London which could not be bought more cheaply and delivered more rapidly from the shops in the Street.

Peering through the apothecary's window, John glimpsed Mr Wright standing at his desk, writing in a ledger. He considered how to enter and what to say, whether to knock like a caller or enter like a customer. As he entered and the bell rang out across the shop, Mr Wright looked up. John spoke quickly. He did not want the confusion of being taken for a customer and having to explain Mr Wright's mistake.

"Good day, Mr Wright. I'm John Stevenson. Tom Hutchinson told me that you were looking for a servant or assistant."

Mr Wright looked at him closely and seemed quite impressed by the tall, serious looking man in front of him.

"What the correct title will be, I'm not quite sure myself. This is my son's idea. Do you know my son, Anthony? No? He's in London, apprenticed to an excellent man in the Apothecaries' Company and I trust another two or three years will see him home to take some of the work from my shoulders."

A little puzzled, John asked, "You want a servant or assistant until he returns?"

"As I said, I'm not quite certain whether 'servant' or 'assistant' would be the better title. I am inclined to think some people in the profession would call it 'quack'."

As each minute passed and as each vague answer was given to his questions, John was becoming more certain that he was on another wild goose chase. The old man seemed inclined to ramble and not to be at all certain himself that he needed help.

"I can see you're confused," Mr Wright said. "Let us start from the beginning again." He sat down and invited John to pull up a chair. "From my understanding, you have helped surgeons and helped tend the sick on the battlefield?"

As these words were followed by a pause, John gathered this was a question and, taking Tom's criticisms to heart, decided to answer as fully as he could, without being shy or modest. "The surgeons and their apprentices did the skilled work, of course, and we mostly held men down and carried the wounded, but, in battle, there can be few set rules of who does this or that. A surgeon would sometimes take a quick look and let us dress a wound or even extract a piece of shot near the surface. One or two of us, being considered conscientious and capable, were entrusted with looking after the wounded and calling the surgeon if he was needed and if he could be spared."

"So you would not faint at the sight of blood if a labourer has scythed off his foot or a boy has been crushed under a cart?"

Mr Wright seemed pleased with John's answers and with the thought, which he voiced next, that John would be used to taking orders and doing exactly what he was told. "Insubordination is so rife among the lower orders these days. I am glad there are some men not yet infected by that particular disease."

There was another pause and John was about to ask directly if he was to be employed and what his duties would be when Mr Wright spoke again.

"My son should be here to explain his idea, but he has returned to London. You see, Anthony says that the profession of medicine is changing. He was to have been my apprentice, but, by the new Act of Parliament, he must take the examinations of the Society of Apothecaries of London and must have been apprenticed for five years to a member of that Society."

"Though I know my craft well and have practised it with, I trust, some measure of success, I learned my trade from my father, who learned his from his father. Each of us enlarged his knowledge and perfected his skill by experience, but it seems that is no longer good enough for these modern times." At last, John thought he could see what the apothecary was trying to say. "So, as you can no longer take an apprentice, you want an assistant to help you until your son returns?"

Mr Wright answered, as seemed usual for him, indirectly. "When Anthony visited me recently, he told me that he thought I was looking tired and suggested that I should take an assistant. Naturally, I reminded him that no father would be willing to apprentice his son to a man who was not a member of the Society. He said he would take an apprentice when he himself was qualified, but he also had this idea of an assistant." The apothecary looked doubtful. "I am not at all convinced of the wisdom of such a course."

There was, in fact, no work for him here, John decided, but he patiently heard the man out.

Suddenly, as he seemed to be repeating his son's ideas rather than his own, the man's meaning became clearer. "As medical men must now undergo a more exacting training and as men without examination qualifications disappear from the profession, Anthony argues that fees will rise. This must mean that, as the flow of private charity and public rates cannot keep up with the rapid rise in population, the poor will not be able to afford an apothecary's fees and will fall victim to every quack, witch and trickster with a cure-all." Shaking his head sadly, he added, "The poor are so gullible and superstitious that they are all too ready to fall prey to anyone who offers a magical potion or enchanted ointment."

"I'm sure that what your son says is correct, sir."

"Anthony therefore wishes to train a man in the simple arts of healing. He suggested a man of humble stock who will work with us, charging a modest fee for medicines for common ailments. He will be able to separate minor from serious ailments, treating only the former and calling us when we are required."

"We have never gone in for cure-alls," John said, trying to establish that he was from ordinary stock, but no superstitious fool.

"My wife," Mr Wright went on, "is eager for me to take up this plan. She thinks it will lighten my load and help the poor. She realises too, as I do, that, without such a plan, Anthony will give his services free when he returns." Again, Mr Wright seemed lost in his own train of thought and it was some moments before he added, "I understand you would be able to start at once."

"Yes, sir."

"So would you like to work for me?"

"I would most certainly, sir." John tried to stay calm to avoid any possible disappointment if the apothecary suddenly changed his mind.

"I see no harm in your starting as soon as you wish, John. Let us say that you will be on trial."

John wondered about wages, but he knew that he would take the job at any price. Like his new master, he approached the question indirectly. "Can you recommend any lodgings, sir?"

"You are not planning to marry, are you?" It seemed from Mr Wright's tone that this would not be welcome.

"No, sir." As briefly as he could, John explained his family circumstances and his marriage. Mr Wright expressed sympathy and also indicated that a man who had been married, but had no longer the expense of a family, was the one best suited to the work.

"The wage will not be sufficient to support a man and his family. For a single man, part of the wage can be paid in board and lodging to the benefit of us both. You will eat with us at table. As to a wage, that is a very difficult problem."

It was clear that Mr Wright was weighing up several factors to arrive at a figure. He pointed out a few of these to John.

"You have no education."

"I can read and write, sir."

"Those are useful skills, John, but they do not constitute an education. A wide education with Latin and Greek and mathematics trains and broadens the mind. An educated man can apply himself to any subject and problem, whatever its nature."

That point settled, Mr Wright went on to the next. "You have a little experience, but no training. In many ways you will be an apprentice, but you will have paid no premium. I think it fair that the cost of the training you will receive should be deducted from your wage. However, you are a grown man, not a youth and I must take that into account. Most difficult. Most difficult."

He looked at John and John hoped it was not too obvious that he would agree to anything.

"Let us say your board and lodging and eight pounds a year. That, I think you will agree, is more than generous."

John agreed at once.

"You must not, of course," Mr Wright pointed out, showing that, in spite of his absent minded air, he covered all details of importance most effectively, "ever start any type of business using the skills which you learn from me within fifty miles of here. It would be quite wrong for you to take advantage of any connections you may make for your own ends."

John agreed to this condition, but there were others to come. "I shall not expect you to frequent ale houses or inns and I shall expect you to do nothing which will lower the esteem in which I and my profession are held in this district."

Having agreed readily to all the conditions Mr Wright made, John took his leave and covered the distance to Tom's house in no time at all. Everyone hugged everyone else and a little wine had a large effect on John's spirits, and even more on Henry's.

CHAPTER SIXTEEN

While John no longer looked at the sky each morning for signs of perfect farming weather, Will Dodds had searched it anxiously every day of that year. January had come and February and with them deep winter. Day after day the sun had risen reluctantly onto an earth buried in bitter cold, dawning with a pale glow too thin for vision or warmth, and slowly summoned all its strength to reflect in a hard, low glare the frost which traced every blade of grass, each gnarled trunk and each leafless branch in white relief. It revealed a landscape of shape and form, with trees standing bold from the colourless earth as though this were the season when they were alert and it was in summer that they dozed lazily beneath their covers of green.

March had come in like a lion and gone out in the same fashion. April, when it had come at last, had tinged the air with warmth and smudged the scene with a mist of clinging droplets. Moisture glossed the holly leaves and seeped through slits and pinholes in soaking wood to make a mockery of every shelter for stock and grain. Plants and crops, waiting for the warmth of the spring sunshine, stayed dormant in the ground, while the beasts sought shelter under hedges and trees. May, in its turn, had brought squalls to flood the ditches to the brim and fill every hollow and rut with squelching mud. June, July, August had merged together, not into a long, hot summer, but into a strange, misplaced, alien season of thick, glowering clouds, which burst angrily forth in storms of hail and rain. From time to time, when the sun had broken through to force a steamy dampness from the ground and warm the birds into song, it had revealed a landscape of flattened corn and dejected sheep cropping dank, foot-rotting meadows.

On this September day of 1816, the rain seemed to be suspended, unable to penetrate the heavy mist which covered the countryside. Everything was damp to the touch and, from where the moisture collected in trees and hedges, on clothes and hair, droplets fell heavily, direct to the ground, or meandered, skewing jerkily, from step to step to collect in streams before cascading down stems and trunks.

As he sat on the canal bank, Will Dodds stared at the moisture on the back of his hand and seemed to rouse himself to shake it off, but he did not see his hand or feel the damp air slowly drawing warmth from his skin. His anger divided him from all but his consuming thoughts on how he had lost his farm. In this, the wettest year that even folk much older than he could recall, he had fought to keep his birthright, handed down from generation to generation, employing all the skill and patience handed down with that inheritance. In desperation, he had even listened to the advice of young Richard Hammond and dug ditches to drain his fields, filling them with brushwood and straw. In his heart he had known it would do no good and when he had seen the sparse harvest, scarcely enough to feed the rats and mice let alone pay his debts, he had known that he was beaten. He cursed the weather and his bad luck, but most of all he cursed enclosure which had hung debt like a millstone around his neck.

Glancing, at last, around him and at the sky, Will knew by this time the sale would be over. Neighbours and strangers would have left and there would be just his family and a few friends gathered there for the last evening in his own farmhouse. Facing them would be bad enough. He had always been convinced he knew why others had failed and every man would have his own idea why Dodds' Farm could bear that name no longer. But his return could be put off no longer.

Sarah, determined as ever to serve his meal at its hottest and best, chivvied him the moment he entered the door to change his clothes and thoroughly dry his hair with all speed. Then, the food before them, they discussed the sale. To the name of Richard Hammond, the highest and successful bidder for the farm, Will reacted as quickly and predictably as Sarah had reacted to his wet clothes.

"Improvements, improvements. That was all I heard from that young gentleman when he looked round the place. New methods. New breeds. New strains. As though we don't know the best animals to keep and the best crops to grow."

"They ain't got an ounce of flavour, neither, them new breed of sheep," Edward announced, chewing toothlessly and with obvious enjoyment on his far tastier mutton from Will's flock.

"Gentlemen know nothing about farming," Will went on. "What can he know, coming to farming with a gentleman's education at twenty five? I told him straight, 'Ask any farmer. The best men are those who start in the field at seven. Little striplings who learn the feel of the soil and the smell of the weather. They grow into honest men with skill in their hands and strength in their backs.'" Here, Will did his best to imitate a young, over confident gentleman. "Such men make excellent labourers, Dodds, I grant you."

Not for the first time in the past year, John stayed silent. They all knew his views on having an education, but only Beth agreed with him. It seemed his ideas didn't fit in neatly with anyone's anymore — neither Will's nor the gentry's.

"Give Hammond a year, or maybe two," Charles stated, "and the farm'll be on the market again."

"Maybe we'll get it back," Frances said, as though thinking aloud to herself to disguise the fact she was joining in the grown-ups' conversation.

"You're full of your Ma's dreams," Sarah told her, dismissing the child's fancies for what they were. Letting the conversation drift, Sarah looked around her. She had always been taught to count her blessings and she tried to now. There would be work for Will and Charles with Richard Hammond — he'd been gentleman enough to promise that. Her glance moved on to Sam and quickly to John. She couldn't bring herself to separate poaching and stealing with the ease the young men did and she wouldn't admit how great a blessing Sam's offerings would be in the future. But there was nothing to stop her being grateful to John. Without a word to her, he had bought back her chickens at the sale and told her they would find a spot for them somewhere in Beth's garden. Sarah's eyes turned to Frances and Billy. Only farmers' daughters could go into service in the best houses. Frances would not follow Becky into the vicarage now. And what would become of Billy, with his naughty ways, no one could tell.

Gradually, Will's voice took over again from Sarah's thoughts. He was warming to his subject. "They always had plenty to say."

"Who's that?" Sarah demanded.

"The man in the moon. Who do you think?" Her husband resented being stopped for foolish questions. "The Hammonds and the vicar and the rest of the gentry. They all had plenty to say, right enough, when they wanted us small men to agree to enclose the common fields. 'No more a strip here and a strip there,' they said. 'You'll have your own land all together in your own fields. You'll be master of your own land and your own future. No more parish meetings with the worst holding back the best. No more arguments about what to grow and what to plant. No more diseased stock infesting the healthy on common land.' They knew what to say, alright." Dodds waved his arms around. "Then, suddenly, there were lawyers wanting payment for this and payment for that to make it all legal and telling you you'd agreed, without you knowing it, to fence your new land, whatever the cost. How could we improve anything without money for beasts and money to pay for the fodder they used to get free on the common?"

"A bad business," John sympathised.

Will hadn't finished. "And I'll tell you another thing, John, for you weren't there at the time. When the open fields were parcelled out, there were some who did better than others. Look at the fields they gave me — a mile from my house and not the best of soils. Then look at Simpkins. He....."

It was seldom Sarah joined in the men's conversation, but her resentment at her husband's talking so freely now when he had been so silent with her for weeks, burst through her tiredness. "I don't say much, but I think a great deal."

The men laughed at this, one of Sarah's sayings, not realising the depths of her feelings.

"You may laugh, but it's us women who take the time to think."

"A man's too busy," Will told her.

"We work. I've worked on those fields, next to you since we were married. I've done my share of stooping and bending, hoeing and clearing and sitting up with the lambs and piglets. You've been glad to have my labour all these years."

"I'm not complaining about you."

"Nor am I complaining. These are facts, not complaints. You talk so much about experience, but women have plenty of that, too. When we wash and sweep and glean, we're turning things over in our minds."

"Ready to tell us what mistakes we're making," Will commented.

The other men thought it wisest to keep out of this argument between man and wife.

"What man would admit to his mistakes? God knew what he was doing when he created women. There's always pride stands between a man and his mistakes."

"Well, everyone else has been quick to tell me mine, so you might as well join in. No reason why my wife should be the only one to hold back." Will leaned back to listen.

"You should have sold up at enclosure or stuck to the old ways. Kept to working just to feed your family and keep a roof over our heads. What more does a man need while he's on this earth? Things went right before they filled your head with all their talk of profits."

"I never wanted enclosure, but what could I do against the gentry?"

"But you went along with them. We never heard all these complaints when you were getting high prices in the war. Then you were all for borrowing money to make money. You didn't complain in the good days."

"What man wouldn't try to better himself? In the war, I thought I could provide for you all and save to buy a few extra acres to leave to Charles and Beth. What was wrong with that?"

"The same as is wrong when anyone wants what he hasn't got. There's two sides to every coin, Will, but what do you do when you see gold held out in another man's hand? You agree to anything just to snatch it and put it in your own pocket." Sarah paused a moment for breath, but she had not finished yet. "We saw the good side of enclosure in the war. Now the wars are over, we'll see the other side of the coin. You mark my words!"

CHAPTER SEVENTEEN

With a kiss and a bear hug, John swung Frances from the barge to the firm ground of Gressingford quay. The hug he received in return, given with all the strength in the little girl's body, made him laugh. In fulfilling his promise to take her to the bookshop and in the pleasure of sharing her unsuppressed joy, he could forget the selfishness he felt in clinging to his poorly paid, but totally satisfying, work for the apothecary while his family needed every penny its members could earn.

Eagerly, his boyhood memories of a trip to the town reviving as he spoke, John told the child of the watchmaker, the saddlemaker and all the other craftsmen who worked magic in the row upon row of workshops in the back streets and alleys, but Frances was not listening. Thinking she might be interested, instead, in the dressmakers and milliners, he scraped together what little knowledge he had of them, but she still paid no attention to him. Frances, like Sam's dog after its prey, could hear or see nothing but the treat she had been promised — the bookshop.

Suddenly, she had it within her sights, and, had it not been for her uncle's grasp, would not have checked her pace for any horse or carriage. As it was, she steered them on an erratic course between two heavily laden carts to stand triumphantly and delightedly before the window.

From within the shop, Charlotte Elham, the sister of the new owner, Mark Elham, saw the man and the little girl arrive. Already, within a few days of her arrival, she knew many people by name, sight and reputation. John Stevenson, by sight, she knew as quite handsome, but too serious, and by reputation, from her neighbour Mrs Wright, conscientious and hardworking. If all was to be believed, he was devoted to his work from early morning to late evening, was well behaved and sober, and spent every spare minute in study or visiting his family. To them went every penny he could spare from his wages. In short, by reputation, Charlotte Elham knew John Stevenson looked after his own family, but showed no interest in raising the general conditions of working men.

If she had thought about it, Charlotte Elham would have realised that John Stevenson was quite as aware of her reputation as she was of his. It was the talk of Gressingford that the bookshop was sure to become a centre for radical thought. Although the Elhams were the children of parents who were well off and were of good birth and education, the only formal education brother or sister had received was learning their letters at their mother's knee. From thence forward, they had been free to sit on the floor of their father's bookshop or on the window seat of the house or even on a stile in the fields reading any book they fancied. When they did not fancy reading at all, they had been allowed to mingle with adults, to be heard as well as seen and to expect straight answers to straight questions. On Sundays, they had communed with God morning and evening in the Methodist Chapel and with Nature in the afternoon in wood and meadow.

It was to no one's surprise that brother and sister had grown up with opinions, which they were only too willing to express, on every subject on earth and beyond. These opinions were shared only to a certain extent by their new neighbours, enlightened and liberal as these people considered themselves to be. Fortunately, the people of Gressingford all agreed, Mark, having been trained as a lawyer, was a radical without being a law-breaker. He would take his head from the clouds now he had the responsibilities of business. He would soon find that his profits in the bookshop came from novels and religious works, rather than from radical pamphlets and works of self-improvement for working men. No one doubted that he would mature even more when he married and had a family. Sadly, they all agreed, unless Charlotte took the advice every woman in Gressingford was eager to give, her upbringing had quite lost her any chance of marriage.

A step within the bookshop door, Frances stood still. The little girl seemed to hold her breath and gazed wide-eyed in amazement and awe at the books. Her eyes followed along row after row of books, from tier after tier of books to pile after pile of books. John watched the child with obvious pleasure in her delight at finding such a store of treasures. At last she drew breath and, putting out her hand, carefully, caressingly touched a book. Laughing up at her uncle and bolder now, she ran her fingers, still as gently, along a whole row of books.

"May I please open one?"

As the little girl asked, John looked at Charlotte with the laughing, loving, open look for the child still in his eyes.

Charlotte found herself hurrying forward.

"Which book would you like to see?"

The question was too enormous for the child. Once again she gazed from book to book. At last, she stated firmly, "I don't want a baby's alphabet book."

"Then you'll not want one off that shelf." Charlotte gathered a selection of books. "We have stories to entertain you, stories to astonish you and stories to make you good." She opened each book in turn and laid it before the child. "What is your name?"

"Fran...," the child started and then corrected herself. "Miss Stevenson."

Charlotte and John laughed together.

"There, Miss Stevenson, take as long as you like."

Favouring first this one and then the other, Frances could not make up her mind and, at last, Charlotte chose one for her. It was a scarcely marked second-hand book, which Charlotte priced according to the coins the child held in her hand rather than by its real value.

With obvious reluctance, asking her uncle in a loud whisper if they could come back soon, Frances walked slowly to the door. As the little girl took one last look around, Charlotte heard herself saying, "Would Miss Stevenson like to stay and help me for a while? I'm just minding the shop while the assistant is out and my brother will expect me to have tidied all these piles of books from the floor by the time he returns."

In a quarter of the time it had taken her to move from the counter to the door, Frances had retraced her steps to stand next to Charlotte and stared pleadingly at her uncle.

Admitting he had a job or two to do for Mr Wright, which would not interest Frances, John thanked Miss Elham for her kindness and left the two new friends together. For a few moments the child's shyness sealed her lips, but this did not last long. Frances knew all about helping. She helped Ma and Grandma often enough. While your hands were busy you chatted away to each other, exchanging information and bringing each other up to date until the chore was finished.

"There's no work for the men again today," the child announced, lifting books from the floor to a shelf. "That'll be the second day in a week for Grandpa. Not a penny coming into the house today." The tone and words were an exact imitation of her mother's. Charlotte expressed her sympathy.

"Do you know?" Here Frances's indignation so overcame her that she was forced to stop dusting and look at Charlotte. "Do you know Joe Braithwaite has worked every day? He's even been given an indoor job today. That's his reward for marrying too young and having five children by the time he's twenty two." Mistaking Charlotte's efforts to stop smiling as a failure to understand, the little girl felt the necessity to explain the facts of poor relief, well known to every country child, to this better-off lady from the town.

"The parish has to pay more for a large family than a smaller one, so masters give work to men with large families to keep them off relief and keep the taxes down. And," she added, the indignation in her voice growing greater, "They take advantage. The overseer knows a Stevenson would rather die than go on the parish. So would a Dodds." Glancing around, Frances lowered her voice. "Uncle Tom — he's not my real uncle, just Uncle John's best friend He lives by the canal. He's always telling Uncle John that he ought to join the revolution......"

Here Charlotte did butt in. "Not a revolution, surely, Frances. Such talk might mean trouble for your uncle."

"That's what we call it." Frances was matter-of-fact. Like all her family she did not take the subject seriously and could not believe anyone else would. "He keeps asking Uncle John because he's special." Knowing the gentry could be very ignorant on some practical aspects of life, she paused in her narrative to ask, "Do you know anything about muskets and things, Miss Elham?"

"No," Charlotte admitted in all honesty.

"Well," Frances patiently diverted from the main topic to pass on one of the hundreds of pieces of information which clung to her like teasels, "rifles are better than muskets. They shoot farther and straighter. Uncle John was a rifleman. Riflemen have dark green uniforms, not showy red coats." Frances's voice conveyed all of her uncle's contempt for show. She went on, returning to the subject of Uncle Tom's revolution, "A good rifleman's worth a dozen labourers with pitchforks in a fight."

"No doubt of that," Charlotte agreed.

For once, Frances was considering if she should say more on this subject. Charlotte assumed the girl was afraid of giving away information about Tom Hutchinson, but Frances was not doubting for a moment Charlotte's ability to keep a secret. It was her fear of what Uncle John would say if she boasted about him which made her choose her words carefully.

"Don't tell Uncle John I told you. He hates talking about the war. Uncle Tom told us about it."

Without hesitation, Charlotte promised not to speak of their conversation and Frances, deciding she would have to proceed without the customary crossing of hearts and oaths to die before telling, went on with the story she had heard from Tom Hutchinson.

"It was at Bandajoz….."

"Badajoz," Charlotte corrected. "It's in Spain."

"I know," Frances sighed impatiently. "That's where the war was. There were hundreds and thousands of men dying. Most of the riflemen were taking cover." Frances shivered. "Behind dead bodies. Uncle John stood up — right up straight in the open. He kept on shooting at the Frenchmen up on the walls. They had been killing lots of our soldiers. The other men loaded the rifles behind cover and Uncle John stood and fired. He fired and fired. Uncle Tom said that the men who saw him said he'd killed at least a dozen Frenchmen. Uncle John didn't have a scratch."

"Then it's no surprise Uncle Tom wants your Uncle John on his side," Charlotte remarked, as impressed as the child by this story of bravery.

"The other men looked up to him," Frances boasted. When Charlotte did not reply, she explained to her as she had explained to herself. "It wasn't cruel to kill Frenchmen. They were killing our soldiers, you know." To give weight to her argument, Frances added, "They shot first, I think." No one had told her that, but she was quite sure her uncle would not have started shooting at people for nothing. To show how kind her uncle usually was, she told Miss Elham what her uncle had given her for Christmas and what he had given Henry. "Mind you," the child added, "Uncle John can see red. Just sometimes, he loses his temper with Grandpa Stevenson, but Ma says, 'Who wouldn't?'"

Recalling another story, Frances continued, "Right after Uncle John came back from the wars, he had a row with his Pa. On the very first day."

"What was that about, Frances?"

"About Henry. Uncle John said Grandpa shouldn't have a climbing boy. He was really cross, Henry said. Henry was frightened of Uncle John at first."

"It isn't wrong to be angry in a just cause," Charlotte explained.

"That's how my Pa broke his leg working in the chimneys. It never mended properly and he limps, now."

A thought struck Charlotte. "Did your Uncle John have to sweep chimneys as a boy?" That would explain the seriousness of John Stevenson's expression and his eagerness to apply himself to another and far more congenial trade.

"Yes, but he grew too big ever so quickly. Grandpa said that was because he never wasted money on show. It all went on good food for their bel — stomachs." Reflecting on the truth of this, Frances continued, "Henry eats like a horse, but he doesn't grow an inch."

"Some young boys grow up suddenly," Charlotte remarked.

"Hope it's not when he's up the chimney," Frances giggled, planning to tell her joke to Henry.

The laughter of the little girl and the young woman made John feel at home as he entered the shop. He liked to form his own opinion about people and had already dismissed all he had heard about Miss Elham being so unlike most young ladies.

"We have spent a very pleasant hour, haven't we Miss Stevenson?" Charlotte said.

"She's a great chatterbox, isn't she?" John laughed. "In my young days children were brought up to be seen and not heard."

"Dear me!" Charlotte commented. "That does makes us opposites."

CHAPTER EIGHTEEN

Today, John decided, was a day for his second best jacket. When he had come to work in Gressingford, this very jacket had been his Sunday best, but, considering it not sombre enough for a respectable trade, Mr Wright had advised him to buy a dark one and had advanced him money from his wages for that purpose. It was the first time in his life that John had owned two best jackets and it pleased him greatly to see, hanging neatly from the peg, these symbols of his rise in the world.

The hour still early, John went down to the shop to mix the medicines and ointments from the list his master had instructed him to take to the poorhouse in Mannington. News of smallpox in a village a few miles away had bought a sudden demand for inoculation and John had been entrusted with the task of inoculating the inmates of the poorhouse who had missed the last general inoculation, while Mr Wright carried on the everyday work of the town.

As he worked, John hummed very softly to himself. No amount of admonitions from Mr Wright, who tended to see evil in any bright colour or cheerful noise, could stop this expression of John's pleasure in his new life. He had little enough money, but ample food, a place in a well run household and even a small room of his own.

Often, as a child, he had pressed his nose against the window of this very shop, moving his head a little this way and a little that to make the colourful bottles and the painted crests on the huge jars mix and sparkle through the distorted window panes like a giant kaleidoscope. Now the marks on the labels along the great rows of drawers and shelves had meaning for him and he worked, knowing just where to reach for the annabar of antimony, the cassafras and the hellibore root, knowing the origin and use of each, deftly crushing and mixing the pastes and potions and feeling himself part of that once remote world of mystery and learning.

Returning the list to his pocket, John felt a piece of paper and, wondering what it was, took it out. The first sight of the grubby scrap in his hand made him recall the message. Smiling, he spread it out and once more read the words scrawled in unevenly sized and roughly formed letters. "for jhon form is fiend henry."

It was the note which Henry had tucked into the packet of bread and

95

cheese he had put on the table over night for John to take early in the morning when he left after his last visit to Abingfield. The affection so obvious in each labouriously formed letter had endeared it to John so that he had kept it as a lucky charm. So far it had certainly brought him nothing but good luck. Henry. Pa. Frances. Beth. John had to admit that he thought of them less and less and he had just not had the time to go to Abingfield as often as he would have liked. They seemed a greater distance away than that represented by two miles or one year. He had to admit he felt further away from them now, in his new life, than he had ever felt when separated by land and sea in the Peninsula. But it was only if he applied himself and learned all he could, John convinced himself, that they could all share his good fortune in the years to come. Surely, there was no selfishness in that.

Above his head, John heard Mr Wright preparing to come downstairs and he smiled to himself. His master would come down, praise his conscientiousness and then check everything for himself. When it came to it, the old man just could not leave him to get on by himself.

That was just how it turned out. Mr Wright checked that John had sufficient serum gathered from smallpox pustules and instructed him, yet again, in the correct method of inoculation. "Remember now, merely scratch the skin. Do not cut deep. A deep cut causes, at the worst, a severe form of the disease and, at the best, a troublesome wound. Worried in case his assistant had not realised the importance of carrying out his instructions to the letter, Mr Wright bared his arm, ordering John to demonstrate the method he would use. Finally satisfied, he quickly checked John's bag, giving information on each box and bottle as he lifted and returned them one by one.

"Antony tells me that, in London, vaccination is now more generally accepted, but inoculation works well enough."

Laughing, John repeated to Mr Wright his father's opinion on the inevitable effects of vaccination with cowpox. "Pa thinks," he started, "that it makes you grow horns." About to add, "or udders," he stopped, realising Mr Wright would think his family ignorant. "Country people prefer inoculation," he ended.

"Country people have a natural wisdom of their own in such matters." Mr Wright, himself, saw little merit in vaccination.

John was bold enough to ask a favour. "Do you think, sir, that, if I pay of course, I could inoculate Beth, my brother's wife? I was thinking of paying them a visit and she'll be frightened when she knows there is smallpox nearby. I know she's never been inoculated."

"Abingfield. Let me see. Isn't that Dr Gray's territory? There was talk of his wanting to vaccinate some poor people free of charge to prove its safety and effectiveness."

"Beth'd be afraid of anything new, sir."

"Nonsense. You must persuade her, John. Speak out against ignorance. You know Dr Gray? A fine young man and building up a fine practice. He has put a few patients in my charge recently — labourers and paupers at a distance, whom he was too busy to visit with the great burden of the work he has." The apothecary gave John's request careful consideration. "No, John. I think we must not trespass on Dr Gray's work. Tell Beth to call at his house."

An ample breakfast consumed with satisfaction, John set off on horseback for Mannington. He soon wished he had walked instead. In the continuing rains, traveller after traveller had been forced farther and farther out around the mire of water-filled ruts until the line between lane and verge had been lost and mud stretched from hedge to hedge. Time and again, as the drag of the squelching mud on the horse's hooves slowed progress to a walking pace, John dismounted to lighten the load on the horse's back. Not having been used to riding everywhere, he still thought of the horse's task of carrying him as a favour from the horse, which he had no right to take for granted. Talking to it, he led it along the firmest footholds and encouraged it through the overflowing fords. It was an hour and a half before the tower of Mannington church came into view.

John found the House of Industry without any difficulty. It was a pauper palace, just as people said. Higher, wider, more splendid than many a gentleman's house, symmetrically balanced by two wings stretching from the square, central facade, its high, flat windows reflecting the sunlight, it stood as a monument to good intentions and to the common sense of local overseers in channelling work and taxes back into the hands and pockets of local, taxpaying businessmen. The idea of the House of Industry had been to put the able-bodied to work, but, money running out with the end of construction, the only work provided for the inmates was the repetitive, endless scrubbing and cleaning of the great building itself.

"For the Encouragement of Industry in the Able-bodied and the Relief of the Old and Infirm," proclaimed the wrought iron letters spanning the wide gates. Riding beneath them, John realised that he had never been in a poorhouse before. That struck him as strange when warnings against idleness and thriftlessness he had received from his father in his childhood and youth had always ended with the threat of the poorhouse. Still, he knew a great deal about Hell and he had never been there either.

John set the horse's head from the main path to a little side door. Children swarmed from nowhere. Most offered to hold his horse or to show him to the Master's office for a farthing. Some offered no help, but simply begged for a farthing with a smile or a sad tale. Eventually, for no other reward than the relief of their boredom, they led him into the building, fighting to hold his hand.

Whatever the outside of the house had promised, the inside had none of the trappings of a palace. There was nothing but space filled with cold, damp air, cut into sections with vast wards and long, narrow corridors of high, whitewashed walls. John walked past the kitchens where women washed dishes, past the laundries where women washed and ironed, past ward after ward where women brushed and scrubbed. Women did everything, it seemed, but look after the children. These, unless old enough to be set to work, roamed where they would, the youngest and meekest following the oldest and cheekiest. Suddenly, calling to each other, the children ran away. Letting them go, John walked on until he heard their shouts again from a ward and stopped to look in. A great open room stretched before him, bare except for, on either side, a row of coffin-like cots. At the very end, their bodies shrunken by age and the great emptiness of the room, a few men huddled around a small stove. They paid no more attention to him than to the screaming children, dancing around the nearest bed. It was covered completely by a neatly patched blanket which hung down the sides to the floor. The children pushed and shoved each other aside to poke at the body beneath.

"Put your 'and over the breathing 'ole," one urged.

Obediently, the oldest girl pressed down on the corner of the bed, where the blanket was raised the merest inch.

"'E'll suffocate," a child warned. "Come on. Leave 'im alone."

"Leave him," John ordered. "You'll be old yourselves, one day."

"I'll be miles from 'ere," the girl declared. "Won't catch me a 'undred miles from this place once they let me out."

John started to lift the blanket to reassure the old man. For a second, he

98

glimpsed the tiny, stark white face before it disappeared, whimpering, beneath hastily raised, bony, stark white arms. Carefully replacing the blanket, reforming the small tunnel at the corner, John wondered what had become of the old woman who had so carefully darned the blanket with bright wool. Perhaps she was dead or as good as dead in the women's ward, somewhere along the maze of corridors.

"'E's daft," the children told John. "The Master 'olds 'is food just out of reach and this 'and comes out just like a dead chicken's claw." They giggled nervously.

In their room a few doors down, the Master, Abraham Williams, and his wife were drinking tea. They offered John no refreshment nor greeting as he came in. "You're late," Mrs Williams accused him.

"What's wrong with the old man in his bed?"

"Nothing that calls for your attention," the Master replied.

"He's warm and fed. He don't like prying eyes no more than the rest of us don't." A stare at John emphasized the woman's point.

"Is there no one who cares for him?"

"Cares? I care for him. The Master cares for him."

"It's melancholia," John announced with all the assurance of a man who had read a few paragraphs on the subject. "Have you tried an infusion of balm leaves? Or, if that fails," he suggested, "nitre and vinegar?"

When these ideas met with no response, John added with feeling. "Just give him something to occupy his mind"

"His mind! That's gone past recall," Mrs Williams asserted. The exasperation left her voice as she fell into a gossiping tone. "Came in here with his old lady. Not a penny between them. And they'd had a bit off the overseer. They found he'd been giving it away to any quack or old woman who came to the door claiming to have a cure for his wife. He hadn't been looking after himself properly. The overseer knew they'd have clean beds and wholesome food here. She died in her sleep in the women's ward one night just after they came in. He'll go in his own good time, too. Can't keep himself clean and they say his cottage has been let, anyway."

"Can't bear to see anyone like that," John said.

"You? What about us? And the other men and children? What an example he's setting them, keeping to his bed all day." After a moment's consideration, Mrs Williams went on, "Spite, that's all I think it is."

"Spite!"

"Spite. Went like that when we told him about his wife. Said he should have been sleeping along side her as he'd always done. At his age, mind you!"

"Is there nothing to occupy him? A little bit of gardening?" John persisted.

The Master's wife had no doubt about the answer. "There's me and him," she began, but, seeming to feel these words did not convey the dignity of their positions, she rephrased them. "There's the Master and myself to see the paupers are fed, lodged and the place kept clean. Between us we have to see they learn working habits and that's a full time job in itself!"

"Can we get on?" the Master asked in a tone of exaggerated politeness.

"I'm at your service," John answered in a matching tone.

Immediately, Mrs Williams called in a child whose job in life seemed to be waiting outside the door to run messages and sent him to summon the other children. "Tell them to come one at a time," she called out after the boy. "We don't want them hanging about wasting time."

From his experience in the army, John knew that if you were in charge of people and had a job to do, it was best to begin as you meant to go on. "If you please, Mrs Williams, we'll have the children with their mothers."

"There's no need for that," the Master answered, obviously following the same theory. "Most of the women bought the infection last time. There's no need for them to leave their work."

"Mothers with children," John repeated, irritated by the man's attitude.

The Master grumbled, but he gathered together the women with young children. The children clung to their mothers, laughing, chattering, whining or grizzling, using any method to gain attention for a brief while.

Last of all, John came to the children with no parents, or none they were likely to see again, huddled together for protection against this stranger who wielded a knife.

Before John could encourage the first one forward, Mrs Williams grabbed a child from the pile and rooted it firmly to the ground by pressing one hand heavily on its head and using the other to tug the child's arm out to the side.

"Mrs Williams," John said as gently as he could, "if I'd wanted their arms held in a grip of iron, I'd have brought the blacksmith. Let their arms relax."

"Perhaps you should have brought him," Mrs Williams agreed. "I've other things to do besides standing here, you know."

As Mrs Williams tugged one arm after another straight out before him, John gently broke the skin and dropped a small portion of serum into the wound.

"Will me arm drop orf, mister?" one boy asked. "Billy Banks sez your arm comes right orf next day."

Placing his hand on the boy's head, John tilted it back so the child was looking directly at him.

"This stuff I'm giving you is a little piece of smallpox. In a few days, you'll feel hot and maybe have a spot or two, but you'll soon feel better and you'll never get the bad sort of smallpox which can make you very ill or even kill you. No more stories now."

"How about Mrs Williams telling us you'd cut us to get the badness out?" Billy Banks asked, innocently, always willing to get someone else into trouble.

"There's plenty of badness to come out, you can take my word for that, Mr Stevenson."

Once finished, John gave instructions to put those who had been inoculated on a light diet and keep them cool until any fever or spots passed.

"For the rest," he added, looking Mr Williams straight in the eye, "see those youngsters and the old people get the food that's meant for them. You don't only have the overseer to answer to."

"Meaning you and that brother of yours I've heard about will find us on a dark night?"

"You heard me," was all John answered. As Mr Wright's assistant he had to be a little careful what he said.

Riding home with the horse able to find its own way, John imagined, as he had so often over the past few months, that he was returning, not to his small attic room, but to a house of his own. There was a woman there, but her face, as always, was not clear. At one time, it had looked like Sarah's and then a little like Beth's. Very recently, the features had resembled those of Charlotte Elham. To her he told the day's happenings, his pleasures and his sorrows.

CHAPTER NINETEEN

"The Lord teaches, does he not, 'And every man that striveth for the mastery is temperate in all things'?"

Those of Mr Wright's neighbours who had dined as a fellow guest with the apothecary before recognised this, with no resentment, as the introduction to his customary 'moderation in all things' speech. The lengthy speech provided an excellent opportunity to enjoy a plentiful and delicious meal provided by their hosts, the Elhams.

"The earthly body is a temple created by God to house our immortal soul in its journey through this life. Intemperance of meat and drink, as any indulgence, destroys that temple and sullies the soul within. Experience, at every turn, confirms the truth of God's message. How often have I seen, in my work, the gouts and distempers which result from gluttony!"

Expecting and receiving no contradiction, he continued, "Like most men, brought up in the English tradition of moderation and temperance, I abhor the example set to our youth and to the lower orders by those in places of power and influence in our nation. There are some, I regret to admit, who abuse their position and wealth to indulge every passion and vice known to man and the devil."

"The Prince of Wales, you mean?" The question came bluntly from one of the two Northern artisans visiting political societies on their way to London. The other guests jumped, not just at the question, but at the clash of his knife dropped heavily onto his plate. All eyes turned to him, only to be quickly averted as he roughly pushed his plate away and just managed to restrain himself from wiping the back of his hand across his mouth.

Averting his eyes with the others, John inwardly thanked Beth and Sarah for the hours of teaching they had given him on such matters. They had been delighted to have a use for all the experience they had accumulated working for the gentry.

The man waited no longer for an answer. "Prinny," he concluded. "His days are numbered. There's a new day dawning in England for kings and princes."

The soft footsteps of the maid and the gentle clink of plates, sounds usually lost in the babble of conversation, rang loudly across the silence like the death knell of monarchy. Carefully and silently, John let his knife and fork come to rest on his plate. Watching him, Mrs Wright smiled approvingly.

At last, Mr Wright considered it his duty to reply to the remark, however much he might regret having to share a table with men of such extreme views. Stiff with disapproval, he still managed to speak with restraint. "When I am called to a sick man, I recommend medicines to cure the diseased parts and strengthen the healthy ones. I do not suggest killing him as the only sure way of stopping the progress of his illness."

"How about when the rottenness is so deep you have to cut it out, even at the risk of killing the patient?"

Mr Wright smiled as though giving a professional opinion. "When the choice is surgery or certain death, then a drastic remedy must be faced. But England is not dying, sir. England is a great nation and will, with a strong dose of medicine, be strong enough to destroy corruption."

The Northerner was not silenced. "England?" he demanded. "What is England without her people? And the People are dying."

"When did the King give an order to release just one English child from misery?" the second Northerner asked, simply and to the point.

As his companion's voice broke with the strength of his feelings, the first man resumed, "How can there be an England without her children? England is her children and they're being sold into slavery for profit — for a few pieces of copper, not even for silver." His voice faltered, in turn, and he waited, collecting his thoughts and controlling his feelings. He wanted his message to be heard by these people who seemed full of theories, but without any knowledge of the real England.

"Machines. Britain's great inventions. Do you think steam drives those machines? I'll tell you who drives them. Little children drive them — little children with legs and arms working those machines day and night, that's who drives them. Their limbs grow deformed." The man stared at his own arms and hands, as though seeing them as stunted and twisted bones. "Their limbs are forced around those machines hour after hour, day after day, night after night and week after week."

"Children who should be running and shouting in the fields under the sky," his companion put in, as the second the first man stopped for breath.

"The design of the machine wants a cog, needs a movement, calls for an action beyond the ingenuity of man to fashion in wood or iron? Then put a child there, that's the answer. Their young limbs and minds are supple enough to adapt to any design. It'll leave them deformed and diseased, but what does that matter? There's plenty more to be had." Again the man tried to control his shaking voice and trembling lip, but he could not. "Blasphemy, that's what it is." He spoke slowly, emphasising his conclusion. "It's blasphemy against God and His creation of Man."

While Charlotte Elham asked what help could be sent to the mothers for their children and Mrs Jackson wondered aloud why mothers allowed their children to work in such places, where, she had heard, morals were very lax, Mr Jackson, the curate, thought it time to return from emotion to reason.

"A widening of the franchise will bring an end to injustice and corruption. Republicanism, as in France, will simply replace one evil with a worse. No," he concluded confidently, "all that is needed is a widening of the franchise." Unlike the Northerners, Mr Jackson had no need to pause to control his emotions. He paused only for effect, considering himself a first rate public speaker. "I am quite firmly convinced that the right, the privilege, of voting should be tied to property. Ownership of property is in itself proof that a man is successful in practical affairs. It is proof, too, that a man has the breadth and depth of mind to consider the problems of a nation and give advice. Above all," Mr Jackson continued, "men of property are men with something to lose. They will not vote for ill thought out, ill judged measures and squander the country's money in taxation. The country's wealth is their wealth and the country's property their property. They will nurture the nation's inheritance as their own, to the benefit of all." Generously, he concluded, "I would give a vote to any man owning even the smallest property."

"Property? What's property to do with it? We have rights from just being born. Every man born has a right to work, to a fair wage and to see his family fed and clothed, as well as to vote and govern himself."

"It is a question of principle, surely," Mark Elham agreed. "Men are born equal and each has an equal right, with his neighbours, to choose the government under which he will live."

A patient smile flickered on Mr Jackson's face to politely mask the irritation he felt for this young man who seemed too often to court favour with men of inferior rank and who put theory before sound business practice. Slowly he explained, "All men are certainly equal in the eyes of God and of the law, but it does not follow that all are equally capable of framing laws.

That is folly."

Stubbornly, to Mr Jackson's way of thinking, Mark Elham maintained his point of view. Charlotte supported him and declared, "As all men, and, I must say, all women are affected by laws, surely all should have a say, by their votes, in their making."

"Come, come," Mr Jackson retorted, looking at Mark as though Charlotte had not spoken. "Children are affected by laws. Women are affected by laws. Are you saying they should vote at elections?"

Charlotte was about to reply, when Mrs Jackson put in, "I'm sure that I know as much about government as the man who digs my garden. And that," she stressed amidst laughter, "is very little."

"The voice of the people will make itself heard," one of the Northerners declared. "And before very long."

"And what will it say?" Mr Jackson demanded. "Come, John, you have been silent until now. What do the common people say? Come, speak up."

To John, the common people were the Donkins and the Braithwaites of this world and he answered to the best of his knowledge, "Some have no thoughts beyond their ale." He reckoned his family above such people, but he knew those looking down from higher up the social ladder did not make these distinctions. Knowing, without looking, that Charlotte was awaiting his reply and suddenly wanting her to get to know his opinions and feelings, he gave a brief account of the views of himself and his family. "For most people, forms of government are not as important as whether a master is fair and whether you have a family and friends to care for you. They like to be responsible for their own lives, not to be dictated to by either a minority or the majority."

"There," Mr Jackson claimed triumphantly, "the common man is concerned with simple, everyday events and keeping God's laws. The higher reaches of government do not concern him."

The Northerners looked at John with contempt, but Mark took Mr Jackson up on his conclusion. "Oh, no," he answered, like Mr Jackson convinced he knew exactly what John meant, "Mr Stevenson clearly feels with Montesquieu, that the tyranny of the majority may be as great as the tyranny of the few."

Deciding it was time to say exactly what he thought for himself instead of leaving others to turn his words to prove their points, John explained, "I do believe in men governing themselves, but a man must first have knowledge, must know what can be said on both sides of an argument to come to a correct decision. Perhaps education, rather than property, should be the qualification."

"I think that many agree with you," Mr Jackson said approvingly. "The franchise should be limited to university men with a sound classical education."

Over the sounds of approval for that proposal, Charlotte stated firmly, "There should be no qualification other than citizenship."

Mrs Jackson made a comment on the excellence of the meal.

"So you're the John Stevenson we've heard so much about as an example of how working men can improve their lot," one of the visitors sneered, before John could explain himself further.. "There's too many like you. The ladies and gentlemen pat you on the head and you grovel like a puppy dog. You think you can crawl up to their level, even if it's on the backs of the poor."

"No," John interrupted, stung by the allusion to a puppy dog. "I'm for extending education, reading and writing, to everyone, so that they'll agree to give everyone the vote."

"'They'll agree.' You condemn yourself from your own mouth. When they've drilled us at school into what we should think, then they'll let us vote to elect them."

"No," John began, feeling his words were being twisted yet again.

Before he could add more, the other visitor told him, "You'll come to realise, John, you're either with us or against us. You'll learn, you have to make them listen, with force, if necessary."

"Not force," John declared. "It's the innocent who get hurt. I'll wager you've never been to war."

"And I'll wager you've never put your head around a factory door."

Hurriedly, to avoid the argument becoming more heated, Mrs Jackson took it upon herself to suggest the ladies might like to retire. The moment all the ladies were assembled in the drawing room, she began a conversation which would lead her to the points she had determined to make to Charlotte once they were away from the gentlemen.

"We have just returned from a visit to Fanny. The baby, my dear, the baby is so lovely. I shall take you with me on our next visit, Charlotte. How you will enjoy seeing the three children!" Leaning forward to pat Charlotte's arm kindly, or perhaps pityingly, she explained, "It will be a break for you, my dear, from those musty old books of your brother's. Mark should employ another young man to free you from such business."

Again patting Charlotte's arm, Mrs Jackson spoke almost in a whisper, as though not wanting to make a spectacle of Charlotte's ignorance on a point so obvious to all the other ladies, "A house needs children, not books, my dear."

Aware that her house, as well as herself was now an object of pity to Mrs Jackson, Charlotte replied, "My brother is grateful for the help, I am sure, and I am happy to have something to occupy my mind."

"Mark is so kind. I'm sure he is kind enough to let you believe that. But I am quite certain," Mrs Jackson added knowingly, "that he will not expect it of his wife, when he comes to marry." Considering it her duty to guide this young woman, who had no mother or sisters, she rebuked Charlotte, "Leave politics and business to the gentlemen, my dear. We ladies have sufficient to busy ourselves."

At the moment, John, returning with the other men, came within conversational distance. Seeing it as yet another duty to speak to this young man who must be feeling out of his depth with the gentlemen, Mrs Jackson addressed him. "I'm sure your women folk are too busy with their families to worry their heads about anything else, John."

"They like to have their say," he replied honestly. "My brother's mother-in-law gave her opinion on enclosure very freely and...." He was about to say it was all part of sharing the burden of work and the family, but he was not allowed to finish.

"But surely her husband chides her on such occasions," Miss Jackson suggested, not sure of the habits of the lower ranks of society.

"It depends whether she's agreeing with him or not," John laughed.

By her rather remote smile, Mrs Jackson conveyed to her daughter that this conversation was not one to pursue.

Joining the company, Mr Jackson took charge of the conversation with his turn to have a kindly word with John. "Mrs Wright tells me you were in the Peninsula, John."

Not waiting for his reply, Miss Jackson enthused, "The officers who dined with us last week, Mama. They were so brave!"

"Very gallant gentlemen," her mother agreed.

"They told us such stories of courage and daring. Where was the place, Papa?"

"Badajoz, my dear."

"John was there," Mrs Wright declared, hoping John could be persuaded to tell stories he occasionally told to people he knew.

"You were there!" Miss Jackson was almost overcome, anticipating stories of courage and daring.

"I was there, Miss Jackson," John answered, adding not another word. Deeply disappointed, Mrs Jackson looked at her mother in surprise. In a whisper, which carried around the room, Mrs Jackson explained, "John was not an officer, my dear." Smiling at John to reassure him she was casting no blame, she continued, "You cannot expect a soldier to have the same stories to tell. It is the officers who must lead their men through every danger and set the soldiers an example."

Charlotte felt furious with Mrs Jackson and furious that she could not tell everyone the story Frances had told her. Her anger left her at once when she looked up and saw John smiling to himself. He smiled at her and she laughed, suddenly pleased to think they were both misunderstood by the other guests.

"I'm not certain whether I am fish or fowl," John remarked to her ruefully. "Those above me in society treat me like a child, to be smiled at if I do well and, largely, to be seen and not heard. Those on my level see me as a puppy dog."

Charlotte smiled as she agreed, "I am not allowed to express my opinion to the gentlemen and am pitied by the ladies for suffering from the disadvantage of a liberal education."

John and Charlotte talked to discover, as people who feel drawn to each other always do, how much they shared in common. Together they marvelled that they both loved nature and gardening, reading and walking miles on a summer evening beside the cool canal. Both were more than disappointed to be interrupted by Mark, reminding his sister to fulfil her duties as hostess and mix with all the guests.

CHAPTER TWENTY

"If there's one thing I miss, now I'm not working for myself," Will told his son-in-law, nodding his head in Joe Braithwaite's direction, "it's being able to choose who I work with."

The words stopped Joe talking for just a minute, until he saw Colonel Benson riding into view on his way to the Big House. That was too much for him. "That's the third. First it was Simpkins, then Mr Gray and now the Colonel. What's 'appening up at the Big House, Will?"

"Nothing to do with us, that's certain, Joe."

"Maybe," Joe ventured, "it's a ball."

"In the middle of the morning?" Will turned his head to heaven in disbelief at the man's stupidity.

Charles laughed, but in a few minutes he commented, "Joe's right in one thing. There's something going on."

The 'something' was a meeting of the local gentry and leading farmers and tradesmen of the district to discuss Colonel Benson's plan for a volunteer defence force to counter the rick burning and unrest in the villages around. Although Sir Philip Hammond's inclination was always to let things ride, the Colonel's persistence and canvassing of everyone of importance, had forced a meeting upon him. For his own part, by nature and upbringing he was suspicious of enthusiasms and was equally convinced that cold logic led to foolish conclusions. Sir Philip believed that a good season would put things right. Until that time, a rough and ready compromise, a word to a profiteering tradesman here, an agreement there with a tenant farmer to delay asking for his rent if he, in turn, delayed laying off men, was all he thought necessary. They had always had years of plenty and years of poverty, but life levelled out in the end without interference.

The meeting assembled, Colonel Benson looked around. To his annoyance, he noted that not all present could be termed gentlemen. Even Simpkins, with all his new found wealth, had no claim to that title and there were a good few of lower rank than Simpkins.

In his turn Sir Philip glanced around. Perhaps it was old age, but meetings, even people, bored him so. People nowadays seemed to be self-seeking, like Simpkins, fanatical like Colonel Benson or always talking of improvements and abandoning the old ways like his own son, Richard. A meeting had been forced upon him, but he intended to keep it short and guide it to a suitable conclusion.

"Gentlemen," Sir Philip began, looking at everyone, including the tradesmen, and immediately winning their warm approval of his words, "all of us, reading our newspapers will realise these are sad times. Some people," he went on, indicating the Colonel, "feel we are seeing a re-enactment in our own country of those dreadful events which brought revolution to France just a few decades ago."

Colonel Benson nodded in agreement. One or two others nodded with him, but the others, more circumspect, waited to see on which side Sir Philip would come down, if, indeed, he decided to descend from his customary position of sitting on the fence itself.

Sir Philip had been leaning forward, tense and serious, now he suddenly relaxed, smiled tolerantly and set the tone for his conclusions. "However, gentlemen, this is not my reading of events. Let me put it to you that we have lived through such times before. When revolution destroyed France, there were many who predicted that the common people here would rise up and turn on their masters. But," he smiled to show the true facts had always been obvious to him, "Englishmen are practical men, down-to-earth men, not given to theories and enthusiasms. What happened? Did they imitate the Frenchmen? They did not. They followed their masters to war against the French and defeated Napoleon and the pride of his army."

Those who saw the way Sir Philip was arguing began to smile and look wise, as though they, too, knew the minds of the common people.

"Our nation's salvation lay," Sir Philip concluded, "with the common people. They may, from a life of toil and labour, be ignorant men, but I believe them to be loyal men. There is no need, no need at all, to defend ourselves against Englishmen"

As his listeners murmured their approval, Sir Philip looked at his watch. This always made would-be speech makers aware that long contributions were not welcome. It would take more that a brave man to disagree with Sir Philip. It would take a stubborn one.

Colonel Benson was already clearing his throat. Avoiding his eye, Sir Philip thanked his audience for its approval, said that he would see where the feelings of the meeting lay and looked towards Mr Simpkins.

"Perhaps we might have your opinion, Simpkins. You are, after all, an overseer and hear all the claims for parish relief."

"As you say, Sir Philip, times are bad. To make things worse, we had four men return from the war and there are more children than there used to be all expecting to be given work as soon as there're old enough."

"Temporary difficulties. Temporary difficulties." Sir Philip did not want to start a discussion on the rights and wrongs of the labourers having large families.

"What do you suggest, Simpkins? An allowance from the poor rate to men with families to supplement their earnings from time to time as we have done before?"

This was agreed with Mr Simpkins, but the muffled murmur of disapproval it brought from the tradesmen, who thought they would be paying labourers' wages for the farmers, urged Colonel Benson to raise his hand and indicate that he wished to speak.

"Sir Philip, diffident as I am to detain you from the cares and duties which go with your rank, my concern is so great that I feel I must speak, even at the risk of your displeasure."

Sir Philip's smile suggested that he was all too happy to hear the Colonel's views, but it was at times like these that he recalled someone telling him the Colonel had never attained a higher rank than that of captain.

"Nonsense, Colonel," he said. "I expect every man here to speak his mind like a true Englishman." He hoped, given a free rein, the Colonel would go too far as he usually did.

Putting aside his speech on the imminent approach of revolution, which Sir Philip had already answered, he brandished a pile of letters in his hand. "Here are letters received in the last week or two, some signed, 'Gentleman Jack' and some 'the Captain'. They threaten to take property from those who own it and give it to the poor. They threaten to punish any farmer who lays off men, even though there is no work for them to do. They have a leader. They organise to destroy property and murder innocent families in their beds, while we do nothing."

A tradesman ventured to support the Colonel. "You have your servants, Sir Philip. You can defend yourself. If this villain comes at dead of night, who will defend us?"

"Come, my man," Sir Philip urged. "Are you afraid of bogeymen? There is no Gentleman Jack . It is a name based on a foolish prank and used by any villain or malcontent who has a grudge against his neighbour. My servants, my sons, I, myself, will come to the aid of any man in real danger, but it will never come to that."

"Oh, Gentleman Jack is real enough," the Colonel assured everyone, "and I have a good idea who he is. I shall reveal his name in good time. My man, Walker, keeps me abreast of this fellow's activities and of the Captain's."

The consensus of the meeting was shattered. Hurriedly, Sir Philip fell back upon a well tried and tested argument. "Times are bad, gentlemen, and that is why I feel it is the wrong time to put you to the expense of such a scheme. We do not want to have a toy army, the laughing stock of the area. No, let us wait until there is evidence to justify a defence force."

The mention of expense had given his audience food for thought and Sir Philip took the opportunity to bring in Mr Gray. The vicar, for weeks a supporter of the Colonel, saw it as his duty to support his patron in public.

"I must remind you," he began, "at such times, those of us who have been provident and blessed should follow our Lord's example and care for the poor and needy. Lady Hammond has very graciously met with Mrs Gray and the other ladies of the village to organise funds and distribute relief to those in need. It would not be inappropriate — I trust Sir Philip will forgive me for taking the initiative in his house — for us to contribute our mites to aid these unfortunate people."

Sir Philip could see that some of his guests were now eager to hurry away and he closed the meeting, smoothing ruffled feathers and leaving the way open should the Colonel prove to be right in his opinions.

"No one will dispute, I think, that we must take action of some kind. Let Mr Gray, the Colonel, Mr Simpkins and my son meet to discuss these matters further. Meanwhile the ladies, ably led by Mrs Gray, must do all they can to help our poor." As the servants hurried forward to bring carriages and horses to the door, Sir Philip courteously sped his departing guests. He had, he assured Colonel Benson, taken all that had been said to heart and he would be the first to call on the Colonel's services if the need ever arose.

The Colonel was left to console himself that his plan had not been definitely rejected and it was not the first time in history a man of foresight had stood alone. He would be active in his efforts to root out discontent and revolution. He would give Walker orders to confirm the identity of Gentleman Jack and the Captain. They did exist, he was sure, and he had a growing conviction that the first was John Stevenson and Tom Hutchinson was the Captain.

CHAPTER TWENTY ONE

"If it's free, it ain't worth nothing," Eliza declared. "That stands to reason, that does."

Turning the remark over in her mind, Elizabeth felt that was too simple, but she wanted to agree.

Seeing her friend's hesitation, Eliza pressed her point. "If it were worth anything, you'd be asked to pay for it, mark my words Beth."

Eliza's theories always had a powerful appeal. They were short, to the point and usually in keeping with Beth's instincts, if not her reasoning.

"I can't think now why I was so worried," Beth conceded. "When that man in the poorhouse died of smallpox it scared me. I'd have agreed to anything. Now it doesn't seem worth the bother."

"That it ain't," Eliza stated with a certainty Elizabeth always admired. Eliza shunned the safe, narrow path, but seemed to survive so well on the wide path to Hell.

"Look at me," Eliza went on. "Never a day's illness. Tough as old leather. Our Ma had twelve and lost seven. You 'ad to be as strong as an ox in our 'ouse not to die in your cradle."

"I could kick myself for ever agreeing. Still, I can't back out now, that's for sure." Beth knew she should be on her way, but she sat, thinking of Becky and Dr Gray waiting for her and trying to see a gap in the arrangements through which she could escape. She had jumped at the chance of free vaccination when there had been news of deaths and disfigurements, but, now the danger seemed to have passed, all she could think of were the rumours of strange happenings to those who were treated with this stuff from cows. It was not natural, she had to agree with Edward there.

"Just don't turn up," Eliza urged. "Say you forgot. Ten to one, they'll have forgotten themselves."

"Do you think so?" Beth asked hopefully. "Better go and see though. Our Becky would never forgive me if I just didn't turn up."

"Well, you asked for my advice and I've given it."

"Free. You gave it free, Eliza, so it can't be worth anything." Beth had known there was a flaw in Eliza's argument.

"Everyone'll tell you the same. Ask old Ma Fletcher. It ain't natural nor Christian."

"You sound like Charles's Pa."

"Well, he might be an awkward old devil, but he's no fool."

At the word "devil" Beth's thoughts came back to Billy.

"Where's he got to now?" There was no need for Eliza to ask who both of them were talking about.

"He's alright, Beth. What 'arm can 'e do in 'ere? The silver plate's been put away out of 'is reach."

Everything was a joke to Eliza, Elizabeth thought as she looked around. Who else could laugh in this hovel with its mud floor and its roof covered with dripping sods of earth?

"It's no palace," Eliza said, making Beth wonder whether she had spoken her thoughts aloud, "but I've got a dress fit for a princess. Look." She held against herself the loveliest gown Beth had ever seen except on a lady from the Big House.

"Eliza!" In the gloomy interior Beth moved forward for a better look and Eliza obligingly moved to the door. She twirled around, holding out the skirt.

Eliza hugged herself. "Josh is a generous man."

"Not free, I'll be bound." Suddenly good fortune and cheerfulness irritated Beth.

"Not free," Eliza agreed readily enough," but some coin you can use again and again."

"It'll run out one day, Eliza." Beth sounded just like her mother,

"'Ere 'e is, the little love." Eliza lifted William in her arms and cuddled him. "My, ain't we shining like a new pin for the gentry."

"Don't know how long he'll stay like it," Beth sighed. "If you can't have him for a while, I might as well be on my way and get it over with."

"Oo, look Billy. You're covered with cat's hairs. If that old cat's back there'll be rain. She must smell it coming." Eliza put Billy to the floor and did her best to remove the hairs one by one.

"I might have guessed that's where you'd be, Billy." Beth joined in the task of tidying up her child. "He's mad about cats," she explained to Eliza, knowing she was only talking and working to put off the moment when she had to start for the vicarage. There had not really been much chance that Eliza could keep an eye on Billy. Josh Langford, the pugilist, came every afternoon.

Seeing that her friend felt she must go through with it, Eliza urged her on. "Go and get it over with, then, Beth. If it's going free, you might as well 'ave it."

Elizabeth laughed. Half of Eliza's sayings were meant to excuse her own wayward behaviour and the other half to cheer up her friends and help them through whatever they had to do.

At the door, Beth made as though about to speak.

"What were you going to say, Beth?" Eliza asked.

"Nothing really." She still hesitated. "It's this feeling something's going to happen...."

"Then you don't want to miss it, Beth. God knows little enough 'appens around 'ere."

"No, listen, Eliza. Something terrible, I mean."

"It'll be the vaccination. Don't worry about all the stories, Beth. Can you see Dr. Gray killing off the gentry? That's who's having this vaccination. Old Ma Fletcher's only spreading stories to keep people paying her for inoculations. That's all it is, Beth." Eliza gave her friend an encouraging pat on the arm. "Look, if Josh has gone when you're finished, drop in and have a spot of gin. 'E always brings some. Nothing like a dash of blue lightning to make a new woman of you, Beth."

"Eliza," Beth laughed as her friend had known she would," where do you get those names from?"

"Josh. 'E's a card. 'Is stories about 'is boxing, Beth, they'd make you laugh. 'E's mixed with the gentry, Josh 'as. God knows why they put on their airs and graces. Just as bad as we are at 'eart, that's for sure." She stood a moment watching her friend walk off along the lane. "Don't forget. Look in on your way back, Beth. And you be'ave yourself, Billy. There's a good boy."

Even if Eliza's theories were often wide of the mark, Beth thought, the cat had been right. A sudden storm had blown up and the rain cascaded down on them. She had just wasted time at Eliza's. She should have asked her mother to mind Billy as well as Tim, but Sarah had made it so clear that she disapproved of the whole idea. She had been quite put out when Beth had preferred to have free treatment instead of borrowing a few pence and going to Martha Fletcher.

"William. William." The child had run ahead and his mother's words were lost in the blustering wind. "Frances, go and get your brother, before he falls flat on his face in the mud."

Grumbling, Frances ran, trying to jump the puddles and dodge the glistening patches of slippery mud. She did not bother to call or scold. Her brother never took any notice. Grabbing him by the shoulder, she tugged him round to drag him back to his mother. William's face, as he was spun around, showed surprise and shock which, at once gave way to resentment. He tried to pull away and looked to his mother, but, seeing her annoyance, gave in and allowed Frances to hold his hand and lead him along to his mother's side.

Elizabeth swept both of the children under her cloak and they peeped out, walking with tiny steps so that they did not trip over each other and laughing as they went, the best of friends again. Poor William. He was always in trouble, Beth thought. She hated to see fear in his eyes as she corrected him, but what else could she do? Charles and her own mother told her often enough that she was making a rod for her own back, but heaven knew she tried to check him. It was just that she could never look at him without seeing the cheerfulness and generosity which was a part of him, too.

The trees in the churchyard bent in the wind and the incessant beating of the branches against the wall made them hurry along. The storm had been building up all morning and perhaps that was why Beth felt an edginess, an oppressive tightening in the temples which had started yesterday and been with her still when she had woken that morning.

"We'll all feel better now spring's nearly here," her mother had said, but winter had not loosened its grip completely. The weather was so bad, Beth wondered whether Charles had been sent home, unable to work. She thought of calling in to see if he was there and could keep an eye on Billy, but she dismissed the idea as soon as it came to her. Everyone, was on edge just now, after the cold and hardships of winter. There would only be another row over Billy's disobedience.

Then she became aware again of the children laughing as they sheltered under her cloak. She wrapped it tight so that they could not see where they were going. They laughed all the more and she joined in. Not until they reached the vicarage gate did Elizabeth hush them as they giggled, squeezing tight to go through the gate, still hidden under her cloak. From the window Becky saw them coming and hurried to door to snatch their wet clothes and rush them into Dr. Gray's study. They were late and Elizabeth's heart sank as she saw her last small hope of backing out taken from her.

"Oh, Becky, I've got this awful feeling….."

"Beth. It isn't going to hurt, you know. Dr. Gray….."

"I don't mean that." Beth dismissed her sister's reply almost angrily, making Becky stare at her. "Like something hanging over you. This feeling of dread."

"Have you left a pot on the fire? Ma'll go in and check, Beth. Don't worry." Seeing the troubled look had not left her sister's eyes, Becky asked, "Is it something Charles has said that's upset you?"

"More likely to be something he hasn't said. He's in a bit of a mood, what with the weather and little work to be done."

"We'll all be better now spring's nearly here."

"Just what Ma said."

"You know Ma's always right." Becky was glad to see Beth smile at last. "Here they come," Becky warned in a low voice. She looked round quickly to see that everything was neat and tidy. Dr Gray and his sister came into the room and Elizabeth and Frances stood quietly until they were addressed. Miss Gray began to inquire about the family's health and to tell Beth how Frances had learned by heart more verses of the Bible than any other child in the Sunday School. Her words were drowned by a shriek from William. With delight, he rushed impulsively towards the large dog which had come padding in after his master. The dog's eyes fixed the child and hardened menacingly. A growl started deep in its throat, rumbling threats to the child to keep away. Showing no fear, William held out his hand to pat the dog.

"Here, Major," Dr Gray ordered the dog.

"William. Leave the dog alone," Beth ordered.

The dog had obeyed instantly. To Elizabeth's shame William did not.

"I'll take the children into the garden, now the rain has stopped," Miss Gray suggested to everyone's relief. She led the way and her little King Charles dashed onto the grass with Billy in hot pursuit.

For a few moments, full attention was on the vaccination to come and Beth chatted without pause about the weather and the Sunday School and how grateful everyone was to Miss Gray. From Dr Gray, in reply, there were smiles, but few words until he said, "That's all there is to be done. There was no need to have been afraid, was there?"

At once Beth felt foolish. "You hear such stories, sir."

Once again, Dr Gray smiled. He was about to speak when the spaniel rushed back into the room with William at its heels. Neither heeded Miss

Gray's call to come back into the garden at once.

"William. Don't think I won't spank you in front of the gentleman." Beth added her threats to no effect. As excited as the boy, the spaniel ran under the desk and, keeping just out of reach, barked defiantly. Without hesitation, William ducked in after it, sprawling his full length as the dog, playfully dodging his grasp, rushed out the other side.

"You were certainly right, Becky, when you warned us that Billy was a very naughty boy," Anne Gray remarked pointedly, her voice emphasising her disapproval. Beth moved to the door, opening onto the garden. The sooner she took Billy home, the better. She thanked Dr Gray at length and he smiled and told her not to listen to old wives' tales. Turning to leave, she apologised for Billy's bad behaviour.

Dr Gray smiled. Shaking his head a little sadly, he said, "Deaf children can be very wayward."

Beth heard no more. That one sentence stayed on the air, echoing around the garden to the heavy beat of rain drops still trickling from the leaves. Her mind rejected the harsh words, questioning their meaning. She had not heard them properly, Beth convinced herself. Sometimes it was hard to make out what gentlefolk said when you were used to rougher voices. "Deaf children can be very wayward." That could not be right. "Deaf?" "Deaf children?" Perhaps he had said "Some children" or perhaps, that would be it, he had meant children who would not listen. That was true. She had to admit that William never listened to a word anyone said.

Now Beth could reply to the gentleman. He would think ill of her for not answering before this. Her mind had been numbed, but now impressions of her surrounding touched her again. What a lovely garden. If her ship ever did come in, she would have a garden just like this one. The sun was shining, but the chill she had felt when Dr Gray had spoken those words, still crept beneath her skin.

"You'll think me foolish, sir," Beth began, not certain of the words to use. "Please, sir, what did you say?"

As Beth looked at the doctor, she saw the scene before her as though at a distance. She was detached from it, just as if she was looking through a window. There was Becky with her hands to her mouth, as white as a sheet. She was crying. Dr Gray stood by the door, his eyes turned from her, gravely listening to his sister.

Frances's hand on her arm brought her back amongst them. Beth looked

118

down to see her daughter's tear-stained face. "Ma. Billy isn't deaf is he?"

"Billy isn't deaf, is he, sir?" Beth wanted to plead, just as the child did, but she spoke very calmly. "Deaf, sir? Nobody has ever told us Billy was deaf." Her own words, her own voice reassured her. The warmth of the air began to reach her and the wave of sickness passed. "Oh, no, sir. No one has ever said Billy was deaf and dumb. He's not as quick to talk as Frances was, but then boys never are, sir." This time Beth smiled at the doctor. "You'll learn that yourself when you have children, sir."

From behind the bushes, the little spaniel dashed across the garden with William almost upon it. Suddenly the child stopped and looked at his mother. He was breathing as rapidly as the dog, gulping the warm, fresh air. The animal wanted to stay in the game. Its back high in the air, it rested its chin between its front paws, yapping and begging its new friend to play. William, his whole face lit with excitement, laughed in the joy of the game. There was no evil in the child. Deaf? It explained so much.

The dog still stayed a little out of reach, teasing the child. A shriek of excitement escaped William's lips. The chill touched Elizabeth again. That was why she had felt so fearful. That was what she was refusing to hear.

Dr Gray was speaking to her. He looked so young and he spoke hesitantly, without the assurance of a few minutes before.

"I am newly qualified, Mrs Stevenson, without the experience of an older man."

Anne had urged him to withdraw his statement, but he was sure he was right. "If you step back into the house, I will gladly examine him."

"We've troubled you enough today, sir."

"Let Dr Gray examine Billy," Becky pleaded. "He knows all the medicine those London men could teach him, Beth."

Elizabeth hesitated. She had admitted the truth to herself now. There was no need to bother the doctor.

"Come on, Beth," Becky urged. "You'll regret it if you don't. Charles and Ma will want to know."

Frances had already run to fetch Billy and, while Beth sat bolt upright on the chair Miss Gray had provided, she led her brother by the hand to Dr Gray.

"Has the child ever had a severe fever?"

"Only colds and chills, sir."

"Scarlet fever? Measles?"

"No, sir." Elizabeth looked puzzled

"I ask to find the cause of his deafness. It may be the result of a fever. Has he ever spoken?"

"No, sir."

"Then it was before he was a year or two old Turning to his sister, the doctor said, "It is congenital in all probability." He explained, in response to Becky's blank expression. "The child was probably deaf from birth."

"Oh, yes, sir," Beth agreed, without hesitation.

Astonished, Dr Gray asked how she could be so sure.

"It was the hare, sir. There's no doubt of that now, sir."

CHAPTER TWENTY TWO

Through the small square window, Elizabeth watched the dawn light pick out the dull, grey clouds which passed like huge, ragged flocks of sheep. They moved now slowly, in an orderly fashion, now in haste and disarray, as though surging forward before a dog snapping and barking at their heels. The rain, sleeting against the window, kept pace with the flurrying clouds, at times tapping gently, at others beating and stinging against the pane.

As for so many long nights and slow dawns, Elizabeth lay awake. Yet again she closed her eyes, shutting out the light and desperately seeking sleep, but there was no shutting out sounds. Her son would never hear her voice, never hear the warmth of encouragement and love or hear the chiding which would guide him from wickedness, but here she lay, aware of every sound of that wild night. The dull thump, thump of the garden gate hurtling to and fro in the storm, the whistling of the wind forcing its way between door and frame and the sharp, metallic rattle of the latch had kept sleep away. Now it was the screeching of the wind across the earth which beat at her ears and at her mind. Tired and exhausted, she admitted herself beaten by the gale's howling insistence, but it showed no more mercy to her than it felt for the trees which, even though they bowed before it, were still harried and harassed until they shivered and shook to their very roots.

Her mind raw from tiredness and worry, Elizabeth pressed her head against the bolster, folding and squashing the covers into a thick pad over her other ear. Just a moment's quiet, if she could have a moment's quiet she would fall asleep. Her breathing lengthened and the restless movements eased. Was that a cry on the wind? Beth had to listen again. Her hand released its grasp on the cover and her head eased from the pillow. Was that the cry again? If only the wind would drop, she would know for sure. There, wasn't that a scream, a desperate moaning carried away to the hills beneath the blustering wind?

The gusting, screaming winds of March. March, the month of the hare. Day after day Beth had seen the bucks prancing on their hind legs. The men laughed, "Milling", they called it. Milling like the prize fighters. No woman ever laughed at the hare and risked its curse. Across the fields the cry echoed again on the wind. Some poacher would be out there, hunting the hare. Pray God it was not Sam. If one was harmed, another woman's son might pay for it as William had.

Elizabeth thought of the day in late March four years ago when William had been born. She had looked first at his lip. It had been perfectly formed, his mouth so small and his lips moving as though already eager for the breast. She had kept to herself how, when she had first known she was with child, she had heard the leveret's scream, so like a child's. As she looked from the window, she had seen the cat drop it, not to let it go, but simply to snatch it up again in a tighter hold. Perhaps she could have saved it, but she had turned away, pretending not to see it and had not gone to its aid. That way it could not cross her path if it escaped, she had told herself, or die in her hand if it was already past saving. It had been nothing to do with her. She had done it no harm. Later, when she had considered it safe, Elizabeth had opened the door, only to find the small, warm body on the step. Its head, huge to its body, had lain limply to one side and its large, pained eyes stared blindly at her. Just one small stain of blood showed on its fur. Terrified, Beth had shut the door and waited. Perhaps she should have buried it, but she had not dared to touch it. It had disappeared. It would have been a relief to tell someone, but she had kept it to herself and almost forgotten it once William was born and she could see no mark upon him. How was she to know that he bore the mark of the hare, hidden from view?

Billy was deaf and there was no doubt in Beth's mind that it was her fault. She had let the leveret die and every woman knew that witches could take the shape of a hare in the twinkling of an eye. That leveret had been a witch's child and now she was being punished for letting it die.

Dozing restlessly, Beth thought of how, straight from Dr Gray's, she had rushed to Martha Fletcher's. At once Martha had said ,"I guessed. I saw you look at the child when it was born and I knew what you feared." She had added, knowing Elizabeth's question, "What's there for me to say, my dear? There's none of my herbs or cures can work against a witch. Children marked by the hare carry the scar to the grave."

"But he has no mark." Beth had pushed William towards her "His ears are as perfect as yours or mine."

"There's things made worse by meddling, Elizabeth. You'll find no cure, if you give every penny you have to quacks and gypsy women."

Elizabeth's thoughts drifted into sleep. Her hand fell from the covers around her head. As she slept the wind dropped and there were no more cries to be heard.

Without disturbing his wife, Charles Stevenson got up from his bed. There was little enough for them to say to each other these days. There were things which needed to be said and questions which needed to be asked, but he would bide his time, dig back into his mind for the facts so that there would be no getting out of it when he faced her with them.

Leaning down, Charles rubbed his leg, trying to work strength into the sluggish muscles. These last few days it had given him so much pain. That was an injury though, and everyone knew how it had happened. They knew that, as a lad, he had caught his foot in a loose brick in the chimney: and, slipping, had wedged with his leg twisted under him. It could have happened to anyone. Many a man and boy carried the scars of their trade. But why was William deaf? No one could tell him that. Sarah and Will had not said much, but he felt sure they blamed the Stevensons. The Dodds had been healthy and strong for generations and they could prove it, but Edward did not even know his father and mother. Everyone would blame the Stevensons. They would say they came of bad stock.

His son Billy was deaf. Charles busied himself with fastening his belt and putting on his boots, trying to shut out his thoughts. That story would keep coming back into his mind. That silly, foolish story he had heard as a youth was always in his thoughts however hard he tried to close his mind to it. There had been this woman, a good few miles away, with three deaf children. She had claimed it was hearing the grunts of a deaf and dumb beggar which had frightened her when she was carrying each child. The lads had sniggered over the story and wagered she had done more than listen to the beggar's cries. No one was going to laugh at him, Charles swore. He left his wife sleeping and went to work.

It was a few hours later when Sarah Dodds set out. She had to give Eliza time to be up and about and Eliza was never an early riser. The women's first reaction had been to grasp William to them to give him little treats, smiles and kisses to make up for all of life's hurts which lay in store. They had drawn away from the neighbours, fearing the stares and calls and the gossip which followed them everywhere. Now Sarah could stand it no longer. She hated uncertainty and indecision. Whatever burden God put upon you, you took it up and carried it with you. God would never make the burden beyond your strength, however heavy it might seem at first.

Taking Frances and Billy and young Tim with her to let Beth sleep,

Sarah set out for Eliza's. Knocking briefly, she went in, scarcely heeding Eliza's weary apology for the untidy room.

"Well, Eliza?" There was no point in beating about the bush. "What are they saying about us?"

For a second, Eliza averted her eyes, but then recovered her cheerfulness. "You know people, Mrs Dodds, they mean no 'arm. It'll blow over. Better take no notice." Laughing, she added, "Think what people 'ave said about me and God ain't struck me dead, yet."

"Out with it, Eliza. I'm too old and thick-skinned to be hurt by words. Sticks and stones."

"Why come to me, Mrs Dodds? It's a bit of an insult thinking I'm the one to come to about gossip."

"And I'm right, Eliza, but there's no malice in you and you're Beth's friend."

"That's something you've never wanted to accept."

"There's a good many things I'd rather not accept, but I have to. She'll need all the friends she can get from now on and it's best to sort out who they are."

It was tempting to gossip and persuade yourself you were doing it for the best and Eliza was never one to resist temptation. "Some sez it was the 'are. Sez if Beth had made the sign of the cross on it and buried it, Billy wouldn't 'ave been 'armed."

Sarah had wondered about those things, herself. "Go on Eliza."

"Dolly Braithwaite" Eliza blurted out, "sez your cousin was simple and Billy's taking after 'im."

"What about her sister's boy? There's plenty wrong with him," Sarah retorted.

She had meant to stay calm, but the thought of Becky Braithtwaite made her cheeks burn. "Any way, Billy's no fool. Got as much sense as you or me and a good deal more than some."

"A few — name no names, Mrs Dodds, so don't ask me — recall a deaf beggar on a canal boat that passed through about the right time."

Sarah stiffened. "What's that supposed to mean?"

"I said I knew for a fact that Beth's not that kind, but you know some people like to think evil of everyone."

"The wickedness of it all!" Sarah's armour of calmness and determination proved useless against such evil. She snapped angrily, "Are they saying they saw this creature with Beth?"

"No," Eliza hesitated. "Someone saw a woman 'anging about the barge, but no one says for sure it was Beth."

"God strike dead anyone who does." Sarah could understand Charles's hurt now. He would have heard all of these stories. It was to his credit that he had kept them to himself.

Turning to Eliza again, Sarah protested, "Beth was married with little Frances when this is supposed to have happened."

"They say Charles guessed at the time and that's why he broods so much."

"Tell them all from me, it's a wicked, evil lie. May God strike them down."

"Don't tell Beth."

"She's a right to know, as I had."

"I wouldn't 'ave told you if I'd known you'd tell 'er. It'll break 'er 'eart."

"We'll see," Sarah sighed and got up. "Where are the children?"

"They ran off to play with Jem and George." Eliza never named more than her first two children, as though she had given up identifying them after that.

Outside, Sarah found Tim sitting happily making mud pies and she picked him up without a word of reprimand.

"Send Billy and Frances home the minute you see them, please Eliza." She was too near tears of anger and sorrow to stay and call them.

By the time Sarah returned, Beth was up, sweeping the floor. Sarah did not sit down, but stood, moving aside whenever the broom was pushed in her direction.

"What's the matter now, Ma?" Beth stood up straight as her broom almost touched her mother's feet for the third or fourth time. She had not meant her tone to be so sharp.

"Don't speak to your mother like that." The words, so often snapped at the children over the years as a stern warning, came out as a feeble plea for consideration and mercy. In a second, mother and daughter were weeping, holding each other to give and receive comfort. Elizabeth hugged her mother to her, gently patting her as though she were a child.

"Oh, Beth," Sarah Dodds cried, sobbing, "They're saying such dreadful things."

"I know. I know, Ma."

"They're......"

Elizabeth let her mother go. Her tears stopped as suddenly as they had begun. Looking for the piece of wood onto which she brushed the dirt, she said quietly," Don't tell me, Ma. Spare me any more."

"Isn't it better....?" her mother began.

"No, Ma." Her voice was muffled as Beth straightened up from bending with the square of wood held tightly in her hand. All her mind and thoughts seemed to be concentrated on carefully balancing the dirt on the flat surface until, opening the door, she threw it onto the soil.

The control Beth was struggling to keep over her voice made her tone brittle as she spoke. "I can't take any more, Ma." She could not trust herself to say another word.

"I meant it for the best, my love."

Going to the door, Beth breathed slowly and deeply. The warm spring air soothed the smarting in her throat. Still staring into the lane, her back to her mother, she asked, "Do you remember, Ma, what you said when James Collier used to call names after me when I had that blue dress you made? You made it with room for me to grow, remember?"

"Ignorant that one was and always will be."

"You said, 'Sticks and stones will break your bones, but names will never hurt you.' It's not true, Ma. It hurts deep down. I feel raw, Ma, raw. The thought — just thinking of what they're saying puts me on edge — makes me draw into my self to deaden the pain. No, Ma. I can't bear to hear all that evil and ignorance put into words. I've had enough, Ma."

"I'll say no more, Beth." She set about helping Beth with her tasks, passing time with the normal things they did on a normal day. "Time will heal a lot, Beth. You know what people are with a nine day wonder."

Elizabeth nodded, but Sarah sensed there was something else on her mind.

"Amy was here while you were out," Beth spoke at last, trying to keep her voice even.

"Your sister Amy? She hasn't been over for months. Didn't she wait to see me?"

"She went off in a huff."

Without a further question, Sarah waited for her daughter to go on in her own time. Beth was trying to calm herself, she knew, and she was not deceived by the detached tone of Beth's words when they came.

"Asked if I couldn't tell everyone Billy was deaf of the fever."

"Well?" The query slipped out before Sarah had time to think. How many times had she wanted to ask the same question?

"Billy's never had a fever."

"Every child has fevers. Heaven knows, when you and the others were little...."

"Ma. it was the hare. I've always known it."

"Who'll know, Beth? What harm will it do to say he had a fever?"

"You're as bad as Amy. She wanted to know who'd marry Frances if they thought we came of bad stock."

"There is that to consider, Beth." Sarah spoke in a gentle tone, but she was as insistent as Amy had been. She waited, hoping and praying that Beth would agree. "Is it so much to ask?"

"I'm frightened, Ma. Who knows what a witch will do, if you lie? You can't deny a witch's power without coming to harm, Ma. Where are the children?" Beth asked suddenly. In a panic she demanded, "Didn't Billy come back with you?"

"They'll be along, Beth. You can't tie the boy to your apron strings."

In spite of her own words, Sarah moved to the window and was reassured to see Frances and Billy playing a little way off with Eliza's children.

CHAPTER TWENTY THREE

Sarah, looking out of the window, saw that all the children, Beth's and Eliza's, had followed her home. To Sarah's eyes they were playing as usual and she left them to get on with their games, untouched by the wicked world of grown-ups. A closer look, through William's eyes, showed that the children were playing, but not as usual. Jem and George did not rush at him, their eyes bright and smiling. They did not, as so often happened, come to a sudden stop by him, grabbing his shoulders and gazing into his eyes while their lips moved and smiled. Today they ran after Frances, laughing, and, when Jemima caught her, the others surrounded her, tugging her along.

William, neglected, charged, jumping on George's back, hanging on with his arms and legs clasped tightly around the boy's body. Instead of galloping along, struggling like a highly strung horse trying to unseat his rider, George scratched at the hands around his neck and turned to his sister. Without hesitation, she solemnly and firmly unclasped William's hands and threw him to the ground. When he, still laughing, grabbed George's foot, the boy kicked out at him.

Frances kicked George in return and William concluded this was just a new version of their usual game. He stood up and walked towards George. A hand was stretched out to push him away, not a grasping or a rough hand energetically punching him, but a firm, open hand putting him in his place — a place apart and separate from the others. Gradually, William stopped struggling and reaching towards his friends. Now, as unsmiling as they were, he stood searching their faces. They avoided his eyes and their lips were still. Frances took her brother's hand and pulled him to her side.

It was Jem's lips which Billy saw move next. Then his sister's moved. For a moment it looked as though Jem would walk away, taking her brothers and sisters with her. William looked to his sister, trying to understand what was going on. She shrugged her shoulders then, facing him and calming him, she let the others come close. As usual, Jem took the lead. Holding Billy's ear between thumb and fore finger, she peered into it. Seeing nothing, she poked the forefinger of her other hand into his ear.

"It's just a 'ole," she announced.

"Ears are 'oles," stated George, stepping up for his look. It was disappointing.

"Let's see yours." Jem gave her brother's ear the same inspection she had given William's. It provided no clues. "What's 'is mouth like?" she asked Frances. Placing her finger tips on Billy's bottom lip, she tried to ease his mouth open, but he clamped his jaws shut.

"He'll bite you," Frances warned.

"'E better not try." Quickly, George stepped forward again and, firmly pinching William's nose, forced him to gasp for breath. In a flash, George pulled and held Billy's jaws apart as though he were a horse. One by one, the children went through the motions of examining Billy's ears and mouth. They could see nothing out of the ordinary about them.

"Per'aps 'e's just stubborn," George suggested. It was an idea which appealed to him once he had thought of it. Without more ado, he looked around and picked up a stick. "I'll soon make 'im talk."

Jem suddenly had a brainwave.

"Let's go up the churchyard," she suggested. She turned away from Billy and took a step or two in that direction. Frances could not decide what to do. Her first feeling was one of relief that they had lost interest in Billy, but her second was the creepy feeling up her spine which even mention of the churchyard always brought to her. She hated the dark yew tree and the path around the back, between the church and the high churchyard wall. Jem would dare her to run around it and she could never refuse to run the long, lonely silent distance.

"Come on. Just you and me." Jem always knew the words to swing the balance. She started off towards the churchyard, leaving George and the little ones grumbling.

"Will you look after Billy?" Frances asked George. "Don't fight him."

Without his big sister and bored by the little ones, George was only too ready to promise and Billy laughed to see his friend grinning at him again.

Once sure that Frances was following, Jem casually stopped to pull a leaf or two from the hawthorn hedge to chew and than rewrapped the old stockings around her feet until Frances caught her up and the two girls walked side by side.

"Nobody new's dead" Frances commented. They sometimes went to view a new grave. A few more steps and they would reach the meadow from where the path led to the wall of the churchyard. Frances wondered whether there would be any point in reminding her friend that the vicar had forbidden children to play around the church.

"Give us a leg up." Jem hitched up her skirts and lifted a foot for Frances to hold in her hands.

"There's ghosts in there. Fred Donkins saw one." It was worth trying, Frances decided.

"'Ow can you trust what Fred Donkins sees when 'e's blind drunk?" Narrowing her eyes and leering horribly, Jem raised her arms over her head and spread out her fingers like menacing claws about to seize their prey. Frances stood her ground.

Jemima dropped her arms to her sides. "I'm going over," she announced in a brisk, matter of fact tone, designed to encourage her friend to follow without question. Carefully finding protrusions and holes, Jem scrambled over the wall. More afraid of being called a coward than of meeting a ghost, Frances prepared to follow. Jem's next remark stopped her in her track. Leaning down over the wall and again leering like a gargoyle, Jem whispered, "There are body snatchers, but 'oo'd want to snatch your body? You're too skinny." She took a step away from the wall, listening all the while for the call she knew would soon come from her friend.

"Pull me up." At least, Frances had decided, with Jem she would have company.

"That's where they were," Jem announced as soon as they were standing side by side in the churchyard. She pointed to a tomb as high as the children, just under the shadow of the yew tree. "That's where the resurrection men were standing — a dozen of 'em, at least."

Frances stared at her in disbelief. Jem was a well known liar.

Her friend read her thoughts "I'm not saying they dug up a body," she explained, "so don't look at me like that." She led Frances forward. "But I bet they would have done, if they could 'ave lifted the stone off the top."

"What are you on about?" Frances demanded in the tone her own mother used when she was talking nonsense.

"Last night, me and George was playing dares when Ma had company. We see these men standing around talking. They was mostly old Per'aps that's why they couldn't lift the stone."

Sighing, Frances asked the obvious question. "Who'd come up here just to talk in the middle of the night?"

Jem smiled, relishing her reply. "I was 'oping you could tell me. One of them was your Grandpa Dodds."

Frances fought to control the astonishment she knew would give Jem such satisfaction. No one should get pleasure from sin and Jem was sinning as never before. "You tell lies." Even provoked as she was Frances avoided the word which she had been forbidden to utter.

"I am not."

"How could you see in the dark?"

"It was a little bit moonlight."

"You tell lies."

"There was your grandpa, Mr Ballom, Mr Low and some others."

Jem always could tell a good lie, Frances thought. They were grandpa's best friends. She needed time to think what was the weak point in Jem's story. A look of triumph was spreading across Jem's face.

"He'd have told me," Frances declared. It was the best she could do. "There are no secrets in our family."

"What do you know, then?"

Frances was not to be caught that easily. She was silent.

"There's no secrets in this village, anyway," Jem said, echoing her mother's words. "Someone's watching you even if you go down the garden to...."

Interrupting her friend's vulgarities, Frances pleaded, "Let's go home, Jem."

"Say you believe me."

With her expression solemn and sincere, but with her fingers crossed behind her back, Frances said, "I believe you, Jem"

They walked home, more slowly than Frances would have liked, but at least they were on their way.

"I know a thing or two about your family," Jem claimed. "Your grandpa Stevenson was born in the poorhouse, Billy's a little devil, your Uncle John's stuck up, now, and your Uncle Sam's a poacher. And," she added, tightening her hold on Frances's shoulder to emphasise the point, "your Grandpa Dodds is a body snatcher."

Frances bit back a denial. She did not want to walk home alone. There would be chances to get her own back later.

At last, well out of the churchyard, Frances sprinted ahead. Complaining, Jem turned in the direction of her own home. Gradually, Frances slowed her pace. She wanted to challenge her grandfather with Jem's story, but she hardly dared. Without knowing what she would say, she let herself in her grandpa's front door. He stood filling his pipe by the fire.

"To what do we owe this honour? I thought you had too many friends to come and see your old grandpa."

"Ma wanted to borrow a spot of sugar." Again her fingers were crossed behind her back.

"You deserve a little treat, my love," Sarah said. "You've been a good girl while we've all been taken up with Billy's troubles." Busy at the table kneading dough, Sarah said, "Your grandpa will pass it down if you ask him nicely."

As Frances reached for the bowl, her grandfather held it above his head. "It will cost you a kiss."

Frances hesitated. In her mind's eye she saw her grandfather and the other men lifting a dead body from the tomb.

"What's that old-fashioned look for?" he laughed.

There were many grown-up goings on which you got into trouble for knowing about. Frances was silent.

"No kiss, no sugar." He placed the bowl high on the shelf and resumed filling his pipe. Tears came into Frances's eyes.

"Don't tease the child, Will." Wiping her hands on her apron, Sarah put her arms around her granddaughter "What's up, my love? Are you tired? Aren't you feeling well?"

With her grandmother on her side, the child burst out, "Jemmy says she saw Grandpa in the graveyard with the resurrection men."

A quick glance passed between Will and his wife. Slowly and casually filling his pipe, he smiled at the child. Without giving anything away, he wanted to find out how much she and Jem knew. "I often go to the church-yard, Frances. There's nothing strange about that. Have a breath of fresh air. Think about my old friends and my Ma and Pa. That's never stopped you giving your old grandpa a kiss before."

Sarah Dodds took another approach. She sat by the fire and, pulling Frances onto her knee, dried the child's eyes with the corner of her apron. "Tell your grandma all about it, love. What's that naughty Jemima been say-ing now?"

Soon, Frances had told the whole story. When she had finished, she kept her head tucked on her grandmother's shoulder. She felt guilty and miserable that she knew things she should not know and had upset her grandparents, who were so good to her. The grown-ups were silent.

"No need to cry, dear. Take your sugar and go home to bed. Grandma'll tell you all about it one day. Of course your grandpa wouldn't do anything wicked and those resurrection men are as wicked as any of the Devil's creatures." Sarah reached up for the sugar and gave it to Frances. "How do you know about such men?"

"Uncle John told Ma and Pa."

"He should know better in front of you little ones. Don't you talk of such things to anyone, do you hear?"

Shutting the door firmly behind the child, Sarah turned to her husband. He was bent over the fire lighting a taper for his pipe, his face turned from her. For a moment she seemed about to speak, but she changed her mind and resumed stirring the stew, her annoyance and distress echoing in each bang of the wooden spoon against the sides of the iron pot.

"Don't take it out on the supper," Will told her. "If you've anything to say, say it now."

"Oh, Will, didn't I tell you not to get mixed up in that nonsense? Haven't we got enough to worry about with Beth and Billy?"

Will sucked on his pipe. Hours he had spent struggling with new words and new ideas. He had talked and talked with his friends, with the shepherd and the shoemaker, with John and, after John had left, with Tom. The whole country was alive with ideas, if Tom was to be believed, and Sarah just dismissed it all as nonsense.

To some extent Will had agreed with his wife. He had not been brought up to ruling the country as the gentry had. All he wanted was the freedom to farm a few acres in the way his father had and to provide for his family. Where he and Sarah differed was in his conviction that the men in government had a duty to listen to poor men and right their grievances. If they failed in this duty, poor men had the right to unite and petition those in authority. Will's heart sank at the thought that now he would have to tell Sarah all that he and the other men had decided. They had banded together and sworn, at that secret meeting in the churchyard, to support each other in petitioning the local magistrates and asking them to restore the villagers' ancient rights and bring back the old times when even a poor man, with his own land to work, could support his family and live simply, but with dignity. The children had stumbled on the truth in a way. At the meeting in the churchyard, they had given themselves the name of Resurrection Men and pledged themselves to work for the resurrection of the old days. Slowly and deliberately, Will tapped out his pipe and prepared to tell Sarah all that he and the other Resurrection Men had agreed.

CHAPTER TWENTY FOUR

In the vicarage, Mrs Gray was sewing and Anne and Nicholas were exchanging opinions on the books they were reading, when Mr Gray left his study and joined them. Tired, his eyes aching from several hours spent peering in candlelight at books and writing down and revising his words for the next day's sermon, Mr Gray was, nonetheless, very satisfied with his work.

"There, it is done," he said. "It is time someone with an abiding belief in the unchanging truth of God's laws spoke out against the fashions of our times."

"May we read the petition, Father?" Nicholas asked.

It was a difficult decision. "The paper is on my desk, Nicholas. Fetch it yourself. It is not something which I would wish to see in a servant's hands — or a young woman's."

For a moment, Anne thought that she was not to be allowed to see the petition, but her father went on. "You may see it, Ann, to learn the evil which can result when ignorant, common men read the lies which flood from the country's presses. Let it be a warning never to contemplate teaching writing in your school or reading any book but the Bible. Not only will it lead to a spread of atheistic, seditious ideas, but it will lead to pride and conceit in minds of limited intelligence, degraded by labour. It will breed in such minds the conviction that they know as much as their betters."

Standing, posed like the statue of an orator, Nicholas read, "A humble petition to the Magistrates. Sirs, we the undersigned, simple men of Abingfield, have read and considered many opinions and having seen with our own eyes the distress in our village do most humbly petition you to restore our ancient rights and properties." Here Nicholas stopped and gulped a large breath, emphasising the lack of punctuation in the passage he had read so far.

"In former times," he continued, "our fathers and grandfathers owned a few acres by which they could support their families without resort to charity or the parish and could graze their beasts on the common land and collect wood for their fires." Again he paused and gulped at the air. "In present times honest men have lost their independence, their livelihoods and their hope. We most humbly petition, sirs, that each family is rented an acre of land and is lent money to buy seeds and a pig or two or a few sheep and cattle."

Nicholas looked up. "'A pig or two or a few sheep' that has a rustic ring." Again he read from the paper, "We, sir, beg you to consider this our humble petition and assure you and their Majesties of our loyalty as true Englishmen."

Coming to the end, Nicholas commented, "It is much milder, Father, than many inflammatory letters and pamphlets I have read lately." He looked at the signatures, some mere squiggles, and smiled. "It is simply and clearly set out, not without a little truth in it."

"Simple? Deceitful is a word I would use. Of course, there is a little truth in it, but the Devil knows that a little truth is worse than a lie," Mr Gray declared. "What would happen if we conceded to their demands? Half the men would refuse to work for any master, saying they were too busy on their own land and had all the money they needed. The other half would sell up and use the money in the ale house and then put out their hands for charity again."

"What have you and the other magistrates replied?" Nicholas asked.

"You, and they, shall have my reply from the pulpit."

The following Sunday, Mr Gray having let it be known that he wished all masters to see to it that their servants and labourers attended, there was a full congregation. Each household was neatly penned, as God's flock, in pews, with servants near the doors, from where they could discreetly leave early to prepare meals for the returning families.

The Stevensons were early in their places. Even Edward, whose very low opinion of human nature made him have very serious doubts about a God of a similar image, was there, knowing the gentry preferred their chimneys swept by a member of the Church of England than by an atheist or nonconformist. Beth sat quietly, seeking in the House of God comfort and hope. The cross glinting in the sloping shafts of light eased her soul.

Everyone sat clearing throats and making last minute adjustments to their positions in the hard, wooden benches waiting for the sermon to begin. Mr Gray's eyes swept the congregation and, as he began to speak, silence fell. It was necessary for those who wanted to hear his message to make an effort to listen, his words usually being deadened by high rafters or by low minds unfamiliar with long words, flowery phrases and references to the classical world.

"Righteousness exalteth a nation, but sin is a reproach to any people." Mr Gray's voice was stern and he waited as the words filled the church from the altar to the west door and from the high hammer beams to the stone floor. The faces of many of his parishioners remained as wooden and expressionless as the carved cherubim and seraphim above.

"Has there ever, since Creation, been a greater nation than ours? Classical scholars amongst you may put forward the claims of Rome, that great city which ruled an empire from Asia Minor to Northern Britain, or of Athens, that brilliant jewel set in the crown of Greece. I would answer that, great as these cities were, it was the uncivilised darkness of the ancient world around them, which caused them to shine as stars in a moonless night. They would seem as dim candles against the dazzling sunlight of our own great nation. Our great nation, which shines like the sun, not only over the narrow world of' the ancients, but over the whole globe, over lands undiscovered until recent times stretching from America to the Antipodes. France, Russia, Austria, even these mighty nations pale beside our brilliance." Now the parson's words echoed not only throughout the church, but in the very hearts of his congregation.

"On no other nation has God showered such blessings and to no other country has God given such wealth, power and greatness. No other nation has been raised to such heights. Righteousness! From His Almighty Throne, God looked down upon this island and into the hearts and minds of her people. God saw a people who feared Him, a righteous people and He exalted our nation above all others. He blessed our industries, putting into the minds of humble men ingenious inventions. He blessed our trade, bringing ships from the ends of the earth laden with wealth. He blessed our armies and our navies, giving strength to our swords and victories to our generals and admirals. All this God did in fulfilment of his promise."

Pausing again, Mr Gray took breath so that he could speak with all the authority and certainty of God's messenger. Only those who had already lost the thread of the message thought of moving to ease the hardness of the seats, but they were inhibited by the heavy silence around them.

"But sin is a reproach to any people. At the very moment that God exalted Britain, he set a warning before the eyes of her people. France, that nation of sin, pride and popery, was cast down. God looked across the Channel and, in the hearts of Frenchmen, saw the ignorance, wickedness and superstition which let them fall prey to that most evil of all man's philosophies — radicalism. God rested His hand and let the maggots of equality, fraternity and all other false beliefs grow until worm-like, they ate into the very foundations of the State."

"Sin." Arms outstretched, Mr Gray proclaimed in a mighty voice, "For sin, Lucifer was cast out of Heaven. For sin Adam and Eve were cast from Eden. For sin, the French State was destroyed."

Not a single man, woman or child in the congregation questioned the right ness of God's anger in any of these cases and not one even noticed, let alone questioned, the assumption which Mr Gray had made that, if God had looked across the Channel to France, His home was in England.

"Now, in this year of Our Lord, 1817, after such a brief passage of time, God sees that we have not heeded His warning and He warns us again that, as He hath exalted a righteous nation, so shall He destroy a sinful one. Before it is too late, let us look to the signs He has sent in His mercy and let us pluck out the sin in our society. The signs of our sin and of God's wrath are everywhere. Let all who have eyes to see and ears to hear heed His message. Who is so foolish amongst you that he will not heed the failing harvests, the smoke rising from the ricks set on fire by wicked, envious men? Who has not seen the lanes filled with idle beggars? Who has not heard whispers of false doctrines of radicalism, hidden in the guise of liberty and freedom? You have all seen these signs and more, but few have heeded them.

"How do I know, you might ask, what lurks in the darkest parts of your minds and what passions stir in your very hearts? I do not know." Mr Gray had spoken these words in a quiet, humble tone Now his voice rose, crashing against the roof. "I do not know, but have no doubt your Maker knows. What He has seen has caused Him to send a sign to this village."

For a moment Mr Gray's thoughts seemed to have wandered and his eyes were turned to the wall. The effect, as he had anticipated, was all the more telling when, with a suddenness which startled every member of the congregation, he pounced to the edge of the pulpit, staring and pointing down.

"There is the sign. There is the mark of evil. There is the deaf and dumb boy who walks amongst us. The child has no thoughts, no mind and, worse by far, his soul shrinks and perishes for want of the nourishment of God's word. That boy is no better than an animal — a creature with animal needs and passions, bearing no mark of God's grace. As that being stalks amongst us, let us all look upon him and bless God for His mercy in sending this awful sign of His displeasure."

All eyes were upon Billy. Beth looked away, past Mr Gray to the cross above the altar. "Oh God, Dear God, help us," she said in a whisper. She felt at her side on the bench and gently took Billy's hand to comfort him. He turned and as he smiled at her Beth realised he knew nothing of the cruel words being spoken. That, at least, was a blessing. Charles took Billy's other hand and, in his pleasure, the boy swung his feet so that they clattered, without his being aware of it, against the pew in front.

The sound spurred Mr Gray to greater anguish. "Sin. Sin. The cause of all afflictions and imperfections. Let there be no doubt that this deaf and dumb child, like the cripple, the blind, the halt and the lame, was born out of sin, a punishment to the sinner and a warning to God's people."

"Let the sinners amongst you look on this child and harken to the mother's weeping. Let his parents repent. Let all repent and turn from sin lest the day come when all women and female creatures bring forth monsters, lest the corn rot in the fields and plague and famine and desolation visit this once great land."

"Sin," Mr Gray continued, "or should I say sins, for the Devil has set more snares for man than a mere seven deadly sins?" For a moment, the flow of the parson's speech was stemmed by a restless movement from the Hammond's pew as Maria changed her position. Ever sensitive to any reaction from that family, Mr Gray went on quickly, "Let us consider this morning just one sin, however, the sin of pride. Every man, rich or poor, who looks into his heart will see there the sin of pride." Hurrying on, not wishing to offend, he explained, "Even those who are most pure and closest to God will find pride if they search. Can it be wrong, you may ask, to look with pride on achievement, on the fruits of hard work, on wealth and rank? It is wrong. It is forgotten that differences between men are bestowed by God for his purpose. The wise man," Mr Gray said with a slight smile and inclination of his head towards the Hammond's pew, "praises God for His blessings and keeps a humble heart. 'God resisteth the proud and giveth to the humble.'"

More slowly and with greater emphasis, Mr Gray looked towards the back of the church. "And the poor man, of simple intellect, fit only to labour all his days on the land? Ah, you may think such a man has no cause for pride and so, my brethren, so God intended. He did not make most men poor because He despises them, but because he loves them. Yes," Mr Gray repeated, "God made men poor because He loves them. How blessed is the poor man free from the temptations which wealth brings, free from the burdens of office and the demands on his time which authority brings! How close to our Saviour's own life is that of a humble, simple God-fearing man. How God must grieve when he sees these simple creatures set themselves against their betters, sees them defy and disobey their masters and demand — may God forgive their pride — demand to share power and authority with those whom God has set over them. All a poor man needs do on this earth is praise God, turn from sin and do his duty obediently."

There was more shuffling and movement from the front pew. It was not Sir Philip, Mr Gray told himself, taking breath and continuing with a point dear to his heart. "Pride of intellect, that is the curse of our age. So many and so varied are the triumphs of man's intellect in the last hundred years, so daring and courageous his travels and discoveries of new lands, so ingenious his mechanical inventions and so far reaching the progress of medicine and the sciences that we are in danger of glorifying man rather than his Maker. We forget that man's intellect may be used for the forces of darkness to set up new religions, evil sects and false politics. How easily man, for all his intellect, is tempted to follow fashion, to seek the new and forsake old values, to turn from the Church and from the Constitution established by God."

With renewed vigour, Mr Gray caught his second wind to digress on the topic of former days. "The old days were good. Poor men were content and obedient. Men did not chase every fashionable idea. Men did not think, in their pride, that poverty and sickness could be swept away by earthly powers. In those golden days few were content to eat the bread of idleness. But let us return to the present unhappy times. The danger, it is my duty to warn you, is that man is tampering with God's creation and may destroy the orderliness of the universe. How can the true Christian rejoice to see the annihilation of those very diseases which have always served to remind men of his mortality and forced him, in his helplessness, to turn to his maker? Smallpox, for centuries, has been a part of God's plan to call mankind to throw itself on His mercy, yet there are some who rejoice to claim that it has been conquered by the intellect of man."

The theme was not to be elaborated. A slight movement of Sir Philip's head and Mr Gray pruned his sermon severely, if reluctantly. There was no more time for words on the duties of the poor and no time to point out the tendency for some of the better off members of the congregation to encourage indolence and improvidence by the indiscriminate distribution of charity. Whatever Sir Philip might say, however, Mr Gray was not to be diverted from his final point.

"Let me conclude," he said, "by denouncing a sin rife among the lower ranks of society — superstition. There is no place for superstition in a Christian, civilized nation. I am urged to speak on this subject by the heathen belief, which has reached my ears, that the sight of a hare might harm an unborn child. A harmless old wives' tale, you may think, but think again. What harm such an idea does in simple minds! What is the next step in this fallacious reasoning? The child's disability is a witch's fault. It is not the mother's fault, these people claim. It is not the father's fault or the father's father's, but the fault of a witch in the shape of a hare. Such superstitious beliefs take away all blame, take away all shame and thus take away all hope of repentance. God has told us that the sins of the fathers shall be visited upon the children. These imperfect beings come into the world as a warning to all to turn from sin to righteousness, so that God may once more exalt our nation."

Each word had followed rapidly upon the one before and the last came just within the time Sir Philip had suggested, when he gave Mr Gray the living, was sufficient for any sermon.

Above the usual muffled coughing and shuffling and creaking of benches, the sharp clatter of heavy boots rang out on the stone floor. At first, only a few of the congregation reacted to the sound. In a few more, half asleep, the movement released the set pattern of action and, but for restraining hands, they would have stood up too. Only when Will spoke did every one realise he had risen to his feet to have his say.

"We asked for bread and you gave us stones," he shouted.

Wives nudged their dozing husbands and sweethearts turned from each other at last. The pews heaved as everyone looked at Will and then to Paul Low and a few other men who rose one by one. From here and there in the anonymity of the crowd came the sound of stamping feet and shouts. The words were lost, but the tone of threat and defiance set the hearts of those privileged to sit in the well-sited pews away from obscuring pillars as rapidly as the hearts of foxes surrounded by hounds. They looked to Sir Philip.

Quietly, Sir Philip rose, showing no sign that he was aware of anything unusual. With his back to most of the parishioners he continued the ritual of set actions for that moment of that day of the week in that place. One by one, the congregation joined him.

Will Dodds, surrounded by singing parishioners, felt quite separate from them and quite separate from that part of himself which had watched in embarrassment, warning him that he was showing himself up and making a fool of himself. The endless hymn droned on and on. The damp, stuffy air stifled him, until he was sure he was going to drop to the floor. Breathing deeply and trying to calm his mind, Will told himself that he must gain control of himself, stifle the angry, bitter man who had spoken out with his voice and walk from the church to the sanctuary of his own home.

At the first hesitant step towards the end of the pew, Sarah placed her hand gently on Will's arm and then put her arm through his.

"Stay where you are, Will. This is God's House and you've no call to be angry with Him just because the parson's a fool. When it's the proper time to leave, you take young Billy in your arms so that Charles can take care of Beth."

CHAPTER TWENTY FIVE

As Will entered, he saw Beth leaning over the hearth picking up the iron warming by the fire. Her face, as she looked up, was pale and tear-stained. Even the exertion of bending and the heat from the fire had brought no flush to her cheeks. Will moved towards her, but she backed away.

"I'm alright, Pa, truly, I am." Seeing the hurt on his face, she explained, "I've been to the depths, Pa, and I'm not going there again."

Without another word, Will stood watching his daughter as she wet her finger and deftly touched it against the iron and then, hearing it sizzle sharply, began ironing. Any other time he would have taken the iron from her, grown up though she was, and forbidden her to break the Sabbath. Today he was silent.

"I've cried and cried Pa, not just about what the vicar said, but before that, ever since that day at Dr Gray's." Her grip on the iron seemed to tighten and she pressed her weight more heavily upon it. "And do you know what I feel now, Pa? Anger. Blind anger and I'm glad. I'll thank that parson till my dying day for what he said. It was like a spur — it hurt deep, but now it'll drive me on to do whatever I must do for Billy.

"Perhaps God is punishing me," Beth continued. "I'll know that on Judgement Day. As for now, Billy's my first concern. When people stare at him and point at me, I shan't care any more. That anger is there to toughen me up. Every minute I've got, I'll walk as far as I have to — to Hell and back if necessary — and talk to as many people as I have to, to find help for our son. John sent a message, you know, along with those cures I tried, that there was supposed to be a deaf boy over at Padsett. Said he'd go there when he could, but I don't want to wait. Tomorrow Ma can keep an eye on Tim and the other two and I'll go there myself."

"It's a good four miles each way."

"Then I'll have to start early, Pa."

Beth was as good as her word. She woke the children when she got up to get Charles off to work and chivvied them into dressing quickly.

"Grandma's having Tim, but you take care of Billy, Frances. Look after him and I'll make you bread and milk as soon as I get back."

"With sugar?" Frances asked, sensing her power at that moment. Her Ma was anxious about leaving Billy and only she could calm her mother's worries.

Beth considered the weighty matter as carefully as a merchant making a bargain, but it was only pretend, Frances knew, just part of the fun of having a treat which made it all the more delicious when it came.

With a sigh, her mother agreed, as though making a great concession. "I'll bring some fresh milk and some sugar back with me. Don't take your eyes off Billy. Promise?"

"I promise, Ma."

For a while after her mother left, Frances played in the street, keeping a watchful eye on her brother. She picked up Nelson and, just to pass the time, hugged him and stroked him. The cat struggled and squirmed to free himself, but then lay quiet. Like any cat, Nelson did not waste energy in a pointless struggle, but neither did he forget his purpose. He simply bided his time, summing up the situation and moving, when the chance came, with the speed of light.

"Nelson!" As the cat sensed its chance had come, Frances's hands closed on the empty air. The sleek black body, already across the lane, disappeared into the field.

It had been a movement in the hedge a couple of fields away which had caught Frances's attention so that she had loosened her grasp. For a moment she had thought she glimpsed Jem, but now the movement had stopped and there was no Jem and she had lost Nelson. Perhaps, her mind turned once again to the treat in store, Ma would bring the bread and milk to her in bed. About to join Billy in his game, Frances spotted the movement again, more definite this time. It was Jem and it looked as though she was on her way over.

Just as the very words 'bread and milk' conjured up images and associations of warmth and love and care, of warm, sweet milk squeezed from soft bread on the tongue, so the sight and name of Jem brought their own associations. "She'll go the way of her mother," some said, or, "Poor mite, she hasn't got a chance." "Her little legs and feet are always blue with cold." Jem, Frances knew from grown-ups and accepted as Gospel truth, had been born in sin, and was an inheritor of sin as well as its victim, to be pitied, condemned and, in the end, to gather the inevitable wages of sin. The knowledge gave Frances a sense of superiority in her own goodness and decency, but, such is the unreasonableness of childish reason, or of mature reason for that matter, the name of Jemima aroused, at the same time, envy and admiration and promises of a boundless world of adventure and daring.

"Ma's gone to Padsett," Frances announced as Jem climbed the field gate.

"Has she left you anything to eat?" Jem knew what was important in life.

"Grandma'll give us something. Ma's promised me bread and milk when she comes home," Frances answered, anxious to let Jem know that her mother did not neglect her.

"We 'ad it yesterday," Jem claimed, adding for good measure, "and the day before." For a moment she paused, ready to defend, herself against any charge of telling lies with an even bigger, more convincing one. Frances, she realised, wanted her company and was not going to risk losing it by arguing. She pressed on with her plan. "Let's go and play somewhere better than this."

"Can Billy come?"

To Frances's surprise, she was told that he could and all that remained was to ask where they were going.

"You'll see," Jem told her, linking arms, "It's a surprise."

Once out of the village, Frances felt a little uneasy, but Jem soon made her forget her doubts. "Me feet are killing me Fran," she moaned, lifting her foot to show the sole hanging from the over large shoe. "These nettles are stinging right through. Give us a ride, Frances."

Obediently, Frances stood still and let Jem, facing her and holding her around the waist, stand on her toes. Then, as they clung together, laughing, Frances staggered forward. After that, it was piggy-backs and wheel-barrows and anything except plain, boring walking.

"Where are we?" Frances asked at last. She was quite lost.

"I bet you've never seen the turnpike." Jem stressed the word 'you' to make it clear that she had.

"Pa's going to take us when we're old enough to walk that far." With a cry of triumph, Jem flung her arms wide. "You're old enough now." Frances looked around in disbelief.

"This ain't it." Jemima raised her eyes to Heaven at her friend's ignorance. They were on a path, deeply rutted from cart and waggon wheels, running a zigzag path through the trees and trampled hedges. "This is where the mean old farmers come to dodge the gate-keeper. This way, they get on the turnpike without paying."

It was all beyond Frances's knowledge and understanding. Jemima beckoned her on and in a few steps they were standing on the turnpike. William and George stamped on it until their feet stung. It was hard, harder than anything they had stamped on before, harder than the mud lanes even on a dry, hot summer's day. There was scarcely a puddle or pothole in sight. With her eyes, Frances followed its straight course for as far as she could see. She jumped for joy. A little way along the road was a tiny little house with six sides and a thatched roof rising up to a point. She had never seen a fairy house, but surely this was one. It made no difference that Jem told her it was where the toll keeper took money from travellers wishing to use the turnpike; she was convinced it was a fairy house. Jem gloried in her friend's ignorance and led her to meet the keeper. After Frances's delighted cries and wide-eyed admiration of things she took in her stride, Jem could almost bear her friend's reading all the notices she had never read herself'.

"Soldiers don't have to pay," Frances informed her.

"So?" Jem asked, strolling casually away. It was puzzling her how to make the most of William's appeal to persuade travellers to part with a little money. If he only had staring, unseeing eyes like the blind beggar who passed through each year, or twisted limbs like the cripple who sat all day by the canal basin. You needed something to show for their money and, with William, there was nothing to be seen. Perhaps, if you held a candle close to his ear hole, there would be something to see, if only it was an empty space through to the other side of his head. Jem knew, from side shows at the fair, that people liked to feast their eyes on deformities. Travellers, bored or anxious to have a good story for their stay at home neighbours, would give good money to see a curiosity.

There was nothing for it, Jemima concluded, she would have to use Billy and Frances as straightforward beggars. Her Ma had said that, when she was a child, people chucked money to any urchin, the grubbier the better, but now they held on to their money if you were untidy or idle and then they started talking about the House of Correction or Sunday School. Frances and Billy might be just the kind of clean, tidy children who would be considered deserving of a little help, but Jem's hopes were not high.

From Billy, at that very moment, came a strange, unearthly cry. In a mock battle, George had accidentally bent back Billy's finger and he had uttered a yell of pain. Jem's hopes soared.

At the tollgate, an argument was going on, about the amount due from a waggon. It must have been going on for some time and a carriage and a post chaise waited near by, their passengers anxious to be on their way. Gathering her little flock of innocent lambs about her, Jemima walked towards the carriage. At the right moment, she pinched Billy sharply. He let out the dreadful shriek.

"There, there," Jem comforted him, her arm lovingly around his shoulder. "It ain't your Ma. If only you could 'ear, Billy, you'd know she's dead and gorn and ain't never coming back."

The woman's disgust at being mistaken for a poor child's mother was overcome, as Jem expected, by her curiosity. "What's the matter with the boy?"

With a charming curtsey, Jem answered, "He's deaf and dumb, ma'am. Comes here every day to look for his Ma. He thinks she's just gone on a journey and will be coming back to him one day." She hugged Billy to her, digging her nails into his shoulder to stop his wriggling protest and smiling all the while at the travellers.

"Poor child. How did it come about?"

Jem was not sure if the lady meant the affliction or the bereavement, but she had already learned that it was always best to keep as close to the truth as possible. There was less chance that way of slipping up or being caught out. At least it was true that Billy was deaf and dumb.

"A fever. No fault of 'is or 'is Ma and Pa, that's for sure."

"Where's his father?"

Outrage transformed every feature of Jem's face. "Working, sir."

The couple seemed to be losing interest. Jem hurried on with her tale. "That is, sir, 'e works when there is any work to be 'ad. There's never enough money in the 'ouse to spend on medicines. That's why Billy called out. Pain. Pain something terrible in 'is ears."

"Let me see," the woman demanded.

"There ain't nothing to see, ma'am. If there were 'is Pa would keep 'im 'idden, not wishing to let others see 'ow they suffered."

The man looked at Frances who had just walked up, wondering what was going on. "You resemble the boy. Are you his sister?"

"Yes, sir."

"Why aren't you working, child, to help support your unfortunate brother?"

"She 'as to look after 'im. Keeps 'im out of trouble." Seeing where this remark might lead, Jem added quickly, "Not that 'e's any trouble. She just 'as

146

to keep 'im out of 'arm's way."

"We're ready to go at last," the gentleman announced with relief. As Jem ran alongside the carriage, he seemed about to reach for a coin.

"I always maintain there's work enough for those who want it," his wife told him, placing a restraining hand on his arm. "There will be another three or four children all bringing in a wage, you mark my word." Her husband must have raised a faint protest as she asked him, "How do we know he is deaf and dumb? Anyone can pretend to be deaf and dumb."

Jem stopped running and stood to stare after the carriage and pull a face at the departing travellers. "The 'orses looks ready to drop dead and I 'ope they do as well."

The chaise with its driver in his yellow uniform brought no better luck. At Jem's announcement that Billy was deaf and dumb, the occupants, two young men, giggled.

"The sins of the fathers," one said, looking at Billy.

"And the mothers."

"Looks a shade like you. Did his mother work at the inn a few years ago?"

"I was too young then," the first protested.

"I was thinking of your father."

As the chaise moved away, Frances heard one say, "In that case, Father must have been busy. There are a dozen or more like that at the deaf and dumb asylum in Hunsdon. All young children. A kind of school I suppose, though what anyone could teach the deaf and dumb, I don't know."

"Sir," Frances shouted at the top of her voice. "Please, sir. Wait, sir."

Thinking she was begging, they took no notice. Soon the chaise was gone.

"Jem, I've got to tell Ma." Frances seemed suddenly to remember her mother and her grandmother. She looked at the sun. "Jem, Ma will be back by now. She won't give me my bread and milk."

With Jem acting as though she were deaf, too, Frances had no choice but to start back with Billy. Although she did not know the way Jem had brought them, she knew the direction to aim for and, with Billy's help, soon had the church steeple in sight. Around the corner would be a ford and, from there on, they would be on familiar territory.

"Come on." Frances took her brother's hand as they ran along the lane and around the corner.

The familiar landmarks were not there. Swollen by rain, the stream had risen and spread to fill the hollow and cover path and fence and field. Frances let her brother's hand drop. She stood, wondering what to do, but Billy, impulsive as ever, rushed in, laughing and splashing the water all around him.

"Billy. You'll get your clothes soaked. Pa'll wallop you." His back was towards her, and he could not see her warning. She remembered how her Pa had described how the heavy rain had made potholes in the lane and how he had nearly lost his footing in one and fallen flat on his face. William would have heard none of this, she realised, and she watched in horror as he advanced further into the water, too young to realise that the water would get deeper and deeper as the path dipped and unaware of the holes and uneven ground which might trip him at any moment.

The water was up to Billy's chest and, as he moved into the path of the swollen stream, the current of surging water swirled around him, pressing its weight against him. Until now he had resolutely kept his face away from his sister so as not to be able to see her entreaties and signals. At last he turned, his eyes pleading and his lips moving in a voiceless plea for help.

"Come here. Come here," she called, summoning him with her hands, but he did not seem to understand or dare to move. He gazed at his sister, hesitating in the buffeting of the current. In an attempt to make him understand, Frances turned and walked away in the opposite direction. He, thinking she was leaving him, panicked and tried to rush after her. Just as she had seen in her fears, he tripped, sprawling face forward into the water and disappeared beneath the surface.

Praying with all the urgency of her young soul, Frances plunged in and battled to the spot where she had last seen her brother. From the edge of the water she had fixed the spot where he had been, but, in the swirling mass, as she moved forward, it was difficult to remember where, on the shining surface, it had been. She plunged her face under the water, but it stung her eyes and she did not even have time to find her bearings in the murky water stirred up by her feet before she had to lift her head and gulp in the fresh air.

As she stood, shivering with cold and the terror of Billy's disappearance, time seemed to have stopped. Never, never it seemed, would this terrible moment pass. Except for the whistle of the cold wind and the splash of water against the tree trunks there was silence over the flooded earth. Only

148

when she had looked and listened, desperately trying to imagine what her Ma and Pa would do, was Frances aware of the pressure of water against her side. The current would have swept Billy in its path. At once, she walked with it, leaning backwards to resist being swept off her feet. Edging forward, Frances stopped to feel under the water. She moved forward again and stopped again. Her toe had hit something hard. For a moment she thought it might be Billy's body, but it was too hard and too unyielding. Feeling with her hands, she realised that it was the stile, the one through the hedge onto the path which ran alongside the stream in its quieter seasons. Frances hung on to the stile with one hand and, bending low in the water, stretched out the other to feel right and left. Her hand clutched Billy's jacket. By now her eyes had focused through the water and she saw Billy, his leg caught in the wood supporting the stile so that his whole body was being held beneath the water just where the current was forced through the narrow gap in the hedge.

Holding her breath until her lungs seemed to be bursting, Frances freed him, at first tugging aimlessly, but then methodically working his leg free and lifting him to the surface. To regain her breath and her strength, she rested Billy's still body on the stile, holding his head above the stream. Then she dragged him from the water and laid him face down on the path.

There Frances hesitated, not knowing whether to run for help or drag Billy home. She would be quicker on her own and pulling her brother well away from the flood, she left him in the shelter of the hedge, away from the wind which chilled her beneath her wet clothes and froze her to the bone. She started to run, but her petticoat, heavy with water, clung to her and tripped her. As quickly as her trembling hands would move, she took it off and threw it down.

Running forward again, Frances sobbed as she went. The path was slippery and her tired legs seemed incapable of carrying her any further. Step by step, she forced herself towards the village. "Pa. Please somebody help me."

Rounding a bend, her head low, Frances did not see the Colonel and his servant until she was almost upon him. In a vain attempt to stop, she collapsed into his arms.

"Billy! He's drowned!"

Dropping Frances, the Colonel ordered, "Hurry, Walker. You can move faster than I."

Wearily picking herself up and terrified of what she might find, Frances followed them.

"He's alive, sir. Just about." Walker shouted.

"Freed at last from the responsibility of saving her brother and completely exhausted, Frances began to shiver uncontrollably.

Already, Walker had wrapped Billy in his coat and was carrying him in his arms.

Following his example and taking off his own coat, the Colonel encircled Frances in its warmth and carried her safely home. "There, there, child. You are both safe now."

CHAPTER TWENTY SIX

For the rest of that day and most of the night, Frances passed the hours asleep or only half awake, hiding within herself from the nightmares of drowning and dying and the whispered talk and argument which reached her on her crime and the nature of her punishment. A candle burned all night and from its shadows and the hushed voices, Frances knew that her parents were sitting over Billy. Then, to snatch a few hours sleep before he went to the fields, her father went to his bed.

"I'll deal with that young lady tomorrow," she heard him say. All was quiet and Frances slept peacefully, knowing she was protected from every evil by her mother, still awake to guard her children.

Billy stayed in bed all the next day, but Frances was allowed up in the afternoon. Not that there was anything to do, with Jem and George forbidden to venture within sight of the cottage. Nobody seemed to want to speak to her and disapproval showed on every face and in every voice inquiring how the poor little lad was after his terrible ordeal. As the time of her father's return from work drew near, Frances felt her legs grow weak and the tiredness returned.

"You'd better pop back into bed," Beth advised, understanding the symptoms straight away. "Give your Pa a day or two and he might calm down." She tucked Frances in bed and kissed her. "Not that you don't deserve a good hiding for what you did."

There was no need to ask what she had done wrong. Even if she had not heard her Pa say it many times last night, her own conscience had given her no peace. She might, with Ma's protection, escape her Pa's full anger, but God still knew that she had taken Billy too far, not asked permission to go and let Billy rush into the water and nearly get drowned. And there was something even worse. Frances could hardly face the thought herself and tried to push it away —she had been begging. With all her heart she prayed that this sin was known only to God and never revealed to her Pa.

As the latch was raised, all Frances's strength seemed to drain away. A good spanking was terrible enough, but for things as bad as she had done, it might be a caning or a belting. She had never had one before. She listened, her eyes tightly closed, as her parents discussed Billy's condition and then her own.

"Leave it a day or two, Charles," her mother pleaded. "She's still weak."

"Don't try and talk me out of it, Beth. Do you want to wait until Billy's drowned, or Tim? She's old enough to know better and take some of the cares off your shoulders." Still very angry with his daughter, he added, loudly enough for her to hear, "What's the use of all this learning out of books if she hasn't the sense she was born with?"

Although not daring to peep down the stairs, Frances relaxed a little. It sounded as though her father was sitting down to his meal. Sam had brought in a rabbit, or rather, a skinned rabbit with no tell-tale fur to leave for prying eyes. Ma had planned Pa's favourite rabbit pie, as well as broth for Billy, and Grandma had cooked them to perfection. No-one had spoken of it or laid a plan, but everyone was trying to please her Pa and save her from a walloping. They all agreed that she deserved it, but they could face the thought of the actual beating no better than she could.

Trying to forget the rabbit pie, for it was too risky to ask for even just a spoonful in her weakest voice, she wondered if, for a real belting, you were tied down like Uncle John said the soldiers were tied to the halberds for a flogging. There were plenty of children in the village who did get belted, but they were always too busy showing the wheals and bruises to tell just how it was done. She was fast asleep some hours later when Ma woke her and, placing a finger over her lips, signalled her to be quiet and just eat up her broth as quickly as she could.

By the next day, Frances was playing outside and Billy sitting in the parlour when Colonel Benson and Ben Walker called. Beth thanked them over and over again and made Frances thank them and apologise for causing so much trouble.

"The boy's been pointed out to me before, of course," the Colonel said. "Knew he was deaf and dumb. Been observing him."

Beth listened, all attention to the gentlemen, as she had been trained to do. "Yes, sir."

"Observation. That's the first thing. All conclusions should be based on observation. Avoid mad theories that way." The Colonel, having declined a chair, stood with his back to the hearth, gazing at Billy. Ben Walker stood beside him.

"I've been watching that lad of yours, Mrs Stevenson, and I've observed how you and he behave together." Turning to his servant, he ordered, "Open the door, Walker. There, Mrs Stevenson. Do shut it again, Walker.

The boy will catch a chill from that draught."

"Sir?" Beth was not quite sure what this was all about. Walker seemed bewildered too.

"Smoaker, Mrs Stevenson. My spaniel. When I came in, I told him to sit and stay and there he sits until I give him his next order."

"Yes, sir. He's a lovely dog."

"He's an obedient dog. Disobedient dogs and disobedient children are a burden to their owners, to their neighbours and to themselves. A walk with Smoaker Mrs Stevenson, is a pleasure and a relaxation. A walk with your son — I have seen it — a walk with your son is a punishment. I have heard you shouting, seen you chasing after him. He does just as he likes. This unfortunate incident would not have occurred, I am sure, if he had looked to his sister and not rushed headlong into the water. My dog loves water. As a puppy he once dashed straight in. Now he waits, looks to me and does only what I allow him to do."

"Yes, sir."

"Let us go outside."

From the moment the door opened, Smoaker fixed his deep brown eyes lovingly on his master. As the Colonel gave him a series of orders, each was obeyed eagerly and the next awaited with joyous anticipation.

"Make the child watch you, as Smoaker watches me. Make him alert to your every word and signal. Have a signal for this and that. Keep it clear and simple. Do not fuss, that confuses. Reward good behaviour at once and punish wilfulness with equal speed. Be just, be firm, but affectionate also and that way, you will not break his spirit."

His ideas, based on observation and common-sense greatly pleased the Colonel. To encourage Beth, he explained, "The child may bear the signs of God's anger, but he is still one of his creatures and can be trained like other creatures." Eager not to forget anything, he began again. "Imitation, that is how young children learn. The bird flies, the cat stalks. No word passes. The young watch and imitate. That is why all must set a good example." Remembering another point he intended to make, the Colonel emphasised, "It will be especially important to keep him from bad company. All men are easily led — look around you at all the terrible crimes in the country today — but your boy, Mrs Stevenson, Billy, will copy everything he sees. Keep him from wicked examples."

The Colonel's servant, Benjamin Walker, had listened and seemed to agree with every word his master uttered. Apart from being taller, he was very like the Colonel in bearing, upright and smart, clearly an excellent servant, anticipating every wish of his master and carrying out every order to perfection. It had been known for children, safely hidden at a distance, to shout after him, "Walker. Heel, Walker."

The lecture finished, the Colonel strolled back into the cottage with Walker and Beth close behind.

"Where is it, Walker?" he demanded, standing by Billy's chair.

"Here, sir." From his jacket, the servant gently took a small ball of black fur. It was a kitten.

Frances rushed to stroke it and Billy threw aside the cover tucked around his legs. The Colonel placed a restraining hand on his shoulder. At first Billy tried to shrug it off and shake himself free. Only when he at last sat still and looked up at the Colonel did he receive a smile and a nod which told him he might take it in his hands.

"I found it yesterday, or, rather, it found me," Ben Walker explained. "I was walking along the canal bank when I heard a meowing behind me and there it was dripping wet and trailing at my heels. It had a piece of string dangling around its neck. I'm sure someone had tried to drown it and it had somehow struggled free and clambered up the bank. Would you like it Billy?"

"Don't be foolish, man. How can he hear you? Point to the cat and then to the boy. Smile at him questioningly."

Awkwardly, Walker did as he was bidden. The message was not lost on Billy. Tenderly, he took the kitten and showed it to his mother.

"The bedraggled little thing reminded me of your William after his soaking yesterday," Ben told Beth, "so what better than to give it to him?"

Beth was beginning to think that he could not be as much under his master's thumb as everyone thought, when he spoiled it by adding, "The Colonel said I might. We hadn't the heart to kill it after it had had such courage to fight for its life."

As Colonel Benson and Ben Walker left, the master said to his servant, "If all you have told me of John Stevenson is true, he is the worst example a boy could have."

"I swear it's all true, sir."

In the cottage, the children sat with eyes and thoughts for nothing but the kitten. It lay on its side, its head propped against the fender. As William stroked it gently, it opened its eyes a little until they were small, blue slits and stiffly stretched its legs, letting them relax suddenly and satisfyingly as its eyes closed again.

The little creature was exhausted. As it slept, William traced, without quite touching, the shape of its small round head and the soft, fluffy hairs growing along the edge of its over large ears. With light finger tips, he felt the tiny, black pads on its paws curled beneath its body. At the touch, the kitten stretched until front legs, body and back legs formed a straight line from nose to tail. Like that, it slept again, a small, hard, well filled belly extended for the children to stroke.

"Leave it to sleep," Beth urged, but they could not keep their hands off it. They could see that the cat was not, as it seemed at first, as black as coal, but had greyish, short hairs, hinting at the pattern of a tabby, beneath the long black hair of its chest. Ears, nose and tiny paws twitched violently and the up and down movements of its breathing became rapid and panicky.

"It's dreaming, Ma. Don't be afraid." Frances raised it to its feet, waking it from nightmares such as she had known. Feeling the warmth of her hand, it purred until its whole body throbbed. When she withdrew her hand, it stood up.

"It's all belly and head," Elizabeth commented on the little creature as it launched itself unsteadily on its thin legs. Its neck seemed hardly strong enough to support its head or its legs sturdy enough to take the weight of its body. It lurched forward, each movement ending in a stagger before it wobbled on again towards Billy, sitting on the floor. If it were weak and exhausted, its will was made of iron. Beth's resolution that one cat in the house was enough melted away. It was a sign, just like Billy's adventure, that the weak could triumph.

"It'll have to earn its keep mousing and ratting," she remarked, to no one in particular. "There's enough mouths to feed in this house."

"What shall we call it, Ma?" Frances would have asked her brother, as it was his cat, but it was no good asking him anything.

"It looks to me like the smallest in the litter," Beth answered. "It's the little runt. Shall we call him Runty?"

Frances laughed. "It's a good name, but he must have been the strongest to get out of the water."

"It's a sign," Beth smiled. "It's a sign our Billy will overcome everything and grow into a fine man." Mother and child hugged each other.

There were footsteps coming to the cottage. "There's Pa," Frances shouted, running to meet her father and tell him all about the kitten. Too late, as she saw his stern expression, she remembered her mistake. Too eagerly, too loudly, she talked and talked, putting off the evil moment to come.

"That's enough, Frances," Charles pointed at the chair by the table and stood facing it.

"He wouldn't listen, Pa. He wouldn't listen."

"Go gently," Beth pleaded. "She saved his life."

"His life wouldn't have been in danger, but for her. You don't know the half of it, Beth. Begging, that's what she was doing. Bothering the ladies and gentlemen as they stopped at the tollgate."

"Ma. Pa." Her father's words had brought the memories rushing back." Ma, there's a school for deaf and dumb children like Billy at Hunsdon." The sudden light which had come across Frances's face with the memory, made Charles think she had suddenly been inspired to tell a lie to escape punishment.

"Lies make things worse."

"I've never known the child to lie, Charles. What happened Frances?"

Frances told her mother and father about the gentlemen in the post-chaise and what they had said.

"If it's the truth, Frances, your Pa and me will forgive you anything," Beth promised. "I found nothing out at Padsett. The family swore they had no deaf child. A neighbour said they hid the boy away. That's not going to happen to Billy."

CHAPTER TWENTY SEVEN

"You wouldn't be doing that if the master was here," Bessie, one of the Wright's servants told John as he checked book after book.

"There's something I want to find."

"Your little nephew? It's a shame, poor little lad."

John wondered if that was all she said, gossiping in the kitchen, but her next words reassured him.

"I just thank God all my young brothers and sisters are whole and well. You carry on, John, I'll not tell the master you missed church or read his books on the Sabbath." Looking over his shoulder, she added, "For all I know, it could be the Bible you're reading and that's allowed, isn't it? Have you found anything?"

Closing the book in his hand, John reached for the next in the tall pile he had collected from the shelves. "Only the things I've told Beth already. Eel oil or raw bacon to moisten the ear. Roasted onions. She's tried that, too."

"And they haven't done any good?"

"At first Beth always swears she sees an improvement, thinks Billy turns to her voice, but then she has to admit he's as deaf as before."

"All them books," Bessie commented, running her eyes along the rows of shelves, "and not one any help when you need it." She shook her head. "And what does Mr Wright say?"

"The lad's ears are dead and nothing can bring them to life."

That was not all Mr Wright had said. He had explained that the inner ear was in perpetual darkness, one of God's mysteries beyond the understanding of man. Always glad to catch out the university men, the apothecary had questioned every physician he knew and had concluded with satisfaction that none knew more than he did on the subject.

"A Frenchman suggests a burning substance applied on the bone behind the ear," John said, half to himself.

"What do they know about anything?"

"Is it worth telling Beth such things?" John asked, feeling a woman knew best about such matters. "Is it worth causing Billy such pain with little hope of a cure?"

"If you're asking my opinion, I'd keep quiet. He'll have enough suffering to come in life, you can be sure of that. But if you're asking me what your Beth would say — I've never met her, mind — she'd say what any mother would say." There was no need to ask what that was. Beth would try anything if there was the remotest chance of its helping Billy. John turned back to his books and Bessie patted him on the shoulder. "I'll bring you something to eat in here, John, so you can go on searching."

Grateful for her concern, John continued his reading, but soon, although his eyes were on the book, he was not taking in what was printed there. In his daydream, as usual recently, the scene was in the bookshop and he was telling Charlotte Elham about Billy and asking her opinion. He had thought of asking her for books, but he knew Mr Wright had a far better selection and that the excuse to talk to her was too obvious and clumsy.

Lost in daydreaming and reading, John was not at first aware of Bessie's coming back into the room and talking to him. His thoughts were jolted back to the outside world by Beth's voice and he stared at her blankly.

"Beth. Is anything wrong?"

"No more than usual," she smiled, making John realise how much more refreshed and lively she looked than when he had last seen her.

"You've landed on your feet, John," she laughed, examining everything in the study. "And a servant to wait on you! My, you've gone up in the world!"

It gave John pleasure to find others saw him as well placed as he considered himself and he hated to have to admit that not one of what Beth always called his 'precious books' contained anything of use to Billy. "I've found nothing else, Beth."

"But I have, or, rather, Frances has."

After her initial greeting Frances had remained quiet while the grownups talked, but now she was happy to be the centre of attention for a while. Almost before her mother had asked her, she was repeating the turnpike story, which she now recited with dramatic actions and comments on the gentlemen, but without those remarks of theirs which she had not understood, but which her father had told her were not words fit for a child's lips.

"Do you know who they are?" Beth demanded. "Do you know anyone who could tell us?"

"Yes," John heard himself saying, with the unreal feeling that he was stepping into his own daydream. "Miss Elham will know — not the young men, I don't mean, but if there's a school in Hunsdon. I've heard her mention a friend who's a minister there."

"Will she mind, John? Will Miss Elham mind if we call on Sunday?"

"Let me come, Uncle John," Frances begged.

"No," John replied to both at once. "If I go alone, it will be less of a nuisance." It seemed predestined that he was to see Charlotte and discuss Billy, but he hesitated about the details. What was right and proper about visiting was another aspect of life about which women knew best. "Shall I wait, Beth? They'll only just be back from Chapel."

"Give them time to eat and take a rest," Beth advised reluctantly, "but don't leave it too long. I expect they take an afternoon walk, don't they? And then they'll no doubt have visitors for tea."

"I have noticed Mark Elham and his sister pass by quite often on a Sunday stroll," John agreed casually.

At the very moment Beth judged right, John set off the few yards along the High Street to the house adjoining the book shop. Again, as he rang the bell and was shown in, he had the feeling that he was detached from himself, watching a scene written by Fate. He asked if he might see Miss Elham for just a few minutes and was shown into the drawing room and there Charlotte joined him. So far, each step, each action had been just as he imagined it, but suddenly he wondered why he was standing there making a request which could well have waited until the next day. Miss Elham looked as pleased to see him as in his imagination, but a little more flustered.

As John spoke, emphasising Beth's concern and her impatience to do everything she could for Billy, Charlotte's puzzled expression disappeared. She was obviously ready to accept the visit as one which quite rightly had to be made at once. Her precise questions about Frances's story soon gave her all the information she needed and she promised to write to her friend in Hunsdon immediately.

"The better the day, the better the deed," Charlotte laughed, seemingly in no hurry to end the conversation. "Can there really be a way to teach these children so that they can convey their thoughts and feelings?"

"I have enough trouble," John told her, "expressing my thoughts and feelings and I'm neither deaf nor dumb." The speed and nature of his comment told Charlotte he had been giving the matter some thought before this minute and she waited with interest.

John continued, as though as intent on revealing his character as pursuing a discussion. "The difficulty is that one word comes after another. Feelings and thoughts come all in one tangled bunch. You can't spin them neatly into one long thread of words."

For once, Charlotte was silent, genuinely interested in what someone else had to say.

"You see," John smiled despairingly, "I told you words were useless. I haven't managed to make you understand a word."

"Oh, yes," Charlotte protested, her quick wits working again, "but if you have so many thoughts at once, I'm waiting to hear them all. If I answer the first, the rest may be lost to me and to the world for ever."

Far from being offended by her teasing, John was pleased by it. "There, you do understand. That's what happens to me. I say something, someone answers and, from there, we go off on one line of thought and the rest are forgotten. Afterwards, I remember all I wanted to say."

From all he said, Charlotte was sure that John had, just as she had, repeated their conversation of the other evening over and over, wringing from it every ounce of meaning. She wished, as John seemed to, that they could continue their conversation just where it had left off, but, reluctantly, she had to admit to herself and to John that her visitors would be arriving any second and she was not yet ready to receive them.

As reluctantly, John left. None of those he loved or had loved shared his new world and talking with Charlotte eased the loneliness he sometimes felt in it.

CHAPTER TWENTY EIGHT

There was a prompt and full reply from Peter Hadnam, the minister in Hunsdon and an old friend of the Elhams. Immediately on reading it, Charlotte put into practice the plan which had been forming in her mind over the past few days. Mr Hadnam had suggested that she should meet Billy and make other calls in the village and, obviously, John was the best person to take her to Abingfield and show her around. Ever eager to support a charitable enterprise, the Wrights agreed at once. Everything was arranged for Sunday afternoon.

The day dawned, and remained, bright and beautiful, the kind of day when, beneath the warming, generous sun, spirits soared with the birds and hearts opened as fully to the world as the yellow petals of the primrose. All was such perfection that, for the very first time, Charlotte had to admit to herself that there was, after all she had said to Mark on the subject, some merit in Miss Jackson's water colours of picturesque rural life. The sky was unclouded blue and the grass bright, fresh green. Red faced cottagers, mongrels sleeping at their feet and rosy cheeked children at their knees, did sit before the cottage doors. Fluffy ducklings floated, balls of down, in their mother's wake and the sails of the windmill sighed in contentment.

As John drove, Charlotte read the letter to him, commenting on it as she went. "My friend knows the school well. He visits at least twice a week and knows every child. He writes, 'Left to nature, the deaf and dumb child is wayward and obstinate and most wretched, like all Adam's children born in sin. They are a prey to unbridled passions and quite ignorant of the higher nature of man and the hope of salvation, revealed to us by Jesus Christ."

"Billy is very wayward," John agreed, "but there's no malice in him."

"But as he grows," Charlotte pointed out, "and is less under the good influence of his family, he will be at the mercy of every evil influence without proper instruction." John accepted that was true without further argument.

"The great majority of people," Charlotte read on, "have no idea what can be done for the deaf and dumb. Even if they know a deaf and dumb child, they are not aware that the dumbness arises solely from the failure to hear others speak. Without giving the matter the least thought, they assume the child who cannot learn to speak is an idiot and past all hope. Some are hidden from view for fear of spiteful gossip and remain wretched, animal-like creatures all their days." She added, with her usual enthusiasm, "It will be so rewarding to watch Billy grow and learn, like any other child."

Although Charlotte could not say it, John was sure she felt, as he did, that part of the reward would come from their helping Billy together. He drew the horse to a halt.

"Look here, a moment," he said, jumping down and holding his hand to help Charlotte down. Careful not to trip, Charlotte held it until she was firmly on the ground. Walking across the lane, John stopped where a young ash tree rose from the quick thorn hedge. A blackbird, with a great flurry and flapping, flew into the tree above their heads. With great care, John separated the leaves and twigs with one hand and beckoned Charlotte to look in with the other.

Charlotte peered into the hedge. There, in a nest, were four tiny, writhing monsters, their huge eyeless heads, with gaping beaks, wobbling on thin, featherless bodies, which beat with life through their purple skins. "Ugh!" Shuddering, Charlotte stepped back.

"That's what girls always do," John laughed.

To gloss over her irrational dislike of the small, harmless creatures, Charlotte asked, "How did you know they were there?"

"They've always been there as long as I can remember. I used to prac-tise my counting on them, like Frances practises her reading on every occa-sion."

"And there," John pointed into a field to where a few rotting pieces of wood lay in the tangled undergrowth, "was an old shed. It was falling down then. A half wild dog had taken it as a home for her pups. I came here every day after my work for a while."

As though to explain such behaviour in a young child, he told her, "I brought them water. I played with the pups." Suddenly, in all honesty, he told her, "I was five. My mother had just died giving birth to Sam. I came to cuddle the pups. They greeted me with such a welcome. Licked my hands and face — even though the soot must have been so bitter. We played rough and tumble and then snuggled up to sleep together."

"But the hurt remained." Charlotte's comment was unexpected. From her voice John could not tell whether it was question or statement and, as he turned to help her back into the carriage, hesitated whether to answer.

"My mother died when I was six," she told him. "My father was loving and kind and he gave us so much of his time and his affection. But nothing took away the hurt, did it, that the person you loved best in all the world had left you?"

To anyone else, 'left' would have meant 'died', but John, without being able to blame his mother openly, even now, knew it meant 'deserted'.

"No," he agreed. "Nothing took that away. I gave up going to the pups. Their mother," he explained, "always came back. Whatever the weather, or the danger, she always came back. Then I went home. My mother never came back. I couldn't bear it."

For a long while, they drove along in silence. At last John smiled at Charlotte gently. "There, it proves I was right the other evening about only people who have shared an experience being able to understand."

"Oh! That's what you meant, was it?" Charlotte laughed.

"Along there," John pointed out vaguely, as they reached the village, "is the house where we grew up." He did not add that he had come a long way round to avoid passing it and risk meeting his father.

Quickly and expertly, Sarah Dodds glanced around the cottage and, at last, declared it fit for a visitor of Miss Elham's standing. The carriage arrived almost immediately and, looking out of the window, careful not be seen themselves, Sarah and Beth saw a young woman tallish, but not too tall, slim, neatly rather than fashionably dressed.

The strict rules of behaviour laid down and rehearsed by Sarah eased the first awkward moments and Charlotte needed no encouragement to talk. Partly reading from her friend's letter and partly explaining in her own words, she first told them how signs, made with the hands, were used instead of words to teach the children.

"All the best ideas are simple," Will commented. Such a simple idea gave everyone great hopes for Billy. As Charlotte talked, explaining that, by signs, he would learn religion and right behaviour, language and a little arithmetic and reading and writing, the years of trouble-ridden dependence, which had seemed to stretch ahead for Billy' became a future of independence, work and a wife and family like anyone else.

"They like the children to start at as early an age as possible and they feel they need seven years to complete their education," Charlotte finished. She looked from Sarah's firm, purposeful face to Will's weather-beaten features and Charles's sad eyes and saw hope and gratitude. Only Beth kept her head down. Gently, Charles put his arm around her and repeated quietly all

Charlotte had said about Billy's future. All the time he spoke, Beth nodded in agreement, but, Charlotte realised from the shaking of her shoulders, she could not stop crying.

"It's Billy going away so long," Charles explained.

"I'm most grateful to you, Miss Elham," Beth sobbed. "It's what I — what John asked you, but I never dreamt of sending Billy away so young and for so long." Overcome by her tears, she murmured over and over again, "Seven years. Oh, Charles, we'll never see him grow up. He'll forget his own family."

Giving her time to recover, Will commented on the lovely weather Charlotte had brought with her and she praised the beauty of Abingfield.

"You see," Beth began, unable to turn to a new subject, "it's not natural for us to send a child away. The gentry — they're used to it. But Billy's place is with his family." Once again she sobbed. "How will we explain it to him? He won't even know where he's going. Or why."

There was no comforting her, but they tried. "It's for the best, Beth. You'll see that in a day or two."

John searched his mind for something more convincing. "And an apprenticeship, Beth. You've always wanted that for Billy. They apprentice the children to a trade."

"I know," Beth sobbed.

"It will be a cruel parting," Charlotte agreed, "but there is no other way."

"Sometimes you must be cruel to be kind," Sarah stated. "Beth will do the right thing when the time comes, Miss Elham."

Rising to go, Charlotte explained, "My next call is on Mr Gray."

"He'll not help us," Will blurted out.

"I'm quite sure he will," Charlotte assured them, ignorant of the sermon. "A place at the school will be costly and my friend tells me it is usual for the local clergyman to support a child's application and raise funds to support him." Seeing the family still looking worried, she assured them, "I know Miss Gray. She's most eager to help. If a committee is appointed, I'm sure I'll be on it and I'll see all goes smoothly for Billy."

Watching Charlotte and John climb into the carriage, Sarah commented firmly, "It's not right."

"No," Beth agreed, still trying to control her tears, "It should all be left to Miss Elham and her friends in Gressingford."

"That woman's encouraging John's fanciful ideas," Sarah corrected her.

"God gives each of us a place in this world and it's no good trying to climb above it."

"There's no harm in it, Ma."

"You're too fond of saying that, Beth. No good can come of her encouraging him, you mark my word. It's time he settled down with a good, reliable girl of his own kind. Our Becky. She's the girl for him."

CHAPTER TWENTY NINE

As they drove to the vicarage, Charlotte and John talked about how Beth must be reassured that Billy would be happy and would not forget his family. They discussed the chance of Beth's going to see him, once he was settled in. But at the back of their minds, each was thinking what to say when Charlotte dismounted at the front door and John, who would never be allowed over the front door step, drove around to the stables. This was not a situation covered by the rules of day to day behaviour. Charlotte felt she could not simply dismiss him, giving him a time to return and John wondered whether to tell her when he would come for her, as he would tell his womenfolk, or sit and await instructions.

When the moment came they spoke together.

"I'll send...."

"I'll pass the ti..."

"I was going to say, John, you mustn't waste your time just waiting. The Gray's servant can find you when I'm ready if you tell me where you will be."

"I was just going to say I'll have a chance to talk to Becky."

With that agreed, Charlotte entered the house to a warm welcome. She was plied with refreshments and questions on how she and her brother found the district and its inhabitants.

There was really no need for questions or answers. From the tradesmen's and servants' gossip, the Grays had already learned the Elhams tastes, their spending and their reliability in settling bills. From those who had already been visited by the Elhams or who had visited them, they had learned of their tastes in furnishings and clothes, the number of servants they kept and their opinions on the questions of the day. From further afield, from distant friends and cousins several times removed, who had been neighbours of the Elhams in Hampshire, they knew of family connections, education, income and expectations.

The Grays had concluded that, while it was regrettable that the Elhams dabbled in trade, it was a respectable one. As a keen gardener, Mrs Gray could not believe ill of Charlotte, the possessor of many rare plants from which cuttings might be obtained, and, as an Oxford man himself, Mr Gray realised that any faults in Mark Elham, from the very same college, could be put down to youth, a factor always cured by time.

It was some time before the real subject of Charlotte's visit was approached, even indirectly. "You must tell Charlotte the time of the Society's meeting, Anne," Mrs Gray prompted her daughter. "It's to be held here at the vicarage. In that way Mr Gray and I can give advice and help when required."

"Society?" Charlotte queried politely.

"Your brother must come, too," Mrs Gray insisted.

It was left to Anne to begin to explain the purpose of the society. "We have so many parish charities…"

"And more springing up every day," her mother interrupted. "A society for baby clothes for the newborn, a society for medicines for the aged, a society for…"

"Quite so, my dear," Mr Gray interrupted in turn. His heavy features took on an even weightier expression as he explained, "It just will not do. Men, women, children going from one charity to another and receiving help time and time again. One simple cold, one ailing child provides a more ample income that a week of honest work."

Mrs Gray was quick with an example. "I know for a fact that Eliza Braithwaite's Jemima received tuppence from the Ladies' Society and a pair of boots from the Boot Fund on the very day she was begging at the turnpike. I'm sure that child can collect more in an hour than is placed on my husband's collection plate on a good Sunday."

"Charity is easily abused," Charlotte agreed. Such stories could be repeated in every town and village.

"Just so," Mr Gray nodded. "For that very reason, we plan to consolidate all the parish charities."

"We are to run it," Anne told Charlotte with enthusiasm. "The young people of Abingfield," she added pointedly for Charlotte's sake.

At that moment, Nicholas Gray entered to play his part in providing the scraps of information Charlotte was putting together. "We shall seek out new causes if need exists. This young deaf and dumb boy you have brought to out attention is a most interesting case. We shall discuss the matter at our very first meeting of the….What was the name we finally decided upon, Anne?"

"The Society for the Improvement of the Conditions and Morals of the Poor."

"Morals and Conditions," Mr Gray corrected his daughter in as gentle a tone as his deep, serious voice allowed.

"And we shall see those aims are fulfilled," Nicholas pointed out. "There is an excellent scheme which I met with in London whereby an applicant for charity must be supported by two people of standing — a master, a doctor or the local clergyman. In this way we shall be able to influence the lives of those who receive our help in the direction of morality and religion."

Charlotte had the distinct feeling that the plans for Billy were being taken out of her hands. "The Stevensons," she began firmly, preparing to keep her plan under her control, "are of good repute, I am sure."

"That, my dear young lady," Mr Gray replied, "you must leave us to judge. I am sure I know every detail of my parishioners' lives and must be left to know what is for their good." Before Charlotte could reply, he went on humbly, "I must admit, I had not realised — although I should have had faith in the Lord's mercy and pity — that these children could be taught to praise His Holy Name and follow His commandments. But first steps first. My son is a physician and well qualified to judge the usefulness of the education provided at the school you have discovered. He is to visit next week."

With as much gratitude in her voice as she could summon, Charlotte said," I was planning a visit to the school myself. I had hoped you would help me raise the funds necessary for the boy's fees."

"We have such plans," Anne told her. "Dances and picnics and a concert with recitations."

"I am sure," Mr Gray said graciously, "Nicholas will not mind if you visit the school, but I think we must leave it to him to judge those matters, which only a doctor can judge. He will, too, be able to look into the management of the school and discover whether the funds we provide will be wisely and frugally spent. By all means visit if you wish, my dear. I am sure it will provide an interesting curiosity for a visit."

With Mrs Gray pressing her to visit the garden, Charlotte was forced to leave the matter there. With Mark and just the young people at the Society meeting, they would have a chance to say what they wished. She followed Mrs Gray into the garden, aware that, by the kitchen window, John was deep in conversation with Becky.

CHAPTER THIRTY

News of the Society for the Improvement of the Morals and Conditions of the Poor spread as rapidly as any piece of news in Abingfield.

"It was bound to come," Will Dodds remarked. "First they improve the cattle and sheep — they're more important and precious — and then they come to the poor."

"Not quite the same," Matthew Sharp, a young out-of-work neighbour pointed out. "They improve animals by breeding. We're not encouraged to breed. They don't need labourers any more."

"Perhaps," Eliza sighed hopefully, "they'll improve us all into ladies and gentlemen."

"That's not the idea," Charles's friend, Abraham Collins corrected her. "They don't try to turn goats into sheep and that's what we are to them — a different breed."

"They'll just improve us," Charles decided, "so we eat less, work more and ..."

"Drop dead the day we're no longer needed," Will finished for him. On her chair in the corner, Frances sat as usual with her head in her hands, eagerly taking in the words and trying to fit their meaning into her scheme of the world she was building in her head. Somewhere in her own country lived The Poor and, from what she could discover from the conversation, they did not live far away.

"Where do The Poor live, Pa?" she asked.

Looking at her sharply, Charles saw she was speaking in all innocence. "Under our roof, my girl. That's why you and Billy have to go to tea with the ladies and gentlemen and bow and scrape to get Billy his schooling."

"Is that why we're going, Ma?" Since the invitation, Frances had thought of nothing but going to the vicarage for tea. She had imagined she had been invited, just as she always was, to read to the ladies and gentlemen as she did when they visited the Sunday school.

"You can't be poor and proud," her father told her. "The sooner you learn that, the more help you'll get from the gentry."

"Don't spoil the day for her, Charles," Beth pleaded, always guilty nowadays that she had so little time with her daughter. Seeing the disappointment on Frances's face, she assured her, "I'm sure they'll ask you to read. Everyone knows you're the best reader for your age in the whole village. Even the gentlemen's children can't read any better"

"And don't mention that in front of them," her father advised.

For a short while, Beth gave all her attention to Frances. "Let's get you dressed up, then. That dress has washed up a treat."

"That was meant for me," Sarah thought. So often she had urged her daughter to keep to the warm woollen dresses they had always worn, but Beth preferred new-fangled cotton. "There's a chilly breeze," she warned.

Frances twirled round, her skirts billowing. "Look, Grandma."

"It's lovely, my sweet. Just you behave yourself and do what your Aunt Becky tells you."

"Yes, Grandma." Frances took Billy's hand and was about to march him off, when the door opened and a strangely clean Henry bounced in.

"Miss Gray sent a message that I 'ad to go too."

"They can't want just the best readers," Frances whispered to her mother, as she kissed her.

Anne Gray, busying herself at the vicarage, was more concerned with welcoming and settling the members of the Society than entertaining the children. They arrived at the back door and were under Becky's care, while the friends and neighbours arriving at the front door were her concern. A sleepless night had done nothing to increase her confidence in being able to handle the contempt Maria Hammond felt for Lucy Simpkins. Somehow she must cope with Lucy Simpkins' social ambitions and Charlotte Elham's expectations of playing a major role in what were, after all, village affairs and little concern of hers.

Her friend's anxiety was so obvious, that Maria Hammond tried to calm it. "Anne, you're not entertaining the Prince of Wales. Just a few friends and a few clodhopping farmers and tight-fisted tradesmen's sons and daughters." The comment gave an opening for one of Anne's worries. "If only I could feel safe about your foolish antagonism to Lucy Simpkins," she sighed, "I would feel easier in my mind."

"Foolish antagonism! I can assure you it's a serious matter. I dislike — I might say loathe — the creature."

"Come, Maria, you are usually fair and honest in your judgements."

"Don't flatter me to win a point. You well know that I am prejudiced and dogmatic and enjoy being so."

In a low voice, Anne tried to reconcile her friend to Lucy Simpkins' playing a more prominent part in the Society's doings. "Her brother," she admitted, "has had every advantage money can buy and is still an oaf, but Lucy's intelligence and sensibilities have enabled her to take advantage of her chances. I admit money alone cannot transform a farmer's daughter into a lady."

"That it why I despise her. You will welcome her into the Society and she will end up running it and marrying one of my brothers or yours."

"That it not possible," Anne laughed. "Nicholas is quite taken with Charlotte Elham."

"Wait and see. Wait and see."

"That was your reply when I asked you what was the subject you wished to place first on the agenda."

"And that, my friend, is still my answer."

"And there's Charlotte Elham," Anne continued, once she was listing her worries. "Papa insists matters concerning his parishioners are left to him —acting through the Society — to decide." She dropped her voice, "I hear Charlotte Elham is a chapel goer."

"Dear me!" Maria, who like the majority of the Hammond family, was not driven by religious zeal, feigned deep concern to mock her friend. More helpfully, she added, "Miss Elham brought the child to your father's notice and must leave it to his judgement now."

The full Society assembled before her, Anne breathed deeply to calm herself before welcoming them and opening the meeting. Her duty done, she sat down with obvious relief. Had everyone been aware, as she had, of her burning cheeks? Had she fallen into the habit, which Nicholas warned her against, of always talking like a Sunday school teacher? Absorbed in her own thoughts, it was a few minutes before she realised the point Maria was making.

"My project is a serious one and one of which you will all approve, I am sure," Maria beamed. She smiled directly at Lucy. "It is the failure of farmers' daughters to enter service as they used to do."

To avoid being stopped, Maria hurried on. "With a Sunday school, we have tackled the problem of religious and moral education. Now we must give some training for work. Every day, I hear complaints of the bad quality of domestic servants. Let me read just a little from this book to show the nature of the problem we must tackle. The author," she added, smiling again at Lucy, "puts the matter most succinctly." As she began to read, shuffling of feet and rustling of dresses ceased completely. Maria Hammond was about to put Lucy Simpkins in her place. You could have heard a fly settle on the wall and a pin dropping would have sounded like an iron beam.

In a very clear, pleasant voice, Maria read, "In my youthful days, farmers' daughters put their red cloaks on, and the milking pails on their shoulders, went out before dawn of day into the field to milk the cows, and before they had gone a hundred yards, generally split a cow turd with their feet, — but now, if one of them look out at the door, the servant cries out, 'Miss, pray do not go out, you will....'"

Only another Hammond could stop this nonsense and Richard Hammond did. "Maria, we have a great deal of business to attend to. What is the point you wish us to consider?" The interruption did not come soon enough to stop a red patch appear on Lucy Simpkins' neck and spread to her cheeks.

"My point is that, now farmers' daughters consider domestic work beneath them, we shall have to rely on the daughters of labourers. They will require a good deal of training from someone."

Quite in command of herself, Lucy even smiled quite sweetly at Maria. "Surely, we can leave these matters to our housekeepers. I am sure ours is an excellent teacher for the young girls we employ."

"She should be, at the wage we pay her!" her brother declared, only to be silenced by a withering glance from his sister.

Immediately, Lucy Simpkins indicated that she had a subject — and not a frivolous one — to raise. To compensate for Maria's behaviour, Anne and Richard were more than happy to allow her to speak. That ensured that almost anything Miss Simpkins proposed would be supported by them.

In the remotest corner of the room, Charlotte deplored to her brother the haphazard way in which the meeting was being conducted. They had been shown to their seats with no more than a comment on the weather and Charlotte could only wait for her turn to speak about Billy.

"While I was in London, recently," Miss Simpkins began, "a guest at the wedding of Lord Manton's sister, a great friend of mine from our school days at an academy in Hackney, I was invited by Sir Thomas Street to attend a meeting. It was a meeting of the Society for Superseding the Necessity of Climbing Boys. The stories I heard there," Lucy looked as though she would weep, "were so terrible, I resolved at once to take up the cause of these unfortunate boys in the locality immediately upon my return.

In the Lord's name, you must join me in righting the terrible injustices inflicted upon these unfortunates."

With warm support from Anne and Richard, Maria related the stories she had been told of young boys being goaded into climbing narrow flues, no more than thirteen inches by ten, by having sharp sticks and burning straw held against their bare feet. Vividly and dramatically, she related a story of a boy, no more than seven years of age, who, having become lodged in a flue, could not be removed by efforts to attach a rope and drag him free. By the time an opening had been made in the wall, he had suffocated. As Lucy spoke, Anne almost heard the boy's screams of terror, fading into whimpering, which were answered only by the sweep's curses.

The men in the audience had warmed to Lucy's prettiness and her feminine tender-heartedness and, for the first time, took an interest in the children who had swept their chimneys for centuries. Here, indeed, was an evil to be plucked from society. Only Charlotte felt a need, not to defend sweeps in general, but the Stevensons.

"Henry is a cheerful little imp and…"

Her words travelled no farther than her brother. "Ssh!" This was a subject in which Mark had interested himself for some time. Charlotte was quiet. She could not defend sweeps with any conviction, but, for the first time in her life, she felt uneasy about doing the right thing and riding roughshod over everyone else involved.

The only other person with any reservations was young Simpkins. Lucy always knew best, but he always took his father's pronouncements at their face value. "It's a serious matter coming between a master and his men or telling any man how he must do his work. I'm sure Pa wouldn't like you to interfere, Lucy."

"Papa," his sister replied, determining to remind her brother yet again about his usage of the common term 'Pa', "agrees with me entirely on this matter, as," she added, smiling at Richard Hammond, "any man of feeling would."

Not having heard his father referred to as 'a man of feeling' before, young Simpkins returned to a state of puzzled silence.

"Knowing your hearts would be touched as deeply as mine," Lucy resumed, "I had the village climbing boy brought here today. You will have seen him sent to his cruel work by his master many times, but have you ever thought to ask him his story?"

Maria Hammond returned to reading her book. As the children were led in, Nicholas Gray announced, "We shall have an opportunity of observing the deaf and dumb boy at the same time, before we discuss a request for help for that lad."

"At last!" Charlotte muttered. The others moved their chairs for a better view of the children and settled down to watch.

CHAPTER THIRTY ONE

To Frances's dismay, Henry was called first to face the company. "Why ask him?" she thought. "They'll soon find out he can't recite the Commandments or the Beatitudes."

Red in the face and urgently wanting to visit the closet yet again, Henry moved a step forward, his hands stuffed in his pockets. In the false hope and belief that, if he could not see them, they could not see him, he raised his eyes to the ceiling. He found he could still hear them.

"Such a pathetic scrap of a lad!"

"Why, he's half the size of James and he's barely six."

"He is of a naturally small build," Charlotte told Mark. "And he was in the workhouse for the early years of his life on a diet of...."

"Ssh!"

"How old are you, young man?" Richard Hammond demanded in a kindly voice. Until he saw Henry's matted hair which had defied all Becky's efforts to run a comb through it, he had been about to pat the child's head.

A poke from Frances, who had sidled up to join him in the limelight, jolted Henry into answering.

"I think I'm nine, sir."

"Think?"

"He was born in the workhouse, sir," Frances eagerly joined in.

"Let the boy speak for himself, child."

"Tell us your story,.....Henry, is it?" Lucy coaxed.

At last, Henry saw what they wanted him to tell. It was the story he never tired of hearing himself about how his master had fetched him from the workhouse. Many an evening he begged old Edward to tell him how he had gone to all the workhouses for miles around. "There were some," his master always said, "who will take any boy for money — five shillings I was offered at one place — and then let them run away. That way the sweep and the workhouse get rid of the burden. This one they offered was a difficult lad they said. I looked him over. Don't mind a bit of spirit, but he looked a wild one. Some they offered me was 'uge — so fat they'd 'ave got stuck climbing up the stairs in a church tower. Another 'ad long, skinny legs and such a 'ead of 'air. I were looking for a boy, not a brush."

"Nearly give up the search, I did," the sweep always said. "Then, at your place, 'Enry, they showed me three. One was too know-all, one too weak and weepy and one just right. I could see straight orf you'd make a sweep, 'Enry. Needed a bit of training and a good master, mind you, but you was a born sweep, like me, 'Enry, if ever I see one."

It was a story that proved to Henry that he was someone and someone who, even if they didn't say it in so many words, made Henry more of a son to the old man than his own children, who cared nothing about chimneys. Henry embarked on the story with gusto, but no one seemed to understand a word.

"Tell us, boy, what happens when you are put up a difficult chimney?" a young man asked firmly, determined that he would stop the boy's ramblings with this, his third attempt to put a question.

"I listens carefully to me master cos 'e's climbed every chimbley for miles around. Then I shins up it."

"Tell us, Henry," Lucy prompted, "clearly and holding nothing back. You are with friends who will see that you come to no harm. How do you climb? What do you see?"

"Nothing much. It's all black."

"What do you feel?" a young lady, herself of tender sensibilities, wanted to know.

"I feels me way up to the top with me 'ands and feet."

The boy, all concluded sadly, was an idiot, his brain numbed by his dreadful work.

Lost in trying to make sense of what was happening, Frances had released her hold on Billy. He had watched with mounting interest as the ladies and gentlemen, in their attempt to make Henry understand them, had, as in talking to someone who spoke a different language, waved arms and legs and stretched as though climbing a chimney. This was something he could join in. Too late, Frances heard the sniggers of the young men and the embarrassed squeals of the ladies.

"The deaf and dumb boy is undressing."

Hurriedly, Becky rushed in to dress him. Concerned about the turn events were taking, she had listened at the door.

"He's seen Henry climbing," she explained to Miss Gray. "Henry often climbs na.... He doesn't wear.... Sometimes," she propelled the children to the door, "he takes off his shirt so it doesn't roll up and jam him as he comes down."

The children gone, it was resolved that something must be done to stop the exploitation of the climbing boy. Miss Simpkins had clearly anticipated such determination.

"I have plans for a mechanical means of sweeping chimneys, for which the Society offered a prize. May we ask Mr Hammond and the other gentlemen to study it and give us their opinion?"

"I am sure," Richard Hammond pronounced, "that if the Society has approved the plans, they are practical ones. May I propose we ask the sweep..."

"Tell the sweep," Lucy corrected gently.

"May I propose that we tell the sweep to use the mechanical means of sweeping, making a small grant towards the cost, if necessary."

"Don't see why we should give a grant," young Simpkins protested. Not once before had he questioned Edward Stevenson's methods, but he was a Simpkins through and through. "The old man's been making money out of the child long enough. Mind you, the sweep'll not change his ways, grant or no grant."

"Perhaps," Anne suggested, recovering from the strong emotions she had felt hearing Lucy's stories, "we might make it clear that his services will not be required in the village unless he changes his ways."

This resolved, the company were told, to the relief of many, that Dr Gray would address them on the subject of the deaf and dumb boy after tea. The guests collected in groups. Anne sat by Maria. "What book is that? You've taken little interest in our proceedings."

'It's Colonel Benson's. He lent it to my brothers. Full of advice on horses and dogs and how to stop poachers with a cannon."

"Poachers?" Several young men were drawn by the word, but lost interest when Richard Hammond explained the plan was to shoot wooden cannon balls, which would scare the poachers, but do no lasting harm to them.

Charlotte, still confined in the corner of the room, pleaded with Mark, "Please work your way through and find out what is happening" In the milling throng she had given up hope of attracting Anne Gray's attention.

Before Mark could make any progress, young Simpkins, broad shouldered and bulky and clearly having no trouble moving about, arrived by their side. One by one, he had, over the past year, nurtured romantic ideas about every young lady in the area, but none had shown him the admiration he won so readily from the village girls. Ever hopeful, he had been pleased to see Charlotte, a new arrival in the locality.

"We've made up a party to go to the fight next week, Elham," he announced, addressing Mark, but leering at Charlotte. "Would you both care to come?" Knowing Mark's views on prize fights Charlotte simply smiled and left it to Mark to reply, but Simpkins had spotted their hesitation and added more weight to his request. "There'll be the Hammonds." That, he thought, was enough to make anyone accept an invitation. It had, in fact, been Richard Hammond who had invited all and sundry to come and see his man fight.

"It's most kind of you," Mark began, hesitating which way to answer. He did have a business to run and contacts were useful.

"The Grays will be there," Simpkins continued. Names always eluded him and he paused to think again.

That decided it. Mark had found Anne Gray totally sweet and charming. He quickly convinced himself that Dr Gray was just the kind of young man, intelligent and well educated, that Charlotte should be encouraged to meet. "We'd be glad to come, Simpkins"

"Mark!" Charlotte muttered in desperation, giving him a little push to start him on his journey across the room.

"It's too late, Charlotte. We'll have to sit down. Nicholas Gray is starting his report."

Frustrated, but helpless, Charlotte sat down.

"Ladies and gentlemen," Dr Gray began, speaking from memory except for a few brief notes on the table in front of him. "My visit to the Asylum for the Deaf and Dumb in Hunsdon was most rewarding. Let me describe my visit just as it happened, so that you, too, may realise what can be achieved by dedicated men and women working in the name of Our Lord."

"Visitors are admitted to the school, on payment of a small contribution, on Wednesdays. The house is modest and dowdy, but the proclamation, 'The Deaf shall hear the word of the Lord' and 'The Dumb shall praise His Holy Name,' tell of the blessed work within."

"A demonstration was arranged and it was truly amazing to see how meaning could be conveyed both by signs and by spelling on the fingers. That is the way the child's mind is reached — through his eyes, not the ears. Language is taught through reading and writing, supplemented by signs and the manual alphabet." Here Nicholas demonstrated the few signs he had learned and illustrated how the fingers could be used to stand for the letters of the alphabet.

"Of course," he continued, once his audience had given up their efforts to imitate him, "I looked into the management closely to see no money we contributed would be wasted. Washing, ironing, cleaning and baking provide excellent opportunities to train the girls for domestic work. The boys tend the garden, providing all the vegetables the pupils eat. In this way, Mr and Mrs Webster, who run the establishment, manage with one servant and one young teacher. As the teacher is learning his profession he receives no salary apart from his board and lodging."

"I can assure you every penny is accounted for and not a farthing wasted. Food is simple and adequate. Meat is eaten twice a week and, for the rest, good vegetable stews and bread and cheese provide ample nourishment at midday. At breakfast bread and milk is consumed and at supper bread and treacle. As a medical man, I can assure you such a diet is far healthier than that the children receive at home." Young Simpkins, who adored bread and treacle and despised the diet his family now consumed in their prosperous days, envied them.

"As a medical man, too, I was satisfied to find boarding is the rule. No day children attend to bring diseases, physical or moral, from the poorer areas of the town. The children are isolated from infections and from the vicious influences of parents of a low and ignorant grade."

"At the end of seven years, ladies and gentlemen, children are sent into the world virtuous and industrious. I can recommend the Asylum for the Deaf and Dumb as a worthy cause for your charity and compassion."

About to sit down, Dr Gray spotted one remaining point in his notes. "Ah, yes. The actual means of sending a child to the school. Everyone who contributes one guinea, and I am sure that will include everyone here, gains the right to vote for a child when a vacancy occurs and an election is held. Supporters of each child canvass voters. Naturally, voters seek assurances that a child comes from a deserving home"

Thinking Nicholas Gray had finished, many listeners had questions and Charlotte had almost to shout to make herself heard. "I propose we support the election of William Stevenson."

"I was just about to add," Nicholas said, putting down the glass from which he had sipped a cordial to refresh his throat, "that we must send a visitor to the Stevensons to ensure they are deserving. They must be beyond reproach or supporters of other candidates will use any shortcomings against us. What is known about the family?"

"His uncle's a poacher," young Simpkins called out.

"He is Becky's niece, Nicholas. She would not work for us were the family not respectable. The weakness lies on the Stevenson's side."

"Of course," Nicholas realised. "A relation of the sweep. We must have that matter settled before we can support the child."

"The sins of the fathers," Charlotte began her protest.

"Quite so," Dr Gray interrupted. "We must give the child every chance. Let me suggest that we appoint one or two ladies to visit the Stevensons and make them aware of their responsibilities."

Beforehand, Mr Gray had already decided that this task should be left to his son and daughter and proposed Nicholas and Anne for the work. Immediately Richard Hammond, still angry over his sister's insult to her, proposed Anne should be accompanied by Miss Simpkins.

Suddenly, the meeting was over.

"It's so unfair," Charlotte complained to her brother. "We'll have no say at all. Billy must go to school." At the door, she turned. "I shall talk to Anne."

"No," Mark restrained her, leading her to the carriage. "I am sure Anne has the child's interest at heart."

"But it was all my idea, Mark. The boy is not to blame for his Uncle Sam and grandfather."

"Charlotte. You heard Dr Gray. Can you disagree with him? Unless these matters are sorted out the boy will not win the support of the electors."

At that moment, Nicholas Gray approached Charlotte. Smiling, he assured her she would be kept informed of all that happened. "I shall meet with you myself, when ever necessary."

"But......" Charlotte jumped in surprise.

"Sorry, Miss Elham," John apologised, raising his hat to Charlotte and then to Mark. "I've been waiting out of sight. Is there any news for Beth about Billy?"

Although it would have been a breach of confidence, on her own Charlotte might have been tempted to tell him the briefest details, but Mark had no doubts on what to say.

"I understand members of the Committee are to call on Mrs Stevenson shortly. I am sure they will not keep her waiting longer than necessary."

"Miss Gray and Miss Simpkins," Charlotte told him, trying to add any possible details as John looked from Mark to her.

"Oh." For two hours John had waited for news and for the pleasure of talking to Charlotte. It was not turning out as he had planned, but he continued with the next speech he had rehearsed.

"I wondered, Mr Elham if you and Miss Elham would do us the honour of joining the family at the fight next week." Hastily, he added, "You don't have to watch the fight. It's a great day for the neighbourhood and everyone will be there."

"Thank you, John," Mark replied, "but we'll be in the Hammond's party."

"It's very thoughtful of you, John," Charlotte began. She would have much preferred to go with the Stevensons, but it had all been arranged and it gave her a chance to talk to Anne Gray about Billy. "Perhaps we shall see you there."

John's rehearsal had been ready for a refusal, agreeing, "The Hammonds' is the best party to be in — what with it being Mr Richard's man Langford doing the fighting."

But he was still disappointed by their declining his offer. It must mean they wanted to keep their distance from him. Watching them drive away, he took off his hat, twisting it in his hand by the brim. "Goodbye, miss. Goodbye, sir."

As they disappeared, John flung his hat in the air, kicking it once and then again as it fell. They had put him in his place and, like any labourer he had let them. "Good-bye, miss. Goodbye, sir." He kicked the hat again with even greater ferocity. Who were they, or any of those at the meeting, to make decisions on Billy's life?

CHAPTER THIRTY TWO

Since early morning, Becky had had young Joe, the gardener's son, planted as securely as any of his father's flowers, by the wall in the vicarage garden, waiting to take a message. Beth, having heard the scraps of discussion Becky had heard, did not know what to expect and wanted to be prepared for the ladies' arrival. On Tuesday Becky had sent Joe scurrying along with a message that Miss Gray would call that day, but she had not arrived. At the moment she was about to leave, Richard Hammond had called.

"It's not," Becky had heard Mrs Gray tell her daughter, "as though you had a previous engagement. You can call on the Stevensons any time. You have a duty to your friends, too, you know."

Reassured by this parental advice, Anne Gray had left it until Wednesday to make the call and then until Thursday. Now it was Friday and Becky was tired of making jobs near enough to the family breakfast table to overhear their plans. At last, she heard the ladies would be visiting that day. With an empty dish hastily snatched up, she rushed to the kitchen and sent Joe on his way. The day was heavy with clouds and Anne Gray was almost glad that Lucy, who always had the use of the family carriage just when she wanted it, was going with her. She accepted the ride without taking sides on the argument, started by her mother and father, as to whether Lucy's free use of the carriage meant that she was socially ambitious or that her parents had few engagements themselves.

As the horse bucked and stamped to keep its hold on the muddy street, Beth tugged the children from the window. Heedless of the rain herself, she ran the few steps along the path to help the ladies down, asking them to come in quickly out of the downpour. Once they were seated, Beth forced herself to sit patiently for their decision.

There was not long to wait. Miss Gray came straight to the point. "With certain reservations, Mrs Stevenson, we have decided to support your boy at the Asylum for the Deaf and Dumb at Hunsdon. When Billy is six or seven, we shall put him forward for election."

"Election!" Beth echoed.

"Yes," Miss Gray explained. "An election is held to fill the vacancies."

"Will he be elected?" Beth asked anxiously. She knew enough about elections to know someone must lose if someone else won.

"That," Lucy Simpkins told her, taking on herself the important part of the announcement, "is entirely up to you." Stifling both Beth's and Miss Gray's attempts to speak, she carried on, "Your family must prove to the electors that the child comes from a respectable family and is deserving of help."

"We are a respectable family," Beth was quick to assure her. "Your mother was a friend of my mother's when they were children. They played ..."

This was not the line Lucy wanted the conversation to take. "They will want to know your husband is in work...."

Again to Miss Simpkins' irritation, Beth interrupted her. "My husband works whenever he can. His injured leg..."

"Working six days a week is what electors will expect, as God ordained."

"We never accept relief."

"But you will be taking money from the electors!"

"For Billy," Beth said, swallowing her pride. "We'd do anything for Billy."

"Then your husband must take light work on the days he is not capable of hard work. But we will leave that point, for the moment. You work, of course, when there are women's tasks in the fields?"

"Yes, Miss Simpkins. Whenever possible."

"And the child?" Lucy turned to Frances.

"Frances stays home to look after Billy and help him with his letters."

Lucy laughed. "But that is skilled work. If the child could teach him, we should not be discussing his schooling. Far better she should earn a little money and begin to support herself."

Now Beth was quiet. She wondered what else was coming.

As she expected, Miss Simpkins had not finished. "There must be no more living off crime or cruelty, Mrs Stevenson." Not heeding Anne Gray's attempts to word their message less harshly, she continued, "Nothing your brother-in-law has poached — stolen— must come into this house."

For once, Miss Simpkins paused to receive Beth's words of agreement. For once, Beth was quiet, working out an answer which would not incriminate Sam by agreeing he did go poaching. She found the words. "No meat from poaching will be eaten in this house," Beth agreed. She had thought the word 'cruelty' had covered Sam's activities, but Miss Simpkins made her meaning clear.

"We are going on to old Mr Stevenson's to tell him no one will employ him in this village until he gives up his cruel exploitation of his young sweeping boy."

"Henry?"

"I understand that is his name."

If they were going on to Edward's, Beth knew better than to say anything. Edward could give them his own answer.

"And," Miss Simpkins recommended, "you must keep William and your other children from bad company. I do not think the Braithwaite children or their mother are suitable company for a family who claim respectability."

There was nothing more to be said and the ladies left. As the clopping of hooves died away, Beth reached for her shawl. Without planning it, she was going through the motions of setting out to walk her slow, thoughtful path along the canal bank, where she always went when there was a decision to be made. The ladies had not pressed her to agree, but had left it to her good sense to see, as she often expressed it to Frances, which side her bread was buttered. What was she to say to them? "I'll take this part of the bargain and leave that?" "Keep your Asylum. Billy can go somewhere else." The shawl was dropped onto the back of the chair. There was no thinking to be done. There was no choice. They had done their best to train Billy just as the Colonel had suggested, but it took so much time and every hour seemed to be spent these days in scraping a living.

Frances had watched her mother's every expression. It had not passed her eyes and ears that her mother had not agreed to anything, but now, she realised, her mother, for Billy, was going to keep to everything the ladies had asked. Soon, perhaps even tomorrow, she would be sent into the fields to work until her back broke and her eyes were too tired to look at a book, even if they had the money for candles, which they did not. Her heart hardened against her mother. Harvesting and casual work in the fields was one thing, but slaving every day was another.

"Take the boys outside to play," Beth ordered, "and stay out until your Pa's had his meal in peace and quiet." Silently, Frances obeyed.

Now her prying little eyes had gone, Beth decided she would have some bread and a morsel of cheese. It was not unusual for her to give Charles the lion's share, but, from now on, she would give him all the meat and bacon and tell him she had had hers before he came in. That way she could prove to him that they could manage without help from Sam.

It was an hour after Charles's usual time when he came in. Beth noticed he was quiet as she told him all the ladies had said. "It is asking a lot," she finished, "but if you want something badly, you have to pay for it, Charles."

"It's breaking the old man's heart, Beth, what they said to him."

"But look what it did to your life, Charles. You've him to thank for that leg."

"I know that. Don't you think I've thought that time and again? But there's a lot that's not right in this world and we have to put up with it to make a living. Pa learnt his lesson with me and he loves that child like his own. The care he takes to explain to the boy. Pa sees every inch of every chimney clearly in his mind. It's filthy and hard, but there's no danger."

"Did he say that to the ladies?"

"You know Pa. He said it was none of their business."

"They'll take the work away from him, Charles, and some stranger will start up as a sweep." She spoke quietly, knowing how much Charles would hate it. "You'll have to take over from him, Charles. He has a bit of money put by and we'll look after him somehow."

"I know that," Charles agreed, as helpless as she was.

Frances had been waiting for her opportunity to speak. "Pa," she protested. "They want me to start work."

"Why not?" her father demanded, turning on her. "Why are you so special? Your Ma and me have to swallow our pride, why shouldn't you?"

Tears stung her eyes and her voice quivered. Frances could not accept that her father knew what he was saying. "But Pa, Ma promised. She prom...."

"We all make a good few promises we can't keep. You're too old for make believe, Frances." When she continued to plead with him, he answered sharply, "Do you think we enjoy having to do what we do? Don't let me hear another word about it from you. Who do you think you are, Lucy Simpkins with all her airs and graces?"

185

CHAPTER THIRTY THREE

As far as the weather was concerned, the day was as ordinary as it could be, but to hundreds upon hundreds of people coming to the fight, the day had a glow, a promise in the air, a rare feeling to be held close and enjoyed. Exchanging views and plans over the past week or so, everyone in Abingfield had agreed that a couple of hours after sunrise would be early enough to set out. They would get up at leisure and meet up at the cross-roads, or by the church, at the stile or by the canal bridge after breakfast. Now that comfortable feeling of unhurried composure was cracking as the villagers were caught up in the sights and sounds of the tramping hordes massing on Abingfield from far and near.

At first the strangers had straggled past in twos and threes, then, as the day progressed, in groups and, finally, in the last hour, in column after column. They came on foot, on horseback, on carts and waggons, in carriages and on barrows of every sort and description. As the sound of tramping feet mingled with the creak and rattle of wheels beneath their windows, the villagers resolve was shattered along with their peace. An urgent determination not to miss anything swept them out of their beds and, slices of bread rammed in their pockets or clutched in children's hands, they tumbled into the lane and were swallowed in the buzzing crowd.

"Now stay in here. Don't open that door again," Charles told Frances.

Until now, she had danced about in the lane, dodging between the people and asking where they came from. Such strange distant places, Reading, Nottingham, Norwich and Winchester. They had the novelty and magic of the Spanish names she had heard from Uncle John. These people, though, did not look short and dark and Spanish. They were tall, short, rich and poor, all united in their love of the fancy.

All the information which Frances gathered was called back through the cottage door." There's a man with a wooden leg, Pa." Then came, "There's a lady with a whole basketful of oranges."

Suddenly, Frances dashed in and closed the door except for just a slit through which she peered in silent awe. At first, Charles had imagined that his order was at last being obeyed, but realised Frances had not heard a word he had said. Walking over, he opened the door wider. Frances hid behind his legs.

"It's a bear, Frances. We've told you about bears." He lifted Tim to look and Frances gained the courage to stand beside her father and watch the bear shamble by, its chain rattling as its head turned and small eyes looked over the muzzle straight at them.

"You said bears stood as big as a man Pa."

"It does. You'll see later when you see it on its hind legs."

Caught up in the excitement himself, Charles urged Beth, "Come on. It'll be over by the time we get there. All our neighbours have gone by."

"We'd be quicker if you came and helped me pack the food instead of standing there like a great child, yourself," Beth pointed out.

Willingly, Charles did all he was asked. Several days before he had determined that this would be a day when there would be no arguments, no accusations, but a day when they would find their old happiness. First he had cut himself off from Beth with his doubts and suspicions and then Beth had thought only of Billy, Billy, Billy. Today they would be a family like any other out to enjoy all the day had to offer.

"Come on," he told Frances," you help your Ma, too. You're old enough to make yourself useful."

"I'm ready, Pa. So's Billy and Tim."

"There's nothing for her to do, Charles, except keep everyone from under my feet," Beth told her husband. Sighing, she took cheese from the basket where he had placed it and put it into another. "I'm not sure whether you're meant to be helping or hindering."

Made sensitive to any hint of irritation in his wife's voice by the happenings of the past weeks, Charles had to bite back a, "What's wrong now?" He knew Beth was worried, imagining Billy lost in the crowds and unable to hear her calls. At times it had been tempting to agree with her that he should take Frances and Tim and leave her at home with Billy. There would be no comments, no questions, "Is he daft?" There would be no whispers, "He's a dummy," and no staring at him and Elizabeth to see these wicked, unclean people who had brought an imperfect child into the world. It had been tempting, but no more. Apart from wanting to be with them, he could not leave his wife and boy alone, with all the houses in the village empty. Every villain for miles would be gathered for the pickings.

Elizabeth could bottle up her feelings no longer. "You'll stay with us, won't you Charles? Not go off with Sam and John and leave me alone? Frances, you hold Billy's hand all the time. You know what happened before when you let him run off. I'll have to carry Tim, or, Charles, will you take Tim and I'll take Billy? Perhaps Ma ..."

"Beth. We've agreed time and again that we'll all stay together." To try and make her smile, Charles added, "If John can play the gentleman so can I." Beth did not smile and a note of irritation crept into Charles's voice, "Be fair, Elizabeth. Don't spoil the day before it starts. Think of Frances and me, for once."

At her husband's words, Beth looked at her daughter. Eyes cast down, the child slipped her hand into her father's. She was waiting, Beth knew, to be asked to walk hand in hand with her, but Beth did not call her. It hurt Beth to see them closing ranks and leaving no place for her, but she had to put Billy first. Frances would understand that one day.

As Mrs Dodds opened the door to see if they were ready, Frances flung herself on her grandmother in a demonstration of affection which nearly bowled the old lady over.

"Don't be silly, Frances," her grandmother scolded. "You're old enough to know better. Where's Tim? I can manage him, Beth." She lifted the little boy and snuggled him against her, planting great kisses in his hair until he laughed and wriggled free.

"Come on, Frances," Charles sighed. "We've got our orders. You take Billy's hand and your Ma will take his other one."

Silently, they left the house. Silently they locked the door and silently they stepped into the swarm of people passing by. The grown-ups continued silent, suspicious of all these strangers in their village, speaking only to warn each other to hang on to their belongings and mind their purses and pockets. Gradually, as Frances's questions and Billy's pointing finger drew their attention to one novelty after another, they began to live for the present, not worrying about yesterday or tomorrow. Charles' solemn resolution to mind his temper and be cheerful and Beth's realisation that she was cutting herself off in her concern for Billy and must make amends, gave way to a spontaneous warmth and enjoyment.

CHAPTER THIRTY FOUR

The fight was to be on a field below Hangar Hill to give the best view to the greatest number of people, but, already, a mile away, the family could make little headway through the crowds.

"We'll never see a thing," Beth said.

"That's no loss," Sarah replied. "Who wants to see all that blood spilt?"

"Claret." Henry spoke the word with even greater relish than he would have said, "Blood," in relating a tale of horror. When Sarah looked at him blankly, he repeated, "Claret. That's what them in the fancy call blood."

"Is that Henry?" Beth called along the row, knowing full well that it was, but expressing her surprise that he had found them in this crowd.

"Master's behind and Sam," Henry shouted. Today he had a real excuse for shouting, which was his preferred form of communication.

"Who's been filling your head with all that nonsense?" Sarah asked.

"There's worse things than boxing for a boy to follow," Will claimed, emphatically.

Edward's voice piped up from just behind them. "'Ow do you think we beat them Frenchies, Sarah Dodds?" He pushed his way in beside her. "It's places like this where English lads learn to stand square to the enemy."

"And to fight fair," Sam added, over their heads. "No hidden knives and cudgels for your Englishman."

"Places like this," Edward put in again, "where 'e learns to get up fighting. No lying down and pleading 'e's 'urt."

Sarah knew better than to argue. She never ceased to marvel how men, who never agreed about anything else, could agree over boxing and men, who never said a cross word, could fall out for ever over a dog or a fighting bird.

Henry, feinting and delivering an uppercut to the air around him, did not see that he was in a rider's path.

"Let the gentleman pass, Henry."

The men touched their forelocks and the women curtsied. It was Richard Hammond. Taking a penny from his pocket he leaned forward and gave it to Henry.

"You've the right spirit, lad, but I think God intended you for a jockey, not a fighter."

"I hope your man wins sir," Will Dodds called, as one sportsman to another.

"Have no fear on that score. You can safely put a shilling or two on his back. I've a thousand pounds on him myself."

"How much is that?" Frances whispered to her father.

"More than any of us will ever see in our lifetimes."

"More than we'll ever have if we all put our wages together for a lifetime," Will told her.

There was no pattern or order in the dozens of stalls and side-shows through which they walked. Each salesman and showman parked where his business acumen led him and his strength and readiness to protect his rights allowed him to remain. Some favoured a site close enough to the ring to supply the minute to minute needs of those who refused to leave a favoured spot throughout the two or three hours of the fight, but far enough away to avoid being used as a stand by those spectators ready to climb any contraption a foot or two higher than the ground itself. Others, intent on being the first to part fools from their money, pitched their stalls, carts and barrows by gates and stiles, along verges and lanes several fields away from the ring. Latecomers and opportunists parked by any successful showman already attracting customers eager to be amazed, delighted and entertained.

Frances, as usual, delighted in reading every word, but no one listened. There was no need for reading here. Before each stall and stand, the raucous voice of the owner bellowed to the crowd, describing his wares in enticing words and irresistible phrases. His wife, mother, brother or cousin stood alongside ready, with a soft word in the ear and a hard tug on the arm, to draw into the show anyone who hesitated for a split second.

"The smallest dwarf in the world," called a man in a bright yellow jacket.

"'Ave my job, 'e could," Henry commented.

"You could have his," Frances taunted.

"It's a child dressed up," Edward announced.

"Is it, Grandpa?" Frances was still young enough to take anything her grandfather said as gospel truth, but the man in the yellow jacket looked so open and honest.

"Course it is." Her grandfather's tone conveyed his contempt for the gullibility of the rest of the world and his conviction of his own wisdom. For the child's benefit, to teach her his skill in detecting fraud, he went on,

"Do you know, some years that so-called dwarf is smaller than 'e were the year before?" At Frances's puzzled look, he explained. "One child grows too big and 'is little brother takes 'is place. It's the same in chimney sweeping."

Frances and Henry were impressed by the old man's keen powers of observation, but Charles said in an innocent voice, "Didn't know you ever wasted your money on shows like that Pa?" He would have been willing to bet a hundred pounds that his father had never seen that particular dwarf in his life.

"Over 'ere. You'll get more to look at for your money," a woman called. She was fat herself, with a man's tricorn hat perched on her thick curls, but she promised even greater sights. "You can't miss the fattest woman in the world, dear." Leering enticingly at Edward, she said, "A sight for the likes of you, sir. You like big women, I can see just as they takes a liking to you."

"Padding," Edward announced, walking straight past to pause by the tooth puller's chair. His family gathered around him and the practitioner glanced swiftly along the row of teeth before him, past Beth's neat white set and Charles's irregular but healthy set to Edward's few black stumps.

"'Ave them out for you in no time, sir. There," he murmured, turning back to the large mouth open before him, "'Ave that out in a jiffy." Deftly moving his wrist and pulling at the terrifying tool in his hand, he jerked it free from the man's mouth and, into his other hand, shook a large molar tooth. The long roots lay across his open palm for all to see.

"'Ole and complete. No stumps left behind to fester. Not a murmur of pain did you 'ear did you? Come trembling along, 'e did, trembling like a leaf and begging me not to 'urt 'im. There, did I 'urt you, sir? Did I make you wince and scream like some quacks does?"

Rising from his chair, all smiles, the man paid his money. "Didn't feel nothing," he told the crowd in a strong, clear voice.

"There's no blood on that tooth," Edward smirked triumphantly. "Never got it out of that mouth, 'e never. 'Ad it in 'is 'and all the time." Nodding knowingly, he walked on to join a crowd around the bear.

"Is he real, grandpa?" Frances asked, her faith in human nature badly shaken by now.

"Could be a man dressed up," Henry suggested, taking his lead from the sweep as usual.

"'E's real enough. Nasty things, bears. Nasty mean creatures."

For the first time, Frances doubted her grandfather. No animal with such thick, soft fur and sad brown eyes could be mean and nasty. If it were, it was because no one looked after it and understood it as she would do if given a chance.

"This animal here," the big man holding the end of the bear's chain declared, "is wild — as wild as the day my partner and me captured him single-handed in the forests of North America. Don't be frightened," he urged, knowing full well the appeal and thrill of fear. "My partner has a loaded musket, ready to shoot this bear, this rare and valuable animal, if he goes on the rampage. He'll not get more than one of you." The people thronged closer at this promise of the chance of both a mauling and a shooting.

Charles prepared to pay the man for Frances to stand close and watch. He knew it was as safe to watch as the dwarf or the fat lady and he knew his daughter had talked of nothing else for weeks. To his surprise, she took his hand, "I don't want to watch it, Pa."

"It isn't really fierce. The man just says that to draw a crowd. It just shambles about and pretends to dance."

Even more firmly, Frances told him, "I don't want to watch the poor bear, Pa. He looks too sad to dance. Did God make bears to dance, Pa?"

CHAPTER THIRTY FIVE

John's friend, Tom Hutchinson, having started out at first light for the fight, had intended to climb Hangar Hill by the gentle slope, but he found the way barred by the crowd gathered on this prime vantage point looking down on the field where the fight was to take place. He was forced to skirt round and climb the steeper side by the track through the woods. He overtook many older people and many with children already dragging their feet and complaining. As he always did when about to meet the Captain, he greeted everyone with whom he had the slightest acquaintance. It was important that, when they did talk together, it should look like a casual, friendly chat, which would arouse no suspicion. After so many meetings, Tom took it for granted that it would not be he who found the Captain, but the Captain who found him. He sat at the very top of the hill, looking down on the crowds, but sheltered by the trees, and pulled his breakfast of bread and ham from his pocket. The sparrows, made bold by the innumerable picnics held on this spot, hopped right up to him. He threw a scrap and within half a second a starling had swooped down, scattering the smaller birds to take the prize for himself.

"Life in the raw, Tom," the Captain said and Tom knew he had been there all the time. "Size is power. The big take from the small, unless the small make a stand together."

Tom acknowledged the Captain and the truth of his statement. Breaking off another piece of bread, he aimed it beyond the starling to the sparrows.

"You can't put things right by throwing a few crumbs to the weak, Tom."

"But you can make life more bearable."

"Is that doing anyone a favour, Tom? So long as life is just bearable, things will go on the way they have always done. It's only when life becomes unbearable that people will listen to us. A little charity here, a little charity there. Eighteen hundred years of Christian charity and where has it got us? Just makes life bearable so the people demand nothing else and won't risk losing the little they have."

Tom considered. "There's many a man brought to our side by God's word. They want to help bring heaven on earth."

"And there are more against us who can quote God's word to destroy us."

Knowing the Captain never liked to stay in one place long, Tom stood up and brushed the crumbs from his jacket. He started to walk away, but the Captain stayed where he was and Tom waited.

"It wasn't until he was old that my father read Tom Paine and felt a conviction of the rightness of everything he read, which never left him, even on his death bed. Until then he had searched everywhere for the truth. Methodist, Baptist, Quaker. He had listened to them all. Taught himself to read the Bible and knew every word of it as well as many a parson and a good deal better than some."

For the first time, Tom heard the Captain talking about himself and he did not interrupt as the man continued. "Chapter and verse he knew and he taught me. I've been grateful ever since. Know your enemy, Tom. Those who seek revolution in every individual heart instead of in society are our enemies, believe me. They preach the joy of suffering in this world for the joy of everlasting life. There'd be nothing in Christ's message to support a revolution, even if the Church wasn't entrenched in its own wealth and dogma. We demand bread and Christ's answer is that you cannot live by bread alone."

As he had spoken, the Captain had seemed to have been unaware of the vast crowd below him on the hill, but suddenly he focused his eyes upon the scene and stretched to his full height.

"That's where Christ went wrong." The Captain began to speak in a hollow, clerical voice, "Again, the devil taketh him up into an exceedingly high mountain, and showeth him all the kingdoms of the world, and the glory of them. And saith unto him, 'All these things will I give thee.' If the Devil made me that offer, I'd snatch it up."

Knowing his Bible as well as any man brought up in a dissenting household, and still believing, as the Captain guessed, in many of its truths, Tom quoted, "All these things will I give thee," — he emphasised the next words — "if thou wilt fall down and worship me."

As ever, Tom found, the Captain had his answer ready. "But once you have absolute power, Tom, you don't have to keep the terms. The people gave kings their power centuries ago, but have kings kept their side of the bargain? Once we have power, we can use it against lords and kings and the Devil himself. No more poverty, no more slavery and no more tyranny."

Listening, Tom poked the ground with his stick. "Land," he mused, "that's what the Devil was offering. Land is power. It's those with the land who rule the country."

"Was the Devil offering land?" the Captain thought aloud. "What the Bible says is 'all the kingdoms of the world'. Is that land, or people?"

Silently, for a while, the Captain continued the line of thought, then spoke his conclusions. "Perhaps that was the fourth temptation, Tom. Was it too terrible an idea for the churchmen and kings even to include in the Bible? Perhaps this is what they left out. 'And the fourth time the devil tempteth Jesus and sheweth him the people and the power that rested in them. And saith unto Jesus, all this will I give ye and ye shall overthrow kings and governments and rule in the people's name.'" The Captain held out his hands, as though to receive a gift. "If only the Devil would offer me the power in that crowd down there, I'd not refuse it."

"Even the Devil hasn't got it in his power to offer that," Tom told him without hesitation. "You may get a crowd coming together to watch a fight, but it's harder to get them to join together in a common cause, let alone stay together. A bad harvest and men join us. A good one and they fade away."

"They wouldn't have to come together for long," the Captain argued. "The people only have to come together long enough to tear down the established constitution. Then they can go home, while we build up a new one the way it ought to be."

"Can you see," Tom asked in disbelief, "this crowd coming to hear one of us speak? They've come miles to follow a boxer, but not one of us. We'll just have to work slowly, take years if need be, and gradually build a strong, loyal group around us." His point reminded Tom of something else he meant to say. "Talk to John Stevenson. Take him into your confidence. He could win you a good following in the district."

"He's too independent. We want to build around men who are committed body and soul to our cause. Anyway, isn't he busy trying to make a gentleman of himself? Well, he'll learn they won't let him. He'll turn to us in the end."

As they parted, the Captain stood for a last look down onto the hordes below. "If only they would follow me as they do those fighters."

"They worship them. That local fellow Langford's a hero for miles around." Tom kept going, half walking, half running with the steepness of the hill. He did not look to see if the Captain was following. Perhaps he would see him again that day, just to talk to as any other man, perhaps not.

CHAPTER THIRTY SIX

In the jostling mob, among the groups already seated on the ground and those pushing to select their spots, the pace of the horses became slower and slower, until Mark Elham had to admit that the only sensation of movement was from people passing the carriages rather than the carriages moving forward. The Hammond's carriage was a little way ahead, with the Simpkins' just behind and the Gray's behind them. None had moved for minutes.

Lost in his observations, Mark could offer no resistance when the reins were grabbed from his hands and a large young man began to pull the horse forward, cursing at those who blocked the path.

"This is just what we need," Sam Stevenson yelled above the noise, winking at Mark and grinning at Charlotte. Surrounding the carriage, his friends pushed and pulled with a colourful selection of grunts and curses.

"Take a rest," Sam ordered at last, opening the door and flopping on the seat next to Charlotte. Even he, almost, if not quite, drunk, recognised the look of fear. "Didn't I say, Miss? I'm Sam, John's brother. Thought we'd give you a hand as you're a friend of his."

Still trembling, Charlotte recovered enough to tell him they had no interest in the fight and would stay where they were. "It's Sam Stevenson," she explained to her brother who had rushed up, whip raised.

"Careful, squire," Sam laughed. "You could do a man an injury with that." Stretching his arms and flexing his muscles, he was ready for the fray once more. "Right! Another try, lads!"

"No, really, Stevenson. Leave the carriage here. It's quite close enough for us."

"To be honest," Sam confided with exaggerated secrecy, "it wasn't just you I was thinking of. It's what me and the lads need to stand on and get a ringside view."

Seeing his carriage, in his mind's eye, covered with the scratching, scraping boots of Sam Stevenson and 'the lads', Mark asserted himself. "We — and the carriage — are staying where we are."

"They're charging three shillings — three shillings for a seat up front," one of Sam's friends protested, giving the carriage a shove.

"Let's find another," Sam ordered. "We could do with something bigger."

As they pushed along a line of carriages, one said, loud enough for Mark to hear, "Is that the woman your John has his eye on?" He did not hear Sam's reply. In a few minutes they were bargaining successfully with Richard Hammond to get his carriage through the throng in return for a seat at the ringside. Immediately, another Stevenson took shape from the seething mass. Edward sat himself on the step of the carriage.

"Let the young 'uns wear theirselves out first and let the old 'uns sit down," he joked. Serious again, he demanded of Mark, "Can I 'ave a word with you, mister?"

The strong smell of soot in the air gave Mark his first clue to the man's identity. Edward, the undisputed centre of his own world, assumed he needed no introduction.

"That's me apprentice, 'Enry over there."

Spotting the sweeping boy they had seen a few days before, Mark concluded this was, in fact, the sweep himself.

An audience of one was enough for the sweep to begin a speech he often made. "I owe nothing to no one," he stated with obvious pride. "All I am, I've got by me own efforts. It was me they come to, building the Big 'Ouse. Sir Philip 'Ammond's place, you know. 'E says, 'Stevenson, we can't do nothing without your opinion. No one knows 'is job better than you.'" The old man was well into his stride and Mark had no need to reply. "I told 'im looking after a 'ouse of that size was a full time job for one man. 'Oped one of me sons would take it. A good living it would 'ave been for John, but no, 'e would go 'is own way."

There was a hardly perceptible pause for breath. "Now I'm an open minded man. I'm the first to admit 'e seems to 'ave made the right choice. Determined to do well for 'isself and I can see 'e's done that. A good trade and a good marriage, that's the way to get on. That's what I've taught 'im and 'e's a good learner, John."

The old man proceeded to tell Mark, who, in fact, knew a good deal more about Mr Wright than he did, how greatly John was valued and how much work he had taken from Mr Wright's shoulders. "You'll see. John'll be taking over soon. 'E's always been the one with ambition, John 'as. No labouring job and marriage to one of the village wenches for 'im and 'oo can blame 'im?"

Standing up and leaning closer, Edward confided to Mark, who was forced to back away, "I've a little money put by for any of me children 'oo needs it. John won't come penniless to a marriage even though I can't match penny with penny to your sister's money. Though," he added with a knowing wink, "I know it's not just money the lasses look for in a husband and John's a strapping feller."

At long last the sweep realised Mark had made no answer, but misinterpreted his silence. "Now I can't say I'm pleased with the way things have turned out, but I'm not blaming you or the young lady. Them youngsters pushing their nose into my business. Stuck up miss, that Lucy Simpkins. But I'll sort that out with their fathers. Nobody's complained before, I know that. My John can marry with my blessing. That's all I wanted to tell you." Like a grubby imp, he melted into the crowd.

Speechless, Mark looked at his sister and thought back over the past few weeks since John's arrival in Gressingford. He could not believe she had encouraged Stevenson, but perhaps she had been as deceived as he had about the man's true boastful and ambitious nature, so different from the manner he assumed in Gressingford. Perhaps she had, but she could certainly have had no idea of the characters of Stevenson's loutish brother and grasping father. There could be no thought of a connection between the Stevenson and Elham families. Something must be done for his sister's good name to set matters to rights.

Waving hands above the crowds, the Grays made their way across to the Elhams. "Like us," Nicholas said, "You've decided this is far enough" Shaking his head disapprovingly, he added, "We, like you, had offers of help to move forward."

"Mr Hammond shouldn't have encouraged such behaviour," Charlotte replied, giving up looking for John, an occupation which had taken all her attention while Mark had talked to the strange, little, old man.

The Grays, accepting that in their own village the Hammonds could do as they wished, did not reply directly. Then Anne Gray remarked, "To think Becky, our servant was hopeful of marrying Sam Stevenson at one time. He's the poacher, you know. Mama was most disturbed and talked to Mrs Dodds about it — that's the girl's mother. It seems the plan now is for her to marry the brother, John."

"John Stevenson!" Charlotte heard herself echo. Mark watched his sister closely and was deeply disturbed by her concern.

"Yes," Anne told them, "the brother who works for Mr Wright." She laughed at her recollections. "Where Sam is so free and easy, the brother is pompous. He very nearly wrecked my first Sunday school." Encouraged by Mark Elham's interest in anything she had to say, she related the story of the Sunday school from her point of view. She told how she was just bringing the class under control when John Stevenson burst in. "There was really no need! Such bad behaviour would not have occurred again. Father would have spoken to their masters and that would have been the end of it."

With returning annoyance at the memory of the incident, Anne Gray recalled, "It could have made me a laughing stock. To think — the stupid fellow even said, 'With your permission, Miss Gray,' before clipping the boys' ears."

"He hit them?" Mark's voice reflected the horror of someone who had never felt a hand raised in anger or reproach.

"Quite a blow."

"Such brute force with such a show of good manners," Nicholas remarked, "with such pretence at refined behaviour. Anne laughed so much when she returned home and showed us his attempt at a bow."

"I could barely keep a straight face at the time," Anne recalled, still smiling.

Mark thought it time to point out John's faults, just in case the man had deceived Charlotte into thinking his manner genuine. He had to admit the fellow had deceived him.

"There really is nothing more deplorable than simple men aping their…" Biting back the word 'betters', which, as a believer in equality, he could not bring himself to utter, Mark sought a replacement.

"Betters," Anne finished for him, quite unaware that anyone would consider replacing it.

Unable to think of the word he wanted, Mark rephrased the whole idea, explaining, as he knew from the many books he had read on the nature of man, that simple men, unfettered by society, had a natural simplicity and gentleness of manner.

The Grays were not sure they agreed, but did not openly disagree. Anne began again about Becky and John, determined to avoid any conversation with the Elhams on politics. "At least," she reflected, "If he is planning to marry Becky, he is no longer determined to marry for money."

"Was that his plan?" Mark decided to bring out all the facts to make the man's true nature clear to Charlotte. She was much quieter than her usual self and looked rather pale.

199

"Oh, yes. The Colonel is watching him. Thinks he is Gentleman Jack. Stevenson was behind that little prank, you know. He is a gentleman in one sense, you see," Anne Gray laughed.

"Going to war does unsettle many common men," Dr Gray stated from his knowledge of human nature. "They see the poverty of peasants in Spain and France and feel themselves gentlemen. Some learn to read or pick up a smattering of an education and soon have grand ideas above their station."

"There they are," Anne pointed out, "Becky and John Stevenson."

With concern, Mark noted that Charlotte had risen as though to find a more comfortable position, but was searching in the direction of Anne's gaze. "People are buzzing around the stalls like bees around a honey pot," Charlotte remarked, for want of something to say to cover her search.

"Just the people who can least afford it are spending the most," Anne pointed out.

"Some will have borrowed against the harvest money," Mark explained, having studied the budgets of labouring families.

"But their lives must be so hard," Charlotte commented.

Dr Gray was not at all sure he agreed and pointed out the simple pleasures which can be enjoyed by country folk.

Her voice raised with indignation, Anne was quite certain she did not agree. "But it is a question of principle and honesty. The Stevensons are buying trinkets and sweetmeats, having asked us to provide for their child."

Loud shouts and crashes broke out around them.

"Whatever is happening?"

"I thought we were well back from the fight."

Experienced showmen and travellers were hastily packing up or taking out staves and clubs, kept at the back for just this purpose, and defending their property with a will. It happened every year. The gangs of Irish labourers who came to England every summer met the resentment of the Englishmen whose wages they lowered and whose work they took. At gatherings such as this, a mocking remark, an insult could and did lead to a full scale battle with no holds barred.

Appalled at the bloody and violent spectacle, Nicholas Gray ordered some local men, whose names he knew, to stand around them and protect the ladies. As Anne had averted her eyes, he asked one of the men to tell him the names of anyone he recognised in the fighting.

"Sam Stevenson, sir, and all his friends. They never miss a fight. The

Braithwaites and the Donkins. Same applies to them, sir."

"There's Tom Hutchinson in the middle of it all," Mark pointed out in surprise. "And John Stevenson next to him." With swollen eyes and bleeding mouth, John was battering an Irishman with complete abandon. He was scarcely recognisable as the clean, quietly spoken man he posed as in Gressingford. Suddenly, it was all over.

"Would you believe it?" Mark Elham asked in amazement, "They are patting each other on the back like the greatest of friends"

"And they won't be satisfied until they have seen who, English or Irish, can drink the most ale." It was as though Nicholas had heard an Irishman say to John, "I've two pounds if I can find the thieving Englishman who took my bet. Let's drink it to every last penny."

"Why not?" John had asked, kissing Becky as she came to tend their wounds. For long enough he had watched the Elhams and Grays chatting, making two perfect couples. If this was where they thought he belonged, he would show them he had real friends.

CHAPTER THIRTY SEVEN

Mr Gray, the vicar, rose at five o'clock, glad to leave the bed on which he had tossed without sleep. There had been no dawn, for there had been no night. The glow of thousands of lanterns and torches had seared into the sky, keeping at bay the blessed night which God had given to men for sleep and refreshment. Even now, revellers, determined to wring the last drops of sinful pleasure, still sang and shouted, as they staggered away.

His eyes and brow hot from lack of sleep and his indignation red hot from the insults he had received from strangers in front of his own parishioners, the parson stood at the window looking down into the lane. As a man looked up, he stepped quickly back behind the curtain. The words of abuse which had been flung back at him when he last made a quite reasonable request from that very window for those passing below to check their language and their behaviour were still fresh in his mind. He stopped his inner ear against the wicked, evil words, but could not but think of the evil, wicked hearts of men who had spoken them.

Hurrying downstairs, Mr Gray heard Becky in the kitchen and found his wife dozing just where he had left her. She had preferred to face the mob, if they returned, fully clothed and seated in her chair rather than in her nightdress in bed. Another servant, Frederick, whom he had left to snatch what sleep he could stretched across the door mat, was looking up and down the street. Mr Gray joined him.

The scene was even worse than the vicar had imagined in his most demented visions of hell. Men, women and children slept in doorways and on graves. Scarcely a patch of ground was to be seen beneath the litter and the debris of human pleasure. Just as horrified, the parson realised that there was not a sound from the cottages and workshops. Why were not the men making for the fields and the washerwomen leaning over their steaming tubs?

In the whole length of the lane there was only one man walking along and, as Mr Gray watched, he leaned over a man lying against a hedge and then knelt down beside him.

"Stop, thief!" the parson called. "Quickly, Frederick, after him."

"It's Becky's father," Frederick said, making no attempt to move.

Mistaking his inactivity for fear, Mr Gray urged him once more to apprehend the man. "Come with me and we will take him red-handed."

When they were within a few yards of him, Will Dodds stood up. Mr Gray was determined that he would not escape him and justice.

"Stay where you are," he ordered. "Fetch the constable, Frederick."

Will forced himself to speak to the vicar. "Is your son in, sir? This man needs a doctor."

Immediately, the vicar revised his interpretation of the scene. It must be one of' this man's relations lying drunk on the ground. "No," he answered. His son was above treating such people.

"Frederick," Will Dodds asked," will you run and tell John I'm bringing the shepherd in? John can give him what help he can and then send for Mr Wright." As Frederick came nearer to look, he told him, "It's Paul Low. He's been beaten half to death. Tell Charles and Sam to get down to the Canal Field. Paul was down there yesterday keeping an eye on Richard Hammond's sheep to see they weren't worried by dogs. Something must have happened and he dragged himself this far to tell somebody."

With a sensible errand this time, Frederick ran to do as he was asked. Ignoring the vicar, Will lifted the shepherd, but could not carry him. Send John along here," he shouted after Frederick.

"Evil breeds evil," Mr Gray stated and hurried away to send a messenger to Richard Hammond to tell him to go to the Canal Field at once as there was some evil afoot there.

Once John had come and they had taken the shepherd to the Dodds's house, Will hurried after Charles and Sam to the field. They had not had much of a start and he caught them up just as they were stopping a stranger passing with a barrow loaded with dead sheep. The man dropped the shafts.

"Take them, take them," he smiled, eager to avoid any trouble. "I found them right by that gate. Thought they'd fallen off a cart. You can't pass by gifts these days." When they questioned him about the fate of the rest of the flock, his expression became even vaguer and his smile even more ingratiating. They hurried on to the field.

One or two sheep, their throats cut, still remained by the gate. The others must have panicked and run at the initial noise and flurry and they lay dead along the canal bank. The same rust red stain was smeared on their fleeces. Some floated on the water and others overhung it, pools of red beneath showing where their blood had dripped. There was nothing to be done except to pick the bodies from the water before they putrefied and quickly dispatch those who still lingered in agony.

The news spread as rapidly as any news in the village and men who had turned and tossed in pain all night and feared they would never rise again, forced their sore limbs in the direction of the field, their fretful wives and children with them. Will Dodds, looking for help, could see few farmers or their men. They had rushed to check their own stock. The blacksmith and his son waded in to help.

"Here, make a chain. We can pass these bodies back," Will called. The gaping group of men he had addressed continued to gape back at him.

"Don't stand there like sheep yourselves," he shouted. There was no answer, just the same unflinching, expressionless stares.

Aggressively, the blacksmith made a step towards the group. "Did you hear me?"

"We hear you," one answered in a flat, detached voice.

"So?" The blacksmith took another step towards them.

"We don't work for the Hammonds. Don't work for nobody."

"You'll take your share of the poor rate, though."

"We'd be as dead as them sheep if we didn't."

Two or three stepped forward to help, slowly and without enthusiasm. The rest walked off to stand and stare at a safe distance from the blacksmith, prodding with their boots at the strange sheep which Mr Hammond had chosen to breed instead of the familiar ones the farmers had kept for generations.

Gradually, small groups of farmers and their labourers joined those already in the field. They had found damaged fences, broken gates, the expected trampled crops and missing hens, but nothing to compare with this slaughter. There was, at first, little argument about the culprits. It was the cowardly papists, the Irish, beaten in a fair fight, who had secretly taken revenge in the night. It was certainly not thieves. The sheep had been left where they were killed. When the Colonel suggested this was the work of revolutionaries, evil, envious men, no one seemed prepared to listen. Surprisingly, it was young George Braithwaite who brought the evidence which convinced everyone that the Colonel was right in this matter and had probably been right in all he had said.

"Mr 'Ammond, Mr 'Ammond," the lad called, pushing his way through to Richard Hammond with a piece of paper waving in his hand. He had found it nailed to a tree trunk and, although he could not read it, he realised its importance.

Richard Hammond gave the paper a quick glance. "To al marsters how treat men worse than animals. Here endith the ferst lesin. Jentelman Jack." He handed it to Mr Gray, unable to read it aloud for the anger which choked him. Mr Gray read it and passed it to Colonel Benson. It vindicated all he had ever said.

Along the bank, Sam was still trying to stop his ears to the pathetic bleating of dying sheep when a stronger, angrier bleat drew his attention. Caught in the brambles at the corner of the field he found two sheep.

Better than anyone, Will knew what it meant to lose stock and a farm. He would not have wished this upon anyone. "Here's a new beginning, sir," he told Richard Hammond. "There's a ewe and a ram." He did not look directly at Mr Hammond, knowing he would cry, too, if he saw his own sorrow reflected in the man's eyes.

"You see Dodds, what comes of your ideas," Mr Gray pointed out.

Will stared at the vicar as uncomprehendingly as the men had stared at the blacksmith.

"You see what happens when you meddle in matters beyond your understanding? Once you open the door to the Devil, there is no closing it."

"You don't think ....," Will began in astonishment.

"You and your kind should remember," Richard Hammond told him sternly, "that labourers lose as much, perhaps more, than masters when property is wantonly destroyed. In time, though not in this country, where old ways and values are dead, I shall start again. But what of your work and your daughter's husband's work? From today there is no work for you."

"But why, sir? Surely…."

"Don't play the innocent. If you don't know, ask others in your family. I have no more to say."

CHAPTER THIRTY EIGHT

Apart from an involuntary groan and a wild clutching at his head as he had risen from his bed to Frederick's frantic calls, John had not had a second to think about his aching body or consider how he looked after the fight. Now, with the shepherd made as comfortable as his shattered bones would allow, John faced his master's stern gaze and suddenly felt that dreadful moment of realisation, known in nightmares, of not being presentable to the world. Despite the heat, he tugged at his collar, drawing in his head like a tortoise to hide his bruised eyes and cut lip. It was no more effective than his vain attempts to pull his hat down over his eyes. Mr Wright's gaze was as fixed and stern as ever.

"What I have heard and seen today has caused me great distress," he remarked, taking the reins from the boy who held his horse.

Relieved that Mr Wright seemed to refer to the shepherd and the destruction of the sheep, John replied, "It's a sad business, Mr Wright. My brother Charles and Will Dodds will have no more work because of it. They say Richard Hammond will be off to Australia."

"You misunderstand me, John, perhaps deliberately. If I had known all that has been revealed to me today, I would not have given you employment. The stories I have heard, and there have been many, that you are this Gentleman Jack, I have dismissed as wild speculation."

Completely convinced of the rightness of the case against John on other counts, the apothecary waved aside his assistants attempt to speak.

"Now I hear — and believe them to be true— stories of pranks played on gamekeepers, of clothes stolen from Mr Richard Hammond and his friends. But worse, even worse as you are in my employ and your behaviour reflects on me, I hear of fighting and drunkenness before my friends and neighbours yesterday."

John insisted on speaking. "It will never happen again, Mr Wright. On my word of honour, it will never happen again." He could not explain that his disappointment at seeing Charlotte chatting so cosily with Nicholas Gray had made him feel, just that once, that he had nothing to lose by behaving as his brother and friends behaved. And that Irishman had set upon his brother.

"You speak of honour," Mr Wright mocked. With deep seriousness, he went on, "A neighbour came to see me early this morning telling me of the harassment to which people had been subjected by your brother and his friends and the wild claims and presumptions of your father."

"My father!" John burst out. "He says a great many foolish things without an ounce of truth in them."

It was not the right thing to say. Mr Wright shook his head sadly. "You add disrespect to your father to your other vices, John."

In desperation, John begged forgiveness for his stupidity at the fight, thinking that was all for which he was being blamed.

"It is too late for apologies, John. I can see you have guessed what I am about to say."

"Mr Wright...."

"You need not return with me, John. I have already apologised to Mr Elham for your behaviour — and that of your family. Let us hope that I do not have to distress Miss Elham with an apology. Let us hope she never hears of the coarse way your father, no doubt reflecting your boasting, spoke of her."

"Miss Elham?" John queried. "How have I offended her?"

Intently, Mr Wright studied John's expression and then spoke more kindly. "Perhaps you do not know, John. Perhaps I have done you an injustice, plucking you from your humble family and placing you in company where you were flattered." He began again, "Yes, perhaps, John, you have misunderstood the interest of people who wish to help you educate and better yourself. Perhaps we are partly to blame for talking of equality without always defining this as equality before the law and in the eyes of God. There will always be, there must always be, rules governing the conduct of those in one rank of society to those in another, especially between men and women."

At last John realised that it was his behaviour to Charlotte Elham which was being criticised and had really caused his dismissal. "I have only respect for Miss Elham. Never, never have I abused her confidence. Did Miss Elham speak to you? Did Miss Elham complain?"

"You are impertinent, John. Now I see how mistaken I was in your character. I am assured that she does not want to see you again. You are not to call or contact Miss Elham ever again." To emphasis his point, he went on, "Male servants must, in their work, be admitted into the company of ladies, often without the chaperone required when a lady talks to a gentleman, and ties may arise of benevolent interest on one side and gratitude on the other, but it would be wrong, destructive of society itself, if this situation were abused with familiarity and disrespect."

"Did Miss Elham complain of my behaviour?" John demanded.

"I will not stand here arguing with a servant. Have you no respect for Miss Elham, who took such a kind interest in you?"

Drowning John's questioning, he told him, "When a man marries beneath him, John, people suspect he is infatuated by beauty and lured into folly by his animal nature. When a man attempts to marry above his station in life, he betrays himself as ambitious and avaricious. The lady, too, finds herself shunned by good company, yet unhappy in that of her inferiors."

John stopped questioning and protesting. All Mr Wright was saying was true. It had all been a fantasy bred of his loneliness and Miss Elham's kindness.

Tightening his hold on the horse's reins, Mr Wright spurred it forward. "Such matters will never alter, John. Those matters which are established by law, they may change, be amended, repealed or even overthrown by revolution. But these matters of social conduct are not regulated by law. They have arisen over the centuries from the wisdom and common sense of our ancestors and wisdom and common sense do not change."

CHAPTER THIRTY NINE

Reluctantly, Frances dragged herself from bed, exaggerating each action as only a child can. Wearily the bed cover was edged back, inch by inch, and painfully slowly her feet were lowered, inch by inch, to swing, as she rested from her effort, above the bare floorboards. Listlessly, she moved her feet and wiggled her toes in the sunlight from the tiny window, but the shadowy patterns gave her no pleasure. Today she was being forced to shut her books and shut her mind and go to labour in the fields and she intended to protest just as strongly as her Grandpa Dodds had protested about the changes in his life.

"Come on my love," her father called again. So it was still 'my love' after five calls, not 'you lazy little girl.' They were trying to win her round, but she would have none of it. Once, twice, three times more, she swung her legs in the sunshine. She was quite safe. They would not smack her today.

Slowly walking downstairs, Frances set her face in its most defiant pose, ready for the glance her mother would give to check her mood and see how much effort was necessary to make her smile again.

"There's bread and milk for you, Frances. I'll get some more for you when you get home. We'll all eat together like grown-ups when we come in from the fields." As she placed the bowl in front of her, her mother kissed the top of her head.

"Or you can have a bite of my juicy fat bacon," her father told her, "Now you're going to be a wage-earner."

Frances pulled a face and shook her head. For the first time in her life, that she could remember, she was not reminded to say, "No, thank you."

Beside Frances, her father talked of bits of news which might interest her. Yesterday he had seen a black rabbit on the edge of the wood and the day before he had spotted a litter of wild kittens in the stack-yard at Top Farm. After work, he suggested, they could go and see them.

"I'll be too tired."

"Here's Runty," Charles noted brightly, biting back the annoyance he felt at his daughter's play acting. The long-legged young cat rubbed himself, purring, against Frances's chair. "Where's Nelson? Did he come back with you?"

"He can do what he likes," Frances answered for the cat. Each word, heavily stressed, underlined her belief in free choice.

At last her father's conversation flagged, dying from lack of encouragement, but her mother did not give up so easily.

"I'll tell you what. When you bring home your sixpence tonight, you can keep a whole penny and put it in the box your Uncle John gave you."

Not quite daring to keep totally silent in case the offer was withdrawn, Frances let a "Yes, Ma," slip from her lips. If she saved every week, she might have enough to run away one day.

For a while, Beth continued to talk cheerfully, seeming not to notice that Frances made no reply to her stories of her own first day at work and her first penny in wages. Exasperated at last, she finished, "Frances, it's not as though you have to go every single day. It will only be at the busy times, when there's hoeing and stone picking or harvest. You used to enjoy coming to those and begged and begged to help."

Beth looked for a response, but the child's expression might have been carved from stone. Somehow Beth had to make her listen to what she was about to tell her.

"You stay with the other girls and the women. Don't go off with any of the boys, do you hear me?"

"Why, Ma?" There were times when it was as annoying to others to pretend that you did not understand as it was to pretend that you had not heard.

"You know why, my girl, as well as I do."

"Just you do as you're told, Frances." There could be no doubt from his sharp glance and tone that her father meant what he said.

"Yes, Pa."

CHAPTER FORTY

To occupy her mind, Frances counted each weed which she dragged by its brilliant white roots from the ground, but there was no one who would be interested in learning the total. The women by whom she sat to eat her bread and cheese seemed interested in nothing but husbands and children and in running down Eliza and the men and women who laughed, out-staring them brazenly, in the corner of the field. Jem and George probably would not have been interested either, but at least they still had the energy to play. Just in time, Frances turned her head to avoid acknowledging Jem's wave.

A minute or two later, Jem stood over her. "Didn't you see me wave, Fran?" The crumb of cheese on Frances's skirt took all her attention. "Are you deaf or something, like Billy?"

One of the women reached out and shook Frances's arm. "Jem's talking to you."

"I'm not to talk to her," Frances whispered, in the faint hope that Jem would not hear.

"Your loss," Jem sang out. "You come or stay. It's all the same to me."

For a few seconds, Frances did not look up, but then she watched Jem and George run back to the other children. Bossily, but efficiently, Jem broke up the game which had started in her absence and organised her own. There were plenty of lieutenants eager to take Frances's usual place.

Frances made herself look away and she turned her eyes to the bank where her fingers, outstretched, supported her. Perhaps there was a daisy, extra special in its colouring, or a four-leaved clover. There was such a treasure. A lady bird walked precariously around the edge of a finger nail. She picked a piece of grass and slowly and gently eased it beneath the insect's front legs. Obligingly, it made its way along the narrow blade and, when she moved her hold to the other end, just as obligingly, it made its way back. Bored by such an obliging captive, Frances shook it onto the hedge. As she did so she caught sight of the shallow shadow cast by the noon sun against the hedge. Along its latticed edge, silhouettes of leaves and flowers fell upon the grass. On her hands and knees, Frances crawled along, naming them one by one. Dog rose, convolvulus, another and another, old man's beard. Further and further she crawled from the women and nearer and nearer to Jem and the children. Leaning back on her heels, she watched them playing. If only Jem could read, she could trace a message out on the ground or even in the air. If she just tried to join in without speaking, they would push her away.

An idea, the perfect idea, struck her. They always let Billy play now and he could not talk.

In the lane, on his way home from work, Charles caught sight of Frances waving goodbye to Jem and George.

"You mustn't talk to them, Frances," he told her as she fell into step at his side. "It's not your Ma and me who say so, but those ladies on the Committee. They've more spies working for them than the Colonel has."

"I didn't," Frances told him smugly. "I didn't talk to them, not one word." Before her father could ask what happened, she went on, smugness giving way to triumph, "I signed, Pa, just like I do to Billy, and they signed back. Miss Simpkins only said not to talk to them and I didn't Pa. I didn't."

Resting his hand on his daughter's shoulder as they walked home, Charles laughed and Frances laughed at her own cleverness and the fact that she was not in trouble.

"Now I'll tell you my secret, Frances, but you must never tell your Ma." Charles held out a small bundle he had been carrying under his jacket and leaned down to whisper conspiratorially, "I've come to an arrangement with Hugh Armitage, with words, mind you, not signs, and he's agreed, when Sam has a little something for us, to do a deal with us and exchange it for a piece of pork. That way he gets a treat and I get a piece of meat to take home to Ma and tell her Mr Armitage gave it to me as part of my wages."

"A little something," Frances echoed, giggling. "She'll...." Frances corrected herself. Many times she had been told not to call her mother 'she'. "Ma will know, Pa." From a lifetime's experience, Frances knew that her mother did know all secrets, especially guilty ones.

"Ma will probably guess," her father agreed. "She's no fool, but guessing isn't knowing, is it? If I know your Ma, she'll not ask any questions. That's something you'll do well to learn from her that you'll not find in all your books. 'Where ignorance is bliss, it's foolish to be wise.'"

CHAPTER FORTY ONE

Stamping his feet and beating his arms across his chest, John stood in the open door.

"Here we are again, Pa. Christmas. May we all live to see many more."

A grunt squeezed through the old man's lips. John interpreted it as a greeting and interpreted the look which went with it as an order to shut the door before they all froze to death. Still jumping up and down, he propelled himself forward and deftly kicked the door to behind him.

"Not ready yet, Pa?" There was really no point in trying to persuade his father, usually unshakable in his stubbornness, but John had to try.

"As ready as I'll ever be." Pulling himself up from his chair, Edward moved to the fire. His hand shook as he poked and raked, pushing the ashes and the dust through the iron basket and releasing into the stuffy air the sweet, crisp smell of burning wood.

"Pa. I've told you before, leave it to Henry." Only just in time, John's hand steadied the old man as, leaning to reach for a log from the hearth, he hovered over the flames.

"Anyway, why are you building up the fire, Pa? We'll be leaving for Charles's soon." At one time, John might have said "for Charles's and Beth's" or even "for Beth's."

"You go where you like, son. I'm staying here." John's supporting arm was pushed away.

"You'll be left on your own, Pa." There was no conviction in John's voices as he spoke the empty threat, but Edward would still not have moved if there had been.

"I've been on my own before, ever since your Ma died. I was on my own all the years I was bringing up you boys. No fine ladies came to help me." He lifted the lid from the heavy iron pot standing on the table, as though it had slipped his mind what he had put in it. "The potatoes can go on when the meat's half done. I've told you. I've told Sam. You boys do as you think best."

"Best, Pa. What's best?"

"Best. Do what you think best. Don't plain words mean anything to you with all your learning? Do what's right. Can you understand that?"

"There is no right and wrong in...."

"If you think that, why didn't you go straight over to Beth's? Go on. Get over there. You always did play up to her."

"Just for the children, Pa." The plea was desperate and useless.

"Ah. That's the excuse for everything these days. That was the excuse for taking away my living. I built it all up myself. Nobody 'elped me. Never chased women. Never spent my money in the ale 'ouse. Always put a little away so not to be a burden on my children or live to see the inside of a poor'ouse again. And why? Just for my children, that's why. I know all about 'elping children. And what's 'appened? My own son's wife 'as turned against me, just to get in that Lucy Simpkins' good books. She's trying to turn Charles, you know, and the children. She's over there, 'oping you'll all leave me and go over. Looking all innocent she'll be, 'oping to see you all leave me on me own. Well, looks as though she'll…"

The old man was not arguing, John realised. He never had argued. He just stated his beliefs over and over like a creed and there was as much chance of converting him as of turning the vicar to Rome.

"Like it or not, I'm going over there first, Pa."

"Take those new farthings I've put by for the children. Don't expect she'll let them come to see me, son. Don't think too badly of me. It's all Beth's doing, she can't deny that."

Beth did not deny it was her decision to abide by the Committee's conditions which had caused the split with Edward. She could not deny it and that was why she had convinced Charles, to ease her conscience, to take the children to visit their grandfather and why she had persuaded him, to ease his guilt, that she wanted to visit the cottage in the wood to see what jobs had still to be done before they moved in there in a week or two.

"It really doesn't seem like Christmas!" Although there was no one beside her and no one in the house as she locked the door, Beth spoke out loud. Often, lately, since Will and Sarah had moved to live with their daughter, Amy, she had found herself acting her mother's part and saying things her mother used to say for all of them.

Without any urgency, Beth walked along the street. Many houses were deserted, but the shouting and singing confirmed that families were gathered together in those houses where candles and rushes were burning brightly, lit extravagantly early to provide a glow to pierce the dark winter ahead.

Through the panes of Edward's window she could recognise the shadows cast on the wall. They were all sitting around the fire.

"Christmas is for families," Beth said softly.

At the top of the village, where the path to the wood left the street, Beth hesitated. Was it worth going now? Already darkness was spreading across the sky and there would hardly be time to start anything, let alone finish it. The damp air chilled Beth's cheeks and clung to the curls around her face. Ahead, the droplets of moisture fused into a soft mist, but, as she stepped forward, its edge dissolved and it retreated to hang always at a distance. Now she had come this far, she might as well go on. The path was open, wide enough for the waggons which had brought timber from the wood to the canal in the busy days of' the war. There would still be enough light for her to see her way back, even in an hour or two.

The fields had lain in silence, but the wood, when Beth reached it, echoed with the brisk pit-pat of droplets of moisture dripping from the branches to the dead, brittle leaves. The noise imitated the sound of people moving unseen before her, behind her, now to the right and now to the left. She must have become a brilliant actress to have persuaded Charles that she wanted to come here today, or any day.

It had been a sensible decision to move here, into the shepherd's house. This way he would have strong, young people to lift and carry him and to free him from the dull misery of the poorhouse infirmary and they would never again have to set aside the greater part of the harvest money for rent before they could buy clothes and boots for the winter. No one could argue it was not a sensible idea,

Off, on a narrower path, the cottage was shrouded in mist. Winter had drained the scene of all colour. In the low, cloud-covered sky, the bare trees, the mud walls and the faded thatch, there was no tinge of green or blue. Only thin grey and dull brown were to be seen anywhere.

From inside the house, as Beth opened the door, the musty smell of decay, which was dispersed on the air in the wood, rose concentrated to taint each breath she took. Her feet slipped on the green-tinted surface of the brick floor. Since the shepherd was attacked, the house had been empty.

Turning back to open the door, Beth found she had not closed it. Against the deep silence of the house, the pit-pat from the trees was comforting.

The pile of logs by the hearth made Beth smile. Each neat layer and each square edge spoke of Charles's carefulness and pride in the smallest task. They were set there to dry, ready to fire the oven. He always drew her attention, whenever they came, to the oven beside the open fire, reminding her how often she had longed to have just such a one.

That was a quick job she could do, blacking the grate. As soon as she had finished, she could go home and she would have an answer for Charles when he inquired what she had done. Absorbed in the thought, Beth reached out her hand and opened the oven door. A mouse flashed along her hand and forearm, plopped to the ground and disappeared. It was gone almost before she had realised it was there, but she leaped away. Shivering, she rubbed her fingers along her arm to rid her skin of the brush of fur and the scratch of tiny claws she could still feel upon it. A fluttering in the grate made her stiff with fear. She was breathing rapidly and trembling and the door seemed so far away. She looked and listened tensely, fearing what she might see or hear. Then, grabbing her skirts, she ran and ran through the open door and into the wood. Leaning against a tree, she sobbed and sobbed as though her heart would break.

For a while, Beth could not have stopped weeping, even if she had tried, but when this desperation passed, she let herself cry until she had no more tears. Weeping was the only way to shed a little of her burden of loneliness. Everyone seemed to be against her.

At last, with the corner of her cloak, she dried her eyes and turned to look all around, at the wood and the path and the cottage. It was as colourless, as miserable and as lonely as her own life had become. She had known nothing would be the same after they had found out that Billy was deaf, but she had never thought that, bit by bit, her family and her old life would be taken from her. What would the next year bring? She could not see more than a few weeks ahead any more than she could see more than a few yards into the mist. For the present, she had no more choice in what she did, than she had had at each turn in the path. There was only one decision to make. Billy must come first.

Beth walked back to the cottage and, with the tips of her fingers, pushed open the door. She glanced back into the wood and then again into the cottage. It was as though, somewhere, someone, something stood watching, watching and waiting.

"There's nothing there. Look. It's just your imagination." This time Beth spoke not her mother's words, but the words she had so often used to her own daughter. Did Frances think her hard and cruel? She had always thought her own mother hard, but perhaps Sarah had kept to herself the doubts and guilt she felt, just as she, herself, was doing now. If she was to send Billy to school, she would need all the hardness and strength her mother seemed to possess.

Hardness and strength? If there was a nest of mice in the oven she had not the heart to light the fire and kill them and she had not a stout enough heart to take them out. At last, with her skirts pulled up, she took careful step after careful step back to the oven and, with a long stick, slowly pushed the door open, ready to flee at the first sight or sound of movement. There was nothing there. She must learn from that and face the future again, without fear.

CHAPTER FORTY TWO

Spring did come at last to the wood and it would have been a soulless person whose spirit did not sing to see the morning sun shining in shafts of light straight from heaven and to share the spring warmth with the bright green ferns unfurling above the dead leaves. Charles had borrowed a handcart and, with Sam's help, after Beth and Frances had padded it with anything soft which came to hand, lifted Paul Low into it and taken him to see the first lambs. After such a long time, he had been reluctant to go, but once out he had been touched by the warmth of the welcome he had received and had visited old friends and stopped at every corner and been taken up the hill to see the view and pronounce on the health of the sheep and the state of the grass. The hours passed all too quickly and it was getting late.

Frances, waiting for her mother and father's return, covered Tim with her cloak. As the sun set, the last of the winter storms had blown up, chilling everything inside and outside the cottage. Tim had fallen asleep an hour ago and Billy looked close to following his example. They had played all day with Henry in the wood and had had more fun than when grown-ups were there to remind them that this was the Sabbath. Henry had left not long since, calling his goodbyes long after he was out of sight and whistling to keep up his own spirits and frighten off the evil ones who lurked among the trees.

Leaning across the table, Frances lifted her mother's shawl from the back of the chair and, pulling William close to her, she wrapped the shawl around them both. Together they peered through the small panes into the wood. Winter was trying to regain its hold. Against a sky already losing its light, the trees leaned submissively to each gust of wind, to fall back shuddering as it passed. The ferns seemed to have curled back to give way once again to last autumn's dry, dead leaves swirling from gully to hollow and back again.

Frances released her hold on William's shoulder and tapped him so that he looked at her. "Dead," she mouthed, pointing to the brittle leaves and making the sign of the cross and the sign they used for sleep. William looked puzzled, searching for the connection between the leaves whirling through the air and the dead rabbits and rats they found in the fields. Leaves were not meant to run and breathe and eat and drink, so how could they die?

As the wind eased, Frances thought she could hear Henry still calling in the distance. Perhaps, if she prayed hard, it would be her parents returning with Mr Low and Sam. She hated being without them in the cottage once it was dark and it soon would be. The noises came closer. They did not sound like human voices, more like shrieking, wailing spirits in hell. She looked from right to left, back and forth trying to find an explanation before she was swallowed up in the terror around them, but the screams and shouts seemed to move, disembodied on the wind.

There, right close to the house, she glimpsed something moving. Suddenly her fear gave way to anger. It was Tommy Donkins and two of those Braithwaites.

"The horrible, coarse, loudmouth toads," she said, borrowing Jem's words.

Billy was content to sign, "Bad."

The boys rushed from the wood and pressed against the window. Letting their mouths hang open, as though stupid, they pressed even closer to the panes and pointed in at William. "Dummy," they taunted. "Billy's a dummy."

Hurriedly, Frances pulled William back from the window into the shadows of the room and lifted her hands to her ears and closed her eyes to blot out the cruel faces and the cruel words, but, as she did so, she caught a new, chilling cry.

"The skinny cat's dead. The skinny cat's dead."

Held above the dark shadows at the window, in Tommy Donkins' hand, was a limp, dangling body. Frances thought her heart would stop beating. It could not be. It could not be. God would never let such a thing happen.

Suddenly there was disorder among the besiegers. Jigging about, the boys had knocked into a water butt and found themselves enmeshed in the horde of gnats which hummed around it.

"They're all up my nose."

"They're getting in my mouth. And my ears."

"Serve you right," Frances said under her breath as she saw them beating the air around their heads and heard them spitting the insects from their mouths.

"Come on," Tommy urged the rest of the gang. "Let's get going. These gnats is eating me alive."

With their victims silent and out of sight in the dark room, no one offered any protest. Content with a last kick at the locked door, screaming and wailing, they disappeared back along the path into the wood.

Signalling Billy to stay where he was, Frances moved to the window. Before the house, in the middle of the path, barely perceptible in the dusk, was a patch of something darker than the bare earth. Still and motionless, without the vigour of life, the form did not match the sleek firm lines of Nelson or Runty. Frances breathed again. Tommy Donkins and his friends had a stupid idea of what was funny. It was probably just a rabbit skin they had round in the wood.

To be on the safe side, Frances signed again to Billy to stay where he was, before she tugged back the bolts on the door and stepped out into the gloom. Leaving the door just a little ajar, for a swift retreat, she made her feet move towards the small, dark shape. It was something dead, she sensed that, and she hated dead bodies, so familiar and lifelike and yet so strange and lifeless. The fur was black.

"Please God, please, please God, let it be that black rabbit that Pa saw."

It was not the black rabbit. It was Runty and he was dead. His back legs were torn and twisted and his fur matted with blood. Frances sobbed. He looked so lonely, lying there on the ground. He must have suffered alone in the trap for so long. Kneeling down, Frances tentatively reached out towards the cat, wanting to give him comfort, but dreading the feel of death.

William's hand on her shoulder made her leap up. He was not crying.

"How?" he signed.

Searching in her mind for the occasions when they had seen traps, she remembered the time when Uncle Sam had taken them to see one to warn them to be careful. Traps of all kinds were set in the woods, not only for poachers, but for poachers' dogs and any stray animal which might disturb the young game. Putting her wrists together, Frances bent her fingers and then snapped them together. From his expression, she could see that Billy understood and could remember too. She was relieved he did not cry and when he indicated that he would stay and bury it, she went into the cottage. Perhaps, she thought, he was like so many boys, fascinated by anything dead and mouldering. If it had been Nelson, she would have cried and cried for days. As it was, she could not stop crying now.

The click of the latch jerked Frances awake. Her mother came in and her father and Sam followed, carrying Paul Low. They were smiling and laughing and still relishing the day's pleasures.

"We'll do it again before long," Charles told the shepherd. "Where's the ale, Charles?"

"We haven't any but you've had enough already, Sam. Sit down and sleep it off."

Elizabeth looked at Tim sleeping and then said, "Sorry we were longer than we meant to be, my love. I'll tell you all about it in a minute. Has Billy gone to bed already?"

"His cat's dead," Frances burst out, so relieved to see them return. "He's burying it, Ma." They got the whole story out of her and hurried outside. The shepherd looked old again, drained of all spirit and colour.

"Wait till I find young Donkins. I'll skin him alive," Sam promised.

A few minutes later, Beth came back into the cottage.

"He's nowhere to be found, Frances. Where did he go?"

"Look at this," Charles called from outside.

There, behind the cottage, was a hump of freshly disturbed earth and on it a cross of twigs bound together with grass. The spade was back in its place, but there was no sight or sound of Billy.

"Billy," Sam yelled so it echoed around the trees.

"He can't hear you, Sam." It was so easy to forget.

A search through the house and in the woods showed only that Charles's heaviest stick was missing, the one he used when his leg ached at its worst.

"Did he think the boys killed it?" her father asked Frances.

"No, Pa. I told Billy it was a trap."

At once Sam remembered what he had done as a boy, what many a boy would do.

"I sprang an old trap with a stick to show him how they could bite into your flesh. He'll be going around trying to find all the traps and spring them."

"Come on, Sam." Charles opened the door. "Don't you come, Beth. We don't want to have to worry about you, too."

"You stay with her, Charles." Sam pushed his brother aside and dismissed his protestations with a shake of his head. "I know every trap Jacob Rush has ever set. I can reach them before Billy and I know how to keep out of sight. If you get caught, it's goodbye to Billy's schooling and goodbye to your whole family."

"It'll be worse if you're caught. It'll be….."

"But I won't be caught. I can move faster and I know the ground like the back of my hand." Sam pushed Charles aside. "I know where to look," he said, sounding reassuringly calm. "We'll be back safe and sound in no time. Have the kettle boiling."

Beth and Charles stood looking at each other.

"He's had too much ale, Beth. He never touches a drop when he goes out at night."

Hesitating, Beth weighed up the chances of her husband's getting caught or hindering Sam. "Go the other way, then, Charles. Cover the other side. That'll be the best thing to do."

CHAPTER FORTY THREE

Running the first part of the way, Sam made for the road. As a warning, he had once shown Billy how the traps were set close to the roads to catch dogs which wandered in and disturbed the game. It was too light and the moon too bright. Billy would not know how to keep from standing against the sky as he crossed ridges and open ground. That might be a blessing. It depended on who saw him first.

When Sam came to the first trap, its jaws closed tight, he knew he had been right. At once he hurried quickly and silently to the next. Knowing where it was set, he had a good chance of gaining on the boy, who had to search in the undergrowth.

The fresh night air made Sam drowsy after all the ale he had drunk. He prayed it would wear off soon. Suddenly, he could not think why he had been so confident to Charles and Beth. That had been the ale speaking. A deaf boy and a half drunk man. What a pair! Sporting man that he was, he would not like to give odds on that combination.

There Billy was, just a hundred yards ahead. Forgetting yet again that the boy could not hear him, he hooted like an owl to attract his attention. Billy kept going forward across the field. He would risk it, Sam decided, and run across the space. If anyone could see or hear him, he would already have seen or heard Billy so there was nothing to lose. At least this way, he would reach the boy and hide him out of sight more quickly.

In a minute Sam had caught up. He threw the boy to the ground.

"It's me. It's your Uncle Sam." he whispered, in an effort to stop Billy's kicking and biting.

Forcibly, his hands clasping the child's head like a vice, Sam turned Billy's eyes to look at him. The struggling stopped and earnestly Billy demonstrated to his uncle what he had been trying to do, what he had to do.

Losing no time, Sam shook his head and acted how he would smack Billy if he went on. Billy was still and Sam relaxed his hold and looked towards the road. In a second, Billy was up and would have been away if Sam had not grabbed his ankle and pinned him down again. A smacking was no good, Sam could see that. Waving his hands before Billy's eyes to get his attention, he made as though picking up and loading a gun and then fired. Billy stared at him.

"He thinks I'm threatening to shoot him," Sam thought. "He'll never have heard of spring guns that rip the stomach out of anyone who puts his foot on one."

Patiently, Sam mimed the setting of a trap and then went through the pantomime of firing the gun, this time at himself. Surprisingly, Billy laughed and repeated the actions himself. His face as he pressed the imaginary trigger was stern and full of hate.

"He thinks I'm promising to shoot Jacob Rush," Sam smiled, shaking Billy's hand. "We'll sort that out later."

Signalling to Billy to stay very still, Sam looked around and listened. He could feel his own heart beating so hard that, in the silence, it was as though he could hear it. There was no other sound. Slowly, showing Billy how to move low to the ground, Sam guided him from tree to tree, from bush to bush, listening, always listening.

With the road and safety in sight, Sam stood straight against a tree and pulled Billy close into its trunk beside him, ready for the short dash to the hard mud lane. Silence and then the clear, hard chime of eight o'clock from a watch held in someone's hand. Rush had a watch like that. He never tired of showing it off in the ale house. You could make it strike the hours to tell the time in the dark.

So the gamekeeper was just a little way away and standing in the shadows. If he had been in the open he could have seen the time by moonlight. And he had not seen or heard them, or he would not be bothering with the time. For a moment, Sam thought of pushing Billy in the direction of the road and then running at full speed in the opposite direction to lead Rush away, but he could not be sure that Billy would understand and there might be another man nearby, anyway. Touching Billy's shoulder softly, so that he did not startle him, Sam lifted him under one arm and took the few steps to a thick clump of bushes. They would be safe there, all night, if necessary.

Billy let himself be dragged through the brambles and eased into the small space beneath the canopy of leaves and thorns. Realising the boy could no longer see him, Sam put his hand across his mouth and then, releasing it, held the child's arm to keep him still and give him comfort. Not far away the gamekeeper stirred. He had heard a sound and was listening, not being sure what it was,

Twenty, thirty minutes must have passed. The gamekeeper moved, stretching his numbed limbs and making himself more comfortable. Sam, almost unable to stifle a sigh of relief, snatched the opportunity of moving his leg. It was lifeless and he had to lean a little forward and move it with his hands. The tingling and pricking in it made him wince, but, as quickly as he could, his movements still drowned by Jacob Rush's own, he took hold of Billy around the waist to ease him into a new position while they had the chance. Half asleep, thinking it was time to move off, Billy stood up, the cracking twigs beneath his feet sounding clearly for yards. In a second, Sam had pulled him back to the ground.

There was silence, then the sharp, controlled click of a safety catch released from its position. Very slowly, very carefully, with only the muted sounds of cloth brushing against leaves and boots scraping over earth, Jacob Rush was crawling forward. Sam was immobilized by the realisation of his own stupidity. Just a second's thoughtlessness, a split second's lack of concentration and there was no undoing it.

Pushing Billy firmly to fix him to the spot where he sat, Sam stood up and moved forward, parting the overhanging brambles before him.

"Good evening, Squire," he smiled, walking towards the gamekeeper and away from the bushes.

Jacob Rush stopped. He was clearly afraid this was some sort of ambush. Not taking his eyes off Sam, but listening all the time for any movement from behind, he called his dog to flush out anyone who might still be hiding ready to spring from the bushes. The dog's excited whining told him he had been right and, unwilling to see the animal killed by a desperate man who might be hiding armed with a knife, he called it back and pointed his rifle into the bush.

"For God's sake, no," Sam shouted, rushing forward. "It's a boy. My nephew, Billy."

"Stand still." The gamekeeper had Sam and the bush in front of the rifle now. "Call him out."

"He's deaf. He can't hear me."

Rush thought for a minute. He could not believe, he just could not believe his luck. Nothing was going to rob him of this.

"Go over there slowly and bring him out. I'll shoot you both if' I have to."

In a minute, Sam stood with William beside him. The gamekeeper's laughter rang out strangely in the night against the rustling leaves and the distant hooting of an owl, but he was determined to enjoy this moment and fix it in his mind forever.

"The poacher and his apprentice — a master poacher and his apprentice." Confident, at last, that there was no trap, he lowered his gun, but kept alert. He either did not hear Sam's attempt to explain or did not want to know. "How long is it, Sam Stevenson? How many sleepless nights have I given up for this? By God, it was worth every one. He who laughs last....! You forgot that when you were making a laughing stock of me, didn't you?"

"And how long is it since you were my age, Jacob Rush? I could knock you down in a second."

"I'd shoot you first." The gamekeeper raised his gun again.

"Me? An unarmed man? There'd be a riot. You'd be murdered in your bed."

"And if you attacked me you'd be hung as you deserve."

"If it wasn't for the boy you'd never have caught me."

"But I did, Sam Stevenson, I did. Where's your nets?"

"I've no nets, Mr Rush." Sam's tone was reasonable and one he had never used to a gamekeeper before. "There, that'll prove I'm telling the truth."

"Whether you were poaching or not is no concern of mine. You're on Sir Philip's land at night and that's good enough for me."

"No jury will convict."

"The one Sir Philip chooses will. Let's be on our way."

Sam led Billy by the hand, the gamekeeper's gun a few feet from their backs. If Billy was charged, even if they refused to convict, there would be no school for him after this. Sam stood still.

"Let me turn round. I'll offer you a bargain."

Jacob Rush said nothing. He was offering no deals, but he let Sam turn round.

"It's me you've been after. I'm your prize. Let the boy go. Don't even say he was here. I'll admit I was poaching."

"Admit what's known for fifty miles around. Now, if you were to show me where you've hidden the nets and the booty, that would be another matter."

"I've got no nets."

"A good try, Sam Stevenson. I let the boy go and he gets the nets from where you've hidden them and you plead your innocence with that friendly, open look of yours." He poked the gun at Sam, careful to keep it out of reach. "Go on." he told them and Sam turned and walked forward with Billy copying him.

By the time they had reached the gamekeeper's cottage, walking to a chorus of barking from the row of kennels beside it, Rush had thought things over. The triumph of the capture was fading. His mind was on a conviction.

"Let's see if you're telling the truth. I'll let the boy go if you admit to having nets with you."

"It'll be transportation."

"You criminals are regular lawyers, aren't you? If New South Wales's going to be good enough for Richard Hammond, it's good enough for you." As Sam weighed up the offer, he added, "Come on. It's only a matter of time before you get caught again and, this way, the boy goes free."

"Do we shake on it?" Sam asked.

"Fetch them nets we found hidden in the wood the other night," Jacob Rush told his wife, giving his son the gun to keep Sam covered.

"Take the nets in your hand," the gamekeeper ordered Sam when his wife returned. "Do you admit they're your nets and you were poaching on Sir Philip's land?"

"They're my nets and I was poaching."

"Take the boy home," Rush told his wife. "We'll take Sam up to the Big House before anyone tries to rescue him. They can do what they like with him. It'll be nothing to do with me, once I pass him on."

CHAPTER FORTY FOUR

Every one had risen in unquestioning respect as the judge, gathering his scarlet gown around him, had walked in majestic solemnity from the small courtroom to be escorted to his lodging, where he might dine and sleep the sleep of the righteous. This was the time of day which John and his family had come to dread, when they were hustled and jostled by strangers pressing around them. Mercifully, today, the voices and faces were dulled and obscured by their need to comfort and be comforted and to weep for Sam.

Elizabeth, Tim at her skirts, cried on Charles's shoulder and he, the shyest of men, lost in their common sorrow, wept too. Next to them, Frances clung to her grandfather, feeling, with no word from him, that his was the greatest loss, the deepest sorrow.

"That'll be the father — the little old man."

"Is that the one who's deaf and dumb?"

"That's the boy who's an idiot."

Today they were all deaf to the remarks and blind to the stares. John, who had come, in the last weeks, to take over the leadership of the family, made an effort to guide them across the street out of the path of carts and carriages, which forced their way along as though this were just an ordinary day.

"Where are the people from Abingfield?" he asked.

Each day a small crowd had walked the two miles from Abingfield, some to watch sullenly and some to shout abuse at witnesses and judge alike. They said that Jacob Rush slept with his gun at his side and walked the woods at night in fear of his life. Knowing the verdict was due, Sir Philip would have thought of a way to keep everybody at home. Farmers would have been encouraged to take on extra hands and ladies to dispense food and drink to those who collected it personally. For once, Sir Philip had done them a favour. Any trouble, any drunken villagers — or sober ones for that matter — damaging property would put off respectable townspeople from signing a petition. The only hope, now, was a petition.

"Come on, Pa. There's Mr. Elham." It was Mark Elham John had turned to as the only man he knew to guide them through the maze of courts and the law. Obediently, the old man roused himself and made as though to elbow his way through the crowd, but did no more. He had seen Sam as the judge spoke the sentence. Sam, the one who had always had a smile for him when he came home, the one who had never kept him at arm's length as Charles and John had done as lads, the one whose smile and cheerful, "Sorry, Pa," had usually stayed his hand, the one whose disobedience and even defiance he could always excuse. There had been no smile, no defiance from Sam as the judge spoke. The lad had stood there, leaning on the rail for support, too ill to care what happened to him. That stinking prison was to blame. Half the prisoners had been sick and lying in their filth when Sam had been locked up.

"Just a shadow of himself, the lad is," Edward put his thoughts into words, addressing no one in particular. Turning to look at him, John was startled by the contrast between the man he saw before him and the image of a father who lived in a child's memories in his head. It was hardly believable that this shrivelled, tired, old man was the stern giant of a father whose words he had obeyed in fear. How had it been possible that the bullying and discipline of the army had once seemed a hundred times gentler to him than the tyranny of this man. 'Just a shadow of himself.' That was what the old man was, too. No man could feel his own helplessness more than a man with no power to help his own son.

John reached out and, touching his father's elbow, supported him. Perhaps they could not put it into words as he, himself could, but John could see that, in their bewilderment and behind their tears, his father and brother felt the same frustration, anger and helplessness he was feeling.

The sentence had been inevitable — seven years transportation. The judge's expression had been stern, showing the assembled spectators that he was not a man to shirk his duty.

"I see no cause to extend to you the leniency which I might have been tempted to extend to a man of previous good character who had lapsed but once. You are, there can be no doubt, a confirmed bad character and a notorious poacher, who has repeatedly defied the law and the brave, conscientious gamekeepers who struggle against such odds to bring evil men to justice. In imposing the full severity of the law upon you, I show my admiration for those men, like Mr Rush and Sir Philip Hammond who do not stint of their time and money to bring criminals of your type before me.

"In your refusal to show repentance by naming your fellow conspirators, I see evidence of the depravity and depredation to which you have sunk. It is nothing to your credit to plead that you do not carry a gun. In a young criminal of your strength and recklessness, bare fists must surely be classed as fatal weapons.

"Your only redeeming feature is that you do not put forward in your defence the lame and fanciful story that you were not poaching, but searching for a dumb child. Let me warn others that, were there an ounce of truth in the story, I would have expected to see the child standing before me in the dock. Let me also warn those who try to arouse the sympathy of the ignorant and gullible with such tales, that they will find that the English Judiciary does not quake and waver before the mob.

"I am here to enforce the law, which you have mocked too long, and to teach you a lesson, which may be taken to heart by any other man who mocks the laws which protect property. Let poor, simple men who lend an ear to radicals and let atheists, who claim that private property is evil, take note and be warned.

The sanctity of private property underpins our English constitution. It brings stability and gives hope to every poor man in this kingdom that, by hard work and thrift, he may eventually come to possess a small share of the wealth which God has bestowed on this land. Were I to show leniency now, I would be failing in my duty, not simply to every landowner and gentleman in England, but to every poor man who has a pig and a chicken or two scratching in his back yard.

"Seven years transportation and the county — indeed, the country — are well rid of you, Samuel Stevenson."

Charlotte looked at the forlorn group on the pavement in front of the court. It seemed wrong to stare at people forced to display their private grief in such a public place. Already, the Hammonds and the gentry from Abingfleld had been whisked away in their carriages, surrounded and protected from prying eyes and from abuse by their servants, but the Stevensons stood together like a little pile of leaves swept up and dropped by a gale. Charlotte's heart went out to them, to each of them equally. These past days had given her a chance to test her resolve and her feelings and they had stood the test. From her seat at the back of the court room, she had been able, in quite a detached manner, many times to study the back of John Stevenson's head. Quite dispassionately, she had been able to trace how his dark hair, glistening in the bright sunlight, curled gently on his collar and to notice, when he bent his head forward, how the hairs seemed even darker in the nape of his neck, a neck more delicate and sensitive than the red, bull neck of so many men. From making these observations, she had been able to look at the back of Charles's head and then at the sweep's, without any more or less emotion than she felt when looking at John's.

It was natural, Charlotte went on to tell herself, that she should feel hesitant and even awkward as she moved slowly through the crowd towards the family. It was to be expected that she would have to search for words, to rehearse her speech as she approached them, for no words would be adequate to give comfort in such an extreme situation. Forcing herself forward, Charlotte expressed her sympathy briefly to John and the men and took more time to speak to the women. Beth and Becky were scarcely able to reply, but Mrs Dodds drew her a little aside and thanked her for her concern and for her brother's work on Sam's behalf.

"At least something good has come out of this," Sarah concluded. "It's brought John and Becky even closer. I'd always prayed that I'd live to see those two married and now, I'm sure, the day's not far off."

Charlotte saw no reason to linger. There was so much to do in the shop, with Mark's having been so busy helping Sam. So that was why Becky had sat close to John and why he had comforted her when she had leaned towards him, sobbing. Charlotte had noted it several times, but it was no concern of hers.

At last Mark Elham finished talking with other lawyers and pushed his way through to the family. He spoke encouragingly and John, in repeating his words to the others, copied the smile and the tone.

"Mr Elham says there's hope of a petition. He says there's strong feeling amongst the townspeople against landlords and farmers."

No one smiled back at John. The idea was, in reality, as foolish and pointless as all the wild plans the family had brooded over to rescue Sam by sending Henry over the roof tops or overpowering the guards.

"Let's talk to Sam. Give him a word of hope," Charles said. "Ill as he is, he'll see little enough to live for today."

They made their way through the thinning crowd to the heavy door of the gaol. Two militiamen, called in case of trouble, stood guard. They listened stiffly to attention, but spoke in tones of coaxing reasonableness. "Now we don't want no trouble, do we? You're sensible folk, I'm sure. We've orders there's to be no visiting today and orders is orders. Tomorrow, perhaps, or the next day, when things are calmer." As John pushed forward, the guard spoke more strictly. "I don't give the orders, but I am here to carry them out."

The other guard took over the role of friendly ally. "Go round the back lane and have a quick word. We can't let you in here if we wanted to. Them doors are bolted and barred from the inside. That's to stop anyone who's thinking of making trouble."

Obediently, doing everything with Sam's good in mind, the family made its way around the side of the courthouse and along an alley of timber houses with overhanging jetties closing in above them. A few yards along, a grille in the pavement let a little fresh air into the prison and a little of the foul air out. As their footsteps sounded on the stones, hands reached up through the bars and voices begged for mercy or for money. The sickening smell turned their stomachs so that the women hung back until the men had bent down and persuaded those in position at the grille to give way and call Sam.

John found himself looking into the haunted, excited eyes of a madman, who clung to the bars, refusing to make way. The man's knuckles wrapped tightly around the bars as he pulled himself up from the pit in which he was imprisoned and whispered," Are you the Christ?"

"Is Sam Stevenson there?" Looking past the man into the dark cell, John managed to avoid his eyes. From among the people sitting, sleeping or just staring into space, Sam was staggering up.

"Please let him through," John begged the man. "He's had the fever. He's weak."

"It's me," the man whispered more loudly, his eyes blazing. "It's me." His voice dropped again. "John the Baptist. I'm John the Baptist."

"Move over, you fool," Edward told him. He could see Sam, giddy on his feet, too weak to push the man aside. Suddenly and viciously, the old man kicked at the hands on the rails until they opened and the man dropped, whining and protesting, to the floor.

John and Charles reached their arms through the bars and pulled Sam up as close as they could. They talked hopefully, encouragingly of the petition and Sam tried to smile and listen, but he seemed past caring what happened to him. As they prepared to leave and let him rest as best he could among the crowded bodies on the filthy floor, Edward tried to press a few pence into Sam's hand to give to the keeper for food.

"Take it back!" Sam begged, too ill to be burdened with the worry of guarding the money. "It'll be stolen the minute I close my eyes."

John took the money back and, as they turned to go, threw a penny to the mad man. At the movement of his hand, a dozen bundles of rags scattered about the floor came to life and hurled themselves to the place where the coin clinked to rest on the ground.

Without a word, for each knew what the others were suffering, Edward and his sons began to walk on the road to Abingfield.

"Who's there? Who is it?" The voice of the man in uniform was tentative, pleading.

"Watch there's no one coming up behind or round the side. That's what the Colonel told us to look out for," warned a second guard. His shortness of breath and the jerkiness of his speech showed that his comrade's nervousness had added to his own.

Before Charles could answer, John moved up quickly. "Don't do anything silly," he called. "It's the Stevensons. Edward, Charles and me, John. There's Beth and the children here."

"Oh, my God." The guard who had challenged them snatched clumsily at the musket which was slipping from his sweaty, shaking hands.

"Don't do anything silly," John urged again. "I've known you all my life David Round and you know me."

"Put your arms up in the air, John." The guard's panicking mind struggled to remember the Colonel's instructions. The use of the Christian name brought a touch of normality and released a little of the tension. "We want no trouble. We're only doing our duty."

With his hands in the air, John stood and faced the guards. "Can't people walk to their own homes, nowadays?"

"There's been threats, signed by Gentleman Jack. Say they'll kill the Colonel and Sir Philip and Jacob Rush in their beds. Slit their throats from ear to ear."

"It's nothing to do with us."

"It's all been worse since Sam was took away." Suddenly the guards remembered Sam. "What happened today? Heard they'd give the sentence."

"Transportation for seven years."

"We'll never see him again," Beth cried and the children sobbed at her side. It was the sight of the old sweep, of the hard, unsentimental old man crying which affected the guards most.

"I'm sorry, you know that," David Round said, letting his musket rest on the ground. "Bess'll be sorry when I tell her, I know."

"He had a good run for his money," the second guard added, attempting to cheer them. "We told him, everybody told him, that Rush was bound to catch him at it one day."

"My Sam was too smart for that one," Edward answered, his anger stopping his tears. "Sam never took a drop of ale before he went poaching. They sent 'im out when 'e should never 'ave gone. That woman it was." He pointed his finger at Beth.

The orders, snapped by a voice right beside them, stopped any reply from Charles and sent the guards searching on the ground for their weapons.

"Pick up those guns. Have you searched them? Are they alone?" As David Round seemed about to search in the bushes the Colonel clucked impatiently, "There is no need to search now. I have been searching and listening to your idle gossip." Smugly, he turned to John. "If you had expected some other reception, you will be disappointed, I'm afraid. You'll have to cross the Channel to find an audience for sedition, Stevenson. Ah, my apologies, I should call you Gentleman Jack! English men have too much good sense. Openness and fair play is what they value. I left most of them not ten minutes ago at the fancy, cheering on their man and arguing who should be next to test his skill. That's what your average Englishman is concerned with, challenging a champion to a fair fight, not challenging the government and magistrates."

Beth, knowing this story would be recounted to all the gentry with whom the Colonel dined and who would have to vote for Billy, told him, "We'll be on our way, sir. The children are tired."

"You," the Colonel indicated Beth, "and the children go on. The old man too, but you, John Stevenson, we'll search you. Search him, Walker."

"What right have you ...?"

"John, don't make trouble, please. Don't throw away all Sam's going through for Billy's schooling," Beth pleaded.

"A sensible woman," the Colonel nodded approvingly. "If all women were as sensible, they would calm their hot-headed menfolk."

Reluctantly, John let himself be searched by Walker.

Once in the cottage, there was no talk of sleep. Over and over, they told Paul Low all that had happened, how Sam had looked and what he must be feeling. It was only when they paused, at last, that the shepherd told his news. "Beth, better tell you now than in the morning. Better get all the bad news over in one day. There's to be no school for Billy." His gentle voice could barely be heard. "Miss Gray called today. She said the Committee couldn't support Billy's election. They say there's more deserving cases from honest, respectable families. It's to make an example of Sam and let people see that poaching doesn't pay."

CHAPTER FORTY FIVE

"Is she there again?" Charlotte asked as Mary drew back the curtains and the early morning light fell in neat squares of yellow on the bed cover.

"She's there." The servant's tone indicated that there had never been any doubt in her mind that Becky would be standing in the street below, waiting, as she had been for some days, for Mr Elham to return with news of the petition. "Why they send her, I don't know." As usual Mary was free with her opinions. "She looks so pale and sickly to me."

"The men cannot take time from work to wait about," Charlotte reasoned aloud. "Becky has no work and responsibilities and is the obvious one to send."

"Thought she worked at the vicarage."

"Becky did, until recently." About to go on to explain, "No doubt she has given up work to prepare for her marriage to John Stevenson," Charlotte stopped. The words had formed on her lips, but that part of her mind which had returned to Sarah Dodd's statement time and again, as though to find a flaw in it, warned her that telling others would give it a finality she could not yet accept.

"Give her tea and something to eat," she instructed the servant. Hearing the calmness in her own voice and the generosity of the thought restored Charlotte's faith in her own rationality, which she seemed to come close to losing each night as she lay awake at the mercy of her unhappiness.

"I'll just pop out with something for her, then. Your tray's there, Miss Elham."

At the moment the bedroom door closed, Charlotte hurried across to the window. She saw Becky greet Mary with just a wisp of a smile and then, shaking her head, thank the servant for her concern. She did look very pale, as though she, too, found it hard to sleep at night.

Always forgetting the niceties of training at the least excitement, Mary bounded up the stairs and flung open the door to face her mistress, by now seated at the small table beside the bed and greatly occupied with replacing a cup on the tray.

"If you ask me," the servant blurted out, "it's the old story. There's a baby on the way, that's why she was dismissed."

The set expression on her mistress's face warned Mary of a reprimand to come and she waited patiently for it. If Miss Elham was not interested in her news, cook would be.

"Mary," Charlotte said, speaking slowly and deliberately, "I have told you before that there is to be no gossip under this roof. Now take the tray and return to your work. I have a good deal to do today myself."

Not waiting to be told twice, Mary grabbed the tray, eager to pass on her opinion in the kitchen. The food on the tray was untouched.

Few sounds pierced the intensity with which Charlotte studied her brother's accounts that morning, but the sound of her brother's carriage at the door brought her instantly to her feet and she rushed to the window. John Stevenson was with her brother and, her back to the house, Becky was already questioning them. Suddenly, without warning, Becky fainted.

Very gently, John picked her up and, at Mark's insistence, carried her into the house. Somehow, Charlotte forced herself to go into the room and offer her help. John was kneeling beside Becky, his hand holding hers and Becky, her eyes not moving from John's face, took in every word he said.

Mark, having assured Charlotte that there was nothing she could do, told her the petition had failed and suggested that they should leave the two alone together until the other Stevensons arrived to visit Sam for the last time before he was moved from Gressingford gaol.

A short while later, Mary, returning to report the arrival of Edward and the rest of the family, found Charlotte in her room, her head on her hands weeping and unable to stop.

"Ooh, Miss." Mary, unsure whether to pretend not to notice or point out that the entries in the ledger were being smudged by tears, stood by helplessly.

"That poor young man sent away from his family and friends," Charlotte managed to say, trying in vain to wipe away the signs of her crying.

Approaching the prison, John, as gently and unobtrusively as he could, tried to tidy the old sweep, attempting to tuck his grubby shirt into his breeches.

"Leave me alone. Sam never minded 'ow I looked. 'E's the only one I bother about." He pushed John aside, showing in his refusal to conform to their standards, the contempt he felt for his son and Mark Elham for their uselessness and empty words.

The prison gate opened and Mark came out. They all knew, from the way he looked at the ground as he walked towards them, that something was wrong. "Is he worse?" John asked, meaning, "Has the fever killed him?"

"He's much better, I'm told," Mark replied without hesitation, relieved to find his news might have been even worse than it was.

His words gave John a clue to what had happened. "You were told? You mean he isn't there?"

Before Mark told them about Sam, he looked around at the groups of men hanging about, ready to join in any trouble which might be sparked off by the family's protests.

"Please, go home quietly when I have told you what I have to say. The military is standing by and will be called at the first sign of unrest."

"What 'ave you got to say?" the sweep demanded aggressively.

"To avoid any disturbance, they moved Sam several hours ago."

"You promised," Edward shouted. "Don't tell me you didn't know something like this was going to 'appen."

John tried to restrain him, "Mr Elham has done all he can."

"What 'as 'e done? Tell me that. Nothink. 'E' ain't done nothink for us."

"I'm afraid there is truth in what you say," Mark agreed sadly. "I've achieved very little."

"Where have they taken Sam?" John asked.

"To Portsmouth, I understand, to the hulks to await transportation." With the resignation of people who know their protests achieve nothing, the family turned away to return to Abingfield. John was relieved to find that his father did not shrug off the hand he placed on his elbow to guide him. From the glint in Edward's eyes, he imagined that the old man was lost, for the moment, in cursing Sam's oppressors in silence. Only when they were through the crowd, did Edward offer any resistance to the pressure that John was exerting on his arm. Then he slowed his footsteps, lengthening the distance between them and the rest of the family. Shrugging his arm free, he felt in his ragged coat and thrust something into John's hand.

"No. Don't look at it now." The old man darted glances all around to make sure they were not being watched. "Keep it out of sight."

In the second John had glanced down, he had glimpsed a leather bag and, from the feel of it, guessed that he held a bag of coins.

"It's Sam's money," Edward whispered.

"Sam's money?" To John's knowledge Sam had never saved a penny in his life.

"From his poaching. There was always plenty ready to buy, even though no one come forward to 'elp 'im."

"He saved some?"

"In't that what I'm saying?" In his disappointment and grief, the old man was tired and irritable. "Well," he admitted, "Sam didn't never save on 'is own account. I made 'im give me some to put by for 'im and I took anything 'e left lying about in 'is pockets. That amounted to a pretty penny. I ain't saying 'e wouldn't 'ave 'ad a good deal more if 'e 'adn't wasted it on ale and wenches, but it comes to a fair bit to see 'im through."

"It'll certainly buy him extra food and better treatment. It's Mr Elham, you realise, Pa, who'll know best how to get this money to him."

"If it 'as to be, it 'as to be, but you see it gets to Sam some'ow."

CHAPTER FORTY SIX

It was surprising, Charlotte considered, how many tasks could be completed quite successfully while one's mind was several miles away. Throughout her childhood, it had been impressed upon her that concentration and application were essential in all things, yet her eyes and fingers were working deftly together, while her thoughts wondered beyond her control.

Always strictly honest and in the habit of considering questions from all sides, Charlotte corrected herself. It was true that concentration was sometimes essential. It was essential for writing letters, making up accounts, reading and all those tasks to which she could no longer settle and which she had avoided over the past weeks. How many times had she found herself staring at the paper on the desk and realised she had no idea how to finish the sentence or no idea of the total of the column she had added? About as many times, she supposed, as she had read the same paragraph of a book without grasping its meaning.

"Miss Elham," Mary blurted out as she exploded into the room, "it's John Stevenson just arrived."

Scarcely able to believe the real subject of her thoughts had arrived without her being aware of it, Charlotte forgot to feign indifference. "For me?"

"No, Miss Elham. For the master."

All through the trial, ever since John had asked Mark for help and advice, the two men had met away from the house. It would be best, now, Charlotte decided, if she left the house, but she did not move. The life of busying herself with everyday matters, the life of small events which passed the time, the life which she had so carefully constructed for herself had begun to collapse when they had called John in to care for Becky, but she could not bring herself to go out now. She was terrified of being swamped by the loneliness she knew waited for her beneath the ritual of everyday things, but she could not walk away from the house while John was there.

In the next hour, Charlotte walked from study to kitchen, from drawing room to garden, making herself carry on as though this were any other morning. The only indulgence she allowed herself was to stop in the hall, each time she passed through, and listen to the hum of voices below the strident tick-tock of the hall clock. The words were blurred, but she could make out John's voice as he talked earnestly to her brother. 'Tempus fugit' the clock face proclaimed, but the hands seemed barely to move.

Even having waited so long, Charlotte was startled by the click of the door and disturbed by the sounds of footsteps approaching through the hall. The door opened and Mark came in.

"Have you a moment to speak to John?"

"He wishes to speak to me?"

"I suggested he did, Charlotte. He has a request to make."

Aware that John was just outside the door and could hear all they said, Charlotte murmured her agreement.

"How are you, Miss Elham? I hope you're in good health."

Carefully and deliberately, Charlotte matched her silk, holding the strands to the light as she replied and said that she hoped he would not mind if she continued with her task. Nothing he said, she determined, would make her reveal her feelings.

"First, Miss Elham, I'd like to say I regret my behaviour at the fight more than I can ever express. And, Miss Elham, if ever I have shown anything but the deepest respect for you, I apologise most deeply."

Charlotte wanted to say, "Your behaviour does not concern me," but it was not true and she was not quite sure what the second part of the apology was for. "You had a request to ask of me, Mr Stevenson?"

"Yes, it's Billy. The Committee will not support him at the school."

"I knew nothing of this. You want me to speak to them?"

"Once Mr Gray has made up his mind, there'll be no changing it. No, Miss Elham, I wondered if you could write to your friends and find out how we could help Billy ourselves."

"I'll write at once."

"Beth will be so grateful. We all will, Miss Elham."

Now it was settled, John sat down, although he had declined to earlier. As he turned to her, he looked so tired.

"It seems an eternity since Sam went looking for Billy," he began. Charlotte stood up. A long conversation which might lead to his plans for marrying Becky was something she did not seek. She had something to busy herself with now.

"I'll write to the school at once."

Wearily, but accepting that Charlotte did not wish to renew their friendship, John left.

As Mary closed the door behind the visitor, Charlotte was already at her needlework again. She needed the calming discipline of an occupation before she wrote her letter.

"What did you say?" Mark asked, as he returned to the room. When Charlotte told him, he commented, "I knew you would agree." Intently, he watched his sister's every expression and movement.

"You did care for him, didn't you Charlotte? And you still care."

For a moment, Charlotte seemed about to deny she even knew what her brother was talking about, but she looked at him and questioned him, in turn. "Was it — is it — so obvious?"

There was no point in protesting. As she had talked with John she had realised all the acting and denials had amounted to nothing. She did love him and always would.

"Then I must tell you, Charlotte, he was not dismissed just for his behaviour at the fight — although that was enough for Mr Wright. He was dismissed for his behaviour towards you."

"Towards me?" Her anger flared immediately. "What concern was that of Mr Wright? John has always behaved as well, if not better, than any gentleman." Preparing to take the brunt of her anger, Mark went on to tell her about the sweep's words, his own concern and his talk with Mr Wright. "I am so truly sorry, Charlotte."

For a moment, Charlotte's delight at being given a reason why John had not called on her after his dismissal made her forget about Becky, but the memory rushed back.

"He's to marry Becky."

"Did he tell you so?"

"There was no need. Mary guessed Becky was having a baby and Mrs Dodds told me they would marry."

"I'm sure she hopes they will." Sighing, Mark sat by his sister. "I can't agree that it is a right and proper thing for him to do, Charlotte, for John to allow, even encourage people to think it is his baby."

Her expression of amazement told her brother that Charlotte had believed it was.

"They thought no one would help Sam if they knew the truth. Sam and Becky planned to marry in the summer. It would not be the first baby to arrive just after the wedding."

"But are they to be married, John and Becky?" Charlotte's tone revealed her desperation.

"Perhaps. I am sure that is what Mrs Dodds intends and the others will not be sorry. There is little chance of Sam's ever returning and the child will have a father."

"The family may think it will be best, but what does John think?"

"He is fond of the girl, I believe. I sense that he does not want to marry her, but he may let himself be pushed into it as the honourable thing to do for his brother and his brother's child. Where else is the girl to go? Walking over to his sister, Mark comforted her.

"We must just wait for him to decide, Charlotte, but, whatever he does, I shall try to help him. He has become so angry and bitter, he might well join Tom Hutchinson and the other hot-heads."

Shaking out the crumpled cloth, Charlotte attempted to resume her embroidery, but the bright colours and slender threads were blurred by her tears so that her needle would not go where she intended.

"I'll have to unpick it," she sobbed. "What a tangled mess it all is!"

CHAPTER FORTY SEVEN

Several times, John had protested that he had already eaten and that, at this late hour, he had not expected anything more, but Sarah Dodds insisted on giving him ale and bread and cheese. She was willing to give him, whether he wished it or not, everything she had set aside for herself for the next day and she did it because he was a man who needed his strength to work and not because she wanted him to ask Becky to marry him. Such a marriage, she considered, was his duty to his brother and Becky and to the child not yet born and, while she prayed for it every long, sleepless night, she left a man's duty to his conscience. She was not a woman who had ever schemed or flattered to get her daughters married. John had been a long time in coming to see Becky, but now he was here, she, a woman of strong conscience herself, was sure he would do what was right.

"Don't dwell too much on Sam when you speak to her, John," she advised him. "She's cried her heart out over the past weeks, but time will heal. What's past can't be undone, but we must all put it behind us and think of that poor, innocent child."

As Becky came into the room, Sarah quietly left. John, disturbed to see how ill Becky looked, realised how alone she was and what a burden she would have to face without a husband. He stood, trying to frame the words to ask her to marry him. Suddenly, for the first time since Sam's capture in the woods, she laughed. John told himself that, if he married her, there would be many good and happy days. She had been so happy and lively and would be again.

"What's funny, Becky?"

"You, wondering what to say. Even now, you haven't made up your mind, have you, John? If you're going to let Ma and duty push you into marrying me?"

As though to prove her right, John hesitated in replying. Becky looked at him. When he was not there, she could convince herself that marrying him was for the best and that they would be as happy as any other couple. Perhaps it might have been true at one time, but now she knew she loved Sam.

"Don't think I haven't thought about it, John, especially for the baby's sake. I know how marrying you would take a great weight off my shoulders.

I'd have someone to lean on and be free of the staring and gossiping and the fingers pointing at me. But what if Sam ever came back? I'd wait for him for ever, John, let alone seven years."

"How will you manage, Becky? Where will you live?" When it came to it, he could not try to persuade her to marry him. Her words had come as an inestimable relief.

Perhaps I would have let Ma push me into marriage yesterday, but Miss Elham calling gave me time to think again." Becky watched John, wondering if he had asked Miss Elham to help her as he had asked for help for Billy. It was obvious from his expression that he knew nothing about it.

"She asked me to work for her, living in and having the baby with me, when it's born. Said I needed time to think and not rush into things I might regret later. She said people could make mistakes when they were upset and when there seemed no future to look forward to."

Still watching John closely, Becky went on, "Beth thought at one time that you and Miss Elham were quite taken with each other."

"So did I."

"What happened?"

"Nothing happened. The world stayed as it was and Mr Wright reminded me of my place in it."

"And that was that?" Becky asked. John was certainly not Sam.

"Mr Wright reminded me that I would be living off her money. I could never do that, Becky. No man with any pride could do that. Anyway, one look at Pa and the rest of us at close quarters and that seemed to have been enough for her." After a second, he added, "Did she mention me when she called?"

"No." Becky was back to thinking about Sam. "You should have seen Sam's imitation of your Pa."

"He was always Pa's favourite. Pa's not the same man now Sam's gone."

"His Pa didn't know him very well, did he?"

"Pa doesn't know any of us very well."

"None of you know Sam really," Becky persisted. "You all talk of him as though he was still a child. You always talk as though it would have been better if it had been you or even Charles, as though you would have been able to manage better putting up with all Sam's had to face. You forget he chose to look for Billy. He decided what he would do to make them let Billy go free. Sam's a man, not a boy."

John smiled and heard himself saying, "Then he'll be well settled in when you get to New South Wales."

Becky dare not let herself believe what she was hearing.

"Could I go, John? I used to plan, when Sam was first sentenced, how I'd do something wrong and get sent there, too. But it would break Ma's heart and there's the baby to think of."

Plans formed in John's mind as he spoke and all he said was as new to him as it was to Becky. "Pa has some money. That will give you a start. You can work your passage out there. Perhaps Charles and Beth will go too. Perhaps me as well. There's nothing for any of us here. We'll work it all out Becky, you'll see."

Sarah must have been nearby for, when Becky sang for joy and hugged and kissed John, she hurried in, smiling.

"It's all settled, then?"

"Not quite how you wanted it, Ma, but it is settled. John, I could almost marry you."

"And I could almost ask you."

Sarah sat down. Perhaps they would explain it in their own good time, before she and Will returned to Amy's. She was not going to ask. She had had enough shocks in the last few months to last a life time.

CHAPTER FORTY EIGHT

"So now we're all here," Tom Hutchinson began, rising from his chair to see and be seen by those gathered in the Stevenson's parlour. "Let's get started." In the dimly lit room, his shadow stretched huge against the wall, making Frances stand closer to her Pa. It was just how she had imagined it on dark, howling nights with the Devil coming for their souls. Perhaps Grandma Dodds was right and Tom Hutchinson was about the Devil's work.

Against the meeting from the very beginning, Sarah was not going to let Tom rush the men along to some folly, which might lead God only knew where.

"Will and Edward are the heads of this household, Tom Hutchinson."

"Not this time," Will told them. "It's the young men's turn now, unless Edward wants his say first."

Absentmindedly, Edward shook his head. So often now he seemed lost in the past. "It won't bring back Sam — any of it."

"Then John must decide," Sarah suggested and, as usual, her suggestion had the force of law. "He's led us through these terrible times so far, and done as much as any man could."

"John?" Tom queried, hoping he too would stand down.

Keeping his seat, John looked around and began to speak. At last Frances dropped the hand that had been trying to ease the tightness in her chest. Her breath came more easily. Uncle John would not do Satan's work.

"Sarah's right," John told them. "It takes a shock like Sam's trial and sentence to make a family realise how much each one of us loves and cares for every other one, man, woman or child. God knows, we have our differences," he nodded to his father and they laughed, "but we're a family and that's our strength, not to be thrown away lightly. Tom, here, wants us to join him and the Captain. Like Sarah suggests, all the menfolk join, or none does."

There was warm and total approval of his words.

"So, Tom, here's the chance you've been waiting for, but you've got every man, and his family, to convince."

The dark shadow rose, looming over them. Frances slipped onto her father's lap and was comforted as he smoothed her long hair from her face, to let it fall neatly across her shoulders.

"You know, all of you have seen what's happening in Abingfield. Each week less work. Each week lower wages. Each day greater poverty and suffering. You don't need telling this story, you're living it. There was Will losing his farm. Then Will and Charles — and John— losing their work and looking for a daily job here, there and everywhere. Living hand to mouth it's called, and you all know what it means. Then, the bitterest blow of all, Sam sent to the ends of the earth for trying to help Billy. God alone knows if we'll ever see him again."

Leaning forward, John patted his father's hand while Henry pushed a grubby, well worn rag into the other. The old man sobbed noisily.

"Who will be next? Who will stop the suffering? Not the gentry. They'll give no work. They just take work from the old man and Henry. They won't even help a deaf and dumb child. In the old days, perhaps, there were ties of duty between them and us, but no more. You owe them nothing."

Nobody attempted to deny the truth of what Tom said.

"So," John asked, to make it clear to the others, "what are you suggesting as the remedy, Tom?"

"A vote for every man. Power, that's the key. Where does power lie? In Parliament. How did Will lose his farm? Because Parliament voted an Enclosure Act for Abingfield, paid for by the likes of Will. How did Sam come to be sent to New South Wales? Parliament voted in Game Laws, transporting a man for netting a few birds put on this earth by God for all men."

Taking his time to win them to his way of thinking, Tom paused, letting his words sink in. Then he followed them up. "If we had the vote, we could put it all right. Whoever voted for poverty, for starvation or for suffering?"

"And how do we persuade them to give us a vote?" John asked, for the benefit of the others. He had heard this from Tom many times before.

"We march to London, to Parliament itself. Then, if we've no success, we march to the King. There'll be thousands upon thousands of men. There'll be no work done until they give us the vote."

"A peaceful march?" John asked.

"Peaceful," Tom answered. At heart he was an honest man and added, "If they send soldiers, then we shall defend ourselves."

"Ah!" John murmured. His own views were clear in his mind, but he put the points one by one to the others.

"A vote for every man. Will. Charles. Paul. What are your views?"

It was accepted that the women could, as on any other family matter, try to persuade the men to their point of view before leaving them to make the final decisions.

Sarah put her view first. "If the Braithwaites and the Donkins of this world have a vote a man, let's leave things as they are. The Hammonds and the gentry are born and bred to this work. Who knows what the Braithwaites and the Donkins would vote for. Free ale? They'd sell their votes to the first offer of a shilling. No, leave things as they are — or as they used to be when Will and me were young."

"Will?"

"I'll decide when I've heard all the arguments."

"Charles?"

"I don't know. Yes, by God I do. I'd know how to use my vote to feed my family and help my son."

"Paul?"

Seeing the shepherd struggling to sit up, Sarah hurried over and made him comfortable.

"Thank you Sarah. Thank you all for asking me. I'm not a Stevenson or a Dodds— well, no more than a second cousin of Will's — but you've been mother, father, sisters, brothers and children to me ..." As he spoke, the shepherd's voice broke with the strength of his feelings and his love for them. As one, they assured him he was one of the family — all his days.

Recovering himself, he moved on to the question he had been asked. "It's easy to forget we were young men once. We asked ourselves these questions once before. The French and their uprising, remember? All these ideas were in the air then. Some of us thought long and hard about them until that Napoleon marched his armies against us."

Looking around, Paul, always diffident about imposing his views on others, saw they all wanted to share his conclusions. "I read a great deal in those days. Caring for sheep's that sort of job. Half the time it's panic and not knowing how to fit everything in the day. Then it's days with time and peace to read and consider what you've read. There was one thing I read I came to know so well I recited it over and over again. The words had a ring — they seemed to travel on the breeze and echo across the hills."

Raising himself slightly from his chair, as though once again whole and well, sitting beside his sheep on Hangar Hill, Paul recalled the words, "'or really, I think that the poorest he that is in England hath a life to live, as the greatest he. And, therefore truly, sir, I think it clear, that every man that is to live under a government ought first, by his own consent, to put himself under that government.'"

Its light now flaring, now dying, the candle spluttered, reaching the greasy surface of its holder. Softly, Sarah rose to light another from its wick. It was as though the sun shone in the parlour.

"And you, John?" Paul asked at last. "What do you think?"

"Yes, I agree each man should have a vote," John replied without hesitation.

Glancing at Beth and seeing her nod, Charles said, "And me."

"Aye," Will agreed. There was no point in seeking Sarah's agreement. She would never give it.

"And you, Pa?"

"Our Sam was as good as any man," he muttered.

As Tom smiled, Frances felt the fear she had known when her father had not returned at his usual time when the canal was flooding and the ditches full to the brim. Quickly, she looked to her Uncle John. She was not disappointed.

"But there, Tom, I think you'll find our agreement with you ends. When it comes to trying to win the vote, I stand shoulder to shoulder at meetings. I'll be the first to sign a petition, but I'll not march to London. It will all get out of hand. They'd slaughter us. The innocent will get hurt and who will care for our families when we are dead? I've seen enough of fighting."

"Not if there's enough of us."

"And how will you get poor men to follow you, Tom? They'll not leave the harvest, or the haymaking or the threshing when there's work to be done and money to be made for their families. What use is an army, Tom, that can't gather till the morning milking's over and deserts when the cows' udders are full again in the afternoon?"

"Most of 'em's never bin any further than Gressingford," Edward said suddenly. Everyone saw the point.

Desperately, Tom spoke again. "That quotation of Mr Low's. Those words were spoken two hundred years ago. Unless you join us they'll be just words for another two hundred — two thousand, maybe. Who'll stand up for you, if you don't stand up for yourselves?"

No one answered and he taunted them, "Will you leave it to Mr Elham to sort things out for you? Give him and his friends and a few more of his kind the vote, is that all that's necessary?"

"Perhaps," John agreed, stung by the words, "change will, indeed, come bit by bit."

"God help you all." Controlling stronger language in front of the women, Tom pushed his way across the room. "But remember, God helps only those who help themselves."

"God helps those who put their trust in Him," Sarah called after him.

CHAPTER FORTY NINE

A few minutes later John caught up with Tom and fell into step beside him. "I never seem to settle, now," he explained. "I usually take a walk about this time." Putting his hand on his friend's shoulder, John asked, "No hard feelings?"

"No," Tom answered, trying to hide his disappointment in his hope of still recruiting John. The others would follow if John would join and take on the role of Gentleman Jack. Some thought he was Gentleman Jack. And he could bring in other men, all those who had heard of Sam and his harsh punishment.

"You have to admit," John put it to his friend, "They have the troops, the arms, the power and the money. We have nothing."

"But we do have thousands of men — and a good hard core of trained men."

"Thousands of men! Trained men!" John just did not believe him.

"Swear not to tell. Not to tell your family or a living soul."

"You've got my word," John promised, prepared to hear, what he had so often heard in rumour, that an army of men would march from North, South, East and West to join them in London. It was the stuff of the rumours with which the Colonel scared the gentry into supporting his militia.

"The Captain has a plan. Most men think no further than their own noses, but the Captain looks far ahead. He's cool and calculating — you could say cold and calculating. The Captain asked himself how he could get men to follow him. Their minds are too twisted and distorted by the parson's sermons and the gentry's lies to follow for reason's sake."

Tom saw he had John's attention and smiled in anticipation of his surprise. "What," he asked, "rouses men to passions? What will make them travel across country, putting up with discomfort?"

"You tell me."

As Tom still waited, John thought of a foolish answer to a foolish question. "A horse race? A boxing match?"

"Correct in two." Tom laughed.

"A fight? The fancy?"

"The fancy, John. All the men of Abingfield follow the fancy and those of villages for miles around. The Captain had the idea at the fight."

"Are you serious?"

"Think, John," Tom urged him. "Langford gets more praise for every punch he throws than Wellington ever received for a battle. They go to the barn to see him train, winter and summer, rain or shine. If Langford told them to rise, they'd follow him anywhere."

Silently, John considered the plan. Was it a mad scheme or a brilliantly simple one? Sometimes there was not much difference between the two. A point struck him.

"Are you telling me you'll persuade Langford to lead a rebellion or that you'll let the men think they're following him to a fight in London?"

"Does it matter? The Captain will persuade him to make a speech to work them up. Once we reach London, the trained men will see things go according to plan."

"So, where are the trained men? If just three men walk along the same path, the Colonel's men stop them in case they're going to a meeting."

"Right under the Colonel's nose. The fancy again." Tom stood and laughed. "And the Colonel encourages it. The sport of true Englishmen. Keeps men out of trouble."

Standing still and signalling to Tom to stop too, John tried to get the facts clear in his mind. "You're telling me, when the Colonel's men check the men's movements, they say they're going to watch Langford train. Then they train in arms at the barn and plan the march to London."

"That's about it."

"And when is Langford to lead this march?"

"It won't be long. He's learning his speech that the Captain planned. The Captain says there's enough poverty and starvation for the tinder. All we need is a spark to set that tinder alight. The Captain has a plan he's keeping to himself, but a spark will come — and soon." Facing his friend, he asked, "Are you with us John? We need men like you as a backbone to strengthen the waverers. Langford is no leader. We'll want to get rid of him and take over ourselves."

John looked his friend straight in the eyes.

"You heard of Penrith. When was it? Two years ago. Poor fools were led into rebellion. A few miles and they pined for home. The rest ran at the first sight of the Hussars. The leaders were executed as an example. Others were transported and some still rot in jail. You didn't mention all that to my family, did you, Tom? Don't you think one man transported is enough for any family to bear?"

CHAPTER FIFTY

At the beginning of the working day, forty men or more leaned or sat around the graves in the churchyard, where headstones, wooden head-boards or simple grass mounds stood as the last badges of rank of those lying equal in decay beneath.

Against the great, ancient yew tree, Matt Sharp leaned, his bored hands feeling behind him to its twisted and tortured trunk.

"Just once more especially for you, Joe Braithwaite. We're here to be auctioned. Each labourer looking for work will be auctioned."

Joe's face showed no sign of enlightenment. "With the farmers doing the bidding?"

"Who else?"

"Don't make no sense to me."

"For once, you're not alone in that," Charles told him.

By now, Joe was ready to make another stab at understanding. "So, say I stand up and says, 'I'll do a day's work.' Then a farmer says, 'Right, Joe. I'll give you twenty pence.'"

"You've got a rough idea, Joe," Matt agreed at last. "Only say fifteen pence."

"I ain't working for that. Me and Mary and the little ones can't live on that."

"You don't have to live on it, Joe." A farmer sitting on the churchyard wall walked over and added the little information he had gleaned. "By what us farmers can make out, if you can't live on it, you can go to the overseer and get it made up out of poor relief."

"That sounds alright, then," Joe replied.

"That, Joe," Matt went on, "is why there are so many happy, smiling farmers collected here today."

The farmer defended his kind. "We'll be paying more in taxes."

"But the poor rate taxes will be spread out amongst the tradesmen and the gentry as well. You'll save more than you lose."

"It's just so the landlords can tell us we can afford their high rents," the farmer complained. "You're not the only ones having to tighten your belts."

"'Oo wins, then?" Joe asked, knowing someone usually did.

Patiently, Matt ticked each point he made against his fingers. "First, Joe, the whole idea is to lower wages. A big lad like you going to a farmer's door asking for work might frighten him into giving too much. Here, they can all stick together." He let the tree trunk take more of his weight. "You want to know who gains? Not John Stevenson, here, he's single and they'll not make up his wage. Not Will, here. There's only him and Sarah and they'll get no more."

"I'd not ask for poor relief," Will assured everyone around. "Sooner starve first."

"They depend on that," Matt nodded wisely.

"So do you reckon I gain or lose?" Joe was anxious to know.

"You work it out, Joe. Instead of getting a fair wage for your work to do what you like with, you'll get a wage too low to live on."

"But they'll make it up."

"Only if you can prove you need it for food and drink for the family. They won't dish out your ale money, Joe. It's goodbye to that."

As Matt explained it more and more simply to Joe Braithwaite, Charles and John took the time to pluck the few weeds which had dared to grow around the short, stubby stone on their mother's grave. In contrast with the others, it was carved with no name and embellished with no skull or hour glass. Edward had seen no need to pay the mason to inscribe a name his family knew well enough nor to provide, in a place inhabited only by the dead, superfluous reminders of man's mortality.

Still the labourers and farmers waited, complaining at the delay in starting the day's work. Although he was the overseer of poor relief in the parish, Hugh Armitage was loath to carry out this new duty. It was Simpkins who, while hobnobbing with the gentry and magistrates, had been told of this scheme used in some parts of the country and told to try it out. The Armitages in the churchyard would turn in their graves to hear it.

Impatiently, to get things moving, Simpkins looked around for a hard surface on which to crash his stick for attention. His eyes rested upon an iron grille raised over a grave by the bereaved in the unshakable faith that the iron bars would break asunder on Judgment Day, yet prove immovable by mortal men intent on the premature resurrection of the body. The heavy tap-tap brought silence.

"Shall I begin high or low?" Hugh Armitage appealed to Simpkins. His voice, half prepared to address the crowd, rang out loudly.

"Are we cattle to be auctioned?" Matt Sharp shouted. The remark provoked the grumbling and protests he had intended.

"Start at fifteen pence," Simpkins ordered in a quieter voice.

One labourer pushed forward. "I'll be first, Hugh."

"Are you going to list his good points like a pig at market?" someone called out.

"Leave us some dignity," Will Dodds protested. "If you have to do it, do it like picking men for tug of war. Let the farmers choose men until there's no work left."

"That's the first sensible suggestion I've heard today, Will," Hugh Armitage said gratefully. "To start with, I'll take you, Will."

"And the price — the wage," Simpkins reminded him.

"We'll agree that between us, as we've always done."

To speed things up, Simpkins began choosing his men and offering a shilling and tuppence for the strong and healthy and less for the boys and old men who could be put to lighter or less skilled work.

As men began to leave the churchyard to walk to their work, James Fox walked in, looking more solemn than anyone had ever seen the young man look before. "Where's Simpkins? Is he here? Or Hugh Armitage? Any of the vestry men will do."

"What's up?" Simpkins asked, sensing trouble and knowing the gentry would blame him if anything went wrong with their plan.

"It's Pa," the young man answered. He blurted out, "He's hung himself." The men crowded around the grieving son who had collapsed on the ground. When he could talk again, he screamed, "It was this that did it. He couldn't face being sold for a few pence just cos he was old and ill."

Simpkins swore under his breath. He had known all along the scheme had more holes in it than a sieve, but he had been given no choice.

"Give us a leg up," John Stevenson ordered Matt angrily. He scrambled up onto a large, square tomb, heavy enough to take his weight and stood looking down at the men.

"Right, gentlemen," he shouted. "An auction they wanted and an auction they shall have. Gather closer and make your bids."

There were cheers and jeers from those who pressed forward to join in, leaving those who wished to keep out of trouble sitting on the wall.

"Your attention, gentlemen. I shall name each item, give a brief description and invite your bids. Do not hold back, my friends. There are, for auction today, some prize specimens. As fine a selection of masters as you will find anywhere in the country."

The cheers, which came as the men realised they were to bid for the masters, forced John to pause and raise his hands for silence. The men obeyed at once and more men made their way from the wall to the circle around him. "What have we here, gentlemen? That well-known local farmer, Simpkins, and his job at seven shillings a week. What work will you bid for him? Come, gentlemen, I offer you Simpkins. Have I a bid?"

"Describe the goods," Matt shouted.

"This gentleman reminds me of my duty. What is there to say? A man much esteemed by his betters. A man…"

"You're selling him to us, not the gentry."

"Ah, that is certainly a different matter," John agreed. "You force me to admit this item has deteriorated with time. It used to include a bed in the outhouse and good, square meals morning and evening in the kitchen. Now you take your seven shillings and keep your dirty boots out of the house."

"Isn't there a daughter with this item?" a young man called, grinning.

"Not for marrying to the likes of you. Only a gentleman can bid for Lucy Simpkins."

"Who said anything about marriage? I was thinking of half an hour in the hay loft."

"Send for the Colonel and a few of his men," Simpkins ordered a servant.

"Your bids, gentleman!"

"It's half a wage, so I bid working at half the pace."

"I'll come late, watch the sky all day until it tells me it's time to go home."

A man well hidden in the crowd called, "I'll offer him a bang on the back of the head on a dark night."

"How about a fire in his barn to warm him up a bit?"

"A fair bid, sir. Knocked down to you. Let's hurry gentlemen. By this time in the morning most farmers will be disappearing into the ale house to spend their profits."

"That's enough foolery," Simpkins shouted.

"The gentleman wants me to speed things along. The next item, my friends. Mr Gray and work at Glebe Farm for the customary wage of….." John cupped an ear and listened.

"Seven shillings," the crowd roared.

"The job of jobs, this one. Advice on every aspect of life and conduct thrown in with this bargain."

"Is the advice of any value?" Matt Sharp demanded.

"Thou shalt labour from the cradle to the grave." The familiar exhortations were recalled by men in the crowd.

"Thou shalt not be insolent to your master."

"Thou shalt not take an apple from the orchard."

"Be about your business, Stevenson," the Colonel shouted.

"I've no business to be about."

"He has," Hugh Armitage answered, tugging at John's leg and then helping him down. "I'll set him to work alongside Will."

"My God, you're asking for trouble if ever anyone did," he told John as he dragged him away. "That temper of yours will get you into real trouble one day. There'll be a mark against you in Simpkins' book from now on. You'll put a noose around your own neck, one day. You know there's a rumour that you're Gentleman Jack, or, even, the Captain."

When news of this auction reached the real Captain, he felt he knew how to win John Stevenson to his side. All he had to do was to make the man lose his temper. Once John joined, many others would follow.

CHAPTER FIFTY ONE

At the end of a working day, John sat on the bank, cooling his feet in the canal basin and watching the world go by. As a child, he had often sat here, caught up in the noise and bustle and wondering what lay beyond in the far distance where the barges disappeared. Perhaps, the way things had turned out, he should board one of the barges and go wherever it took him.

"I thought I'd find you here." Spreading out a large, white handkerchief, Mark Elham lowered himself onto it.

"Some news of Sam?" John asked.

"Nothing new. He's in the hulks at Portsmouth, awaiting a ship to New South Wales. His money has been sent to him, but, as I said, it will grow less and less as it passes from hand to hand."

"If that's the way things are done, we have no choice. It was his money. I'm afraid," he confessed, "it's what Sam saved from poaching. That's why I couldn't offer it to you for all your help and expenses."

"The least said about it, the better." After the briefest pause, Mark continued, "I'll come straight to the point, John. From Miss Gray I heard about the auction today. Please don't make trouble for yourself. I'm sure everything can be worked out."

"I lost my temper."

"The auction was inhuman, John, no one is denying that, but you must take care. You know the Colonel has been told that you are Gentleman Jack."

For answer, John dangled his feet in the water, moving them slightly until an ever increasing circle of ripples spread around them.

"Some people have power like that," he commented thoughtfully. "A word and their decisions spread to affect everyone around. You know, Mark," he went on, forgetting his resolve never to become over familiar with the Elhams again, "I used to think — well, take it for granted — that Charles and Will, Sam and I decided our own futures."

Delaying telling John what he had come to say, Mark listened.

"Within our own four walls, with our own kind, perhaps, we can imagine ourselves independent. 'I'll dig the potato patch today.' 'Let's go to the ale house.' 'I'll clean my boots tomorrow, not now.' That's about the extent of it, Mark. Such great decisions in a world of overgrown children. We've no more say in the big world outside than Frances and Billy have in the family. The trial proved that.

"Do you know how I see England in my mind, Mark? Like one vast gentleman's estate, where we can labour all our days. At the centre, just like on Sir Philip's estate, there's a huge maze. That's the law and the courts. Only gentlemen and lawyers know their way through it. Here and there, there's a sign promising fairness and rights, but they're just blind alleys."

"But it can be changed, John. Slowly, perhaps, and gradually."

John turned and faced Mark. "Do you truly believe that?"

"Yes, I do, John. But be patient. Resist any call to violence. You know, better than anyone, that war is a blunt instrument. It destroys the good with the bad."

"How did you learn that?" John demanded, so loudly that Mark was startled.

"How did I learn that?" It seemed a strange question, but the answer was clearly important to John. "From history, I suppose."

Lifting his feet from the water and hugging his knees, John laughed, mocking himself rather than Mark. "You read it in comfort and I have to go off to the wars for years to learn the same lesson."

"How did you learn it, John?" Over the past weeks it had struck Mark more and more how much he had to learn from John, who had seen so much more of the world than he had.

"As Pa would say, I learnt it the hard way," John laughed. The memories of war came, pushing their way into his thoughts.

"How did you learn that lesson?" Mark asked again.

"I think of those days less and less," John said, leading indirectly to his answer. "Then I'll see a broken cart by the roadside or see the dust rising from horses' hooves and the pictures of the battle fields come back as clear as day. Do you know, I couldn't wait to get away to the war? That enthusiasm stayed with me for months. It was all so new and so very different from Abingfield. The older men — the old soldiers, I should say. Some of them weren't much older than me — showed us the ropes. They told us what the army was like, what the officers were like, what foreigners were like. They were our guides in a new world and we took in every word they said as the absolute truth. When they laughed, we laughed. When they jeered, we jeered. When they were pleased, so were we. All we wanted was their admiration. 'He's a good lad.' 'He's as brave as they come.' That was all we wanted to hear."

Mark listened. There was no need to speak.

"It was a bit like Sam saying poaching wasn't stealing. Killing in war wasn't murder. It was winning a victory — showing your bravery and courage. After the battle, there was the joy of being alive. It's only the dead who can't say what they thought of the battle."

Stretching his legs back into the water, John swung them to and fro.

"What happened to change all that?" Mark wanted to know.

"Badajoz." At once, John went on to explain. "Badajoz. It started the same as any other siege — the usual camp a little way from the town, the usual rain and the usual mud. There were all the usual preparations to keep us busy while the artillery bombarded the walls. The noise was deafening, with the ground vibrating under our feet from the thudding. That was comforting in a way. While the cannons were roaring, we weren't needed. It's only when they stop you know it's your turn and your stomach tightens."

With a glance at the darkening sky, John continued, "The assault on the breach was planned for dusk, but then someone decided that the cannons hadn't done a good enough job. It was all off for that night at least. We drew up ready again the next day and waited. That was the moment when part of me seemed to be outside of myself, watching, whispering I might die. It got louder and louder until it was screaming to me to run away. I looked around at my comrades, wondering if they heard the same voices in their heads.

"They were doing ordinary things, saying ordinary things, being just their usual selves. The voice I'd heard quietened. Someone made a joke about the Frenchies. Making them out as stupid gave us confidence and making them out to be animals left us free to slaughter them like cattle. Some grumbled at having to hang around. An officer made a speech telling us he knew we'd be brave lads and win a great victory for our country.

"We chatted about the job ahead. Somehow you felt everything was under control if you rehearsed it in your head. There'd be a climb, then another steep climb over the rubble from the walls. That would be the worst bit, we said, just marching forward in the open while they threw everything they had down on us. But, once inside, we said, we'd give as good as we got."

Recalling that Mark Elham had never seen a rifle fired in anger, let alone been in battle, John asked, "Have you ever heard of the forlorn hope?"

"Yes. They're the volunteers who go in first." Mark laughed, mocking himself. "I read that, too."

"I might have guessed you'd know. Did you know they get an extra ration of bread and rum, but it's the glory they're after? Anyway, we moved up to give them covering fire."

"It was just as we'd thought. Once near the fortress our men had no defence against the fire from the ramparts. The bugle sounded and we went forward. George Jackson was on my right and Dick Murray on my left. In the first step, George went down. I saw him drop. He was clutching a great gaping hole in his chest, his bloody hands against the bare, jagged ribs. Then a cannon ball hit the ground a little ahead. It scythed down a line of men, with Dick Murray on its end. I don't know quite how he died. He was just gone.

"I kept going forward, stumbling, blinded by the earth flung up in my face and stinging my eyes. Musket balls and grape shot whirred like a great wind, but it couldn't blot out the screaming and moaning. Men prayed aloud and called out the names of their womenfolk. It was the only comfort they had in their agony.

"At every explosion, the darkness burst into light. Everywhere there were men flung in the air, their bodies stretched out by the jolting shock, or men sinking to the ground with blood oozing through their fingers. There were bodies — no longer men — with their heads shot off. 'At least,' I remember thinking, 'they can't scream!' There are so many ways of dying in war, Mark, so many ways."

"In the flare of lights, I could see the French on the ramparts. They were goading us on as if we were animals being driven to slaughter. They knew it was slaughter. In the day we had waited for the cannons to do their work, they had filled the breach with every invention of the Devil. There were heavy beams stuck all over with jagged metal. Sword blades and knives embedded in wood. We were marching into a dead end of death."

"As usual, us riflemen were in front. We took a pride in that. We weren't sure what lay ahead. I reached the ditch. It had been flooded by the French, you understand. Bodies floated thick on the water. I recall noticing the colours of the uniforms, some red and a good few green. On all sides there was shouting and commotion. The slope up from the ditch was covered with corpses and the men trying to scale the ladders had to untangle bodies from the rungs. The dead bodies dropped into the water. The wounded tried to cling on. They knew they'd be buried alive beneath the dead in the moat. Their fingers were prised off and they fell screaming into the water."

His expression showing he was reliving every moment, John continued. "I tried to scramble up the bank. The mud was slippery with a surface of blood. 1 couldn't reach the ladders and there was nothing to hold onto. Now and again a pile of bodies began to slither, pushing more dead and wounded before it into the ditch. I was being forced under the water."

As though reminded by the water, John pushed himself back from the canal. "I fought and cursed. I cursed the generals, the French and the wounded. I cursed the dead. I struggled and I stumbled over bodies. Every living man was doing the same. The front ranks couldn't go forward. The rear was still advancing. The living were being crushed together and the only place for the dead and wounded was under our feet."

Coming back to the present, John looked at Mark. "You know, that ditch must have looked like a rat pit. Have you seen the rats scrambling on each others' backs, clawing each other in a frenzy, doing everything to get away from the dogs and certain death?"

In silence, Mark nodded. To him, as well, the battlefield seemed more real than the English countryside around them.

"Some men moved along the bank, sheltering from the French fire behind the dead. Others tried to push back and stop the advance. Amongst it all, group after group rallied and tried to break through. You had to walk over the dead not one step or two, but ten steps, twenty steps — forever, it seemed. All the time, cannon balls and shot rained on us. It was as if they were trying to slaughter those already dead. Any man who did reach the top was bayoneted and slung back. I returned the way I had come across the ditch, trying to take the information back to stop more soldiers coming."

"I was just pulling myself out of the water, when a rifleman gave me a hand. He must have thought I had been wounded and was coming back for attention. A sergeant listened to what I had to tell. 'Get back to the front,' he screamed above the noise. 'Our orders are to go forward. Get back or I'll shoot you myself.'

"My mind burst in fury. I snatched up my rifle and stood up. Then, they told me later, they passed me their loaded rifles one by one as I aimed at the French soldiers on the wall. In the light of the explosions, they fired back at me. Men edged away from me and took cover. When there was no loaded rifle left to shoot, the sergeant said, 'That's enough. You've done enough for one night.' Eight or nine Frenchmen they said I'd killed. It was enough."

"Later, I've no idea how much later, I heard cheering. Another division had broken through. The fortress and town were ours — ours to plunder. That's the spoils of war. If a town holds out, you can plunder and murder to pay for the lives they've taken."

"And you came through without a scratch?"

"There was not a mark on my body."

"But your mind? Your soul?"

"The next day," John told Mark, "every sight was a hundred times more terrible to me than it had ever been before. The screaming and crying always continue on the battlefield, but this time the voices tore at my very soul. There was no joy that I had survived. Something of me had died with each man, English and French, in that God-forsaken spot.

"The next two days were worse, almost, than the battle. Our soldiers took over the town. They committed every crime an army can commit — plunder, rape, arson — anything from drunken brawling to murder. Young, old, women — the English soldiers showed no mercy at Badajoz. All were lost in a kind of madness.

"Do you understand it?" John asked, still trying to find the answer himself. "Revenge, was that it? I could have understood that, although I wanted no part of it. What I'll never understand to my dying day — explain it to me, if you can, Mark — is why they never heard the cries of our own wounded. The injured lay there amongst the dead. They pleaded for help, begging someone to save them, but few heard them."

"I went back to the ditch next day and pulled out those I could save. Men passed by drunk, singing, boasting of what they had done in battle. No one wanted to be last into the town in case they missed some booty or mischief. They just passed by — passed by their own comrades. Even when officers ordered them to help, they cursed and passed by."

"Surely they showed some mercy!"

"None."

"And after Badajoz?"

"Things turned our way, as you know. The end was in sight and that kept me going."

John's chin had been resting on his knees, but he looked intently at Mark. "Do you see, Mark, it makes a nonsense of everything? War destroys the enemy, certainly, but it destroys the innocent too. In the end, it even destroys what you are fighting for. There were no victors at Badajoz, Mark, whatever they say in the books. I was there and I know. There was no victor at Badajoz, except Death."

CHAPTER FIFTY TWO

"John," Mark exclaimed, leaping to his feet, "I forgot my message. Charlotte is expecting us." Groaning, he closed his watch case. "Please agree to come. After supper we'll outline our plans for your opinion."

"I've nothing better to do." Hearing his own words, John laughed and apologised for sounding ungrateful. "I'd enjoy your company, and your conversation." As he spoke, John realised how much he would, indeed, enjoy talking about something other than the weather and the state of the crops and the beasts.

"Excellent."

"I suppose Miss Elham has had a reply about Billy's education."

"Even better than that, John. But wait until we have eaten to hear the plans."

"I'll just have to tell Beth," John said, meaning he would give his family a treat, too, by letting them share out his portion.

In five minutes, the men were heading back to Gressingford. To pass the time, John began to chat about nothing in particular, but Mark did not plan to leave everything of importance until after supper.

"There was something I wanted to say before you meet Charlotte again. I don't want to embarrass you, or, believe me, patronise you, John, but I've learned some lessons lately and there are some matters I have to set right."

It was John's turn to listen with interest.

"You're right, of course, John, all I know is to be found in books. I've never had to find things out the hard way, as you have. I know I talked and talked of equality, but it was all in theory. When it came to the real world, I was as blind as the next man, John. You are intelligent — quite as intelligent as I, I'm sure. You are brave — probably braver than I should prove to be. You are honest, industrious, ..." Memories of the fight in Abingfield made Mark refrain from saying "sober." "I respect how you have led your family through their sorrow over Sam. But, to my shame, all I saw was your lack of breeding and fortune. That has changed, John. I have changed, I hope. You are certainly my equal, John. I have come to see you as my superior in many respects."

Any man would have been flattered by such a speech and, for John, after the humiliation of the auction and hard days in the fields, it was doubly welcome. Smiling at Mark, he began to murmur modestly that he must protest, but Mark had a confession to make.

"It was I who forced Mr Wright to dismiss you, John. I was concerned because everything I heard suggested you wished to marry my sister to better yourself."

"What?" John turned and faced Mark. For a moment Mark thought John's temper would get the better of him once again.

"I can never apologise enough, John. I swear to do all I can to make it up to you."

The moment of anger passed. "To be honest, Mr Wright would have dismissed me for my behaviour at the fight, without a word from you. He did reprimand me for my behaviour to Miss Elham and I am truly sorry for that, Mark." A few seconds of thought and John added. "But even equality would not give me the right to marry without the means to support my wife."

"So you did wish to marry my sister?"

"In my dreams. Even working for Mr Wright I had little prospect of advancement. I realised that some time ago."

"That is what Charlotte and I decided, too."

Interrupting Mark, John asked, "What does your sister think?"

"Let her speak for herself. But she had no part in your dismissal, John. She has only just learned what did happen and why, to her great distress, you did not return to visit us when you left Mr Wright's service."

Looking back, as things fell into place, the explanations of events that he had built up over weeks fell away in seconds. Charlotte did care for him. Everything between them was just as it was before the fight.

Bending down, John picked up a flat stone and, with skill built from long days of practice as a youth, sent it skimming along the surface of the canal. Then, laughing aloud, he flung his hat into the air and caught it with perfect timing.

"Come on," Mark laughed back. "I warn you, Charlotte is a bully and hates food going cold."

Greeting them at the house, Charlotte looked anything but a bully. A glance at John's smiling eyes told her Mark had explained everything and she felt not one twinge of jealousy when he greeted Becky warmly.

Becky explained, "Miss Elham asked me if I minded waiting on you at table, John. I told her the women at Abingfield are used to waiting on the men. It will come as no new task to me."

"Glad to see you know your place, my girl," John told her, kissing her on the cheek.

"Becky is the proverbial treasure," Charlotte commented.

"You've the Grays' hard training to thank for that, Miss Elham."

"And I value her opinion as a friend," Charlotte added, quite truthfully. From their conversations she had learned a great deal about the family. Through the meal, John caught up with all the news in Gressingford, but, as soon as it was over, Charlotte, saying Mark had promised her she could outline their plan, began to tell it to John.

"Perhaps, John, your being dismissed by Mr Wright was not the terrible tragedy it seemed at the time. Where would it have led? To your being skilled and, no doubt, knowledgeable, but, in the eyes of the new laws, unqualified. You were an assistant and that is what you would probably have remained."

"I had thought perhaps I could have found work in one of the colonies or in America, where there are not enough qualified men."

"But we have a better plan — or so it seems to us. Why, we asked ourselves, do you not apprentice yourself to a qualified man and become an apothecary yourself?"

"But ...."

"No buts, John," Becky interrupted, forgetting for the moment to be a silent treasure. She saw this as a chance for the whole family to break from their poverty.

"You're not fourteen," Charlotte told him, "And five years is a long time. But it will pass, John, and then you will be an apothecary with the whole world at your feet."

"Who would take me as an apprentice?"

"Mr Wright."

"Mr Wright?"

"Mr Anthony Wright!"

"Mr Wright's son in London?"

"He has already agreed to take you, John." Mark could not let his sister tell all the good news.

There was a silence until Charlotte managed to convey to her brother that he had agreed to discuss money matters.

"All that's wanted is a premium — he will accept a modest one. And money to keep you for a year or two. As you are responsible and have some experience, Anthony will begin to pay you a small sum after that, as soon as he considers you are useful to him."

"We thought," Mark continued more hesitantly," that you ...."

"Pa's money!" John announced. "He has always put some by for a rainy day. I'll be able to repay him a hundred fold."

"What a wonderful idea!" Charlotte agreed warmly, indicating to Mark not to continue with their offer of a loan.

Suddenly, Becky was not convinced it was a good idea.

"Are you sure, John? Will he have enough? There's the sweep's machine to buy for Charles and my passage to Sam."

"Of course he will, Becky. He was as pleased as punch when I worked for Mr Wright. We always said he was mean, now we can be grateful for it."

"I must complete the day's accounts," Mark announced. "You two go through to the drawing room."

CHAPTER FIFTY THREE

About to sit down, at Charlotte's invitation, John's eye was caught by the doll's house on a small corner table.

"They're beautifully made," he commented, admiring the perfection of the small table with the tiny drawer neatly dovetailed and lined with contrasting wood. The chairs, with their gently curving cabriole legs, with the finest carving on the ball and claw feet, were smaller than his little finger.

Walking over to stand by John, Charlotte told him, "It was made for my grandmother by a cabinet maker who had a workshop nearby. You can see by the style of dress made for the dolls by his wife, as well as by the furniture." Feature by feature, they admired the craftsmanship of the cabinet maker, passing each piece from one to the other. To explain why it was not in its usual place in the attic, Charlotte said, "Frances was playing with it yesterday, when she came to visit Becky. This is how she left it."

"Frances? I had hoped it was you."

"I?"

"Yes. Look."

Carefully, trying not to knock over the miniature furniture in the tiny drawing room with his large hand, John extracted the lady of the house. Her jointed arm was stiffly engaged, in spite of the inconveniently wide hooped skirt, in that of a doll whose clothes and apron clearly proclaimed him to be a servant.

Charlotte laughed, pretending that she had not noticed it before. "Where is the master of the house?"

Leaning over and closing one eye, John peered down the chimney. "She hasn't stuffed him down there."

"He's in the library," Charlotte observed.

"That will be Mark, then. The brother, not the husband. I think Frances intended these other two to be married and sitting in their own drawing room."

"Do you think so?"

"Mmm, that's what Frances intended, I'm sure."

Fingering the tiny silver candlesticks and cutlery, John chose his words carefully. "To a child it would seem so simple. The servant moves into the beautiful house and they all live happily ever after."

"Children in their simplicity see only what is most important. The man and the woman want to be together and that is enough."

"In this isolated little house, in a play world, it might be, but what if there was a row of houses and gossiping neighbours? Can't you hear them? 'How can she demean herself?' 'He married for money, of course.' My goodness," John exclaimed suddenly, holding out in the palm of his hand one of the miniscule hams carved in wood which hung from a tiny hook on the kitchen beams. "Manna from heaven. That must be shared out with all his family who have a claim on him."

"The lady is not rich, but I would say she has enough for them to live simply and comfortably and provide for their relations in time of need."

"No," John said firmly, picking up the male servant doll and holding it in front of his face. "You look an upright man with a proud, honest face. There is hope if you go about it in the right way, I think. Take the lady's hand and ask her to wait patiently for you until you have established yourself and can support a wife."

Turning to Charlotte, John took her hand.

"We're not dolls, are we, guided in what to do by other people? Will you wait for me? Will you wait until I have qualified as an apothecary and then be my wife? Then we'll start afresh, not as the sweep's son and the gentleman's daughter, but as Mr and Mrs Stevenson, the apothecary and his wife."

"Yes, John. Marrying you is all that matters to me in the world." Without directly answering his plea to her to wait for him, Charlotte unceremoniously shoved the servant's head down the chimney. "He deserves that," she said with feeling. "He's allowing pride and convention to come between them."

John showed no sign of laughing or being won round. "It's not just pride or convention, Charlotte. I've watched Beth and Charles lately. It seems all they talk about is money. They argue over every farthing and yet they love each other. How can we plan a life together, when I have nothing to share with you? Share and share alike is how I want our marriage to be, Charlotte, not give and take, with you always giving."

With a kiss, followed by another, Charlotte left the details of when they would marry until another time.

"When did you first realise you loved me?" she asked.

"I don't know that I thought of it like that, at first," John began tentatively. He was inclined to be honest and say that he could not say exactly, but, obviously, Charlotte was setting great store by his answer. He played safe with a light-hearted approach.

"Do you remember Frances with her books? How she could not take her eyes off them and longed to touch them? That's how I felt, too, about you."

"As Frances would say, 'You tell lies.'" Charlotte had to know and repeated her question, "When did you first know you loved me?"

"Have I said I love you?"

Charlotte considered the question "No, John Stevenson, you haven't."

"Then I say it now, my love. I love you. I'll always love you above all others until the day I die."

"And I began to love you the first time you brought Frances into the book shop," Charlotte confided. Looking down, she added, "I thought you would be such a caring father."

Taking Charlotte's hand, John sat down and pulled her down to sit beside him. "If you had been a milkmaid, I would have stolen a kiss long ago. I was afraid to be too bold with a lady."

"And I thought you a courageous hero!"

As he leaned towards her, John paused for a second and picked up her embroidery.

"Let's get rid of that, for a start. With its needles, it's worse than one of Jacob Rush's man traps." He groaned. "There's Mark. Check the accounts quickly and tell him he must go back and do them again."

CHAPTER FIFTY FOUR

"Make me laugh, Frances," Beth said solemnly.

"You'll not want to laugh when you see Pa's face, or Uncle John's — or even Henry's."

Beth hurried across the room and opened the door. "Is he coming?"

"What do you think?" her husband called back.

"The old man wouldn't come?" she persisted. "Can't he see it's best for him to come and live with us here?"

"He wouldn't come." This time John answered.

"Fetch me a stool, Frances," her father told her, but it was Henry who dashed into the cottage, eager to get everyone settled and start discussing what should be done.

"The master won't come of 'is own accord, that's for sure," he declared.

"Children," Beth began, "should be seen and not...."

"'Out of the mouths of babes' in this case," John corrected her.

Like her mother, Beth was not one to shirk saying what she felt had to be said.

"I did tell you, John. Things should never have been allowed to reach this state."

"The old man valued his independence."

"He might be clear one day — his old self — but then his mind rambles. He even asks where Sam is and I haven't the heart to tell him."

"It's his wandering off all on his own that worries me," Charles told them.

"And," Henry added, unable to keep out of anything for long, "'e's telling any Tom, Dick and 'Arry about 'is money. Shows 'em the key to the door and tells 'em there's 'is life savings 'idden under the floor. You've 'eard 'im, 'aven't you Frances?"

Seeing Henry getting away with butting in, Frances ventured her say. "He smells, Uncle John. Not just hot like anyone else, but a real smell."

"What puzzles me, John," Beth wondered, "is why he's getting so thin. He can't be feeding himself properly although I send him something every day."

"'E eats 'is share. 'E don't buy nothing to cook for us now, but 'e eats 'is share of what you send, Beth, and wipes 'is plate clean as a whistle. 'E won't

273

listen when I tells 'im 'e oughter live over 'ere with you."

"He doesn't listen to anyone. Never has done," Beth told the boy. Coming at last to the main reason for this present visit to Edward, Beth asked, "So he wouldn't lend you the premium you need, John, let alone give Charles the money for the sweeping machine and Becky the money to join Sam?"

"No." John, in his disappointment, added no more.

"I suppose I'm not surprised. But he'll have to change his mind." Guiltily, she added, "It's not for me. It's for Charles and the children. That money means so much to us all."

"We'll 'ave to get him over 'ere some'ow," Henry stated, speaking for all of them. If only money hadn't been involved they could all have spoken more openly.

"The boy's right." Beth, less close to Edward, could see the sense of it. "He has to be washed and fed and cared for. God knows, I never really wanted him here, but he's your flesh and blood and we can't leave him to rot over there. There's not much he'll even let Henry do for him now." Pausing, Beth studied their reaction. "And, if he comes, he can't leave the money behind, can he?"

Charles looked at John. He agreed with his wife, but he was not going to do anything unless his brother agreed too. Seemingly, John was engrossed in finding a dry spot on the ground to sit, but then continued to stand.

"Well, John?" Beth demanded impatiently.

"I'm sure Pa has chimney sweep's cancer."

Beth's hand flew to her mouth.

John went on, "I don't think we'll have him with us much longer."

"It's not my fault he's not here." Beth felt she was being accused of something.

After some discussion they decided they must try again to have the old man over for a meal and then make him stay. They all agreed he would soon realise he was better off, but they could not understand why, when everything was decided to save the old man from himself, they felt they were doing something wrong.

No one had thought it would be easy, nothing concerning Edward Stevenson ever had been, but they had not thought it would prove impossible. Old age and Sam's going had made the sweep even more suspicious of others than he had always been. He refused to visit them and threatened that, if they tried to make him move, or even came near him, he would throw himself on the fire or lock himself in and never come out again.

When they were all at their wits' end, the old man provided the solution. It was Henry's habit to wait outside the cottage of an evening and follow Edward on his walk to keep an eye on him. Everyone had heard him boasting about his money and seen the key he held out so tantalisingly. Someone, sooner or later, would try to steal it and Henry wanted to let everyone know the sweep still had a friend and protector.

Leaning on the cottage fence, Henry prodded the ground with angry kicks. If his master had not been so awkward he could have been out with his friends while the old man rested comfortably at Beth's. A group of boys passed, calling to him to join them. Henry pretended not to hear.

From the cottage there were shuffling footsteps and a touch on the latch. Henry knew every move his master would make. The latch would be raised with a clatter and the door flung open to vibrate violently on its hinges. Smiling knowingly, the sweep would glance at him, judging the distance between them and, imagining himself still quick and active, smirk and plan how he would dash back into the cottage if anyone moved towards him.

Henry was more upset by the old man than anyone knew and more than he could explain. All the apprentice wanted to do was look after his master and all the old man thought was that they were all after his money.

Together, the sweep ahead slow with age and the young apprentice trailing miserably behind, they tramped their evening walk. Now and again, Edward looked back and clumsily tossed the key in his hand. The further they walked, the more frequently he stopped and rested, but, if Henry dared to come close or talk to him, the old man shooed him away.

"Go back to your new masters," he shouted. "How much do they pay you to spy on me, or are you after me money for yourself?"

Angry with himself for being such a fool as to care, and angry with his master for destroying all they had shared, Henry kicked viciously at a stone on the path. Dodging awkwardly, Edward shielded his face and cried out as the stone spun by his head. Sobbing, Henry turned away and walked home. Beth was right. There was no helping some people.

An hour later, Eliza's little girl, Fanny, rushed into Charles's cottage. "The old feller's sitting on the doorstep crying 'is eyes out. 'E's lost 'is key, ain't 'e?" Arms folded, she stood in joyful anticipation of the confusion and alarm her news would surely cause. She was not to be disappointed.

"Has he got ladders there?" John asked.

"No. We've some outside. Fetch them, Henry."

"We'd better carry them, Charles. Let the boy rest his arms." Everyone knew, without needing to hear it said, that the cheapest and quickest way into a barricaded house, without doing any damage, was down the chimney. "Be quick. The old man'll go for anyone who tries to help him get in."

"Run ahead, Frances. Tell everyone your father's coming to sort it out. That way, there'll be no more trouble than necessary."

As they hurried into the village, John voiced what they were thinking. "Once we've persuaded Pa to come over here, Henry can go in and have a look around. Then he can nail up the door from the inside, the barricades at the window are already strong enough to keep out the French."

"It's all happened for the best," Beth said.

At the sweep's cottage a small crowd was laughing at the old man, standing defiantly against the door and swearing to break the head of anyone who came near. His appearance so belied his words that there was no alternative to laughing but crying. His shapeless hat, stained with years of grease and soot, was rammed onto his head so that his small, grimy face peered out beneath the brim. Small and thin as he was, his clothes hung loosely about him, his shirt front and jacket splattered with dried food. Children and women giggled as a damp stain spread at the front of his breeches.

"Take him home, Beth."

Confused and shocked, Edward let himself be led away by this woman who seemed to know him and spoke so kindly.

Most of the crowd turned back to their homes, but a few watched as John and Charles placed the ladders against the wall and climbed to the roof. Henry, stripped to the waist and holding his hands up above his head, let John steady him as he climbed into the chimney. He edged further and further down, his fingers clawing at the bricks until he released his hold and supported himself with his feet and elbows braced against the chimney's sides.

Hollowly, Henry's commentary rose to John and Charles perched on the roof. "Know this chimney like the back of me 'and. Another foot or two and I can drop down into the grate. Good job the old feller's too mean to light a fire. Easiest chimbly in Abingfield, this is."

There was a clatter and muffled cursing.

"It wasn't just chimney sweeping Pa taught him."

No one had mentioned the money. That would not have seemed right, but Henry knew what he had to do. At first scanning likely places quickly and then looking more slowly and thoroughly, he searched every inch of the house.

"Whatever's he doing?" John asked. "I wish I could get down there myself." They heard Henry approaching the grate.

"I can't find nothing. Not a shilling, not a penny, not even a button."

"Try under his bed."

"Tell him to look in that old teapot."

The brothers looked through the room in their minds, remembering the places where their father had been standing when they had come home as children to hear him hide something as they entered the door. Five minutes passed and then ten.

"There's nothink 'ere, I tell you," Henry shouted. "Nothink at all."

"We'll have to look ourselves."

"Break down those planks he's nailed to the window, Henry. We'll have to break the window after all."

"There's the spare key I've found," Henry shouted back. "I'll open the door to you."

As the men and Henry searched, Beth was at the cottage washing Edward and wrapping him in a blanket while Frances washed his clothes.

"Sit by the fire, Pa, or you'll catch a chill. I'll get you a cup of tea in a minute, when we've seen to you."

For a while, Edward sat and watched Beth and, as she placed a cup of tea in his hand he touched her arm and looked into her face, his eyes suddenly alert. "Where's my son?"

"They're fetching you your belongings. Don't you fret. They'll be back any minute."

"Fetching me belongings?" He seemed muddled again. "Oh, no," he confided, clutching her arm tightly, "Me son's in New South Wales," he whispered. "'E's doing well for 'imself. 'Ad all me money to set 'imself up, 'e did." Releasing his hold, he sat back and muttered, "John and Charles won't mind. They're good boys, all good boys."

Beth turned to her daughter.

"Go and tell your Pa, Frances, that he's wasting his time. I knew it really all along. Sam never saved a penny in his life. It was the old man's money he had."

Frances ran as fast as her legs would carry her, praying for all she was worth that her mother was wrong.

"Your Ma's right," Charles told her, as he locked the cottage door. "There's not a farthing in there."

"To think I had it in my hand," John told Beth for the hundredth time.

"Would it have made so much difference if we had known? It was all we could do to repay Sam."

It was then that Frances blurted out to her mother, "You can have my money — all the farthings Uncle John gave me for my money box."

Proud of her own generosity, tears in her eyes with the joy of winning such a victory over her own selfishness, Frances had expected hugs and kisses, murmurs of praise and admiration from everybody. There was silence. At last her Uncle John walked over and kissed her on the top of her head.

"Don't you worry, my love. We'll work something out. You're a good girl to offer."

Frances saw her mother wipe a tear from her eye and felt as proud of herself as any child could.

CHAPTER FIFTY FIVE

"You've already spent it, Ma. You spent all the money Uncle John put by for me each Christmas and you didn't ask me. That's stealing. You stole my money."

"I stole it, did I? Don't you eat under this roof along with the rest of us? I had precious little of it. The food went into your mouth, yours and Billy's and Tim's and your Pa's and everyone else who lives here. I didn't touch it until your Pa was out of work after Mr Hammond gave up farming and your Pa wouldn't go to the overseer. Is that what you wanted? Your Pa to swallow his pride and go hat in hand to the parish?"

"You didn't ask me. That's stealing and that's wicked." Helpless against a grownup who had used her power to steal from her, Frances found some consolation. "God knows you took it," she said, in the voice the parson used to strike terror into the hearts of sinners, "and he'll punish you for stealing."

"Was your Ma to see us all go hungry?" Paul asked. He usually kept out of family arguments, but he could not walk away and he could not sit there and hear Beth blamed for something which she had loathed herself for doing and would never have done just for herself."

"Pa brings in money, and Uncle John."

"They didn't when I borrowed your money. God knows I'll pay back every penny if I get the chance. Money does come into this house and it goes out even faster. It isn't enough, Frances, until everyone pays us after the harvest. I'll try and put it back, I promise you I will."

"It was for me. For me to buy books or anything I wanted."

"You can't eat books." Beth's patience snapped at last. "You're not a baby now. Food costs money and that was all the money there was in the house. It's as simple as that, as you'll realise one day for yourself."

"You always said you wanted something special for me when I grew up. You said you wanted me to better myself."

"I wanted a good many things I never have."

"You were only saying it. You never meant it. You don't care about me. It's always 'Billy. Billy. Billy.'"

"You're your father's child, Frances. You grow more like him every day."

"Good. I don't want to be like you, ever."

"Just don't have the Stevenson's pride, that's all."

"I shall," Frances shouted defiantly.

"Well, you can't for a while yet," Beth told her, explaining what she saw as the rules, "First you have to have someone who'll pay for it, like I always pay for your Pa's pride."

"I'll run away."

"That'll be one less mouth to feed."

"You hate me," Frances claimed, convinced at that moment of the absolute truth of what she was saying. "And I....."

"Honour thy father with thy whole heart," Paul told the child, wanting to stop her saying something which she would regret and which would hurt Beth so, "and forget not the sorrows of thy mother; how canst thou recompense them the things that they have done for thee?"

"Thou shalt not steal," Frances declared, staring at her mother and matching quotation with quotation. They were intended as the last words she would ever speak to her mother, as words which would echo in her mother's grieving heart every time she caught sight of the small empty chair and wept for her missing daughter.

Once outside, Frances was less certain what to do. She realised that it was not easy travelling without money and food and she had neither. Uncle John and Miss Elham had gone walking on the heath and, if she found them and told them of her mother's cruelty, Miss Elham might take her in as she had taken in Aunt Becky. After all, she was a victim of misfortune and not, as people said of Aunt Becky, a fallen woman.

It was a long tramp out of the village and across the heath land before she found them. She felt disappointed. Instead of acting as though they had nothing else to do but comfort her, Uncle John was arguing with Mrs Batch, a woman who lived on the heath, and ignored her.

"You don't think they'd tell you the truth do you?" he shouted.

"The gentleman wouldn't lie. 'E told me 'e got Jack's name from the overseer. Said Mr What's-'is-name was sorry 'e 'adn't been able to 'elp us and me being a widow. 'E said Jack was just the kind of boy they wanted to 'elp. Them with no Pa to look after them."

"He never spoke a truer word," John agreed." He wanted lads with no father to see a life in the factories miles from home is no life for a son."

"When did he go?" Charlotte asked. "Jack, I mean."

"It'd be about noon. The man said 'e 'ad a long way to go. They was putting up at an inn. Jack would like that. I've never stayed in an inn in me life."

"The cart will be left in an inn yard, perhaps, and that's where Jack will sleep, if he's lucky."

"But 'e'll get food. The man lodges all the children in a 'ouse and they get their food and clothing and a few pence a week for theirselves."

"And his wages? What about his wages for fourteen hours a day? You and him share those, I suppose with yours paid in advance."

"'Oo better to 'ave a son's wages than 'is mother?"

"Wages?" John shouted at her. "Wages? It's your price for selling him into slavery."

"There's good money to be made in the factories. The man told me."

"Everyone knows, Mrs Batch, that the children are twisted and deformed with the long hours and the hard work. What will Jack do when he is too old for children's work? There will be no future for him then."

"'Is Pa and me worked for a gang master when we was 'is age," Mrs Batch claimed in her defence. "We was often beat with 'is whip and it done us no 'arm"

"At least you were in the fields in the fresh air and the daylight. Jack will be shut in a dark, gloomy factory all the hours of the day. He won't know whether it is summer or winter in there."

"It's nobody's business but mine," Mrs Batch declared and that was her last word.

"The poor," John said, as he gave up arguing and walked away. "To hear some people talk you would think the poor were all long-suffering saints. The poor are much like the rich, but they haven't as much money."

"John," Charlotte chided gently, "you do tend to see all mankind in a poor light."

"I couldn't bear to look at them in a good one."

"What happened?" Frances asked, trying to gain her uncle's attention from Miss Elham and hers from him.

"Nothing much," John told her bitterly. "Just a mother sold her son to the man who goes around the poorhouses buying up children for the factories."

"Is it true?" Frances asked Miss Elham, deciding her uncle was making it up.

"I'm afraid so, Frances. Perhaps," Charlotte pointed out to John, "you are judging her too harshly. The man might have misled her."

"Only if she wanted to be. She's more sense than that. What other woman would do it? Look at Beth. Can you see her letting Frances, Billy or Tim go with a stranger for a few shillings or for a thousand pounds?"

Charlotte and John walked on in silence, their thoughts with Jack, who was only happy in the fields and woods, watching the animals and studying their ways. Frances found that she did not want to tell them her story any more. From the meadows and hedgerow she carefully picked a bunch of flowers, choosing the brightest and most perfect she could find.

When Frances ran home and held out the posy to her, Beth was tempted to comment, "You're soon back," but the serious look on the child's face stopped her. She thanked her and drew her to her side to kiss her cheek. In return Frances threw her arms around her mother's waist and burst out with the terrible news.

"Mrs Batch has sold one of her children to the gang master from the factory."

This was not the time for harsh or clever words to drive the lesson home, Beth knew. Gently, she said, hugging Frances to her, "So we all have something to be grateful for. Thank God things aren't as bad with us as they are for poor Mrs Batch."

"I'm sorry Ma," Frances said and, remembering Mr Low's words, she whispered, "I didn't know you had sorrows, Ma."

Beth could do nothing but laugh and hug her daughter all the more. "Why should you, my love? Mothers don't tell their little girls about sorrows. That shouldn't be little girl's business. All mothers should tell children are the dreams they have for them. Then, if the mothers can't make them come true, the children can dream them for themselves and for their children and theirs."

"I'm truly sorry, Ma. I didn't mind you tak....borrowing my money."

"I did, Frances. I minded a great deal. If there had been any other way, I wouldn't have taken it. Just wait until after the harvest, my pet. That was always a lovely time, my very favourite time of the year. It's the end of one year and the time for turning over in your mind all that has happened, just like them ploughing the fields. Best of all, just as it's time for planning a new crop, it's the time for new dreams."

Bending close over her daughter, Beth whispered, "Do you want to know a secret? I think your Uncle John will marry Miss Elham."

"I know that already," Frances answered. "Even Tim could guess that."

"Oh, dear. I forgot you were such a wise old lady."

"Will she come to New South Wales with us if we go?"

"Why not?" Beth asked, as though all things were possible. "We'll all go. Our ship will come into the harbour and we'll all climb aboard and sail away to a better life."

"Frances," Beth changed the subject suddenly. She had not meant to mention it yet, but she could not make up with her daughter without telling her the whole truth. "Your Pa and me — we've decided it's time you went into service."

"Ma. I don't mind the fields, honest I don't. I don't want to live with anyone else Ma."

"It's no life for a young girl in the fields, Frances. You're old enough to understand that now."

"Where are you sending me?"

"It's in the village, Frances. Mrs Booth, the widow. She's not rich and she's not gentry, but she's comfortably off and respectable. She'll give you a good training."

Frances struggled to bite back her protests. She was truly sorry for upsetting her mother and knew none of this was really her mother's fault.

Beth watched her for a minute. "It's wonderful having a little girl," she confided. "As she grows up it's like having another sister, another friend you can share everything with, good and bad."

CHAPTER FIFTY SIX

Up and down and round, Frances pushed the dusters over the little table in the hall, hands together, hands apart, hands circling inwards and then out, one hand moving up a leg and one down.

"Are you using both hands?" Mrs Booth called from the parlour." God gave you two hands and intended you to use then."

"Yes, ma'am. I'm doing just what you told me." Catching a sound of her new mistress moving quietly to the hall door, Frances set her face in a serious, dedicated expression, placed a duster on each of two table legs and briskly polished them.

Round the door, Mrs Booth looked disbelievingly at her new servant. No child ever did what it was told without being watched and closely supervised. From her pocket she took a spotless white cloth and ran it, pressing heavily, along the top of the door. Silently and primly, she brought it down again to eye level and opened it out for inspection. A black, dusty line seared its pure surface.

Stifling a sigh, for she had been sternly reprimanded for sighing, Frances fetched an old stool from the kitchen and clambered up to dust once again along the door's hidden edge.

"And the door frame, while you're there. A little thought, Frances, a little planning saves so much energy for other tasks." Mrs Booth smiled what was intended as an encouraging smile at the child. "'If a thing's worth doing,' as a wise man said, 'it's worth doing well.'"

"Yes, ma'am." To herself, Frances questioned whether it was worth doing anyway.

Once more in the parlour, Mrs Booth called, "Come in here, Frances. That is enough there for the time being."

"Yes, ma'am."

Mrs Booth gave her a sharp look as she left. The child could make a simple 'Yes, ma'am' sound so insolent. She paused and looked back through the door.

"You must not resent good advice, Frances. How am I to teach you as your parents want, if you will not take advice? Well?"

"It's just, ma'am," Frances burst out, "I can't see why I have to clean the parlour when it'll have to be done all over again when the chimney's been swept."

"You can't see," Mrs Booth echoed the words in disbelief and stared at Frances. "You can't see? You, Frances, are a little girl not yet old enough to question your mistress who keeps you and pays your wages."

"But, ma'am,...."

"No buts, Frances. But. But. The world would come to an end if we all waited for buts. Don't stand there staring. Your ears are still able to hear me when your hands are busy."

As Frances, her two hands moving in unison until her arms ached, dusted the already gleaming furniture, her ears were given a great deal of advice to take in.

"You are to clean the parlour today, Frances, simply because that is to be your work at this time every day. Habit, Frances, good habits are the basis of order. Everything has its time and everything its place."

Frances felt her mistress's stern eye upon her and dare not pause in her task. "Yes, ma'am."

"You may look at me, child, when you speak to me."

"Yes, ma'am." Frances looked up and turned back to her dusting. She was not sure whether it was correct to stop dusting when you looked up or not.

"I'm not one of your idle, foolish mistresses, who were born with wealth and taught to leave everything to idle, foolish servants. Dishonest servants at that. I learned my place before I was your age, Frances, in a good household and, even if I did improve my position, as you may do one day, by marrying a man who had taken care of his money, I still know my place and maintain it. She glanced in the mirror over Frances's head and seemed pleased with what she saw, a neat woman in a prosperous, but not showy, room.

"You are a clever little girl, I'll give you that, and if you learn to do as you are told and accept good advice, one day you may have a comfortable home of your own like this one. You'll thank me, one day, for all I'm teaching you." She paused, "What do you say?"

"Thank you, ma'am."

"That's better. As soon as you've finished, we'll take up all the rugs and I'll lock away all the trinkets."

"Why?" Frances stopped and stared at Mrs Booth, her look conveying not a willingness to learn, but defiance.

"Because, Frances," her mistress explained patiently, "it is wicked to put temptation in the way of poor men. We cannot watch them every moment and the Devil has a loud, insistent voice."

"He's my Pa." Frances's stare was hard and accusing.

"I know what is best, child." Mrs Booth swept from the room. It only encouraged children in their insolence to argue with them.

That was what grownups always said when they were losing an argument. Frances took some consolation from that, but she was still angry about other things. Her mother had not wanted her to live in yet, but Pa had insisted. Uncle John had told her that, one day, he would give her back all the money her Ma had spent out of her box, but you could never believe promises like that.

Here, at Mrs Booth's, Frances read the Bible every night out loud after prayers, but she was never allowed to touch the books except to dust them. They were mouldy old books, anyway. The Bible, commentaries on the Bible, sermons and uplifting thoughts. She was sure there was no thought which could uplift her except going home to her Ma. Even the dusting and scrubbing and sweeping and scouring might be bearable if she could go home to her Ma and Pa when her day's work was done.

Frances' dusters lingered lovingly on the bureau. It was kept locked, but she had caught just a glimpse of the tiny drawers and cubby holes. For a while she dusted the glowing wood, imagining herself sitting there like a lady writing letter upon letter in a fine hand. Perhaps, if she ever did get her money back, she would buy one of her very own.

Without enthusiasm, Frances moved on to the ornaments with all their tiny hollows and dust traps which would be inspected by Mrs Booth at any minute. If Pa had taken over Grandpa Dodds' farm, she might have gone to a finer house with a mistress who had been born a lady, though that might have been every bit as dull as this.

Reaching up to dust the mirror, Frances saw her reflection, her clean white cap covering every strand of hair. She paused, pulling a face at herself, smiling and then, with a glance at the door, poking out her tongue. Pulling herself up on tiptoe, she pursed her lips and flared her nostrils. That was how Mrs Booth looked when she was annoyed, just as though she had a nasty smell under her nose and a nasty taste in her mouth.

"Tut-tut," Frances clicked her tongue briskly, "Tut-tut."

For a few seconds, she stared at her reflection. She was old enough to know why Pa had sent her to this place. It was not just because he thought she would get a good training here, but because Mrs Booth was a widow with no husband and no sons. They did not know she knew everything, but she did. Jem had told her everything, absolutely everything, with nothing left out.

"Whoops." Frances caught the falling ornament. Good job the angels had eyes in the back of their heads just as Mrs Booth had.

When her mistress returned to the room, together they covered the furniture.

"You may greet your Pa when he arrives, Frances, but then busy yourself in another part of the house. Your Pa has his work to do and you have yours. I am paying you both to work, not to chatter."

Demurely, warned not to dirty her clean apron against the sweep's clothes, Frances greeted her father. Then she went back to her dusting, listening from upstairs to the banging and scraping in the chimney until her Pa came to that room and she moved on to another. For a while it took away her loneliness to know that her Pa was under the same roof and thinking of her as she was thinking of him.

"Come and say goodbye to your father, Frances."

Slowly, Frances came downstairs, stretching out time to keep him close by. At the bottom, she made as though to run to him, but Mrs Booth stretched out her hand and caught her.

"Now, now, Frances. You must behave like a young woman now. That apron was clean only a few hours ago."

Her father smiled at her. "Your Ma sends all her love, Frances, and so does Tim. And I know Billy does. We can all see that. Ma says be a good girl and," he added, seeing the tears in her eyes, "don't cry." He looked across at Mrs Booth, but she was smiling the cold, detached smile of a person bringing a meeting to an end.

"Is she a good, obedient girl, Mrs Booth?" Charles asked, prolonging the time he had with his daughter.

"She is young and young people have a great deal to learn, but she has a good teacher, Mr Stevenson. I am forced to say, however, that you sent her to me not a moment too soon. Any later and her big ideas would have grown to such a size that I would have despaired of ever making anything of her."

As she finished speaking, Mrs Booth stepped in front of Frances and began to close the door. The child saw her father blow her a kiss and stand looking at her, just as she was looking at him, until the door closed between them.

Tears streamed down Frances's face and onto her apron. Mrs Booth softened and made no mention of the smears on the white apron or of the child's using the duster to wipe her face.

"Come, Frances," she said quite gently, leading her away with a hand on her shoulder. "You are ten now, remember, and must stop behaving like a child."

CHAPTER FIFTY SEVEN

It had been another evening passed with Charlotte's trying to persuade John that she would willingly give him the money he needed to study with Anthony Wright and with John's listing all the reasons, including his pride and good name, why he could not accept. The fresh evening air did nothing to calm his spirits and, not in the mood to go home to bed, he made his way to Tom Hutchinson's to see if he and Emma thought his attitude as unreasonable as Charlotte claimed it was.

Knocking on the door, John waited an unusually long time for it to be opened. At last Tom did come, explaining that threats he had received made him careful in letting anyone in after dark.

Before John could begin to talk about his concerns or even pass a few comments on this or that, Tom pushed a newspaper into his hand.

"What is it?" John asked.

Immediately, Tom, angry and excited, snatched it back. "Just a peaceful political meeting in Manchester, it was, charged by the Yeoman Cavalry. Listen. Just listen to this, if you still think poor men have any rights in this great country of ours. 'From all inquiries we can make, there appear to be five or six dead — as many mortally wounded and not less than three hundred severely and slightly wounded.'"

"And this, listen to this, John! 'There was a scene of murder and carnage ensued which posterity will hesitate to believe, and which will hand down the authors and abettors of this foul and bloody tragedy to the execration of the astonished world.'"

Scanning the words a little ahead, Tom read on. "Men, women and children, without distinction of age and sex, became the victims of these sanguinary monsters." Flinging down the paper, he told John, "The 16th of August, 1819. The people will never forget that date. There's no turning the clock back now. This will set the people marching for justice!"

"They'll be brought to justice, the men who ordered this," John said solemnly. He had never thought that such things could happen in England and he could scarcely believe it.

"Justice! The magistrates who ordered the charge. Do you know what the Prince Regent said of them? He commended them! Yes, he commended them for their 'prompt, decisive and efficient measures for the preservation of public tranquillity.'"

Immediately, Tom went on, "This is what was needed, John. This is what the Captain has been waiting for. You'll have to take sides now, Jo...."

"No, Tom," John butted in angrily. "Will you never give up?"

Quite unaware of what the men were discussing, Emma came in and kissed John on the cheek.

"How are your plans going, John?"

"That was why I called, Emma, I...."

Before John could finish, Tom turned on his wife. "You go to bed. This has nothing to do with you."

Resignedly, Emma tidied her sewing and prepared to obey.

"It's me who should leave," John announced, standing up.

"Is it any wonder," Tom burst out, "that I lose my temper with you, John? How many times have you come here, expecting me to listen to your complaints? First it was how nobody would support your school. Then it was how you'd been dismissed by Mr Wright when you were so good at your work. After that, it was Sam, and rightly so, and then Beth. How you moaned about Beth having to turn against her friends and bow and scrape to win support for Billy and his schooling! Do you recall how angry you were when they finally wouldn't help? Then came the auction in the churchyard. At last, at last it seemed you'd had enough. But it was back to your precious plans. You're doing nicely since you became so friendly with the Elhams again. You'll never have to want for money."

"You've just answered the question I was going to ask, thank you, Tom. I needn't bore you with my moaning anymore."

"I'll ask Will and Charles — even Henry," Tom yelled after John. "Someone in your family must have some spirit left."

"He'll never join you," Emma ventured to say, when her husband slammed the door.

"Don't you be so sure. Just wait until he loses that temper of his. Please God something happens to make him lose his temper!"

CHAPTER FIFTY EIGHT

"Aah!" Eliza drew onto her face an expression of bliss as exaggerated and dramatic as all her looks and actions. With studied casualness, she closed her eyes and lay back on the ground.

"You'll get your death on that damp earth," Elizabeth warned her.

"I'll get my death if I don't get more sleep. Boxers!" Eyes tightly shut, her hands swept the air and then, when she had, in this way, attracted the attention of any watching man, she tugged at the laces of her bodice and loosened them.

"Eliza!" Beth glanced about, embarrassed for her friend.

"Eliza!" rang out like an echo. "Unless there's a Peeping Tom flat on his belly on the ground behind me," Eliza pointed out, "no one can see anything they shouldn't."

Beth did not reply and, disturbed by the silence, Eliza opened her eyes to look at her. Usually she would have glanced around, too, taking the opportunity of seeing who was watching her, but her eyes rested on her friend. Beth's head was bent forward and she gazed at a blade of grass she had absent-mindedly picked and was twisting in her fingers.

To herself, Eliza said, "Please, God, don't let me have lines on my face and look as washed out as that in a few years' time." Aloud she asked, "Well?"

"Well what?"

"Well, what's the old devil been up to now?"

"Who?"

"You know who I mean as well as I do."

They both did know that they were talking about Charles' father, but Beth had sworn to herself that she would keep off the subject and keep him and the irritations and frustrations he caused out of the conversation and out of her thoughts.

"Come on, Beth. Get it off your chest." The blissful look was gone from Eliza's face and she settled down to listening. Clearly Beth was bottling up something.

"I was thinking of our little Frances at that moment," Beth claimed.

"Maybe you were, but Edward's never far from your thoughts."

Once she got started, Beth told how Edward would eat everything there was in the house, plaintively swearing she had told him to and how, if there was nothing ready the minute she got in from hours in the fields, he would be sitting over the fire complaining and never moving out of her way while she, tired and aching from head to foot, made the meal. Then he would wolf his before she had even sat down or he would wait, complaining, and make her feel too sick to eat hers with his sucking and spitting and the stew running down his chin. Half the evening he would promise her money she did not want and he did not have and the other half he would check his few coins and, looking accusingly at her, say someone had taken one.

Even Beth, listening to herself, knew that, to someone else, her complaints amounted to nothing. What she could not convey was her misery at the certainty that, however tired, however weary she was, when she opened the door, there would be something else for her to do, some other demand made upon her which she had not the strength to face. It was like being lost in a nightmare wood which covered the whole world. You had to keep on going, keep on trying to get out, and yet, the further you went, the more lost you became. There was no rest and no peace anywhere.

Half her mind on what awaited her at home, Eliza gave little thought to the comment she thought was called for as Beth stopped talking. "Seems he can't do nothing right."

"Are you saying it's all my fault?"

"God," Eliza thought to herself. "I can't seem to say anything right, either."

"Is that what you're saying?" Elizabeth pressed her.

"You are a bit....." Eliza had sat up to face her friend. The deep tiredness in the eyes that met hers made her stop. "It's having Frances away, that's what it'll be. I even missed our Jem when she first went and I never thought I'd ever live to say that. Things will pick up, once she's been 'ome to see you." Eliza spoke in a brisk, confident voice, intended to persuade her friend that all this would soon pass. She smiled. "I'll tell you what. I'll come 'ome with you after work to give you a bit of company and keep the old devil out of your way."

Before Beth could answer they were shouted back to work. All of a sudden, just picking up stones seemed to require more skill and strength than Beth could find. It seemed the hours would never pass and she worked on and on and on in a haze of heat and weariness.

At last it was over and Beth faced the thought of the walk home. The cottage seemed so far away, and, unable to imagine herself ever reaching it, she concentrated on one small part of the journey at a time.

First it was the field to the gate, then the path to the lane and then, breathing deeply, Beth fixed her eyes on the stile ahead. Five steps and she could rest. Her hand went out, half in a welcoming gesture to the wooden post, half for support to drag herself the last step. With a sigh of relief and satisfaction, she sat on the step and leaned back, looking up at Eliza and forcing a smile.

"That's better." Her skin was pale with a hot, red flush on her cheeks. If only Charles was there, Elizabeth thought, she could lean on him.

Seeming to read her thoughts, Eliza stepped up to her. "As I can't see any 'andsome young men, you'll 'ave to make do with my arm." Eliza held out her hand and Beth struggled to her feet. Within a second, she had collapsed back onto the stile and was crying. "Oh, Eliza, I do feel bad."

"Don't go away," Eliza ordered and, never at a loss, she ran a little way along the path.

"I'm not going anywhere," Beth tried to laugh through her tears. "I'll be alright. Just a touch of the sun that's what it'll be."

With her skirts tucked up, Eliza came speeding back with a wheelbarrow. Eliza laughed, but Beth found herself crying again. She just had no strength to do anything. She would have been quite content just to be left where she was but, with laughter and tears, she was lifted and shoved into the barrow and taken home.

The barrow proved easier to propel than to stop and Beth was nearly tipped out as they arrived at the cottage. Carefully releasing her hold on the handles so as not to tip it again, Eliza ran to the door and tried to lift the latch. It did not give. Again and again she tried with no better result. Dropping her arm, she opened and closed her fingers, trying to ease back the suppleness and strength she had lost clutching the barrow.

"He'll have tied up the catch again." Beth's voice was so soft Eliza did not hear. Her face close to the glass, she was peering in at the window.

"There's something up at the pane," Eliza said, turning to Beth for confirmation that anything so odd could really be true.

All Beth could do at first was nod her head. It was true as it often was. "He'll have been counting his gold and not wanting anyone in the crowd out here to see." The lightness and laughter she had intended would not come into Beth's voice.

Eliza laughed and battered on the door with her fists.

"Come on, you old crow. Listen. He's undoing it."

"Company?" the old man grinned, showing the few brown stumps which remained in his jaw. He took no notice of Beth.

"Let me put you to bed, Beth," Eliza suggested, ignoring Edward's attempts to gain her attention.

"Just let me stay here, Eliza. Help me to a chair." She smiled at Paul Low, sitting unhappily watching her now as he had sat watching the pantomime. "Tell him I'm alright. Just the heat, that's all it is."

For a while, Beth dozed, or, at least, she was not fully awake. In the background the old sweep's voice droned on and on with a laugh and a remark from Eliza now and again.

"I've never heard that story before," Eliza said, putting a bowl in Beth's left hand and a spoon in her right.

"Don't expect he has, either. Question him and he'll ask if you're calling him a liar." After a few mouthfuls, Beth let the spoon drop into the bowl. "I can't manage this, Eliza. It's lovely. I'm sorry."

"It doesn't matter. Don't cry Beth. If you ask me, you haven't been looking after yourself. What happened to that piece of bacon you said Amy sent?"

"I was keeping it until Frances came over. Don't go on at me." Tears forced themselves into Beth's eyes and ran down her cheeks.

"Beth, what's wrong?"

"I didn't mean to cry. I didn't mean to." Sobbing, Beth clung to Eliza. It was several minutes before Eliza could settle her back in the chair, while the sweep hovered beside them.

"Don't she want that?"

Taking Edward's enquiry as concern, Eliza answered. "Not for the minute. Perhaps she'll have a little when she's slept. I'll pop back and make sure Charles has got home safely. Perhaps it'll be best if he doesn't collect Tim on his way home."

"Don't want to see that go to waste, do we? Give it 'ere." Talking as he ate Edward went on, "Beth's got no time for me, you know. I remind 'er of what she done to our Sam. If it weren't for 'er, none of that would 'ave 'appened. Now Sam was good to me, Eliza. Charles, 'e does 'is best, but 'e always was under 'er thumb. And John, she always fancied 'im, you know.

Oh yes, she did."

As she opened her mouth to tell him that he was an old fool, Eliza felt Edward's bony fingers clutch at her arm.

"Never get old, Eliza. Never get old."

She left her thoughts unspoken.

CHAPTER FIFTY NINE

After several days tramping the county for work, John was glad to climb the narrow back stairs in the cottage. With working in villages the other side of Abingfield, it had been several nights since he had slept in his own bed. As he opened the door of the room, he could see, in the clear moonlight, Charles stretched asleep, face down, on his bed.

"Come on." John bent down and wearily tugged at his brother's arm, which hung over the side of the bed. "Rows between husband and wife are no concern of mine. I said I'd be back tonight."

For a few moments after he woke, Charles stared at his brother and then struggled up to his feet. "I didn't want to miss you coming in, John. Beth's poorly and shows no sign of getting better. Will you just pop in and see her before you get in your bed?"

Without argument, John followed Charles to their room where Beth dozed, flushed and breathing uneasily. Leaning over, he took her hand. At his touch, Beth, startled and confused, sat up.

"Who is it? Who is it?"

"There, Beth, lie back again."

As quickly as it has risen, Beth's panic subsided and she smiled at John. "You're back?"

"I'm back, Beth. We'll soon have you well again."

John moved to take his shadow from her face. "Bring the candle closer, Charles. I'm in my own light here."

"I'm just tired, John. I've taken all the medicine Mrs Fletcher gave me."

"Shows you've a strong constitution."

"Like an ox." Charles brought the candle nearer and kissed his wife's cheek.

Beth tried to smile. "A very sick ox. I can't seem to stop crying, John."

"You're tired, Beth. It is the middle of the night. Charles," John said, moving a step back to speak softly to his brother. "Open her bodice and look at the skin. Can you see a rash?"

"What is it?" Beth voice was frightened.

"Harvest bugs, maybe, or you've got a flea in there with you," John told her, as Charles nodded to say there was a rash.

"You look, John, it's alright," Charles gave John his permission to look.

Beth pushed them both away and dragged herself up from the pillows to inspect her own arms and peer beneath her clothes at the rash. She lay back, smiling and relieved.

"It'll be chickenpox. I was beginning to wonder whatever was wrong with me. I'll feel better now the illness has shown itself won't I, John, once the fever breaks?"

"We'll soon have you better," John told her, his voice firm and comforting. "I'll tuck these clothes back and…"

"Must you, John? It's so lovely and cool." Beth's voice was pleading, but she gave in without further argument.

"Let's leave Beth to sleep, Charles. She'll be better sleeping on her own. You can get me something to eat. I'm wide awake again now."

Downstairs, Charles soon joined his brother and picked up the knife ready to cut a slice of bread.

"I'm not really hungry. That was just to get you down here. It's Beth. That rash is smallpox."

The knife poised in the air, Charles stared at his brother.

"It can't be, John. Dr Gray did the vaccination."

John sat and thought and Charles stood beside him.

"Wasn't that the day she found out about Billy? Perhaps they never got to the vaccination."

Tired and worried himself, Charles tried to search his memory of that dreadful time two years ago. "She did have it done. Her arm was swollen and sore for days after."

"Then perhaps it didn't take. I don't know much about vaccination, only about inoculation. I did a good few of those." Before he had finished speaking, John put on his jacket and hat. "I'm going to fetch Mr Wright. He can call tomorrow and give us his opinion. I'll borrow Langford's horse."

"We can't pay."

"No one does. We'll have credit until we're paid, like everyone else does. Don't tell anyone what I think it is until we're sure."

First running and then walking and running again, John made for Eliza's. Langford would not get up, but Eliza came to the door and listened to what he had to say.

"That one needs 'is beauty sleep," she said, tossing her head in the general direction of the bed. "It can't be a good omen, 'im lying down so much flat on 'is back. In a fight 'e'll never manage to stay on 'is feet more than a couple of hours."

Coming out to show John where the horse was grazing, Eliza sniffed the air. "What a smell of burning. Someone's stack's on fire."

"Hurry up, Eliza. I haven't time to stand talking."

"Give us a 'and to saddle 'im then. I'll make it alright with Pretty Boy in there. Tell 'im you promised to spar with 'im a couple of evenings next week."

"Tell him what you like, but hurry."

"What's the rush? Is Beth worse?"

"It could be smallpox

"She can't 'ave. She…"

The horse saddled, John rode off in the direction of Gressingford. The smell of burning grew stronger and above the hedges, like a reflection of the rising sun which glowed in the east, a yellow light spread into the retreating darkness in the western sky. As he passed nearer, John could see flames searing the early morning sky and see in them strands of burning straw dancing and twirling in the wind and threatening to set light to the rest of Simpkins' buildings. A clamour of voices told him the fire had already been discovered and he pressed on to the town.

To avoid the deep ruts in the well trampled centre of the lane, John directed the horse in close to the hedge. He had a second to feel the horse resist before it wheeled and bucked and almost threw him to the ground. Again in control, he moved towards the middle of the path and peered down into the hedge. In the deep shadow thrown by the bushes and trees, he could see nothing, but the horse edged away whenever he tried to bring it close in to the side of the path.

"Who is it?" he called, still controlling the horse with difficulty. For just a second, John was sure he had heard a movement, but it was so fleeting that, a second later, he could convince himself he had imagined it.

The horse was eager to skirt away from the hedge and take John off on the way they had been travelling. It must have been a rabbit or pheasant, John decided and let the horse follow its instinct and avoid the hedge.

"John," a voice called very quietly. A man, his face against the light, was unfastening the gate in the hedge a few yards along the lane.

"Who is it?" John demanded, sliding from his horse to the ground.

The man spoke, but so softly that John could not make out the words.

"Speak up," John ordered. "I can't hear you."

For an answer the man beckoned him over. Having been addressed by his name, John, after looking all around, decided it was safe to walk over to the man.

"Don't make a noise," the man said, but his tone was one of fear, not threat.

The voice, together with the outline of the heavy figure, told John that the man was John Braithwaite. Angry for being stopped, he supposed the idiot cousins had been out drinking and fallen into the canal or broken a leg tripping in the ruts.

Having succeeded in attracting his attention, John Braithwaite, in his relief, stood shaking and jabbering incoherently. There was nothing for it, if he did not want to stand there for what was left of the night. John hit him across the face.

"Sober up, man, and tell me what you want so I can understand."

Confused as he was, the man resented the blow. At least in his sullenness he made himself understood.

"Joe's 'urt bad. I've 'idden 'im up. What else could I do? 'Elp us John. You know what to do."

"Where is he?"

"In the field up against the 'edge."

Once he was in the field, John had no need to ask where the exact spot was. The screams of pain and terror from the ditch were plain to hear. Suddenly realising the seriousness of Joe's need, John ran over and knelt down. Even after scenes of battle, John's stomach revolted against the smell of burned flesh which hit him. The man's clothes at the front were scorched, but, as John eased him over, he saw that the back and legs had been so badly burned as to make it impossible to tell which of the black, charred remains was cloth and which skin.

From behind him, John Braithwaite at a safe distance from the dreadful sight and smell, mumbled, "A pile of burning 'ay fell on 'im as 'e was running away." Seeing the contempt in John's face, he added hastily, "It was 'is idea. I begged 'im not to." He raised his voice a little. "'E's one of the Captain's men."

"Who is the Captain?"

"'E didn't tell me. Some say it's Langford. I 'ad 'eard it were you or Tom 'Utchinson. Can you do anything? Will 'e die?"

"Stop whining," John ordered him. He wanted silence in which to think. There was only one thing to do. He could think of the next steps later. Carefully, so that the horse did not kick or trample Joe, John led the horse close in to the hedge.

"Help me lift him up. We'll put him face down across the saddle."

As they lifted him, Joe Braithwaite regained his wits and screamed in terror, "I'm dying, aren't I? 'Elp me, John. Don't let me die."

His hands, burned raw with trying to put out the flames which had engulfed him, Joe tried to claw at John's coat, but the pain of the effort made him lapse again into unconsciousness. The silence after the screams was deep and unsettling.

"I'll take him to Mr Wright's. You'd better come, too. Didn't your hands get burnt?"

"I'm off," was John Braithwaite's reply.

"Let me see your hands."

Reluctantly, John Braithwaite held out his hands.

"You didn't make much effort to help, then."

Before John could say any more the man had run away across the field as fast as his legs could take him. John had no time or wish to stop him. Stupidity was not a crime men should hang for.

CHAPTER SIXTY

For speed, John led the horse along the road to Gressingford and prayed, for Joe's sake, they would meet no one. There was no time to go the back way across the fields. He did consider leaving Joe and fetching Mr Wright to him, but that, too, would take time Joe did not have.

A few minutes after John knocked at the apothecary's door someone came to the window. As he cautiously peeped out, his candle flickered through the coloured jars and bottles. Then the door was slowly unbolted and Mr Wright faced his caller.

"John? Has there been an accident? Is it one of your family? Quickly, carry him in."

"It's Joe Braithwaite. He's a labourer in Abingfield. He's been badly burned." John thought it wise not to go into detail.

At once, Mr Wright took charge, instructing John to put the man on the table and take off what remained of his clothes.

For a moment, Joe opened his eyes, but he still saw himself engulfed in flames and burning straw. His voice rose in a scream. "Put out the flames, John. For God's sake, John."

As he worked quickly and efficiently, Mr Wright's face was serious and concerned. Beside him, John worked as quickly and as efficiently, cutting away the clothes and mixing the salves and ointments the apothecary instructed him to make. At last they had done all they could.

"Is there any hope for him, Mr Wright?"

"It's in God's hands. We can do no more."

As they stood over Joe Braithwaite, shattered and disturbed by what had happened, John remembered his errand for Beth, but gave Mr Wright time to compose himself.

"Let us pray, John." Mr Wright knelt on the floor and John knelt beside him. "Lord God, in thy mercy, let Joseph Braithwaite live a sufficient time for him to recognise and repent of his sin before he is called to the Final Judgement. And, Lord God, let John Stevenson likewise repent of his terrible crime...."

John leaped to his feet. "Me? What have I done?"

Patiently and wearily, Mr Wright patted the floor beside him.

"Pray with me, John. Do not let anger and lies separate you from the tender mercy God shows to all those who truly repent."

"What am I supposed to have done?"

"Very soon, I must call the constable. Let us pray in the few minutes we have. I fear you must pay for this crime with your life."

"I didn't say there had been any crime."

"There was no need. In villages up and down the country, foolish men are burning and destroying property. I am on my guard for anyone seeking help for burns." Sighing deeply, he added, "Reform is a fair, Christian cause, but we must shun those who destroy property like common criminals. I thought, when you worked for me, you accepted my views."

"Your views! I have views of my own. You think because I'm a labourer I can't think any more clearly than him." John indicated Joe Braithwaite.

"Everything points to your guilt."

"And if Mr Jackson or another of your friends stood here and everything pointed to his guilt, would you accept he was guilty?"

"But you...."

"But I'm a poor man, is that it?"

"You brought him here. He called your name to save him from the flames."

"And if I gave you my word I wasn't there? If I tell you it was Joe's cousin John."

"Then where is this other man?"

"Miles away by now, I should think. Where I'd be if I was guilty."

"Can you prove what you say?"

"Why do I need proof? If I was one of your kind you'd be calling me a good Samaritan." He added bitterly, "The word of a common man isn't good enough for you, is it?"

"This bitterness and envy does you no credit, John."

"Poor men aren't allowed credit. It's the better off who live on that."

"If you are innocent, why were you out in the middle of the night?"

"I was on my way to see you when I found Joe. Beth's ill."

For the first time doubt crept into Mr Wright's voice. "Why was it so urgent?"

"I think it's smallpox."

"Was she never inoculated?"

"She was vaccinated by Dr Gray."

"Then I don't understand. Perhaps you are mistaken."

302

"Whatever it is, she's very poorly." The cottage seemed a world away, but John told Mr Wright what he knew of the course of Beth's illness.

"A summer rash, perhaps. It may be no more. I'll call tomorrow, first thing in the morning." Feeling deeply ashamed of his suspicions and seeing how tired John was, he asked him to eat and rest before he returned home. John refused.

"Then," the apothecary warned him, "take care, John. There are some, like me, I am afraid, who will demand that you prove your innocence."

The fields lay in the light of the early morning sun. Dead tired as he was, however hard he tried, John could not hold all the happenings of the last night in his mind at one time. As he listed each fact, his memory lost its grasp on the one before, so that he could form no clear picture of how the facts would look to anyone else or what he should do. If others were going to jump to the same conclusions as Mr Wright, perhaps he had better hide until it was cleared up. On the other hand, that might be taken as evidence of his guilt.

Several times, thinking merged into sleeping and John jolted awake to find himself resting on the horse's neck. Again he dozed and jolted forward, but this time he was awake in a second, thinking he was being attacked.

"John. Keep calm. It's me, Tom Hutchinson." Urgently, Tom took the reins and steadied the horse to a stop.

"You can't go back. The Colonel's men are looking for you. They called at the houses of all the men on the Colonel's list after the fire and you were the only one not in your bed. All Simpkins' stacks were destroyed and his barn. The Colonel is determined to catch the culprits and he's always seen you as a trouble maker. They say he claims you are Gentleman Jack."

Desperately collecting his thoughts, John told Tom all that had happened on his way to Mr Wright's.

"You took Joe in badly burned? That makes it look ten times worse. You're as good as hanged." This was his chance, Tom decided, to bring John into the planned march.

Scarcely able to stay awake, John found it difficult to think and more difficult to make a decision. He watched while Tom sent the horse off across the fields and then obediently followed his friend along the shelter of the hedges to the canal basin. There, pressed in against the wall of the warehouse, Tom told him to wait until he saw the way was clear. He returned in a few minutes and whispered instructions to John.

"This is a bolt hole I thought of in case of trouble. You'll not be discovered. This barge usually takes stolen goods and many a shilling changes hands to make sure it's never searched. The choice is yours, John. Stay on it and get well away or get off as soon as you can and make your way back to join the march to London."

In an even lower voice, Tom confided, "The day after tomorrow, John. At dusk. We meet by Hangar Hill, near where Sam and Billy were taken."

Without answering, John waited, his tiredness heavy on his body and mind, and he breathed deeply and prayed for the strength to run to the barge.

"When I signal, John, run like hell. Now!"

Without looking to right or left, John ran to the barge, scrambled aboard and dived under the cover which protected the load. As he gulped for air, a sickly smell reached his nostrils. He sniffed and sniffed again, but could not place it. Lifting the cover a little, he made a narrow channel through which to breathe fresh air. Carefully, trying not to let the top of the cover move and so attract attention, John eased himself into a comfortable position to sleep. His hand touched something and his heart beat fast and his stomach seemed to churn and heave. His fingers held the fingers of a hand, the hand of a dead man lying beside him. That was the smell! The putrid scent of death. This was how John Wells and his gang took their plunder through the country to eager customers. It took every ounce of restraint John had not to throw aside the cover and run. Forcing himself to move slowly, he edged himself to the side of the barge and dropped silently into the water. He would rather face an enemy he could see than whatever disease lurked in the tainted air around the corpse.

As he pulled himself from the canal onto the bank and looked back, John was in time to see Ben Walker, the Colonel's servant, walk onto the barge. Making straight for the cover, Ben Walker turned it back and then, ignoring the body, let it drop again. Someone had intended to give him away. It couldn't be Tom.

CHAPTER SIXTY ONE

The room was light when Beth jerked awake with a shudder, but, through her fever, although she could feel the terror of being quite alone and separate in her pain, she could not find her place in this strangely remote yet overpowering room in which she seemed to float, an insignificant part of an endless universe of suffering and noise. Slowly and painfully, she recalled through her confusion who she was and where she was. The pieces of furniture took on once again their familiarity and solidness, each piece in its usual place. The pain and the heat were in her own body, gushing over her and then ebbing away. The noise was coming from downstairs and voices echoed through the wood.

There was the sound of boots falling heavy and hard against each step of the stair and threatening to come into the bedroom. Beth tried to rise, but the movement exhausted her and she fell back to the pillow, clutching the bed clothes to her throat. She felt sick, so horribly sick. With a sharp kick, the door was flung open and the Colonel stood in the door way. Behind him Charles grabbed at his shoulder and swore and argued.

"Let go, man. Keep your dirty hands and your filthy peasant thoughts to yourself. What interest have I in whether your wife is in bed or not? The sooner you leave me free to search, the sooner I shall be gone."

Flaunting his gentlemanly breeding and upbringing, he kept his eyes averted from Beth, although he marched around the bed, looked beneath it and patted the covers around her until they lay flat against the mattress.

"He's not here." The Colonel left the room, signalling the men who had restrained Charles to release him.

"Don't worry, Beth," Charles knew it was a foolish, useless thing to say, but he had to hurry downstairs after the Colonel and try and find why they were searching for John.

It was several minutes before Charles returned, minutes filled with more shouting of orders and more cursing and arguments. Then there was silence, except for the buzz of conversation and conjecture from the family downstairs. Charles smiled as he came through the door and sat beside her on the bed to reassure her.

"Seems John's in a spot of bother. We'll soon sort it out. Up to one of his pranks again, perhaps, and the Colonel's no sense of humour. Without protest Beth let him go on. She did not believe him and she knew she should be worried for John, but she longed to sleep. Nothing mattered more than her longing to sleep.

"It's all arranged," Charles told her. "Henry's run for Eliza, and Pa and Mr Low are keeping an eye on Tim for the time being. I don't want to leave you while I to go to work, but you know I must. We need the money now and you need some extras to build up your strength. As soon as Henry gets back he can join me and, later, I'll leave him clearing up while I pop back and see how you are. Just you rest and don't worry about anything. Mr Wright may call later to see you."

Strangely, out of all proportion to what she intended, Beth panicked at the thought. "Mr Wright? Oh, Charles, he can't. With me up here and Frances away, what state is the place in down there? I'll have to get up and tidy it before Mr Wright comes."

"Beth," Charles chided gently, kissing her cheek. "Don't worry. I promise you, everything's as clean as a new pin, even Pa."

As quickly as she had reacted to the news, Beth's worry subsided. She was just too tired and sick to care. For Charles' sake she tried to smile. "That will be the day."

Not long after Eliza had arrived and a few minutes before Charles left, Mr Wright called. His first action on entering the room was, with much tutting and shaking of the head, to open the window and then to look from Eliza to Charles. He knew, from experience, long experience of the poor, that men coarsened by the hardness of their own lives, too readily attributed coarse thoughts to medical men. It was usually best to send the possessive husband from the room and keep a female relation or friend, but this woman, in spite of her fine clothes, was as dirty and scruffy a repository of infection and superstition as he had ever seen.

With a sigh, Mr Wright resigned himself to accepting Eliza, for the moment, as nurse and sent Charles downstairs. Beth stiffened as the apothecary moved towards her and, at his touch, felt her cheeks burn even fiercer and her breathing even more rapid. No man, other than Charles, had ever come as close to her in this room. She avoided his eyes, looking past him to Eliza,

"Don't pull away, Mrs Stevenson. I'm feeling your pulse"

Suddenly and exaggeratedly Beth laughed at Eliza's smile and wink. Serious again, she did not want Mr Wright to think she was making a fuss and she did not want to put Charles to the expense of a second visit from the apothecary.

"It's a touch of the sun, Mr Wright. The sun brings me out in a rash some times. I've told you that, haven't I Eliza?"

Smiling politely, Mr Wright nodded and continued his examination, questioning on this and that. Finally, advising Beth to rest and warning Eliza not to shut the windows the moment he left, Mr Wright went downstairs.

"John was right. It is smallpox." He held up his hand to stop Charles's interruption. "I shall call on Dr Gray straight away while I am in Abingfield. All I can say at present is that it is smallpox and your wife will need every care. At this delicate stage we must do all we can to avoid her losing the baby." Aware that husbands were often the last to be told, he explained. "Beth is two or three months gone with child and in illness a woman can so easily lose the baby." He added, "I was shocked to find her so thin and delicate. I am afraid it is the old, old story of a woman feeding her husband and family first and making do with the little that is left. First, we must replace that woman with a suitable nurse. Becky. Becky will do. No, she will not do. She has an infant, and we must keep him from the infection. Her mother? Another sister, perhaps?"

"Her mother lives with her sister, Amy, just the other side of Gressingford."

"Then we'll send for her mother. I will see that is done. And the little lad there," Mr Wright indicated Tim, "Has he been inoculated?"

Charles looked as vague about such matters as fathers are. "I don't think so, sir."

"Bring him to the light. Let me look at him. Has he been listless or seemed unwell?" The apothecary listened to Charles' replies. "Good. And his food? Has he been off his food? Good. On no account let him breathe the unwholesome air of the sick room. It is pernicious and can, at the very least, weaken the child's constitution. The boy must go to your wife's sister, Amy, unless she has young children who have not been inoculated."

"Yes sir."

"I shall arrange everything as soon as possible. Tell Mrs Dodds to sprinkle the room with vinegar to strengthen the air. Keep the bed clothes clean. Wash them every day and keep the windows open. I know it is the practice to keep the patient warm and not change linen for fear if chills, but that is an old wives' tale. Apart from yourself, let your mother attend Beth and keep others away. Sick rooms to women can be like flies to a honey pot, but do not allow them in."

"Yes sir. And John, Mr Wright? What happened to John? The Colonel was here searching for him."

Mr Wright told him all he knew and that Joe Braithwaite had died. "I'll do all that I can for John. I shall call on Mr Gray and tell him all John told me. I am sure it is the truth."

Alone, knowing her mother would soon arrive and everything would be taken care of, Beth felt a little better. The sickness she had felt earlier had passed. That would be why the sun had affected her so severely that day in the fields.

"Tim," she called, wanting company. "Tim, come and see your Ma."

His foot on the bottom step of the stairs, Tim turned and looked at Mr Low.

"Don't go up there, Tim. You know your Pa told you not to. Your Ma needs her rest."

"Ma called me."

"She's dreaming. You know how you call out when you're dreaming, Tim."

"Ma cuddles me."

"I know she does, Tim, but Grandma will be here soon and you'll go and see Aunt Amy."

"Tim," Beth called. "Can you hear me?"

Slowly and deliberately, not taking his eyes of Mr Low, Tim drew his other foot next to the first and then placed the first on the next step. Mr Low could not walk over and stop him and his grandpa was collecting wood outside. He wanted to see his Ma and she wanted to see him.

"Are you there, Tim? Come up and see your Ma."

Stretching his legs to their full length, Tim climbed up the stairs. "Ma!"

"There you are. Come on. Jump on the bed and give your Ma a cuddle." Mother and child snuggled up together and dozed in the warm summer breeze which blew in through the open window.

CHAPTER SIXTY TWO

With no pause for thought, Mr Wright rode straight to the vicarage. He was convinced that Dr Gray had been sadly negligent. Theory, however diligently studied, was no substitute for experience and the young man, promising as he might be, was quite lacking in practical experience. At least, having discovered the son's fault, he might have greater authority with the father in persuading him of John Stevenson's innocence.

The study into which he was shown and left for some time, was much larger and the bookshelves longer, more thickly layered and fuller than his own. The newly printed, newly bound books contrasted sharply with his own well thumbed tomes. On the desk, sheets of paper were covered with lines of small, urgent writing as though their author had been suddenly inspired with insight into the problems of sickness and health. This was no mere shop for the sale of medicines coated in a little free advice, but the library of a physician whose opinions, if he carried even a half of the knowledge in these volumes in his head, might be worth the fat fees he charged.

When he eventually came into the room, Dr Gray was most courteous in his greeting and in his praise of Mr Wright's reputation. Standing up, Mr Wright felt his age contrasting to his disadvantage with the young man's energy, enthusiasm and new knowledge. Suddenly, he felt his experience of old ways counted for nothing.

"A patient of yours, Mrs Stevenson," he began.

"Mrs Stevenson? Mrs Stevenson?" Dr Gray searched amongst the papers on his desk. "I can recall no Mrs Stevenson."

"Her sister worked here at one time, I understood."

"Becky's sister? There is some misunderstanding, surely. She was never a patient of mine. Beth, I believe her name was. Dear me, no, she was not a patient of mine." The smile which accompanied the statement suggested that he was too polite to question how such a foolish mistake came to be made. "I do, indeed, give my services free, or at a very low fee, to the poorhouses in the district and to charities, but Mrs Stevenson was, I understood at the time, a patient, or rather, a customer of Mrs Fletcher."

Attempting to stick to the arguments he had planned on his way, Mr Wright began again. "I have just come from her sickroom. She was, and there is no doubt of this, vaccinated by you and yet she is now stricken with the smallpox." A slight note of triumph creeping into his voice, Mr Wright said, "I feel some explanation is required." He awaited the answer. Convinced that there was none, he was prepared to uncover any excuses which might be offered.

Behind his large, leather-topped desk, Dr Gray nodded sadly. "It is possible. If you say so, I have no doubt you are correct." He said no more, placing on his visitor the onus of making the next move.

Assuming Dr Gray was trying to avoid the point of what he was saying, Mr Wright repeated, "Her husband is quite certain that you completed the vaccination. Do you remember? You discovered that the little boy, Billy, was deaf."

"Of course, of course. Yes, that fact had slipped my mind. I realised it at once. I remember that I found it surprising that no other medical man in the area had realised the boy's condition. The uncle worked for you, I believe and the family was known to you." Generously throwing the apothecary an excuse, he added, "You were not their medical adviser, of course."

Feeling the initiative slipping from him, Mr Wright repeated yet again, somewhat tetchily, "But the woman is ill, brought to her sick bed with smallpox."

"Ah!" From listening very seriously, Dr Gray suddenly nodded, as though at last able to convince himself that what he could not believe, that Mr Wright was totally ignorant of a basic fact of medicine, was correct. "You did not know that the patient must return to check that the vaccination has taken.. Perhaps," he went on, again generously accounting for a slip which others might consider unforgivable, "you are concerned only with inoculations. We have seen such cases before," he said, speaking for the whole body of modern, well-informed physicians. "It did, of course," he pronounced, shaking his head at the folly and ignorance of mankind, "cause some to question the efficacy of vaccination and to pour scorn and abuse on Dr Jenner. As though the slight expense and inconvenience of a second consultation can be weighed against the great benefits over inoculation."

To cover his surprise at what he learned and the ignorance he had so rashly revealed, Mr Wright immediately let it be known that the benefits of vaccination were well known to him. Clinging to his role as spokesman for all apothecaries of wide experience, he said, "Certainly. We have all seen cases where inoculation, badly administered, has caused a severe wound or has even spread the disease itself among the population at large."

As he spoke, a thought occurred to Mr Wright which might yet reveal Dr Gray's inadequacies in this case. "Was Mrs Stevenson aware of these facts? Perhaps you are not used to dealing with the lower orders of society. It is most important to give them instructions clearly and repeat them several times if necessary. Did Mrs Stevenson know that she had to visit you again?"

There was silence. It was a serious point and Dr Gray gave it serious consideration. "A little over two years ago?" he queried. "That is a long time over which to remember every word of such a conversation, is it not?" Openly and sincerely he looked at Mr Wright. "All I can say for certain is that it is my practice always to tell patients of that I must see them again. I can see no reason why I should have departed from such practice in this case. My charitable work, as I have said," he continued, "brings me into touch with the common people and I am well aware of the difficulties. 'Tomorrow' they will save. 'Tomorrow' they will see to this and that. Weeks, months, even years, pass and they do not attend to those matters, which should have been attended to promptly."

"Will you see Mrs Stevenson?" Mr Wright asked, still feeling Dr Gray shared some responsibility at least in the case.

"What is the woman's condition?"

As clearly as possible, Mr Wright gave the details. Reciting them, he felt like an apprentice again, repeating his lessons to his father.

At the end, Dr Gray rose from the desk, at first smiling and the gravely shaking his head. "Is that so? The woman is weakened by hunger and her delicate condition. Smallpox is but one very minor cause of her generally weak condition. An attack of the disease after one vaccination is very mild and of little consequence. No, Mr Wright, it would serve no useful purpose for me to interfere and take the case from your capable hands. I am sure you will advise your patient to take a light but nourishing diet until her strength is restored."

There was nothing more for Mr Wright to say, although he remained seated, and, suddenly, he was being criticised. "I regret that you have come straight from the sickroom to my house, Mr Wright. Do not misunderstand me, but please leave and tell no one you called here. Some of my patients would be most distressed. The word smallpox still strikes terror into many hearts."

After sitting smiling at his visitor for a few moments and then walking, without any sign of haste, across the room, Dr Gray managed, holding the door open and commenting on the weather, to convey, with no hint of impatience or direct comment, that the conversation was at an end and it was time for Mr Wright to leave. It was a method which generally worked without giving offence to wealthy patients.

Mr Wright stood up and took a step to the door, but then stopped. "I came to make inquiries about John Stevenson, too."

"Ah, then you want my father. We have agreed he will not trespass on my territory and I shall not trespass on his. In matters of law and religion, I bow to him as magistrate and clergyman."

Once again, Mr Wright was left alone, but this time it was only long enough for Dr Gray to tell his father the purpose of the visit.

"Have you news of this man?" the vicar demanded as he rushed in, not allowing any time for greetings or pleasantries or even warnings. "There is a reward put up by Mr Simpkins and other farmers and landowners. It is a sad reflection of the times that duty is no longer a sufficient spur to action."

"If you mean do I know John Stevenson's whereabouts, I do not." Mr Wright was angered by the insult and the tone in which it was delivered. "I do, however, know that he is innocent."

"You know that for a fact, do you, sir?" the clergyman asked. "Everything which I have heard speaks, nay, shouts of his guilt."

"John was on his way to me to tell me of his brother's wife's illness when he came upon Joseph Braithwaite already near death. Is he to be held guilty for going to the aid of a man in agony?"

"Who told you this?"

"John Stevenson, when he brought in the injured man, but his brother can swear to the purpose of his journey and there is a witness who can swear to the purpose for which he borrowed the horse."

"With one brother a convicted felon, I would not place confidence in the word of another. There is no witness of known reliability and standing who can swear to this story, except yourself and I am afraid this man often set out to impress those who might be of use to him. He is an ambitious man and determined to triumph over his betters. The information sworn to me shows that he was barely at home two minutes. He came from the home of a well-known radical, committed the crime, went to his own home for the sole purpose of planning his alibi and then borrowed the horse to rescue his accomplice whom he knew to be lying injured. Your two witnesses, and you yourself, can swear only to what John Stevenson told you and not to the truth. The Colonel's servant, Walker, has been watching this man and swears he is Gentleman Jack, as the peasants call him."

"Circumstances, present circumstances, may suggest guilt," Mr Wright conceded, remembering how he had jumped to the wrong conclusion, "but it is not in his character. He is open and honest."

"Not in his character?" Mr Gray questioned. "Pray, what must a man do for you to see him as a troublemaker?" The Colonel has been aware of this man Stevenson ever since he returned to the village. The Colonel is a meticulous man and has listed every wrong the man has committed. Not only does he openly associate with radicals — birds of a feather, you know — but he is part of their conspiracy to destroy the constitution of this great country and then the nation itself. At first, I am sure, he worked silently as Gentleman Jack, but recently he has been more open in his defiance, almost provoking a riot in the churchyard and now plotting to flout the law with his alibi that he was on his way to you when he just happened to find Braithwaite. Unless we find and destroy this rotten apple, the whole population will be tainted. Let me assure you, Mr Wright, that I shall not hesitate to follow the fine example set by my fellow magistrates in Manchester in quelling rebellion and lawlessness in our midst."

Mr Gray was more obvious in his intention than his son had been and he ushered Mr Wright to the door without further ado.

"There is no more to be said, I think.

CHAPTER SIXTY THREE

As the dawn broke a few days later, John made his way into the woods to the spot where Sam and Billy had hidden from Jacob Rush. Now, in summer, the leaves and brambles grew profusely and thorns tore across his hands as he separated the thick cover and, reaching the hollow beneath, turned and closed it around him again. Settling to an uncomfortable and restless sleep, his memories of Sam's capture added to his unease about the place. Nothing could have brought him back, except the fear that Tom Hutchinson would have persuaded Charles, Will and Henry to join the uprising. This was his only chance to stop them.

The sun rose higher into the sky, gently warming the shade beneath the trees and scorching the harvesters in the fields. Its rays reached through the open doors of cottages and burned through the window panes. Beth looked, as she woke, at the small square of sunlight on the wall. Ever since she had been ill, she had watched it move around the room, marking the passing of each day. The passing of the days? Did it mark the passing of her days on earth? Outside, the birds fluttered and squabbled in the thatch above the open window, but, inside, the house was silent.

"Ma, are you there?" she called, but her voice hardly seemed to escape from her lips, let alone reach down the stairs.

Slowly, Beth tried to raise herself up a little to reach for the pipkin of water by the bed to dab her dry lips and burning face. The movement made her senses reel and she dropped back, her breathing as shallow and her body as weary as if she had run miles and miles. The room moved around her, and, even when she shut her eyes, she had to concentrate her whole mind to fend off the wave after wave of dizziness which threatened to sweep her into unconsciousness.

At last the giddiness receded and she could stare at the pipkin and try, keeping her head still, to reach out and dip her hand into it. The touch of the water on her finger tips was cool and refreshing and she longed all the more to sprinkle the cold water on her burning cheeks. For that moment, she was quite unaware, quite forgetful of anything else in the world. All that mattered was reaching the water. Pausing to rehearse the next move in her mind, she held her hand in the bowl and then raised it to shake the dripping water on her face. The droplets fell, pattering against the wall and onto the bed. One or two touched her cheeks, making her all the more desperate to reach out and douse her whole face with the cool water. In her eagerness, she plunged her hand too hard against the bowl. It tipped too suddenly for her fingers to clasp it and clattered to the floor to vibrate noisily for a second against the wooden boards before it came to rest. The water, a sea of water it seemed, spread across the room, at first in a pool but, gradually, in rivulets between the boards, following the slope of the floor to the door.

Watching it disappear, Beth felt the terrible panic of being alone in a nightmare. She was at its centre but had no control over what was happening. However dreadful the scene enacted around her, she would have no power to halt it. As surely and as certainly as the water had flowed across the floor, her life was flowing away and there was nothing she could do about it.

More terrible still, if she was so dreadfully ill, what of Tim? Those few days ago, when she had still been able to pretend to herself that she did not know the name of the deathly disease which was destroying her, she had hugged and kissed him so lovingly. Were they keeping it from her now that his young life was ending as surely as hers?

"God, please God, take me and not Tim. Let me just live to see Charles again and Frances and Billy. Dear God, let Tim live." She struggled to think of some bargain she could strike, some promise of good behaviour or avoidance of evil. There was none. It was too late to make promises she could not keep.

"What happened?" Sarah asked, looking at the water on the floor. "I only popped out for a minute to hang out the bedclothes. Mr Wright said they were to be washed every day. It's a good drying day."

Beth waited until she could see her mother's face, "Is Tim well Ma? Has he caught the smallpox? Will he die, Ma?"

"Of course Tim's alright. Whatever gave you that idea, Beth? The minute you're a little stronger, Amy will bring him to see you."

"Do you swear, Ma? Swear to me on your mother's grave that Tim is well."

"Beth, my love, whatever nonsense is this?"

"Beth, I swear to you that Tim is well. It's yourself you must think about now. Please, my love, lie back and rest." She busied herself wiping up the water.

As she walked about the room, Sarah said, "I'm going to shut that window, whatever Mr Wright says. Mrs Fletcher doesn't hold with all this fresh air and neither do I."

"Leave it Ma. I can smell the wheat."

Unwillingly, Sarah left the window open and sat down to sew.

"Harvest time, Beth, do you know what that reminds me of?" Sarah stopped in mid-thought. So many sad things had happened since Tim had been born. She glanced at Beth. Her daughter's eyes were open and she was listening. "Once you're better and you've built up your strength and this bad business with John is sorted out, we'll all go away, far away from here. It will give me and your Pa a new lease of life."

Resting her needle, Sarah eased her stiff fingers and looked over at her daughter. "Beth. Are you alright, Beth?" Sarah rushed to the bed. Beth lay between sleep and unconsciousness. Tears flowed into Sarah's eyes, but she knew she had no time to stand weeping. She must fetch help and find Charles.

Again in Mrs Booth's parlour, again polishing the furniture which was already as bright and shining as the sun, again with Mrs Booth popping in every minute to keep an eye on her, Frances wondered why, if this was really what God had planned for her, she had not been born with a duster in her hand.

"If I work extra hard, ma'am, can I go early to see Ma?" she asked.

"You should always work extra hard, Frances. It is not something you do just when you have a mind to, in exchange for a favour. I will not have the work skimped. We have had this all out once this morning. Young people are never satisfied now. My goodness, how grateful I would have been for an evening free to call on my Mama and Papa, but you want the afternoon as well."

With Mrs Booth's constant supervision and instruction, Frances continued the daily routine with a mounting lack of enthusiasm. Her Ma needed her — she had been sure of that ever since Henry had come last evening with a message, but Mrs Booth had questioned Henry closely and discovered that Mr Wright had said that, with rest and nourishing foods, her Ma would be well again. After that she had said that Frances could go at four o'clock and take some broth and calves' foot jelly. That would do her Ma good, Frances had to admit, and she was trying, oh how she was trying, to be patient.

As she moved around the rooms making herself pick up and dust everything which could be picked up and dusted, Frances moved from the shadow into the sunlight shining through the high window which looked out into the garden. She reached out for a small ornament, but her hand never closed on it. Her face set and her voice firm, she turned towards Mrs Booth, folded the dusters neatly, untied the strings of her spotless, white apron and announced, "I must go home to Ma. I know she needs me."

Before Mrs Booth could ask the questions which formed on her lips, "What do you think you are doing, child? Are you possessed?" Frances walked from the room.

In the hall, she seemed to hesitate and glanced back at Mrs Booth who stared at her, speechless, from the parlour and then, with a sudden spurt, she darted into the kitchen, snatched up the food for her mother and was off out of the back door and up the lane.

CHAPTER SIXTY FOUR

Every step of the way, Frances ran and ran, her hand on her side to ease the throbbing pain.

Without pausing, she charged through the wood into the clearing in front of the house and then, at last, reached the cottage door. It was opened before she could grip the latch in her hand.

"Just sit with your Ma, my love." Sarah bit back the more urgent and anxious words on her tongue so as not to frighten the child. "I'm going to fetch your Pa. Your Ma isn't feeling too well."

With her wet skirts clinging about her legs and her wet cap dripping into her eyes, Frances ran up the stairs and into her mother's room.

"Ma. Ma." She flung herself across the room and gazed at her mother lying so still with the bright, shallow blush of fever on her chalk white skin. As Frances touched her, Beth started, tugging feebly at the covers and then, seeming to remember something, reached out, feeling all around her.

"Where's my sewing, my sewing?"

Frances took her hands and held them still.

"Who is —?" Beth searched the child's face. "It's you, Frances. Where have you been? Is Billy there?"

"Mrs Booth's, Ma. It was Mrs Booth's fault. She wouldn't let me come when I wanted to," Frances sobbed.

"Mrs Booth?" Beth could not grasp what the child meant. She could not recall what her daughter had to do with a Mrs Booth. She felt the child's small hands on hers and, smiling, closed her eyes to rest. Frances sat by her, afraid to move her hands for fear of disturbing her mother. Five, ten minutes she sat, watching over her mother's restless sleep.

There were firm steps on the stairs and Mr Wright came in.

"How are we feeling today, Mrs Stevenson?" he began and stopped, the strong, reassuring smile fading from his face as he felt the faint pulse. He became aware of the little girl sobbing and watching his every move.

"Don't cry, child. I shall do all I can for your mother."

Opening his bag, the apothecary took out a sharp lancet, a bowl and a cloth, talking all the time to reassure himself and Frances. His voice was confident, with words of comfort and magic to Frances.

"The poison in the pustules is striking inward instead of ripening and rising in the skin. The matter has been absorbed into the blood."

In contrast, his manner, as he opened the pustules one by one, wiping his blade on the cloth after each cut, was hesitant and agitated. At every move he could hear Dr Gray, questioning, at his shoulder. These modern young men had their new ways and he would not be slow to blame him if he were wrong. Did the fewer spots in this case merely indicate a milder attack after vaccination, or had all the poisons gone inward? Should he take a little blood? The young men seemed set against bleeding these days.

Beth moved restlessly, muttering words too quiet and low for anyone to hear.

"Her skin will be sore for a while," the apothecary said, "but your Mama will rest more quietly now."

Once again, Mr Wright took Beth's wrist in his fingers and placed his other hand gently on her forehead. The fever still burned and the pulse seemed even more rapid, even fainter. The child's eyes were still fixed on him.

"Where is your Papa?"

"Grandma's gone to fetch him."

"Good."

"Are you going?"

"No, 1 shall do all I can for your mama." However old fashioned it might be, he knew he could only do the things he had always done. "I want you to be a good girl and help me prepare some plasters." In as simple words as he could find, he gave her instructions and she obeyed them to the letter. The plasters prepared, the apothecary placed them carefully on Beth's wrists and ankles. Taking his watch from his pocket, Mr Wright considered what to do next. "Ah, at last."

Charles rushed into the room, but Mr Wright placed a restraining hand on his arm. "Leave your wife to rest," he advised and explained the purpose of the plasters to draw the poisons to the extremities. "We can expect no change for an hour or two." Mr Wright repacked his bag methodically, everything in its place. His face was serious. "We must, as ever, put our trust in the Lord."

For a while after Mr Wright had left, saying he would return, Charles and Frances sat by Beth, while Sarah sat a little apart by the window. Henry busied himself downstairs, keeping Edward quiet and talking in hushed tones to Mr Low.

Charles did not take his eyes from his wife's face. Every moment he searched it for a sign that the treatment was having its effect, trying to convince himself that all would be well. "Your Ma's breathing a little easier now, Frances. This time tomorrow the worst will be over and she'll have pulled through."

It was strange to Frances to see her father so unsure and at a loss what to do. She had always looked up to her Pa as someone who always knew just what to do and looked after them all. Now she looked away, knowing it was useless to ask the one question in the world that mattered, whether her mother would live or die.

"What shall we do about Billy?" Charles asked.

Her father was asking her what to do. He knew no more than her, a child, what was to be done, but he thought her mother would die. His question could mean only that. As much as Frances wanted, unselfishly, to fetch Billy, she could not leave her mother now.

"You stay, my love," Sarah told her. "Henry can fetch him from Eliza's."

At the sound of voices, Beth stirred. For a second, Charles's heart soared, but then he saw her eyes. Their colour was as soft and their look as gentle as ever, but the light had gone from them. They turned to him dull, without understanding or question. Beth was going to die. He knew she had accepted it, not willingly, not even welcomingly, but as quietly as she had accepted all that life had brought.

Charles moved to sit beside her and held her head on his shoulder. "Don't be afraid, Beth." For just a moment, the light returned to her eyes and she seemed to want to speak to them. Then Beth died.

As Billy rushed into the house, Frances moved to the top of the stairs to warn him. Her tears running unchecked, she pointed to her ring finger, the sign they used for their mother, and pointed to heaven. Billy ran to the bed, stared at his mother and touched her gently. Then he flung himself into the corner and sobbed.

"Oh Charles," Sarah cried, "how can we comfort him?"

Frances sat beside her brother and, her arm around his shoulder, they both wept.

Later, when the small square of sunlight had disappeared, Mrs Fletcher came to lay out the body. Charles stood and watched as she finished. He had been useless. Billy had seen that. There had been nothing he could do to help Beth. His Beth, his own wife, the most precious thing in his life, had died in his arms and there had been nothing he could do to prevent it. It wasn't his fault he couldn't feed his family. Tom was right. They had no power. But that meant they had nothing to lose. Without a word to the women, Charles slipped out of the house and made his way to the barn where the fancy met and where, rumour said, the march to London was to begin.

CHAPTER SIXTY FIVE

Dressing in his uniform with Walker's help, the Colonel turned over the Stevenson woman's death in his thoughts. He had been one of the first to hear that scrap of news. A few years earlier, it had often been said that it was the Colonel's paying half the men, women and children of Abingfield for news and rumours which kept the villagers from starvation. Now, he chose his informants with greater care and gave his money more sparingly and there were many who brought him news just to keep on the right side of him. He added the news of Beth's death to all he already knew about Dr Gray and the vaccination and the course of the illness. It did not surprise him.

"Society physicians," he pronounced, "know little more of medicine than the quacks who travel from fair to fair, but they know a good deal more about the tricks of the trade of parting the public from its money."

Surveying himself in the mirror and pointing out this and that small detail to be corrected by Walker, he continued, "First they convince every one vaccination is vastly superior to inoculation and then that vaccination is a mystery which can be entrusted only to medical men and not to the old women who have inoculated the poor for many long years. Then, believe it or not, they tell us that vaccination must be repeated, from time to time. The face of it! The impudence! Who but society physicians with a rich, gullible audience could manage to fleece their customers not of one fee, but of fee after fee? A travelling quack would be in prison for less."

Walker nodded silently. It was not for him to criticise the gentry. The Colonel certainly did not expect that and would have corrected him sharply had he done so.

Impatiently pushing his man aside with, "That will do Walker," the Colonel gestured towards the shako on the table and, when it was passed to him, carefully placed it on his head. It crowned the stiff, formal figure.

"Not that the woman's death will do any harm to Gray's business. It will bring all those the doctor has already vaccinated once rushing back to him, eager to pay the fee again and receive on their flesh the magic symbol of immortality. He could not have planned it better."

"Dr Gray's contract to vaccinate all the children in the poorhouse will be worth a pretty penny, then," Ben Walker ventured to comment.

"Certainly. One well-meaning society or another has agreed to pay. No doubt he nobly took only half the usual fee — half the usual fee a dozen times over during each pauper's life time. That is the profession to follow, Walker, medicine, not the army. That is the way to earn an excellent remuneration in peace and war. No years of half pay for those gentlemen."

Before beginning his own patrol, the Colonel gave Walker his instructions for the night. "This is just the time Stevenson might come back, if he has heard the news and has any decent feelings. Fortunately the fancy meets tonight. That will keep most out of trouble, but check as usual, Walker, who is missing and if there are fewer men there than usual. Are the men on duty by the cannon as usual?"

"Yes, sir."

"We don't want to slacken our watch on poachers even when there are worse evils to guard against. A wooden cannon ball hurtling through the air soon makes poachers show a fast pair of heels."

"It does, sir."

Vigilance. That is our watch word, Walker."

"Yes, sir."

CHAPTER SIXTY SIX

In his hiding place, John waited. Looking to where the sun sent long fingers of shadow stabbing the evening light in the fields, he reckoned there was still another long hour to pass until Tom and his men assembled alongside him. Once again he fell to thinking about Charlotte and praying for Beth's recovery.

A movement a couple of fields away caught his attention. A youth moved stealthily along a hedge and, coming to a gate, hesitated, kneeling down to think out his next move. Watching, John could not help smiling to himself. Daniel Reed was never late. Early for work, early for church, that was Daniel Reed. And now he was early for the rising.

Everything to Daniel was a matter for serious consideration and he would be weighing up whether he was more likely to be seen opening the gate a little and sliding through or keeping it closed and rolling over the top, flat against the bar. At last, down on his haunches, Daniel opened the gate and waddled through. Then, to John's surprise, he sat down, not attempting to skirt the field or make his way to where John waited and where Tom had said his men would assemble. Perhaps he was reluctant to venture into the wood alone or feared the mantraps and was waiting for others to join him.

A few minutes later, even from where he was in the wood, John could see a smile of relief on the youth's face. Stephen Ballom, stiffly bending at the waist in a futile attempt to keep out of view, was coming along the path the boy had taken. Even in that ridiculous posture, the man kept his dignity and the youth was calmed and reassured by his presence. Will Dodds followed. Again, to John's surprise, they made no attempt to cross to the wood.

In ones and twos other men came, not to the wood, but into the field. They seemed to be old, talking quietly and earnestly, or very young, fooling self-consciously and idiotically to persuade themselves that this was a better spree than the scrapes and fun of their usual evenings out.

A sound behind him made John drop to the ground. Tom's voice sounded softly through the trees.

"Over here," John answered.

Without any ceremony, John grabbed the food and drink Tom had brought him. It was half eaten before he realised Tom was gazing at him in silence.

"What is it, Tom?"

"Beth's dead."

As John pushed the remaining food aside and buried his head in his hands, Tom gently urged him to eat while he had the opportunity.

"Charles and Will have joined us now. And Henry. She had near starved herself, John, to feed her family. Are you with us?"

"All I'll do," John muttered through his tears, "After I've sent Charles and Henry back, that is, is care for anyone who's injured. I'll not fight, Tom." Remembering the other men in the field, John asked, "Will Charles and the boy come here or over there with the others?"

"What others?" Tom's eyes followed John's pointing finger. "Daniel Reed. He's not mine. Nor's Stephen Ballom."

"There's Charles." John exclaimed. "He's no will to live, let alone fight." Into the field Charles limped slowly, making no attempt to keep out of sight. One leg dragged painfully and to walk at all, he leaned heavily on Henry's shoulder. The boy, all his perkiness gone, kept looking helplessly to the man.

"The old, the crippled and the very young," John told him. "They'll be lambs and old rams to the slaughter."

"Oh, my God!" Leaping up, Tom muttered, "He swore he wouldn't do it. I made him swear he wouldn't do it." As John tried to follow him, Tom pushed him back. "Stay here. We might need you."

Like a greyhound, Tom sprinted towards the men. As he ran, he waved his arms and shouted, "Get down. Take cover."

A great flash of light flared in the gathering darkness across the shallow dip of ground from the Colonel's house and the boom of the cannon echoed to Hangar Wood and back. In seconds, grape shot tore through the air, ripping and searing the bodies of any who stood in the way.

Stunned by the scene, John stood stock still, then rushed along the track Tom had taken a minute before. In the confusion, with the light fading, he could make out little around him, but he could hear the screams, the familiar screams of pain and terror he had known in battle, above the urgent prayers. Where were Charles and young Henry? What had happened to Tom? He knew one man could be untouched and the next torn to pieces.

"Call your names," he ordered. More sternly, he shouted, "Call out your names."

He listened for all the men he had seen assemble. Charles did not reply. Nor Henry. They and Tom had been in the open. A few yards ahead in the gloom, Stephen Ballom waved his arms. "Henry's here. I've found the child."

In seconds, John had reached the spot where the old man nursed Henry's head against his knee.

"I'm alright." In a shaky, uncertain voice, as though he hardly dare believe what he was saying, the boy reassured them. "I'm alright," he repeated, pride and the old perkiness creeping back into his voice at his cleverness in surviving. "I knew you'd join us, John. 'Ave you 'eard about Beth?"

John had no time to answer.

"Come here, John," one of the young men said in a gentle tone he had never used before. A small group, with Will Dodds at its centre, huddled around Charles's body, until, one by one, they turned to be sick. Even their unpractised eyes could tell when a man was cut to pieces. Steeling himself, trying to forget this was his brother, John made himself clear his mind and recall all the ways of checking for a glimmer of life. There was none. He stood up, forcing himself to work out, in relation to Charles and Henry, where Tom had been when the cannon fired. Daniel was already ahead of him.

"He's there," Daniel burst out, eager to rid himself of his knowledge. "His arm's just about shattered, John. There's blood. His blood's everywhere."

"Give me your belt, Daniel," John ordered. Unless he spoke sharply his words did not seem to sink into their minds. As he tightened the belt above the wound, John knew it was too late. Very gently, he cradled his friend's head and grasped his hand.

"Lay quiet, Tom, they're going for help."

The slight smile on Tom's lips showed he knew it was a lie, just a vain attempt to ease his passing.

"I'll kill him for you, Tom — for you and Charles. I'll kill the Colonel, I swear."

For a second, the light returned to Tom's eyes and his lips moved.

"What?" John leaned closer. "What do you want to say, Tom."

Again Tom's lips moved, a little more deliberately and with great effort. "Cold and calculating, John. Swear you'll kill ...."

With the edge of his hand, John closed Tom's eyes.

"I swear it, Tom. For you and Charles."

Boys and old men standing around, eyes averted from the broken body, sobbed. "I've wet my breeches, John," a young man confessed, as though to his mother.

Letting Tom's head slip to the ground, John took his friend's rifle and turned his thoughts to the little band around him. The chances were that the cannon was being made ready to fire again.

"Run to the woods. Don't stop until you're under cover."

Urgently, he ordered one man and then another to help those slightly wounded or too shocked to move and drove them before him like sheep. They had reached safety before the second flash of light lit the darkness.

"What shall we do, John?" Stephen Ballom asked.

"Let's tend the wounded, then, if you've had enough, go home."

"We're too far in it now to back out," Will said. "And Charles was married to my daughter."

"We came to take the cannon," Daniel told him. "Seems there's more reason to take it now."

"I've my own score to settle. No one else need come," John told them.

"We're with you, John. I've known Charles since he was a lad. All he wanted to do was see justice for his family."

"You could be useful, Daniel," John agreed. "You, Henry, go home." He raised his hand. "Don't argue. And you, Peter Black and James Appleby. You're too young to risk your lives. The rest of you, if you're taken, swear I forced you to help me at the point of this rifle, do you hear? No one will hold it against you." Reluctantly, they nodded their heads.

"Now, tell me what you know about the guards on the Colonel's house."

"There's four men on guard," Daniel reported. "One on each corner of the house. They march up and back and stand sentry at each corner."

"And by the cannon?"

"As far as we knew, no one guarded that. It was only supposed to fire wooden cannon balls to frighten poachers in the woods."

"We thought it would be easy to take," Stephen told him.

"Let's hope you're right."

CHAPTER SIXTY SEVEN

By a faint moon, John led his small band around the fields to the front of the Colonel's house. Hidden, they watched and waited. Candles burned in the house, but no guards marched up and down and no sentries stood on duty.

"They're waiting to ambush us," Daniel whispered.

"They seemed to know more about what we were going to do than we did," Stephen Ballom observed.

So far, that had been true. They might well be prepared for an attack on the cannon. The house and grounds lay in complete silence. John looked at his men. Between them they had a couple of hooks, an ancient pike, an axe and a dagger. From Daniel, he took the dagger and hid it under his coat.

"I'll leave Tom's rifle with you. If I should be killed, go home. But some day kill the Colonel for me and for Charles and for Tom.

On his hands and knees, John crawled to the lane leading to the house, then stood up, hands raised in the air. At the top of his voice, he shouted to anyone who might be there.

"Don't shoot. I'm not armed. Colonel Benson, I've come to give myself up." There was no sound outside the house or within. His hands still in the air, John walked in through the gate, up the path and into the house.

In the hall and drawing room, candles burned brightly. Carefully listening, easing back each door with his foot, John moved from room to room to the back of the deserted house. From the kitchen door, he moved out into the neat, walled garden and along the path to a high, solid gate. Pausing there, he listened, but could hear nothing.

The cannon lay on the other side of the gate, just a short distance away and the smell of burning powder hung in the air. Very, very slowly, he lifted the catch and, releasing it, sheltered his body behind the wall while he reached out with his foot to open the gate. Creaking harshly against the silence, it swung away from him, shuddering noisily as the hinges, reaching their full extent, would give no more.

The cannon was there, its barrel raised in the trajectory of the field. Across the carriage wheels, where they had fallen, rested the bodies of two men. As John turned them over, he saw where their blood had run, greenish red, on the iron of the cannon. The wounds told him the men had been shot at very close quarters. Another body lay on the ground. They were all men he knew. Men in the Colonel's defence force.

"Thank God," John said, under his breath. "Someone's done part of my work for me. Now it's just the Colonel himself."

Spinning round to a sound behind him, John saw it was Daniel.

"Come back here, John. We've taken a prisoner." The pride in his voice was clear.

In the field across the lane, the men were crowding around one of the Colonel's men. Already his face was bleeding and he held his ribs where they had punched him.

"I'll kill him myself," a youth offered eagerly.

"We'll string him up," another threatened.

"Listen. Oh, God, make them listen." At the sight of John, his pleading grew more spirited. "Stop them, John, for Christ's sake. They'll kill me."

"Why shouldn't they? You and your kind killed my brother and my friend."

"We didn't, John." The denial earned him another punch to the ribs from a man holding him. "I'm the only one left. I've been hiding here for God knows how long."

As a fist struck his mouth, the fear of dying burned in the man's eyes. "Let me tell you, John. Don't kill an innocent man. Don't have that on your conscience forever."

"Let him speak."

Reluctantly, not without more vicious jabs and punches, they let him speak.

"It was just routine, John. One of the men saw a movement in the field and thought it was poachers going into the wood." He appealed to John, "Make them leave me, John. Wait till you've heard everything."

As John ordered his men to let him speak without interruption, the man talked more eagerly than ever. "We came to get the cannon ready. I swear we thought we had to get it ready to fire the wooden cannon ball as usual." He held up his arms to fend off a threatened blow. "It's the truth, so strike me God."

"We're listening." John had decided he could use the man as a witness against the Colonel.

"Firing that cannon at poachers never does any real harm, John. Just scares them, that's all."

329

"So, what happened tonight?"

"It was like the Devil rising up." The man looked behind him in terror. "A man all in black. His face was covered with a mask. He came from nowhere."

The digs and punches had stopped. Everyone was listening in surprise.

"He made us drop our weapons. He had a rifle. Like that one Dan's got there. And a pistol. Before we knew what we were doing, he made us load the cannon with grape shot. It was hidden there close by. He threatened us, John, and he meant it. He told us how to aim the cannon and just where to fire. Honest to God. It was the Captain."

"You're telling me it wasn't the Colonel gave the orders to fire over the field?"

"No, John. It was the Captain. We thought it was the signal to start the march."

Angrily, John raised his hand to stop his men attacking their prisoner. Everything was coming together.

"Go on."

"When we'd fired twice — we'd no idea what we were firing at— he turned on us. There wasn't a word of warning. Two were shot where they stood by the cannon. Joseph Franks turned to run and he got him in the back. I was through that gate in seconds, John. He fired at me. You look. You'll find the holes in that wooden gate, I swear."

"Liar," one of the youths spat at the man. Another raised his hook and they gathered close around him again.

"Wait," John ordered fiercely, demanding time to think back over all that had happened. Tom's dying words came back to him. 'Cold and calculating.' Those were the words he had once used to describe the Captain.

"Leave him," John repeated mechanically, still trying to make sense of everything. As he had run to warn the men, Tom had muttered, 'He swore not to do it.' Tom never spoke to the Colonel. He certainly could not make the Colonel swear not to do anything. Tom did talk to the Captain.

At last John asked the question he had forgotten to ask before. "Daniel. Stephen. Whose band were you to join tonight? If Tom wasn't to be your leader, who was?"

"The Captain," Daniel answered: This man — dressed all in black and his face covered in a mask. He came up beside me out of nowhere when I was walking home. Told me to tell the others we were meeting in the field to take the cannon."

"How do you mean, the others?"

"He named them one by one."

"Where did he tell you to meet?"

"In the field. We thought that was daft, but he said we would be safe there. He said the wood was full of traps. Some of us, thank God, did shelter by the hedge."

So that was to have been the tinder, the flame to start the uprising. A few men killed and the Colonel blamed. That would have been enough. 'Cold and calculating' the Captain certainly was. Tom was right there. He had even thought of killing only men too young or to old to have been any real use in the uprising itself.

"Let your captive go and go home to your beds."

"Where are you going, John?"

"To find the man with the mask. To find the Captain. I swore to Tom I'd kill the man who planned this."

CHAPTER SIXTY EIGHT

The great barn where the fancy met was packed to the rafters. Here and there, men sparred, hoping their turn would come to be discovered and turned into a hero. Around them, spectators weaved, ducked and jerked with pain along with the fighters. A few, who had come to watch Langford put through his paces, good humouredly stamped and whistled, calling his name.

Above them, where a ladder rose to a higher level of planks raised across the rafters, the Captain waited in irritable frustration, with not a sign of humour. The Captain had always dreamed of his plan proceeding like a well-rehearsed drill.

"Where is that fool Langford?" he demanded. "Has someone gone for him?" Most of them were idiots. Everything had been planned to the last detail. How could he have known that stupid Langford would let him down? And where was Tom? He had sworn to bring Stevenson. Surely Tom would have news of the cannon. With a dozen or more men gathered in the field, there must have been some casualties.

Below, the spectators were losing their good humour. Impatient stamping of feet and jeers rose from the mass of men to the rafters.

"Give them more ale," the Captain ordered. It would do no harm to have some of them fighting drunk.

"They've had most of it."

"They're starting to drift home."

"Keep them here." He was their leader, the Captain told himself. He had planned this uprising for years and wasn't going to see it fizzle out like a damp squib. He didn't need Langford.

A few steps and the Captain was standing before the crowd. At the sight of this man dressed in black from head to foot, his face hidden by a mask, a great murmur of wonder rose up.

The men he had planted cheered and shouted. "The Captain!"

"Tell us what to do, Captain!"

The voice from the mask sounded strange and unreal, but it rang clearly and commandingly to the four corners of the barn. "You came to hear about the next fight, gentlemen. That fight is here — here in Abingfield, here in England."

Suddenly, the Captain abandoned the speech he had written. It had been planned for Langford to recite, not him. In any case, what did these men know about natural justice and man's rights? What did they care for reasoned arguments? He could rouse them, inspire them and lead them forward to victory.

"Beth Stevenson is dead." Pausing, the Captain let his words sink in. "How did she die? Smallpox, they say. Smallpox? But she was vaccinated by Dr Gray himself. Vaccinated just like the gentry."

Again, he paused for effect.

"Do the gentry die after vaccination? No, it protects them. But Beth Stevenson died."

They were in the palm of his hand.

"How did they plan it? What did they say, the lords and gentry who rule us?"

"The poor, there's too many of them," one of his men shouted from the floor of the barn.

"We have to feed and clothe them and they're not even any use to us," another shouted.

"Now the machines are here, there's no work for them. We don't need them."

While his men had called their answers, the Captain had been silent. Everyone else fell quiet to hear what he would say next.

"'How did we used to get rid of them?' the gentry asked. 'War? We've just finished one of those. Smallpox? That always worked well enough. Smallpox will cut their numbers down to size!'"

The Captain had every man's attention. They pressed forward, eager not to miss a word. The air, hot and oppressive, threatened a storm. "That's what they said, my friends, but it wasn't that easy. 'Since the old women and the apothecaries started to inoculate them, they don't fall sick anymore,' some noble lord pointed out."

"Vaccination," his men called.

"That was their answer! That was the answer the gentry found! 'Tell the poor they don't need inoculation any more. Tell them we'll vaccinate them from now on.'"

The Captain was breathing deeply. The crowd, the heat-laden air and his own intensity made him giddy, but he could not let them go from his grasp now. "There is no such thing as vaccination. They inoculate their own kind under a different name. The poor? To the poor they give just water. That is no defence. The poor are left to die."

The deathly silence gave way to shouts and threats and the Captain screamed his conclusion. "That's what happened to Beth Stevenson. Who will be next? You," he yelled, stabbing his finger from one to another of his audience. "You and you and you. And your wives and your children."

It was as though the blindfolds had been snatched from their eyes. The men cursed, threatened, fought to be the first to leave the barn and take their revenge.

"To London!" the Captain yelled. "Forward with me to London!"

Nobody was listening to him any more.

Left on the platform with just the view of men's backs as they rushed out, the Captain's lieutenants looked to their leader. They saw him, eyes alight, standing with arms outstretched like a prophet of old.

"We're losing them."

"They're sliding away, Captain."

"They're galloping away."

The Captain laughed. He held out an open hand and then clenched it. "There. In the palm of my hand."

"But they're off to destroy anyone and anything in their path. You said you would lead them to London."

"That's why we joined you, Captain. To march to London and present our grievances to Parliament."

"Let them go," the Captain told his men. "Give the mob its head. Let them plunder and destroy. Then it will be too late for them to change their minds. They will have to march with us to overthrow the Government or stay to be hanged."

The few men left shuffled uneasily, muttering that this was not what they had intended.

"Follow the crowd," the Captain ordered. "Keep them together. Find Tom." Smiling with pride in his own planning, he added, "He might have news for you which will strengthen your resolve. I'm off to find Langford. They'll follow him to the ends of the earth."

CHAPTER SIXTY NINE

The Captain's words had fallen on the fertile ground of frustration and suffering. Through the village, from person to person, cottage to cottage, it spread like a disease. Few were sufficiently well fed or educated to be immune from its touch or to recover until it had run its course. The horror of it burned in their heads like a fever and only action, wild, blind and destructive, relieved their delirium. Alongside wicked, violent men settling old scores against masters, once good men and once mild men released all the frustrations of a poor man's life.

Nourished by ignorance, the rumour sprouted new shoots which grew, distorted and convoluted, to smother the Captain's words in a covering of even more fantastic growth. Dr Gray's vaccinations were not just water, leaving the poor to fall victim to the smallpox, but, some said, the disease itself. Others said he had made the boy deaf and dumb and would harm all their children when the time came.

How the rumour turned and twisted to its final end, no one could unravel. Who uttered the strange, fantastic version no one ever knew, but, that night, it was on everyone's lips. Beth had been given a disease, which would spread to everyone who came near her. More awful than smallpox itself, it would creep unseen through the village until no one was left alive in Abingfield. They would, if there was anyone to bury them, lie in the graveyard beside the other Stevensons and Dodds and Braithwaites and Donkins, who had been victims of the plague which had stalked the country long years ago.

The shared terror of the crowd overwhelmed individual wills and individual minds and bound all into an unreflecting mob, intent on saving itself. Coming from the barn and gathering others on the way, they marched, driven not by zeal for reform, but by fear.

As she lay awake, weeping and mourning for her dearest friend, Beth, Eliza heard the marchers in the distance. It was at times like these when she craved comfort and forgetfulness, but for two nights Langford had slept on his own outside the cottage. Each night she had listened for his coming, but he never came in. Her pleading, teasing, promising had made no difference, neither had her swearing and mocking.

"You big, soft child," she had teased. "Boast of your courage and strength and you're afraid of a fever or of a few spots spoiling your beauty." Now Beth was dead, he was even more frightened and talked of going away.

She had mocked and belittled him, but she still listened. There he was, coming in. She sat up, letting the bed-covers drop. Within a second, she had snatched them up again. Her scream, "Langford," came hoarse, her throat paralysed by fear.

The man in the black clothes and mask stood at the door.

"Where's Langford?"

"He's only just outside. He'll come at once, if I call."

"Then call," he told her. "It's him I want to see, not you."

"Thank God for that." She thought of shouting to warn Langford, but realised that would leave her alone with the stranger. Instead she called his name from the door and at last he came, cursing her for disturbing his sleep.

"Now you get back in bed and pull the covers over your head," the stranger ordered.

Angrily, Eliza got back into bed. She hated being ignored. Obediently, she did as she had been told and pulled the covers over her head, but there were always ways of conforming outwardly while following your own inclinations. As soon as she heard the low throb of voices, she raised the covers a little and turned on her back to listen with both ears. She caught some of the words. 'London,' 'The People,' 'Tyranny." They meant nothing to her. As the voices grew louder and she knew they had forgotten her, Eliza sat up very slowly and quietly and listened again.

"You promised me a fight against a champion in London. I think I'd do better for meself going to Mr 'Ammond instead of going with you."

"You fool. Don't you realise there'll soon be no Hammonds, no lords and gentry. You'll be like a king then. You're the People's Champion. You must lead them if you wish to be their hero."

"There'd be no boxing except for the gentry."

"There'd be no poverty but for the gentry."

"I don't understand all that. That speech you told me. I don't understand 'alf of it. I'm a boxer."

"But the People love you. They look to you. Just do what I say and you'll be the most famous man in England — and the richest."

From Langford's questions, Eliza knew, he was trying to make sense of all he was being told. He was interested in the fame and the riches, but he wanted to know exactly what he had to do without all this talk of tyranny and liberty. The visitor's tone had lost its impatience and was soft and persuasive. She could not make out all the words or put a name to the voice, but he was talking about smallpox and dying.

He was like a boxer's second, Eliza thought, encouraging and driving his man. Langford always needed a second. There was precious little he could do without one. If the visitor went on talking about illness, the boxer would swoon at any minute.

The note of impatience came back into the stranger's voice. He was very angry again, now, not shouting and screaming, but cold and determined. The shadow of his arm moved across the candle and, when it was still again, she saw the glint of the flame playing on the barrel of the pistol in his hand. Eliza screamed. The man's head jerked towards the sound. As he recovered and quickly turned his face back to look at Langford, he met a blow which sent him crashing sideways to the floor.

Without a word, Langford was out the door, but he dashed back, grabbed Eliza's purse, swore as he found it empty, and ran off again not to come back.

Stealthily, Eliza lowered her feet to the floor. The Captain did not move. She crept towards him, lifted the mask, smiled and replaced it. As softly as she had come, she returned to her bed.

Moments passed before the Captain sat up and stared at Eliza. Eyes wide open, peering over the cover, Eliza gazed back. He scrambled to his feet.

"'E's only this second left. You'll catch 'im if you 'urry yourself." As he left, Eliza added, "Ope you both fall 'ead first in the canal."

CHAPTER SEVENTY

"I warned everyone," the Colonel declared. "With a freer hand, with greater support, I could have prevented this." He paced the library in the vicarage, vainly trying to silence his doubts. Walker must have been ambushed on his way to check the barn. Only a few men had dared turn out or leave their own homes unguarded to follow him and there were no weapons even for those few.

Seated at the table, Mr Gray wondered whether he could ask the Colonel to leave. With a mere handful of unarmed men, he provided no defence and might well attract the anger of the mob.

"Surely, Colonel," Dr Gray suggested, "you should attempt to stop the mob before it reaches the village."

"And show our weakness? That would be death to us all. Bluff. Many's the time a battle has been saved and disaster turned to victory that way. With your servants beside us and your fowling pieces, we can fire warning shots above their heads. That will stop them in their tracks until the military arrives."

"Help will be slow in coming, in my opinion," Dr Gray pronounced. "Since the trouble at St Peter's Field, magistrates are terrified of provoking even further violence or the scorn of the newspapers after the event. No one will act until it is too late, of that I am sure."

"Who's to stop the destruction of property in the village if you don't, Colonel?" Mr Simpkins asked. "Who's to protect the tradesmen and craftsmen and their livelihoods?"

"Protect the tradesmen and craftsmen!" the Colonel repeated with contempt. "The tradesmen and craftsmen are out there in the heart of it." There was no doubt in the Colonel's mind that he was being deeply wronged by this criticism and, like a true soldier, he turned to the attack. "It is the Stevenson woman's death which has provoked this outburst. It is Dr Gray who is the object of their hate. He is being blamed for her death."

"Nonsense." Mr Gray dismissed the accusation in a word.

Dr Gray defended himself, even though he considered he had no case to answer. "Mrs Stevenson was not my patient, so I speak reluctantly, but, as the boy's deafness shows, the family are of unhealthy stock and liable to succumb to any illness."

"My son's only fault has been his generosity," Mr Gray answered his neighbours. "He treated the woman free of all charge and now he is blamed for her death because she did not carry out his instructions."

"Don't let us quarrel amongst ourselves, gentlemen," Richard Hammond advised.

"What does Sir Philip wish us to do?" Mr Gray demanded. Sir Philip himself had stayed to defend his own home with a vast army of servants around him, but he had sent Richard with a handful of servants to be of what help he could. So far he had been of very little.

"He is anxious that we should do nothing to provoke further trouble," Richard answered. "If there is any threat to life, we must act, but, until that time comes, we should do nothing to enrage the mob to further violence. We have had riots before and they burn themselves out. The wrong move and the riot could flare into rebellion."

"There's something in that," Simpkins agreed "At the rate they're going, they'll all be dead drunk in a couple of hours. Their beds will appeal to them more than facing us."

"Place the servants at the window, as you suggested, Colonel, but keep them out of sight." Richard Hammond's tone of authority was not lost on the Colonel. With relief, he carried out the order with speed and efficiency.

"But I must reason with my parishioners," Mr Gray continued to protest. "Why would they wish to harm me? I fear your presence, Colonel, will enflame them to violence against us. My dear wife and daughter are in the next room."

No one was listening to him. From behind the curtains, they watched as the screaming mob came nearer.

"Shall my men shoot over their heads, or pick off the ringleaders?" the Colonel asked.

Richard Hammond lightly touched the shoulder of Mr Gray next to him. "Each man according to his calling. Mr Gray, pray as you have never prayed before. Colonel, you and your men shoot if you have to. Cover those rioters who are carrying arms. Nicholas," he paused, "let us hope your services are not needed."

"What are you going to do?" Mr Gray insisted on knowing.

"The only thing I am skilled in — have a little chat."

No one in the room spoke as, alone, Richard Hammond walked upstairs and out onto the small balcony at the front of the house. They waited for the rattle of the gates being forced, for the clatter of boots on the path and the screams of the mob at the door. They waited to hear Richard Hammond's voice reach them from the balcony. His voice, sounding just behind them startled everyone.

"There goes my greatest hour," he laughed. "Father would have been so proud of me." Dropping into a chair and demanding a brandy, he continued to laugh to hide the slight trembling of his hand as he raised the glass to his lips. "They have gone by. They have gone straight by without a glance in our direction."

A servant rushed in. "They have gone to the Stevenson's cottage to burn it down, sir."

"Let us thank God," Mr Gray exhorted them, falling to his knees.

CHAPTER SEVENTY ONE

Even when, in making his way to the village, John lost sight of the torches and their glare behind houses and trees, the great volume of sound told him where the crowd was. The noise of hurrying feet, of smashing glass and splintering wood, of screams and laughs and howls carried to the boundaries of the parish, terrifying men of property and calling forth those with nothing to lose.

Trying to run alongside the people, to make his way to the front where the Captain might be, took all John's strength and attention. The crowd swelled and heaved so that he was thrown against walls and toppled into ditches. In the dense throng, he tripped on boxes and bottles abandoned by looters and had to fend off the mauling, grasping hands of men and women, too drunk to stand alone.

At times, John found himself picked up by the tide of rioters surging from behind and then dropped down as people stopped, attracted by more plunder. Every man and woman was known to him, but they looked strangely changed, as in a dream, when faces and actions no longer match and everyone, acting out of character, plays out his part to the extreme, fantastic conclusion. Many women wore hats, too small, or big, or costly to be their own and some were clothed in silks and satins over their own, everyday wool and linen. The Captain was not at their head and John stood aside to let them pass.

Suddenly the current of bodies was flowing, coursing forward in the direction of the vicarage and then past it out of the village again. Until then, shouting, screaming, laughter and curses had merged into a great surge of sound pounding at his ears, but gradually, one by one, dozens by dozens, the villagers all took up the same cry.

"The Stevenson's cottage! Burn it down! Burn! Burn!"

As the tail of the mob passed out of the village, Henry stood and watched it go. His body was bruised and sore and he had to struggle to catch his breath. "Where are they going, mister?"

The man was too occupied to answer the question. "Careful where you're standing. Just look before you move your feet. There's good pickings to be had if you use your eyes."

"Where are they going?" Henry repeated, coming closer to the man.

"There's nothing worth having where they're going. Stay there. My God! Keep away from me!"

"Where are they going?"

"To burn your place down — with everyone in it, I hope." Clutching his treasures, the man ran after the crowd.

Henry ran in the opposite direction. A few minutes later, with his hand held to his aching side and his lungs bursting for air, he threw open the gate of Mr Armitage's house and left it to crash behind him. He staggered into the yard and flung himself on the door. There was dead silence in the house. He hammered at the door and wept.

"What do you want?" Hugh Armitage demanded, coming quietly up behind him. Henry, blinded by the lantern, sobbed his reply. As the lantern was lowered, he saw Hugh Armitage was holding a musket.

"Let us in," Hugh called and his wife opened the door at once. In a few minutes, Henry had told his story.

"Please stop them Mr Armitage."

Mrs Armitage watched her husband reach for ammunition and knew there was no use arguing with him.

"Don't be afraid to use that," he told her, leaving a loaded pistol on the table.

A little awkwardly, as they had taken their affection for granted for many years, she kissed his cheek.

"I'll be praying for you — and the Stevensons."

"Don't open the door again, except to me. Bolt it behind me." Immediately, Hugh Armitage set off for the next farm. Apart from a few revellers singing and dancing, the lane was empty. At farm after farm, house after house, he called to the silent, unseen occupants and battered at their locked doors. At most, he received no reply. The few men, who ventured to their windows, told him to go home, telling him no one could stand against the mob without risking his life.

CHAPTER SEVENTY TWO

"There, I knew it would turn to thunder." The distant noise, rolling through the trees, awoke Sarah from her restless sleep.

To Paul Low, who could not sleep, the noise did not seem like thunder, but he kept his thoughts to himself. Before he had left, Charles had told him they were joining the uprising, but Will had told Sarah they were going to tell their relations of the death in the family. In the corner, Edward muttered to himself about his young days.

Easing herself slowly from her chair, Sarah moved over and made the men as comfortable as possible. Gratefully, Paul thanked her.

"I'll just shut that door while I'm up." Her thoughts on Beth, Sarah could not find it in her heart to sit and talk, but she tried to say something for Paul's sake. "The rain blows straight in from that direction."

Leaning out to take the door handle, Sarah listened. That was not thunder and that flickering glow in the sky was not lightning.

"What can it be Paul?" In a second, Sarah was answering her own question. "There's torches lighting up the woods. Screaming and shouting. Is it some sort of procession at this time of night?"

Thankful that, at last, he could tell her, Paul said simply, "It's the uprising, Sarah. They're off to London. Shouldn't be passing this way."

"Oh, dear God! And Will and Charles? They've gone too, haven't they?" She needed no answer. "They've gone to fight. I know they have."

"It's just a peaceful march to London, Sarah. Just to let the Government see how the people are suffering. They'll be back safe and sound, you see." On the rug by the empty hearth, Frances stirred.

"Don't you wake, my love," Sarah whispered. "Thank God Billy is with Amy." For several minutes she had hesitated whether to shut the door or not, whether she wanted to know what was happening or not, but she shut it now to let Frances sleep and joined Paul by the open window.

"They're coming this way."

"They'll be calling at every house. It'll be to collect food and money for the journey."

"Did Will and Charles take anything?" A quick search of the pantry told Sarah they had taken nothing. In dismay, she thought of all the preparations that were necessary for a journey to London. There was food and drink to pack, clothes to wash, an extra pair of stout boots, ointment for their feet. They had given her no notice at all, but perhaps, if she was quick, she could manage to get something to them. Hurrying, Sarah fetched the loaf and cheese. It would stay fresher if she didn't cut slices.

"Sarah. Come here."

About to tell Paul she was too busy, Sarah turned to him. For the first time she made out the words the mob was shouting.

"The plague! Burn their cottage to the ground or we'll all die!"

"Burn them with it!"

"Shut the window, Sarah."

Obediently, unable to think for herself, Sarah obeyed.

Someone, anonymous in the crowd, threw a stone. Its course, as drunkenly wayward as the thrower, lurched high and then dropped to the ground. "Don't break the window," a distraught voice screamed from the mob. "Don't let the plague out into the air."

"Burn it down. That's the safest way."

Drunken, excited, frightened, lost in the mindlessness of the mob, old friends and neighbours took up the cry.

"Set it alight! Burn it down!"

"Ma," Frances called, jerking awake, "what is it?" As she heard the words she had spoken, she remembered her mother was dead.

"Bring wood," a voice yelled. "Let's have the torches here."

To those inside, the words, so loud and clear, gave shape to awful terrors which made their hearts beat faster and their skins go cold. In the brilliant light, so eerie against the outer ring of dark trees, they saw a wall of faces, angry and threatening, mouthing threats and fear.

"What do you want?" Sarah shouted, struggling to believe that these were the villagers she had known for a lifetime and they would do her no real harm. The crowd screamed at her to close the window and a stone hit her cheek, stunning her into silence.

"They must be afraid of the smallpox," Paul told her. "Tell them you'll bury Beth in the morning. Tell them none of us will come out. Promise them anything until help comes."

"Oh, Paul, where are Will and Charles?"

"I'll come and go as I please," Edward suddenly announced, pushing to the door. Before they could stop him, he opened it and faced the mob. For a moment, people drew back, those in front trampling those behind, but, instantly, those behind pushed forward again. Young men ran at him, thrusting their burning torches into his face, and, urged on by the crowd, laughed as they baited him like mastiffs goading an old bull.

With the light of the torches blinding him and their flames scorching his clothes, the old man stood his ground.

"Throw the torch in through the door."

Sarah and Frances dragged the old man, protesting and cursing, back into the room. At that second, Will pushed his way in. Sarah slammed the door and, pointlessly as no one else wanted to come in, bolted it."

It fell quieter as the young men marshalled the crowd back and ordered others, as drunk and vicious as themselves, to collect branches and brush-wood and set it around the cottage. Dead wood, dry and brittle from the August sun, was placed at the foot of the walls and piled high with straw. Tenderly, keeping as calm as she could for the child's sake, Sarah drew Frances to her.

"When I tell you, my sweet, jump out of the little kitchen window and run into the wood as fast as your legs will carry you."

"What about you and my grandpas and Mr Low?"

"You be a good girl and do what your Ma would have wanted you to do."

"Who wants the honour?" One man offered his torch to anyone in the crowd.

A man, who had pushed and elbowed his way through the throng and only that minute reached the front, snatched the burning torch from his hand. "I'll do it," he yelled, but once Hugh Armitage held the torch firmly in his hand, he turned and faced the crowd.

"There's no need for murder. Let's call this by its proper name — mur-der. You've harmed no one yet and there's no need for killing. All you need do is board them in. That's what they did in the old days. If they've the plague, they'll die, with no one here to blame. If they haven't the plague, they'll live, and no harm done."

By now, other torches had been passed forward and were at hand to hold to the wood.

"Burn! Burn! Burn!" Instinct told those who shouted that one word, repeated over and over, was more persuasive than reasoned argument.

The crowd pushed forward and Hugh Armitage was trapped against a pile of wood. A youth raised a torch on high and, screaming in excitement while the crowd watched in silence, lowered it towards the tinder. A shot rang out across his head and hit the cottage wall just in front of him.

"I could have shot you through the head, but you'd have dropped the flame onto the wood," John Stevenson shouted. "Touch the wood with the torch and I'll kill you." He had the attention of every single person in the crowd. "The first man to try dies. I've another rifle ready loaded," he lied.

A man rushed at the tree where John stood, his feet planted firmly in the branches and his body braced against the trunk. "I'll kill the second man who tries," Hugh Armitage shouted, his musket loaded and raised ready to fire.

One of the Captain's men, realising that he had taken up his gun to fight for justice, called across, "I'm with you, John."

From where he had been hiding, one of the Colonel's men, who had been detailed earlier in the day to watch the house, came and stood beside Hugh Armitage, facing the crowd.

"If you're not too drunk to get there, go home. Are we going to fight each other? We'll board them in."

Out-armed, if not outnumbered, the crowd's cry changed to, "Board them in!" Hugh Armitage raised his arms for silence and the noise subsided sufficiently for him to make himself heard.

"A dozen of you, that's all. The rest stay back."

Sarah was on her knees, thanking God, when another voice rang out.

"No need for that, gentlemen." Smiling, with no outward sign of fear, Richard Hammond rode his horse to the Stevenson's door to face the crowd. At the sight of Langford at his side, a great cheer echoed through the wood. As befitted a man who had served as an officer in Wellington's army, Richard Hammond took control.

"Ladies and gentlemen," he shouted, standing in the stirrups, "I give you Langford, the next champion of England!" Enthusiastically, he led the huzzahs and then raised his hand. "Silence for Abingfield's champion. Speak up, man." A few words of the speech in which he had been coached by the Captain mixed with a few of those with which his new patron had persuaded him to ride with him came, muddled, into Langford's mind. As he had seen Richard Hammond do, he rose in the stirrups, but his hold was less certain and, as the horse stepped forward, he fell back into the saddle.

"Too much ale," Richard Hammond called, to shouts of approval.

"Friends," Langford began, hesitantly, "Mr 'Ammond 'as...."

"What about the sickness?" a woman called and others took up the cry.

"Old wives' tales," Richard Hammond laughed. "There is no sickness."

"How did Beth Stevenson die then?"

For a second, Richard Hammond hesitated. He could not explain it was smallpox, although she had been vaccinated, and he could not say she was half starved. The explanation Dr Gray had given to free himself of any blame came into his head.

"The woman died, God rest her soul, from a poison from the unborn child." He roared, "Would I put our champion in danger? He's worth money to every one of you if you put your bets on him. Go inside, Langford."

Before the fighter could protest, Richard Hammond signalled to his servants and they lifted the pugilist onto their shoulders and took him into the cottage.

"There," Richard Hammond yelled, "there's no danger."

No one had known Beth was expecting a child and they did know it was a dangerous time. Joyously, they realised they were not going to die of any disease. In their excitement, men grabbed Richard Hammond and bore him, shoulder high, beside the boxer in a singing, dancing procession. Good humouredly, he capped joke with joke and returned insult with insult, until he shouted at last, "To your beds, neighbours, and let me go to mine. It's been a long night."

"I heard some men had been killed by the cannon," a villager shouted.

"Another rumour," Hammond lied. "Now, to your beds!" They could deal with that tomorrow.

The people, exhausted, the first feelings of shame beginning to stir, stumbled home.

The Captain's man who had stood with John, asked him, "Where's Tom?"

He listened with mounting disbelief and horror to John's account of Tom's death. At the end, John ordered, "Tell me where I'll find the Captain and then go home, hide your weapon, go to bed and have your wife swear you were there all night."

"The Captain was off to find Langford, but Hammond must have found him first. I think the Captain was going to try Eliza's place. God knows, I'll be happy to take your advice and go to my bed."

CHAPTER SEVENTY THREE

If anyone knew who the Captain was and, more importantly, would tell, it was Eliza. Langford had spent many hours with her and the Captain might have visited him there and Eliza was not one to rest until she knew every secret. At John's knock, Eliza staggered to the door. She had drunk enough gin to quench her thirst and drown her sorrows.

"Come in, sir. Come into my parlour." She leaned heavily against the door.

"Be quiet, Eliza," John ordered, fearing there might be someone about who would betray him to the Colonel. "Come inside." Half dragging her, half carrying her, he managed to get her into the house and shut the door.

"Don't tell me what to do. There's bin better men than you in 'ere, John Stevenson. Men of quality."

"Quantity, perhaps."

"'Quality,' I said and 'Quality' I means. 'Ave a drink, John. There's plenty there." Turning up the empty bottle, she seemed about to cry. "It's all gorn. Every drop."

"What concerns me at the moment, Eliza, is whether anyone is about."

"You!" Eliza tried to raise her arm and point to him, but her arm fell with the effort of laughing. "You! Concerned! Since when have you been concerned about anybody but yourself?" She stared, her eyes narrowed and every act and expression exaggerated in her effort to overcome the dulling effect of the gin. "Concerned! It were Beth 'oo were concerned about everyone of you. 'Oo showed 'er any concern in return? Not you, that's for sure."

Eager not to waste time, John ignored what she had to say. "Come on, Eliza," he coaxed, "you know who the Captain is, don't you?"

"So that's it!" The situation seemed to amuse Eliza considerably.

"We both know Langford's a fool, Eliza, but you're not."

"Flattery will get you everywhere, sir," she giggled. Suddenly, her mood changed. Sneering, she mocked him. "You think you're clever! You think we're fools!" Snatching another bottle, Eliza took a long drink. "Men! I drink to them, but," she spat a stream of liquid at John, "that's what I think of them! Oppressed! Downtrodden! What would a man know about them things?" For a moment, she put her face close to John's, as though waiting for an answer and then turned away, laughing. "You're fools as well, the lot

348

of you. A good laugh, that's all you're good for."

John was not inclined to argue. He felt sure she knew who the Captain was. He tried to get some sense out of her, but she sat on the floor, her skirts spread out around her, laughing until the tears ran down her face.

"Look at yourself, John Stevenson, prancing about thinking yourself important. The Colonel's got something better to do than look for the likes of you. 'E knows 'oo the Captain is. It were me what told 'im."

"So you do know!"

Kneeling beside her, John tried to take the bottle away, but she went on laughing, rocking backwards and forwards.

"You're drunk." John stood up in disgust to walk away, but Eliza grabbed his ankle and held it.

"Drunk! A liar! Oh what a reputation I've got!" Sniggering, she took another drink. "'E 'oo laughs last — she 'oo laughs last, it should be. Women always 'ave the last laugh."

Shifting his feet, John tried to free himself, but Eliza even put down her bottle to take his ankle in both hands and hold him planted to the floor. The angrier John became, the more she laughed and he stooped down to tear at her fingers and free himself. When his face was close to hers, Eliza looked into his eyes.

"Shall I tell you a secret? Free to you, John. Anything's free to you." His look of disgust set her giggling again and she grabbed his hand instead of his ankle.

"Mmm, you're strong," she teased, rubbing his hand against her cheek. She tugged him closer. Her face softened and she tried to kiss him. "Free to you, John." She whispered a name. "That's 'oo the Captain is, I swear."

John's expression conveyed his utter disbelief without the need for words. Eliza sighed. "You're all the same. Can't see what's right under your noses."

For the first time, John considered carefully what she had said. Suddenly, Eliza was no longer mocking him. Desperately, she was trying to win his favour, trying to convince him of the truth of what she had said by telling him all that had happened.

"If you ask me," she confided, "it explains a lot."

John considered. It did. "What was the Colonel going to do?"

"'E didn't tell me. Nobody confides in me." For a moment, it looked as though Eliza was about to wallow in self pity, but then she touched her nose, knowingly. "I told 'im to look in the barn where the fancy met. It was the Captain 'oo set that all up. The Colonel's off to the barn. Ding-dong. Ding-dong. You men go at each other all the time, don't you?"

Eliza sat, half collapsed, on the floor and, embracing her knees, rested her head and sang sadly to herself. John left her there.

CHAPTER SEVENTY FOUR

John was determined not to let his resolve weaken. He had to kill the Captain, he knew, otherwise what did his word mean and who would ever protect the innocent if ordinary men like him did nothing? The deep anger and sorrow of the uselessness and waste of it all still stirred him, but the blinding anger had passed. In his heart, all John wanted was to sort out the trouble over Joe Braithwaite and go home to Charlotte and his brother's young children. They were his responsibility now, but he told himself this was like war. You did what you had to do.

The path he took led to one place, the barn where the fancy met. There the Captain must have had a hiding place where he could vanish when the Colonel's man called or where he could change back into his everyday clothes before returning, unrecognised, to the life he had always led.

The trees grew more sparse, but John managed to move slowly from cover to cover, skirting the open, rough ground in front of the barn. He would have liked to face the man, tell him why he had to die, but that was a luxury he could not allow himself. There were Charlotte and the children to consider.

A short distance from the barn door, which swung to and fro in the breeze, John took cover and waited. In just a minute, the door's regular, rhythmic creaking ceased. In absolute silence, John raised his rifle, sighted it on the opening door and held it steady. A figure backed through the door. Cursing, unwilling to shoot any man in the back, John stood up.

"Turn round."

The figure turned. It was the Colonel. In his hand, his sword dripped blood onto the cobbled yard.

"You've killed him? The Captain?" John demanded.

"He's dead."

Pushing past the Colonel, John stepped into the deep shadow of the barn. As the darkness thinned, he picked out the walls and the heavy, low rafters and, there on the floor, a pile of sacks. Beneath them, a stain of blood across his shirt, Ben Walker lay dead.

"He claimed he was spying for me," the Colonel said with hatred. "Said he'd been loyal to me all the time. He'd have gone free. Made a laughing stock of me."

"I came to kill him."

"It was he who fed me lies about you. I can see, now, he wanted me to drive you into joining his men. He swore that you were Gentleman Jack. You'll not give me away?"

"You'll need no witness." With his boot, John touched the body. "I'd already planned how to get rid of this." It was true. At the back of his mind, as he had walked and waited, a plan had been forming to dispose of the body so no blame was attached to him. The plan had another use.

"You can do something for me in exchange."

"You can get rid of him so that no one will know?"

"Yes."

"And you'll tell no one?"

"Never."

"How much do you want? I'll reward you well, Stevenson. You're an able man. Ambitious just like I was."

"Never," John said again, this time with venom. "You two were alike, except with you it was 'England' and with him 'The People'. The cause is all that matters to you or his kind. You care nothing for individuals, like Charles and Tom. The end justifies the means. Two sides of the same fake coin. Keep your money."

"What is it you want?"

"Make sure the magistrates know I had no part in Joe Braithwaite's foolishness and that I can walk where I like a free man."

"You have my word as an officer and a gentleman."

"That will have to do."

In his gratitude the Colonel did not notice the insult. "How will you do it, Stevenson?"

"Ask no questions and you'll be told no lies."

"Shall I help? He'll be heavy for one man."

"There'll be others involved. They'll not trust you. Come later and get rid of his clothes."

After the insane night before, there was no one about as John dragged the body to the canal. Checking it was safe, he called softly to a man on the barge.

"Who is it?" a voice demanded.

"Give us a hand."

A man came out and took one end of the sack and they loaded it onto the barge. "How much?" the man asked casually. In the rising sun he inspected the body, but made no comment.

"So," John Wells called, coming from the cabin and glancing into the sack, "you've joined the resurrection men after all. Your handiwork?"

"I understood the charm of your business was no questions asked and no answers expected."

"A few days with them young saw-bones and there'll be precious little to ask questions about."

"That's just what I thought."

CHAPTER SEVENTY FIVE

Eliza wondered why she had not turned spy before. The pay was good. She clanked the gold sovereigns together in her palm. The trouble was, you needed a good secret to get money like that. The Colonel had bullied, cursed like no gentleman should and threatened the troops would come and take her off to prison, but she had stood her ground. If he wanted information about the Captain, it was only right that he should pay for it.

As she made her way to the Stevenson's cottage, she could smell the traces of the night's destruction and passed the smouldering remains of the baker's from which white trails of flour led to many of the houses nearby. She walked on, passing the smashed windows and battered door of the carpenter's. Outside pieces of wood and nails still lay where they had been thrown, but the coffins made for old Mrs Find and old man Smith were still there in the workshop. Until he saw her gold, the carpenter protested that they were already sold, but as soon as he glimpsed the money in her hand, he agreed with Eliza that he could make two more.

"A good send off with all the trimmings," Eliza told him, "That's what Beth deserves." She jingled the coins. "I'll give you 'alf now an' 'alf when it's all over." All that money had not spoiled her feel for a bargain. "You'll have to look sharp, mind you," she went on. "Dr Gray says she 'as to be buried today and Sir Philip is just as anxious. Wants to get back to being like we always was. Wants to send the military packing — the old spoil sport."

The carpenter took the half payment. He knew she would never pay the rest, but he knew, too, that Mrs Find's relations would not have accepted the coffin. It was damaged at the corner, on the side he had placed in the darkest part of the workshop, where men had carried it into the village swearing they would see Dr Gray buried in it.

By mid-morning, the funeral procession made its way through the trees where Beth used to sit sewing in the sunshine in summer and along the rutted path where she had run, skirts lifted above her ankles, jumping the puddles in winter. It passed into the village and in front of the cottages where Beth and Charles had been born and on to the house where they had moved on their marriage and where Beth had given birth to Frances, to Billy and to Tim and had dreamed her dreams for them.

In the cold light of day, many villagers were too shocked by all that had happened even to admit their shame. They stood aimlessly around attributing blame or swept up the debris as though some unseen enemy had come at night and left them to clear up the destruction. As the coffins passed and the bells tolled, men stood, hats in hands, and women wept. All prayed that death would not come as early to them as it had come to Charles and his wife.

The unreality of the night's events added to the unreality of death for the family gathered in the front pews. Certainly, Beth's body lay in one of the coffins there in front of them with Charles close by her just, as everyone knew in their hearts, he had wanted to be. Tim's small coffin rested between them. But, surely, the two of them, hand in hand with Tim, were there standing beside them in the church as they had always been. Within the hour, surely, the family would walk out together, leaving the musty, gloomy church to emerge, side by side, blinking before the sunlight and breathing in the sweet, fresh, country air. Then, wouldn't Beth hurry off to check the pot she had left simmering on the hearth, calling to the men not to hang around until the food was cold? And wouldn't Charles walk with her, renewing his strength from his wife just as he always did?

"I am the resurrection and the life, saith the Lord; he that believeth in me then he were dead, yet shall he live."

Mr Gray's voice echoed hollow as the grave, threatening as hell fire. Death, so certain and so final, was the most powerful weapon God had given his ministers on Earth and the vicar used it with awesome effect.

"We brought nothing into this world and it is certain we can carry nothing out."

"Poor Beth," Eliza thought. "She enjoyed precious little in between her coming and her departure." The vicar would come to the other words later, the ones that had struck her in other burial services. "Let us eat and drink, for tomorrow we die." What good had all Beth's resolutions and all Charles's hard work done them?

His mind drifting into thoughts of how he could provide for his brother's children, how he could ever marry until he could support a wife and how he could escape from the cycle of soulless and unprofitable toil to the life he really wanted, John forced himself, out of respect for the dead, to take in the words of their burial.

"and verily, every man living is altogether vanity."

Perhaps it was just as simple as Charlotte made out. Perhaps empty pride or vanity were all that prevented him reaching out for the happiness he wanted for them all. It was not honour, but pride and vanity which prevented him borrowing money from the Elhams.

"they are even as a sleep. and fade away suddenly like the grass. In the morning it is green and groweth up: but in the evening it is cut down, dried and withered."

His first wife and child had been taken from him. Beth and Charles were dead before he really knew them. How, when he had first returned from the war, Beth had loved to chat. How quiet, he realised now, she had become, as quiet and self-contained as Charles had always been. It was pointless, surely, not to accept Charlotte's help and give the children a better life.

"we bring our years to an end, as it were a tale that was told." That was Pa. Two months, maybe three and he would be dead, too.

"I meant Beth no harm," the old man declared, loudly enough for those around him to hear. His son was looking at him so accusingly. They said Beth was dead, but wasn't that her, there right next to him, her hair shining down her back? His son planned to marry her some day. Why did she look so sad? He smiled at her.

"Oh, grandpa!" The child was crying. Was it Beth? He couldn't remember any more.

"The days of our age are three score years and ten and though men be so strong that they come to four score year, yet is their strength then but labour and sorrow so soon passeth it away and we are gone."

Once again, John forced his mind back to the service.

"then shall be brought to pass the saying that is written, Death is swallowed up in victory. O death, where is thy sting? O grave, where is thy victory?" Glancing at a movement along the row, John saw Charlotte signing to Billy. She was telling him his Ma and Pa were in Heaven with Jesus. John prayed Beth, Charles and Tim had found peace. Pray God they were together in peace.

"Man that is born of woman hath but a short time to live. He cometh up and is cut down like a flower."

It was true. Life was too short for pride and vanity. He would marry Charlotte as soon as the mourning time had passed. What talents God had given him he would use as precious gifts, not waste in empty pride.

Yes, Beth with her common sense was beside him. He could not spend years as an apprentice to Anthony Wright. He would take over the book-shop and run a little school. People were beginning to have a little spare money again to spend on their children's future. He would fulfil Beth's dreams for her children. Frances could work in the bookshop and read every volume, if she wished. Billy would live with them and they would find out every way deaf children could be helped and taught. Perhaps other deaf children would join his school. Will and Sarah had moved into the cottage in the woods to care for the shepherd and Edward and to take over the sweep's business until Henry was old enough to run it himself.

"Yet O Lord God most holy," Mr Gray boomed, "O Lord most mighty, O holy and most merciful saviour, deliver us not into the bitter pains of eternal death." Many a parishioner swore to turn from the wide, inviting path which led to Hell.

For the last time, John, Will and the other bearers took the coffins on their shoulders. They brought them to the graveside and lowered them into the earth. John scattered a handful of soil, while Frances and Billy, clutch-ing each others' hands for fear of falling, tossed posies of wild flowers onto the coffins.

"earth to earth, ashes to ashes, dust to dust."

Sarah clasped the children to her and they wept for Charles and Beth and for Tim, their dear child.

"even so sayeth the spirit, for they rest from their labours."